PROLOGUE

The first murder came to the attention of the police on the afternoon of Tuesday, 7 July 1987, when the victim was discovered by her ten-years-old daughter, Sarah, who returning home from her primary school, had to push against the front door of the ground floor flat, to open it.
Elizabeth Bradley, a single parent, just twenty-nine years of age, was lying where she had fallen in the hallway of her ground floor flat, killed by several blows to the head with a brass candlestick that lay close to her crumpled body.
According to the initial statement from the neighbour who lived in across the landing, the little girls panicked screams alerted Mrs Yvonne Church, who persuaded Sarah to come into Mrs Church's flat from where she summoned the police and an ambulance that unfortunately, whose crew was several hours too late to be of any assistance to the dead woman.
The first police officers on the scene, local beat men Constable Joseph Docherty and his nine-week probationer neighbour, Constable Paul Gunnion, arrived on foot just six minutes later and no more than thirty seconds after the ambulance crew.
Docherty, a veteran beat man with twenty-six years' service, heavy-set and florid faced, who was prone to flatulence and whose heart was beating far too quickly for someone his age, peeked past Bradley's open door at the prone figure, then cautioned his neighbour to remain outside the flat.
Drawing his baton, the portly officer squeezed through the space between the door and victim that permitted him entry without disturbing the body too much, then ensured the victims flat was clear of anyone else who might have been hiding beneath a bed or lurking within. Deciding there was little point in him contaminating the locus any further, he returned to the hallway where stepping gingerly over the corpse, he stepped back through the ajar front door and into the close.

After a brief examination of the body and hearing Sarah's distraught wailing from the flat across the landing, the senior ambulanceman confirmed he would be of no use to the mother, so informed Docherty, "Looks to me like you've got a murder here, pal. We'll head in next door and see if we can calm down the wee lassie." Startled, Docherty turned to see his young, twenty-one-year-old neighbour, pale faced and in obvious distress, bent double and projecting vomit onto the wall of the close.

"For Christ's sake, son," he uncharacteristically snapped, "if you're throwing up, go out into the front and do it!"

Retching with one hand to his mouth and his tunic already stained, the unfortunate Gunnion stumbled to the close entrance while Docherty unclipped his radio and taking a deep breath, contacted his control room at Govan Police Office.

CHAPTER ONE

Detective Chief Inspector Mary Wells, her usually short dark, brown hair now grown and loosely resting on her shoulders, sat at her desk and re-read the Divisional statistical crime reports for June. Uncommonly pleased, Mary read that while statistically, a little over two hundred further crimes had been reported for June, the detection rate had increased by five percent, mainly due to a number of roll-up's when a particularly active gang of housebreakers had been arrested by her Detective Sergeant, Elaine Fitzsimmons, and her neighbour, DC Alan Hamilton. Lengthy interviews conducted by the two Detectives, as well as the recovery of a large quantity of property that yielded fingerprint evidence, had resulted in two members of the gang of three admitting their part in over forty housebreakings.

And worthy of a Chief Constable's commendation, Mary mused as she smiled at her Detectives success.

She shuffled the paperwork across her desk and eyes narrowing, glanced at her wristwatch while she wondered what shopping to take in for her kids' dinner.

Her head rose when the door was knocked, then pushed open by her CID clerk, Alex McCormack, who poking his head into the room, said, "Ma'am, that was the control room on the phone. They're needing a CID presence at a flat in Cessnock, 42 Clifford Street. It seems the beat men there have a suspicious death. A woman found lying behind her front door with her head bashed in. No other details."

But good of Alex to at least find that out, she thought, then inwardly sighed before nodding, said, "Okay, Alex, who have we got through there?"

"The DI's in his room and I think Colin Baxter has just arrived back from court."

"Right then," she pushed herself up from the desk, "inform the DI where I'm going and he's to hold the fort and tell Colin to meet me down at the yard. If this is going to be a long evening, I'd better visit the ladies."

Grinning, McCormack nodded and politely replied, "Will do."

****

Now almost forty-eight years of age, DS Colin Baxter had accepted that with twenty-eight and a bit years' service behind him, it was unlikely he'd progress in the CID. Yes, he often told his wife, there might be the opportunity to finish his career as a uniformed Inspector, but after twenty years as a Detective, he definitely wouldn't be happy returning to uniform and so at the last two annual appraisals, made it known he was not overly ambitious and wished to remain in the CID.

Drawing up behind the parked ambulance, he turned to the DCI and asked, "Once we've confirmed murder, boss, I'll call out the circus, but given the time it is now, do you want the dayshift to hang fire at Govan?"

"Yes," she nodded then thoughtfully added, "but let's see what we've got here first."

Getting out of the car, DCI Wells led the way towards the close and unaware that behind her, Baxter's eyes narrowed as he stared and wondered, what was different about his DCI?

At the close entrance they were greeted by the young Constable Gunnion, who with his notebook in hand, said in a nervous voice, "I've been told to take your names, Ma'am, and your time of arrival, if you please."

"Are you okay, son?" Wells replied as eyes narrowing, she stared at him, seeing his hands shaking and what looked like stains on the front of his tunic.

"Aye, it's just…" he took a deep breath. "Sorry, Ma'am, I've just never seen a dead person before. Well, not like that, I mean. And the smell," his face distorted, then gulped as though fighting his bile.

As Baxter later related to his wife, it was typical of Mary Wells' thoughtfulness when she rested her hand on his shoulder, then softly told the young officer, "Look, away you go and sit in the CID car to catch your breath and don't be feeling bad. No matter how long you intend being in the job, the day you get used to seeing violent death is the day to decide you've had enough."

"Okay, Ma'am, thank you," he muttered with a nod, then holding up his notebook, continued, "But…"

"It's okay, son," Baxter interjected from behind her with a raised hand. "I'll take notes of the comings and goings."

As Gunnion walked away, they entered the close, their noses twitching at the smell of the expelled vomit and were met by Joe Docherty, who politely greeted them with, "Ma'am, Colin thanks for coming."

Baxter supressed his grin, thinking, we're the CID; we could hardly ignore a shout about a murder.

"No problem, Joe," Mary nodded. "What we got and eh," she turned her head to ask, "where's the ambulance crew? Inside the flat?"

"No, Ma'am," he shook his head, then pointed when he added, "they're across the landing."

She turned to the white PVC double glazed door opposite and smiled when she saw the empty milk bottle on the doorstep, awaiting collection for the next morning.

"I didn't think people still had their milk delivered in bottles."

Docherty nodded when he replied, "Oh, aye, it's a local dairy down in Helen Street," then added, "Sorry about the mess here."

He grimaced when he nodded to the vomit stains on the wall and the ground.

"The young lad's new to this game. Anyway, it was the wee lassie that found her mother. The ambulance crew couldn't do anything for the victim and by the way, they got no further inside the flat than where the body's lying," he explained, then knowing the DCI would want to be aware about any contamination of the crime scene, he added, "I went into the flat, Ma'am, to determine there was no one else in there, but I didn't touch anything."

When Wells nodded, he continued, "The ambulance crew went in next door to see if they could help the wee girl who understandably, was completely distraught. She's with the neighbour, a Mrs Church, the woman that called it in. That and with respect, I didn't want to pre-empt you making your own arrangements, but I've also taken the liberty of calling out the duty Casualty Surgeon. I'm sorry, I've not got any more details about the victim other than the name on the door," he pointed to the plain, unpainted wooden door upon which was attached a cheap, black plastic nameplate that bore the name in white lettering, 'BRADLEY.'

"Most of the flats in Clifford Street," he continued, "are bought, but there's quite a few that are rented out by landlords. I can't say for certain, Ma'am, but I suspect this might be a rental."

On numerous occasions, Wells had read Docherty's name on arrest reports submitted by her officers as a witness or arresting officer and knew him to be a hardworking and conscientious cop, one who though never entertained the notion of sitting his police promotion exams, nevertheless could probably lose most of her Detectives when it came to general police work.

And so, she courteously replied, "Thanks for that, Joe, and don't be worrying about not collecting more info. I'm sure you had more to do than run around noting statements and you've done well, protecting the locus and summoning the doctor. Right, the body," she nodded towards the open door, "time for us to have a look."

"Ah, when you go in Ma'am," Docherty frowned, "prepare yourself. There's a possible murder weapon lying beside the victim and eh," his face contorted as though embarrassed when he added, "the poor woman's bowels have loosened; I'm suspecting it happened when she was attacked."

****

The body lay directly behind the door, splayed out as though tossed aside like a rag doll with her head pressed against the bottom of the door. Wrinkling her nose against the foetid smell and choking down the nausea that threatened to overwhelm her, Wells could see that the blood from the woman's battered head had seeped in clotted rivulets through her short, dyed blonde hair and then run down across her face, neck and onto the pink coloured dressing gown she wore. It didn't escape her notice that there appeared to be small slivers of bone adhering to the congealed blood in the victim's hair, an indication of the force used to murder the victim. The cheaply made, knee-length dressing gown had risen to the woman's groin and Wells also saw she wore a pair of white underpants that as Docherty had intimated, were now stained by her excrement and sodden by her loosened bladder. One arm was tucked beneath the body while the left arm was stretched out to its fullest extent, the hand clenched as though in terror.

The bloodstained candlestick lay beside the woman's body that apparently, as she correctly assumed, been simply discarded after delivering the fatal blows.

But it was the face that caught the DCI's attention.

Lying on her right side, the woman's eyes were wide open and staring as though in terror, her mouth also open in a silent scream. It seemed to her that the victim's expression was also one of surprise, as though unable to grasp that whoever was behind her, then struck her with such force, had not been considered by the victim to be a threat.

"You'll gather, Ma'am," Docherty's voice spoke from outside the door, "she's been moved a bit because of the wee lassie pushing against the door when she arrived home and to be honest, when I turned the house over and in case there was a suspect still within, I think when I shoved the door open to get through, I also moved her a bit too."

She stared at Joe and slowly nodding, realised that with him being a stoutly built man, it was likely then that if when exiting the flat, the killer used the door, he or she must have slipped through the door with the body pressing against it.

Does that mean the killer was a slim individual, she wondered?

Stepping into the dimly lit hallway with the light green artexed walls and the faded beige coloured carpet, Wells indicated with a nod that Baxter join her before she replied, "It couldn't be helped, Joe, because you needed to get in here, but when you were checking the place out, did you notice any windows open?"

"Eh, no, Ma'am, I didn't."

Taking the hint, Baxter stepped past Wells to check the flat's windows and a few seconds later, returned to confirm with a shake of his head that they were all tightly closed.

"So," Wells' eyes narrowed, "we must assume the killer left by the front door which means she can't have been pushed too far from the position in which she fell."

"Okay, Colin," she turned to her DS, "nip back to the motor and summon the circus and the duty PF. Have Sammy Salmon and at least four of the guys attend here and when he arrives, you head back to Govan and start setting up for a…"

She suddenly smiled, then taking a breath, shook her head and said, "Sorry, Colin, here's me telling you what you've done a dozen times before. Just ignore me, eh?"

"I'll get the murder box out, Boss," he grinned at her, "and the incident room will be ready to go when you arrive back at the factory."

Nodding, she replied, "In the meantime, I'll pop next door and speak with the daughter and the neighbour and get things rolling."

****

Carefully stepping over the body, Wells and Baxter exited the flat to find that Docherty's outdoor Inspector, Kenny Herdman, a cheery man in the twilight of his career, had joined the Constable and greeted Mary in his lilting Inverness accent with, "Thought I'd pop by, Ma'am, to find out if you need any more of my people here."

"Thanks, Kenny, but for the minute, I'm happy to have Joe and his neighbour standing by the locus. Colin's just off to call my guys in and we'll start some preliminary door to door inquiries for witnesses."

They both turned as a man and woman entered the close, with Mary inwardly pleased to see DS Elaine Fitzsimmons and her neighbour, DC Alan Hamilton, striding towards her.

"Heard on the radio about you being called here, Ma'am, so thought as we were close by?" Fitzsimmons stared at her.

"Good call, Elaine. Woman in the flat there," she jerked a thumb towards the ajar door "lying behind the door with her head bashed in. Murder weapon seems to be a heavy brass candlestick. We're waiting for the Casualty Surgeon to confirm death, but I'm satisfied we're looking at a murder. Her daughter, aged…?"

She turned with raised eyebrows to Docherty who replied, "The girl's ten, Ma'am."

"It was the daughter who discovered the body and the neighbour in there," she nodded to the opposite door, "who raised the alarm."

"Alan," she turned to the young Detective, "can you take a turn upstairs and start chapping on doors, please, while Elaine and I speak with the wee girl."

"Okay, Boss," he nodded and began to make his way up the first flight.

"Elaine?" she nodded at the DS.

It was then that Docherty politely coughed to attract Mary's attention, then said, "The woman there," he nodded at the closed door. "Strikes me, Ma'am, as being a bit of a torn-faced old git, if you get my drift?"

Choking back her laugh, Mary instead smiled when she replied, "Thanks, Joe, I'll bear that in mind."

****

They found the ambulance crew in the kitchen, the senior medic making a note in his folder, who then quietly told Wells, "The wee girl's in there with Mrs Church. We're done here and then heading out, unless you need us for something else?"

When she shook her head, it was Fitzsimmons who stepping forward, replied, "Just give me your names and contact details, guys, and we'll have someone take a statement from you later."

While Fitzsimmons dealt with the ambulance crew, Wells courteously knocked then pushed open the door to the front room where she saw the little girl sitting alone on the three-seater couch and softly weeping while the woman sat on an armchair, her hands clasped on her lap.

With a soft smile, said, "Mrs Church, I'm DCI Mary Wells. And you," she continued to smile, "must be the brave girl that I hope is going to be able to tell me about your mum?"

Yvonne Church, a stick-thin woman now turned seventy-two with her grey hair neatly piled into a tight bun on top of her head, was dressed in an all-encompassing, ankle length black dress that for some curious reason, reminded Wells of photos of Amish women she had seen in a book.

That and the creases in her pale face seemed to be a fixed frown. Involuntarily glancing about her, Mary thought it might explain the abundance of religious artefacts on the walls and displayed on the large, almost antiquated sideboard set against the opposite wall. In fact, as she glanced around the room, all of the furniture seemed to be dark wood, solid and old-fashioned.

When Mary stepped towards the little girl, she saw her to be thinly built, wearing the uniform of Bellahouston Primary School and whose fair hair was tied back with a bright yellow scrunchie into a loose ponytail.

The girl's dried tears shone on her face and even some thirty minutes after the discovery of her mother's body, Mary saw she was still shaking.

Shock, she presumed and mentally warned herself to be careful of her questioning of the girl.

She didn't ask, but sat herself down beside the child, then addressing the little girl, said, "I'm sorry, sweetheart, but nobody told me your name."

"Sarah," the girl lisped in a quiet voice.

"And you're ten, Sarah, is that right?"

Behind Wells, Fitzsimmons quietly slipped into the room and moving around the back of the couch, occupied the second armchair. The girl fearfully glanced around at Fitzsimmons, then seemingly accepting she was not a threat, her wide-eyed attention returned to be fixed on Wells when she nodded that yes, she was ten.

Knowing there was no easy way to break the news, Mary apologetically reached out and clasping the girl's hands in hers, held them tightly when she said, "Sarah, I'm so very sorry to tell you this, but I think you already know that your mum's dead."

Her heart filled with unspoken compassion, she watched the girl curl up into then lean against Mary and sob more tears.

Wrapping her arm around the girl's bony shoulders, she held her close and thought, God almighty, I'm breaking this wee lassie's heart. Yet there is no other way I might have been able to tell her the bloody news!

Minutes passed, then as Sarah's sobs eased and with as much gentle persuasion as she dared, it took Wells all of half an hour to interview the distraught child, during which time she learned that to the little girl's knowledge, there was no husband, boyfriend or any man who was seeing her mother and no, Sarah had no idea who might have wanted to hurt her mum.

During this time, Fitzsimmons was called from the room twice, once for five minutes and another for just a few minutes, but returned on each occasion to resume her seat, informing Mary on the second occasion that the DI had arrived at the locus.

"And when you left for school this morning," Wells asked Sarah, "did your mum say if she was expecting any visitors or does she have a job?"

"She goes into old people's houses and cleans for them," Sarah whispered.

"Right," Mary drawled, then asked, "and do you have a granny or a grandad, Sarah?"

Sarah nodded before she replied, "Granny Bradley. She lives up in Pollok."

"Do you know the address?"

Sarah shook her head before she replied, "We get the bus there, mum and me. The number fifty."

"If I asked you to go in one of my police cars, sweetheart, could you show the driver where your granny lives?"

Continuing to stare at Wells, the young girl thoughtfully nodded.

"Right then," she sighed, "I think that's probably enough for now, eh? Why don't I organise one of my officers to take you to your granny's house and we can let her know what's happened, eh?"

She saw years biting at the little girl's eyes and her lips compress as Sarah fought to maintain her composure.

"Elaine," Mary turned to her DS, "can you show Sarah out and introduce her to DI Salmon and his neighbour, please? I think it would be best if he takes Sarah to her granny's house and have him break the sad news."

"Okay, boss," Fitzsimmons nodded.

****

When the Detective and the little girl had left the room, Mary turned to Church to ask, "How well did you know Mrs Bradley?"

She wasn't prepared for the spiteful response, but almost immediately Joe Docherty's warning came to mind when the older woman sniffed, "For one, I seriously doubt she was *Mrs* Bradley."

Pokerfaced, she ignored Church's hostility when she retorted, "You didn't like her?"

As if realising she had perhaps spoken out of turn, Church took a breath before she offhandedly replied, "I didn't really know her that well, let alone dislike her and we seldom if ever exchanged a word. Look," she stared at Mary, "this is a respectable close and apart from the flat across the landing, we are all owners. In fact, the neighbours upstairs, some of them have been here as long as I have. Those that haven't, well," she shrugged, "at least they take their turns keeping the close tidy. In the year and a bit she's been here," she sniffed again, "that woman never took a turn cleaning the close and the state of her garden at the front? My God the state of her flat too. I wouldn't step into a complete pigsty like that. And don't even ask me about the bins, the sloppy way she left her rubbish out there," she scowled.

At that point Mary thought it unwise to mention the young Constables vomit all over the wall and ground outside the irate woman's door.

With a frown, Church continued, in a huffy voice "While I don't like speaking ill of the dead, Inspector…"

But she got no further for the door was opened by Fitzsimmons who said "Boss, a word?"

Excusing herself, Wells followed her DS into the hallway where in a low voice, Fitzsimmons said, "I could hear that old bag from out here and thought I'd better rescue you before you said something you might regret."

"And thank you for that," Wells exhaled with some feeling, then asked, "What's happening?"

In the same low voice, Fitzsimmons replied, "The DI's away with the wee girl to break the news to the victim's mother. Alan Hamilton only got two replies upstairs, neither of which were any use so we're looking at call-backs later this evening. The Casualty Surgeon's been and pronounced life extinct with the caveat that death was due to an as yet undetermined number of blows to the head. The Scenes of Crime are in the flat the now, processing it. The doc also opines death occurred within the last eight hours, which might explain why the victim is still wearing a dressing gown. I'm thinking if the doc's timing is correct, she's likely seen her daughter out the door to school and her killer has turned up shortly after."

"Seems logical, yes," Mary thoughtfully nodded, then asked, "Anything else?"

"Colin Baxter reports the incident room is up and running and with your permission has arranged your initial briefing for six this evening?"

Glancing at her wristwatch, Wells tiredly nodded while thinking, she better let her mother know to keep the kids that bit longer, then heard Fitzsimmons tell her, "Oh, and the PF Depute arrived to agree murder; a young lassie by the way who after seeing the body, was a bit green looking when she left," Fitzsimmons forced back a snigger. Mary smiled when she replied, "Okay, and thanks, Elaine. Now, can you note a statement from her in there," she nodded back at the front room, "while I liaise with SOCO and you can run me down the road when we're done here."

"No problem, boss."

****

The photography of the victim completed and though the flat had already been entered by a number of individuals, Mary pulled on a one piece white Forensic suit and nitrile gloves before following the SOCO supervisor through each room.

In the living room, the curtains were tightly drawn and suggested that the victim had not yet opened them from the previous evening. It was in this room on one side of the mantlepiece Mary saw the matching brass candlestick that seemed to be the neighbour of the one used to bludgeon the victim and formed the opinion the murder was opportunistic, that the killer had decided perhaps to commit the murder rather than having planned it.

As she toured the flat, what was apparent to Mary was the victim was either a lazy tenant or more likely, had no domestic skills, for the house seemed to be in disarray, with discarded clothing lying about the floors of the bedrooms and the bathroom badly needing a good clean. However, in both bedrooms and the sitting room, she saw an array of photographs of the victim, some framed others lying loosely, sometimes blonde and other times dark haired, laughing in some, posing provocatively in others; some with female friends or the victim alone and even some of her who as a child, her likeness leaving no doubt she was indeed the mother of Sarah. What was clearly obvious was that Elizabeth Bradley had indeed been an extremely attractive looking young woman.

A good many photos also featured the victim hugging and cuddling her daughter and appeared to have been taken through the years, recording the young girl growing up.

However, it was when they were within the third and smallest bedroom that the supervisor said, "Something that might be of interest to you, Ma'am."

When he pulled open both doors of an extremely large, free standing wardrobe, she saw it to be a heavily built piece of furniture and though no expert, guessed it to be made of dark oak and at least fifty to sixty years old; perhaps even older.

Barely concealing his smile, the supervisor said, "These big wardrobes were all the rage in the thirties and forties, Ma'am, and I've come across more than a few in tenements throughout the city. They're a bit too large and cumbersome for smaller houses and not the type of thing that you'd find in a modern semi or detached house or flat, but they're more popular in the older houses and flats like this, with high ceilings. Kind of art deco, as it were. Now," he turned with a wide grin, "tell me what you see."

Puzzled, she turned to stare at the interior of the wardrobe and saw that where the hanging space had been, it was now crudely shelved with inexpensive pine wood and upon each of seven of the eight shelves was a collection of ornaments; dozens of them, thought Wells, ranging from what to her seemed to be cheap bric a brac, to more expensive Lladro, Nao and other unnamed figurines, some of which to her amateur eye she guessed were certainty worth three figures.

On the eighth shelf lay a jumbled assortment of jewellery; brooches, rings, necklaces and watches, with some of the jewellery quite obviously gold and sporting what seemed to be genuine diamonds or emeralds. Other pieces, though again to her untrained eye, seemed to be cheap costume jewellery. However, at least one expensive piece was a large, ruby dress ring and Mary found herself staring at it with undisguised envy.

"The ring," the supervisor interrupted her thoughts, "wasn't with the rest of the jewellery. It was hidden here," he prised back a small, rectangular piece of wood from the side of the inner wardrobe to reveal a tight compartment, no more than four inches deep. "Quite a few of these old wardrobes had secret slots in them in which the mistress of the house could keep her most precious jewels, letters, that sort of thing. When I say secret," he smiled as he shook his head, "they weren't *that* secret, because the bloody things were *advertised* with having secret compartments, so they were more a kind of curiosity than a safe place, if you will."

"And that's where you found the ring?"

"Aye, it is. We maybe wouldn't have noticed it but for the fact the wee flap hadn't been tightly closed. Now, regarding all the productions we seize, with your consent we'll take them back to headquarters, dust them there and send our results to the Fingerprint Department. Once that's done," he paused, then brow furrowed, he asked, "Will it be DS Baxter who is to be your incident room manager?"

"Yes, that's correct," she nodded.

"Then when we're finished with the dusting, I'll contact Colin and have him send your production officer to our Department and for continuity purpose, we'll hand everything straight over to him."

"Good, but can you begin with the candlestick by the body, please? If there's any prints on it, I'll want to know ASAP and also, not that I'm in any doubt, but just in case send a blood sample from both the candlestick and our victim to the Laboratory to confirm that *is* the murder weapon."

"Roger, Ma'am, I'll ensure that's our number one priority."

"Anything else?" she heard herself mutter, then turned when the supervisor said, "We'll photograph each item, Ma'am, then bag it, but I have to warn you, we're already an hour over our finishing time, if you're okay to authorise the overtime?"

Nodding, she frowned when she replied, "Not a problem, but before you leave, turn this place over in case there's any more hidden items and if it means tearing up the floor, do it."

Grinning, the supervisor replied, "Will do, Ma'am."

CHAPTER TWO

Leaving the flat, Mary found Elaine Fitzsimmons standing at the close entrance speaking with Joe Docherty and two of her DC's who awaited the arrival of the undertakers that would remove the body to the City Mortuary at Saltmarket.

Docherty's young probationer stood nearby and clearly still looking a little sheepish, she smiled to herself.

Turning as she approached, Fitzsimmons informed her, "Inspector Herdman is making arrangements with the Chief Inspector for a replacement for Joe and his neighbour to stand by the flat overnight, Ma'am. So, ready to go?"

"That's as much as we can do this evening, Elaine, so yes. Back to Govan, if you please."

Fitzsimmons was turning onto the Paisley Road West when with some hesitation, she risked a glance at her, then said, "Ma'am, sorry if I'm overstepping the mark, but are you okay?"

Wells eyes narrowed when she replied, "What do you mean, okay?" She couldn't fail to notice Fitzsimmons face redden when the DS stuttered, "It's just that, well, this is just me asking, woman to woman; you understand?"

"Go on," her brow knitted when she slowly replied.

Fitzsimmons, her concentration on the bus that suddenly pulled out in front of her, exhaled before she said, "I can't help but notice, that suit you're wearing, it's hanging on you and your face. Look," she grimaced and irritably shook her head, "I'm not being cheeky, but your face has got thinner and…are you really okay? I mean, you're not ill or anything, are you?" she risked another glance at Mary, who saw the DS nervously lick at her lower lip.

Stunned, she stared for several seconds at Fitzsimmons then to the DS's surprise, she began to laugh.

Unprepared for the reaction, Fitzsimmons pulled the car over to the side of the road and the car now stopped, turned to her and said, "You *are* unwell, aren't you?"

Exhaling, she finally composed herself and holding up her hand, grinned when she replied, "No, Elaine, I'm not ill, but thanks for asking. Phew, you've no idea how that's cheered me up."

Fitzsimmons face expressed her surprise when she replied, "Cheered you up?"

"Elaine, you're probably thinking that with my face thinning and this suit," she plucked at the jacket's material, "that's hanging loosely on me, that I've got some sort of debilitating disease, maybe the big C or something."

She shook her head, then still smiling, she continued, "The truth is and please, don't be spreading it among the Department, but on the advice of my doctor, who scared me shitless when she started suggesting the possibility of the onset of diabetes, I've been attending the gym. That," she blushed, "and I've hired a personal trainer who quite frankly, is beasting me like I'm some sort of an Olympian in training."

She smiled again when she added, "To date, I've lost over three stone and a half and not only have I dropped to a size twelve, the fact you've noticed pleases me no end."

She paused when she stared down at her suit then with a quiet sigh, said, "And it's prompting me to throw out some of my old stuff and maybe look at a new wardrobe."

"Good for you and why not treat yourself," a relieved Fitzsimmons grinned at her, then tapping with a forefinger at the side of her nose, admitted, "There was some talk about you not looking yourself and you know what men are like. They'll not see themselves getting bigger, but if a woman as much as puts on a pound, they're not slow in noticing."

"And they've noticed me getting a bit thinner?" she dared to hope.

"Aye, but men don't understand slimming. As far as they're concerned," her face clouded when she frowned, "you're not getting thinner, you're unwell."

"Well, here's hoping that they continue thinking I'm unwell, at least till I reach my target of size ten, though to be honest, at my age maybe that's a wee bit optimistic."

"Well," Fitzsimmons grinned at her, "for your age as you say, you're doing okay being a size twelve."

"Aye, we live in hope anyway," Wells sighed.

Nodding, Fitzsimmons agreed with a wide grin then staring the engine, continued their journey to Govan Police Office.

****

The Detectives of G Division CID were gathered in the DS's room that Colin Baxter, an experienced incident room manager, had already claimed as his own and sat ready with his selected staff that included Constable Janey McPhee, a member of the Female and Child Unit who acted as his assistant, and two civilian staff from the typing pool.

Poking her head into the room, Mary loudly called out, "Sorry to keep you guys waiting, but if you can give me a few minutes with Colin before I brief you on what we know so far."

Joining her in her office along the corridor, Baxter glanced at his notebook before he related, "DI Salmon just phoned in from the mothers house in Langton Crescent up in Pollok to let us know he's broken the news about her daughter. He's leaving the victims daughter with her granny and making his way back here as we speak."

Nodding she understood, he continued, "A PNC check on our victim reveals her to be Elizabeth Anne Bradley, aged twenty-nine, with five convictions for minor theft; three for shoplifting when she was a teenager and two for theft of handbags from city centre pubs, but nothing in the last eleven years. No custodial sentencing; just a couple admonishments and fines only."

"Antecedent history?"

"According to the mother, who is Angela Bradley, her daughter is…" he shook his head then said, "*was* a single parent and was working for the last year and a half with a domestic cleaning company called 'Sweeps 'n Dusts' that's contracted by the City Council on behalf of the Social Work Department. I've got details of the company, but given the time now," he sighed, "they're likely closed, so it'll be tomorrow before we can visit them at their office in Bath Street."

And that, she thought, ties in with the daughter Sarah's comment about her mother cleaning old people's houses.

Mary glanced at her wristwatch then nodding, asked, "Did the DI say if the mother mentioned anything about a boyfriend or partner?"

"No, boss," he shook his head.

Probably forgot to bloody ask and saw it in Baxter's face he had the same thought, but instead said, "Anything else before I brief the team?"

"Not at the minute. I haven't arranged the team into neighbours yet. I thought I'd wait till you got back and made your decision."

"Okay, fair enough," she agreed with a nod, then sighing, added, "Right, let's not keep them waiting any longer."

****

Realising that it was of little use sending her team out to conduct inquiries so late in the day, she gave a five-minute synopsis of the little she knew, then dismissed the dozen Detectives she intended using for the murder investigation with the instruction they be promptly back at work the following morning.

Now seated at her desk, she composed a telex message to the Force Intelligence Bureau about the discovery of Elizabeth Bradley's body that would be summarised by the Duty DS at the FIB and included in the Chief Constable's next morning's twenty-four-hour major incidents bulletin.

That completed, her door was knocked then pushed open by her Detective Inspector, Samuel 'Sammy' Salmon.

The thirty-seven-year-old, university educated Salmon, tall, good looking and a sharp dresser was a fast-tracked officer of the Strathclyde Police Graduate Entry Scheme. Though such officers normally progressed through the uniformed ranks, Salmon and a half dozen others, were just a year previously promoted from uniformed Sergeants into the rank of Detective Inspector in an experiment suggested by the incumbent Chief Constable, Charles Pettigrew, himself with a background in administration and who was of the opinion the role of DI was simply that; an administrator.

Needless to say, most experienced CID managers and those of the experienced rank of DI believed such an experiment to frankly, be ridiculous.

Now standing before her desk, Salmon told her in his easy manner, "That's the victim's mother informed, boss, and the victim's daughter left with her, poor wee thing," he frowned.

"On that we can agree," she nodded in reply, then casually asked, "The mother say anything about her daughter having a boyfriend or anyone she was seeing at this time?"

It was clearly apparent by his expression that Salmon hadn't posed the question and when he blushingly replied, "Sorry, boss, I never thought to ask."

And that's you all over, she angrily thought; no initiative and bugger all common sense, but too tired to get into an argument, blamed the system that sent her an inexperienced DI and instead said, "Right, we'll have someone attend tomorrow and obtain an official statement from the mother. Now, I suggest we call it a night, Sammy, and meet here sharp and bright tomorrow. Okay?"

"Boss," he nodded, then turning towards the door, stopped when he turned and, his face reddening, said, "Look, boss, I know I sometimes let you down, but give me time."

He spread his hands and exhaling through pursed lips, continued, "I sometimes get the feeling I've been thrown into the deep end, coming into the CID and that you rightly expect more of me as a DI, but I promise. Each days a learning curve for me, so if you can just bear with me for a while longer?"

She realised it must have taken some pluck for him to admit his failings and fair play to him, she thought, at least he doesn't try to waffle his way out of his mistakes, so slowly smiled when she replied, "Every day for *all* of us is a learning curve, Sammy. I'll see you tomorrow."

****

Exiting the Clyde Tunnel then driving along Crow Road towards her mid-terraced, red sandstone house in Ancaster Drive, Wells reflected on her day.

It *had* been her intention to get off home earlier and persuade her mother to watch the kids that little bit longer to permit her to spend forty minutes at the gym in Jordanhill, but the murder had put paid to that notion.

Now she'd have to explain to her mother, Natalie, why she was so late and likely face the petted lip and moody silence that went with the disapproving scowl.

Thank God for dad, she inwardly thought and though her father, Michael MacDonald, was not one for standing up against his wife, at least he would always step in when Natalie found some excuse not to look after her grandchildren on the very few occasions when the childminder wasn't available.

She involuntarily smiled when she thought of her children.

Jamie at five years of age and just about to start school in August and Morven, about to turn three. Even at their tender age the children sensed their grandmother was not overly fond of them and it remained a mystery to Mary why her mother had borne three children, though already knew the first, Mary's brother Alan, had been a complete accident.

Mary herself had always wanted children, but after a half dozen miscarriages and having almost given up hope, then to the delight of both Harry and herself she unexpectedly found herself pregnant with Jamie. A menopause baby, the obstetrician had smiled and they'd settled on having just the one child. However, to her delight and Harry's disappointment, Morven arrived, but the pregnancy had resulted in gestational diabetes and the condition had worn her out.

It had been her choice to work through the pregnancy and on hindsight she now believed it had been a bad idea and combined with the worry about birth defects, at that time her mental health suffered dreadfully.

But of course, she had not known then about Harry's infidelity with their neighbour, Beth, her one-time close friend; or so she had thought.

Though the labour and birth had been difficult, Morven was born a healthy baby, but the stress resulted in severe postnatal depression, compounded just days after her delivery of her daughter when Harry announced he was leaving her.

Ten months ill-health leave followed, ten months of days passing without showering.

Days of intensive counselling.

Days of frequent telephone calls and supportive visits from her boss, Keith Meadows.

Ten months of self-flagellation that it finally took for her to first consider, then agree returning to work.

However, the shock of Harry's departure had so devastated her that her burgeoning dependence on comfort food had caused her weight to rocket until she was disgusted by her own reflection.

It had been both the calm and comforting chats with her father and her GP's referral to counselling that finally decided her to return to work, persuading her to once more take charge of her life; if not for herself, they had both cautioned her, then for her children.

She vividly remembered that first day she returned to Govan CID. The smiling faces, the handshaking, even the relief on the face of Sammy Salmon, who ably assisted by Colin Baxter as well as the recently promoted Elaine Fitzsimmons, had run the Department in the acting DCI role.

She recalled that less than an hour after arriving at Govan, she had locked herself in a toilet cubicle and wept, wondering if she had done the right thing by returning to work.

Then crying tears of self-pity, had startled when the door had knocked and the young Constable, Janey McPhee, of the Divisional FACU and herself the mother of a three years old daughter, had ushered her to the sink, helped her to both wash her face and compose herself and assured Mary she was not alone, that what she was experiencing was not that unusual.

Satisfied that her DCI was now presentable, Janey had left her alone with the promise no one would know what had occurred in the toilet and for that, she had been forever grateful.

It was then her thoughts turned towards the children, for without them she couldn't imagine where she would be these days. She involuntarily sighed and her thoughts turned again to the children's father, Harry.

The love of her life, or so she had believed, but who in those first few days after the birth of Morven, callously took off with their next-door neighbour, the woman she had considered to be a close friend.

She had also been fortunate that the divorce court judge had recognised the mental stress caused by his abandonment of not only his wife, but his children too and to Harry's dismay, awarded Mary not just full custody but also took the unusual decision the children were to remain at their place of abode; in essence, their father was not permitted to require his former wife to sell the house and so deprived him of his share of the profit of any sale.

Of course, Harry, now re-married to the bitch, had fought tooth and nail for his share of the house, citing his need for the money to purchase a new home. It was some months after the *decree absolute* that with some bitter satisfaction, she learned from a former friend of theirs that Harry's plumbing business had failed and he was now employed on a building site.

With his new, much younger wife pregnant and them getting by on just his income alone, Harry's misfortune also meant that his child support payments dwindled.

Much as it pained her, Mary made the decision not to make an issue of Harry's default with the payments, telling herself that as he had no apparent interest in seeing his children - though she suspected that was his new wife's influence - the little contact he had with Jamie and Morven, the better for them.

Perhaps it was the effort of changing her name or later explaining to the children why she was Mary MacDonald and they, Jamie and Morven Wells, but whatever her reason, she retained her married name, though a part of her believed it was simply to spite Harry's new wife.

On hindsight, though it was some time after the divorce was finalised and though she had always denied the thought, she had come to accept she'd married a morally weak man and though she might have forgiven him for such weakness, she would neither forgive nor forget the awful names he had called her during the time they were separated, citing her post-natal weight, her lacklustre appearance and even accusing her that throughout their marriage, of her indifference in bed; an accusation that was particularly hurtful because of its falseness. Names that when repeated by her lawyer during his presentation to the court, had quite clearly been noted by the middle-aged female judge, whom from her expressions upon hearing the accusations, Mary suspected might just also have suffered such indignities.

Turning into Ancaster Drive, she slowed as she approached the house, a little disappointed that her usual space outside her front gate was occupied by a black coloured Ford Capri, a car she didn't recognise as belonging to any of her neighbours.

It was an unwritten rule among the neighbours in the mid-terraced block that the space outside each house was unofficially designated to that house.

"Must be a visitor," she grimly muttered as she parked the nearside wheels of the red coloured, three-year-old Toyota Corolla on the pavement on the opposite side of the road.

Switching off the engine, she glanced at the mid-terraced house adjacent to her own and her brow furrowed when she saw lights on. The house had previously been rented by Harry's new wife prior to them moving away when he'd abandoned Mary and his children, then lain empty for some weeks. The most recent tenants, a lovely young Indian couple who had both been employed at the nearby Gartnavel Hospital, had occupied the property till a month previously and when they'd moved out to return to India, the absent owner had decided to again let the house.

With the departure of the Indian couple, not only had Mary lost good neighbours and friends, but also impromptu childminders when she was late home from work, for the couple had adored the children and had been only too happy to feed them dinner and care for them till their mother returned home.

For the weeks the house had been on the market, she was aware a succession of viewings had taken place and it surprised Mary that the house had not quickly been leased, but now with the estate agents rental sign removed from the small front garden, it seemed she had new neighbours.

Having often visited the house when her former friend and the Indian couple occupied it, she knew it to be much the same size, though not as spacious as her own home that after improvements through the years by Harry and herself, now boasted a large formal living room downstairs, a moderate sized dining room and extended kitchen to the rear, while on the first floor there were two good-sized bedrooms, the master bedroom with a bay window. A bathroom was situated on the landing between the ground floor and the first floor and a professional conversion in the roof space had resulted in two further bedrooms, as well as a second bathroom.

Staring at the home that both she and Harry had through the years lovingly renovated and considered to be their 'forever home,' she idly recalled Harry's pleading that it be sold and thought, no wonder you wanted your share of the place.

She smiled at the satisfying memory she got from telling him to fuck off; she wasn't for selling, a decision endorsed by the court.

Getting out of her car, she strode across the road and with a quick glance at the neighbour's window, peeked inside the Ford Capri.

It seemed almost immediately to her that the car was owned by someone who quite possibly had children, for the leather seated interior was dull and she could see at least two empty crisp packets on the well of the passenger floor and what looked like a crushed plastic juice bottle. The bodywork of the car was dull and dusty too. Now why, she wondered, does that make me smile?

****

Before unlocking her front door, she glanced at her wristwatch and saw it to be ten minutes to eight.

Bugger, she frowned, for she knew what kind of reception she faced. Though her mother was likely aware, she had been the last option as a childminder, for neither Jamie nor Morven actually liked their disapproving grandmother who found fault with them where there was none and whose idea of caring for them was to slip on a DVD and sit them down to watch television with the warning not to leave the couch and to remain seated there till the time it took their mother to return home.

Unlike her father who openly adored the kids and found any excuse to spend time with them, particularly since Jamie had recently discovered football, Mary was acutely aware too that Natalie had little in common with her grandchildren and would find any excuse to avoid spending time with them.

Not that her own relationship with Natalie was any better, for she had always known that her mother believed that with Harry being a plumber, regardless that he had worked hard to establish his own business, her daughter had married beneath her, that her postnatal depression was all a piece of nonsense and that the failed marriage was Mary's fault.

And this from a woman who had grown up in a two-bedroom council flat in the Gorbals; a flat that had accommodated not just her workshy father and put-upon mother, but also three siblings and who upon marrying her father, insisted on adopting a *lah-de-dah* accent.

"Sorry I'm so late," she greeted her mother with a fixed smile, but who stood in the hallway with her coat already on and her handbag slung across one arm.

With a theatrical glance at her wristwatch, Natalie, her blue-rinsed hair perfectly coiffured, snapped, "I put your children to bed," then continued, "Perhaps if earlier today, dear, you had warned me you would be late then I might have had time to cancel my bridge night with the girls a little earlier."

"I'm sorry you had to cancel," she continued to smile at her mother, though now through gritted teeth, and resisted the urge to tell Natalie in great detail of the woman with the bloodied head and crushed skull.

Without even a glance at her daughter, Natalie strode past her and wordlessly exited through the open door.

"And goodbye to you too, mother," she sighed as she fought the angry urge to slam the door shut then glanced up the stairs in front of her.

Slipping off her overcoat and dumping her handbag on the hallway table, she trudged up the stairs, still peeved at her mother's attitude when she'd arrived home and not for the first time, thought about her parents' marriage.

It was an open though unspoken family secret that marrying just six weeks after they had met, that seven months after Michael and Natalie's registry office wedding in Martha Street in the Glasgow city centre, her older brother Alan was born.

Family protocol and good manners never questioned the early arrival, explained by Natalie as a premature birth. However, as the baby grew into a toddler and then a young boy, it could not help but be noticed by the families on both sides that Alan did not have the hair colouring and complexion common to the indigenous people of the West of Scotland. Instead, Alan's dark swarthy looks and black coloured curly hair completely differed to that of the children of both families.

Not that it made any difference to Michael, who loved and continued to love him as he loved his daughter Mary, born a year later, and his youngest son, William, now aged thirty-eight.

Even as a child, Mary realised that her mother soon cut herself off from her own parents, for still living in their council home in the Gorbals, at the time that an area with a high incidence of poverty and crime, Natalie reinvented herself as the posh Mrs MacDonald, whose husband was a successful insurance broker and whose in-law's resided in a bought, semi-detached bungalow in the Kings Park area of the city.

As the years passed, even as a child Mary often wondered at her mother's brash assertiveness over her father, though it was several years before she really realised that assertiveness was just another word for bullying. And her mother's bullying carried on to her own children as she attempted to dictate their lives too.

These days, neither Alan nor his wife, Morag, seldom if ever visited her parents at home with their two children, though she was aware her father was a regular visitor to their home, just as he regularly visited William and his lovely young wife, Kathleen, a Belfast born Catholic who nursed in the Sothern General Hospital.

Their marriage had been another bone of contention with the religiously bigoted Natalie, letting all and sundry know that her first concern was if they have children, in which religion would the children be raised.

Not that Natalie herself had come from a deeply religious upbringing, for her own awakening to the Church of Scotland was more to do with the family moving house to the affluent Newton Mearns and recognising the opportunities belonging to the local church offered socially, rather than any sudden closeness with God. This bigotry, as well as her disdainful behaviour towards her new daughter-in-law, had resulted in William cutting himself off completely from his mother who, he privately vowed to his big sister, "…will never again set foot in my home."

At the top of the landing, she paused outside the children's bedroom then eyes narrowing, curiously wondered if her father had ever been happy married to her mother.

Softly exhaling, she irately noticed the closed bedroom door, then gently pushed it open and was immediately angry.

Her mother had not switched on the dull nightlight, even though Mary had expressly insisted she do so.

Natalie's argument with Mary was that, just as she had done with a timid William when was he was young, children slept better in a darkened room.

It was then in the crack of light shining through the door from the hallway, she saw Morven's eyes were wide open.

Furious though she was she forced a smile and went to the little girl, then sitting on the edge of the bed, reached for her and drew her into her arms.

"Still awake?" she whispered.

"Grandma wouldn't put the light on," Morven replied through trembling lips, "and I was scared the bogeyman might come in the dark."

She realised from Morven's breath her mother hadn't even bothered getting the children to brush their teeth before bedtime, another failing that annoyed her no end.

"Well," she smiled in the darkness, "the *bogeyman's* away home and I'm here now, so the light is going on and then you can get some sleep, eh?"

Morven nodded as her mother laid the little girl's head back down onto the pillow, then moving towards the duck shaped lamp, switched it on.

Leaving the room, Mary left the door slightly ajar, another thing she and her mother disagreed on.

For the time being, the children shared the second bedroom on the first floor, though Jamie, soon to be a big schoolboy he frequently reminded his mother, had recently been making overtures about moving upstairs to one of the second-floor bedrooms.

Returning downstairs, she entered the kitchen to check what was available in the fridge, something that wouldn't take long to cook. Since her healthy diet had kicked in, she had a selection of healthy fast foods from which to choose and finally settled for a salad and cold chicken dish, prepared just the previous day.

Seated at the breakfast bar, she was about to start eating when the phone rang.

"Hello?"

"Hello, sweetheart," her dad replied, "has your mother left yet?"

"Thirty seconds out of the door when I got in," she sighed. "I think she's going straight home because I was late getting in and she's missed her bridge night."

"Her bridge night? That's not till Thursday. Is that what she told you, hen?"

The lying old bugger, Mary angrily thought, but forced herself to be calm when she replied, "Maybe I got it wrong, dad. Anyway, she's away so she should be with you soon."

There was a slight pause before her father softly asked, "Hard day, Mary?"

"I've had better," she sighed, then lied, "Sorry, dad, I've something on the cooker."

"Oh, aye, right. Away you go, hen, and I'll speak to you tomorrow."

When she replaced the phone in the wall cradle, she felt tears biting at her eyes and bit at her lower lip, surprised that her father's concern for her was moving her to tears.

Taking a deep breath, she used the sleeve of her blouse to wipe at her eyes then loudly scolded herself with, "Right, Mary Wells, have your dinner, then away upstairs and have a half hour on the exercise mat, then bed."

Thirty-five minutes and one hot shower later, an exhausted Mary returned downstairs in her pyjamas and barefooted to ensure both the front and back doors were securely locked, when in the hallway, she stopped and listened.

She held her breath then sure enough, heard the faint strains of music coming from the adjoining house. Moving closer to the hallway wall, she placed an ear against the wall and listening intently, thought she could make out the sounds of classical music.

At least, she thought and smiled, it's not rock n roll, then made her way back upstairs to bed.

CHAPTER THREE - Wednesday

"It's only me," Mary heard the voice call out and dusting the spilled cornflakes from her daughter Morven's tee shirt, glanced up as the portly, redhaired childminder, Eileen McAulay, entered the kitchen. Her hair piled untidily on top of her head and wearing a brightly coloured, ankle-length kaftan dress that swished as she walked, with open toed sandals, a home-made necklace of colourful beads and a hessian bag hung over her left shoulder, Eileen swept Jamie into her arms and smothered the giggling wee boy with kisses before greeting his mother.

She grinned at Eileen and shaking her head told her, "They've had breakfast, so don't let them kid you on they're hungry."

"I know I'm a wee bit early," Eileen frowned, "but I heard on Radio Clyde there was a murder in Cessnock yesterday. Isn't that your area?"

"Yes, it is and thanks for getting here," she nodded, shying away from the high chair and Morven's milk stained fingers that threatened to stain her black suit jacket.

"Right, away you go, hen. I've got hoddit and doddit here," Eileen blew a raspberry at the squealing Morven, "so give me a phone later to let me know if you're going to be late. I'm not doing anything this evening, not that I ever do," she theatrically sighed, "so don't be worrying about the time, okay? However, if you *do* get the opportunity, phone me anyway to let me know if I've to put the kids to bed or not."

With a relieved sigh, Mary nodded then with a final kiss of both her children, hurried through to the hallway to collect her handbag and overcoat, thinking once more what a God sent find the widowed Eileen had been.

A widow for almost ten years and childless, Mary had been introduced nine months earlier to Eileen by the postnatal counsellor and almost immediately, they'd become good friends. In Mary's eyes, Eileen McAulay was the grandmother the children really wanted and deserved.

Though they had become good friends, Mary knew little of Eileen's personal history, but was aware she lived in an upper conversion of a large detached house in Cleveland Gardens, a relatively well-heeled area in the north side of the city and where property wasn't cheap. She often wondered why it was that Eileen, who drove a brightly yellow coloured Volkswagen Beetle that was festooned with painted flowers and badges, would work as a childminder when in Mary's mind, she was capable of so much more. Yet, rather than risk their relationship, Mary kept her questions to herself and instead continued to be grateful for Eileen's friendship.

Of course, Mary's mother completely disapproved of the fifty-something hippy who regardless of the weather, had the children out of the house most of the day, either dressed in shorts, tee shirts and hats for the sun or rain jackets and wellies for stamping through the puddles in the rain.

"Television," she was fond of telling Mary "is for days when even I won't venture out."

Stopping at the full-length mirror in the hallway, she stared at her reflection, seeing her face to be free of make-up and her skin for the first time in years, clear and fresh looking. Her shoulder length brown hair, now with flecks of grey at the temples, was tied back in a tight ponytail. To her relief, her white blouse had survived Morven's sticky fingers; however, thanks to her punishing physical regime and healthy diet, she saw to her dismay the black skirted suit now looked, as Elaine Fitzsimmons had pointed out, to be hanging on her new figure.

"Nothing I can do about that just now," she muttered with a sigh, yet inwardly pleased that at least she could recognise she now had an hourglass figure.

Pulling open the front door, she stepped out into the short path just as the door opened in the adjacent house and a man stepped out into the adjoining path.

Taller than Mary's five feet six by about five or six inches, she thought him to be in his early to mid-forties, clean shaven with a swarthy complexion - or is he sun-tanned, she wondered - with neatly trimmed brown hair and wearing a three-piece dark grey suit with a light grey shirt and red coloured tie. In one hand he carried a black leather briefcase.

She thought at the time he seemed to be the very epitome of the modern businessman.

"Hi," he greeted her with a smile. "I'm your new…"

"Sorry," she crisply interrupted with her hand held high. "I'm a little late for work. Bye."

The heels of her black patent block heel shoes tapping a rapid beat as she hurried across the road, she felt her face redden, realising that she had been a little rude.

A *little* rude?

Sod it, she thought; that really *was* rude of me.

Now angry with herself she turned the key in the ignition to start the car, acutely aware that the man had now entered the Capri and was himself about to drive off.

If she were honest, the forty-four-year-old Mary Wells had no desire to make new friends, neighbours or otherwise and particularly men. That and since the break-up of her marriage, over the years social invitations had all but dried up, mainly due to the fact that mutual friends had either deserted Mary or following her period of postnatal depression, were either too busy or too embarrassed to maintain contact with her.

Yes, she still had two married brothers and two sisters-in-law who were more than supportive, but like Mary they tactfully avoided family functions because of the usual disapproving behaviour of their mother, Natalie.

The middle child, she was close to her siblings and sympathised with her father, who his children adored, but acutely knew as did her brothers that Michael was locked in a loveless marriage.

Settling herself into the journey, she mentally prepared herself for that day's task and the conversation she was sure to have with her boss, the Assistant Chief Constable in charge of the CID, Keith Meadows.

****

That Wednesday morning, the seventh of July 1987, had dawned clear and bright with the promise of sunshine and a warm day. But of course, this was Glasgow where the locals, rather than trust the TV or radio meteorologists, usually made the decision to stick their heads out of the window to check the weather.

Parking his five-year-old, silver coloured MG in Orkney Street outside G Division Headquarters, DI Sammy Salmon checked his reflection in the rear-view mirror before exiting the vehicle, flicking back a lock of fair hair that had come adrift and checking his teeth for any sign of trapped food.

Not quite a narcissist, nevertheless the DI believed his appearance to be a major feature of his job and quickly realised if he were to progress through the ranks, he must be seen to be smartly turned out. With a final adjustment of his golf club tie, he climbed out of the car and made his way across the road towards the front doors of the office, gallantly holding open the door for the two uniformed female Constables who exited and to whom he graced with a bright smile.

However, he might not have been so pleased had he heard one quietly comment to the other, "I hear he's all balls, but nae brain." Making his way upstairs to the DI's room, Salmon prepared himself for yet another day of disappointing Mary Wells, who truth be told, he both liked and admired. If nothing else, he was a realist and as he had admitted to her the previous evening, often felt himself out of his depth when dealing with his CID subordinates, most of whom were far more experienced than he was.

In fact, since the unsolved murder in 1986 in the Penilee area of the Division of a local man, Edward McCreadie, the subsequent year had reinforced Salmon's belief that he was not cut out to be a Detective. The only thing stopping him from requesting a return to uniform was that the scheme must succeed, for not only was the Chief Constable the driving force behind the idea, but it was also his directive it *must* succeed.

For Salmon to admit he wasn't capable of performing the function of DI would be a direct disputation that the Chief had been wrong and such an admittance would therefore effectively end the DI's career. He'd had numerous conversations about the issue with his partner, Julie, a Veterinarian, yet still had to decide and though she never said, he suspected she was becoming bored with him and particularly because of his indecisiveness about his career.

Never would he have known or realised that he was an honest man who knew his limitations and could openly admit to them; his one strength that even his CID colleagues would agree upon.

Pushing open the door to the DI's office, he hung his overcoat on the metal hook attached to the wall and with a final deep breath, left the room to make his way to the incident room.

To his surprise, he met with DCI Mary Wells walking from her own room and who greeting him with a smile, asked, "Ready for another day, Sammy?"

****

DS Colin Baxter glanced up as the DCI, accompanied by DI Salmon, strode into the room, causing those officers present to sit up as the general hubbub tailed off to a quiet hush.

"Morning all," she began, then with a smile, picked out one of her senior DC's, Kenny Maxwell, and squinting at him, said, "I hear you've brought your sleeping bag to work, Kenny, in preparation for some more overtime?"

The Department's Detectives knew that Maxwell was the top earner where OT was concerned and so the room burst into laughter as an envious Salmon realised that the DCI's simple joke had so easily and within seconds, united the Detectives as a team.
Glancing at Wells, he couldn't help but smile and wished he had such ability.
"Right, Colin," she began by turning to the incident manager, "any phone calls yet on the murder incident hotline?"
"Nothing so far, Boss," he shook his head, "but I managed to catch Charlie the mortuary attendant first thing when I got in and made the arrangement this morning for the post mortem. Eleven o'clock at the Saltmarket and its Mr Morgan who will perform the autopsy, boss."
"Morgan?" her face registered her surprise. "I thought he'd just retired?"
Baxter grinned when he tapping his nose with a stubby forefinger, he replied, "Charlie says Morgan's just taken on a new wife, so he's needing the cash."
"Aye, like all us women are money grabbing harlots, eh?" she pretended to scowl.
"Sorry, Boss," Baxter had the good grace to blush.
"Right, anything else I should know?"
"Ah, no, boss. I've sorted out teams as agreed and the actions and were you saying that you wanted the victim's mother re-interviewed?"
Ignoring Salmon's embarrassed glance, Wells replied, "Yes, allocate that action to…"
Her eyes danced around the room then settled on Elaine Fitzsimmons. "DS Fitzsimmons and her neighbour and before you leave the office, Elaine, come and see me, please."
"Boss," Fitzsimmons nodded.
"Right, folks," Wells addressed the team, "here's the little that we know."
She took a breath, then began, "Elizabeth Bradley, aged twenty-nine years, lived with her ten-years-old daughter Sarah in the rented, ground flat at 42 Clifford Street, Cessnock."
Her brow furrowed when she turned to Baxter to say, "On that point, Colin, most if not all the flats around there are privately owned, though likely there will be a few that are rented. Have an action raised to find out who rented the flat to our victim, what rent she

paid and try to establish from her employer what her salary was. I'm thinking that with her having previous convictions for theft and with regard to the items discovered in the flat, she might have had a wee business peddling stolen property."

"On it, boss," he scribbled on his pad.

"Now, where was I," she took a deep breath. "The time of death and the manner in which the victim was attired suggests she was killed not long after putting her daughter out the door to school. Now, you guys who will be on the door to door. While there's no suggestion yet the victim had a man friend, let's not forget to ask anyone who knew her if that is correct. One more thing on that. Whoever is allocated the close that is the locus, pry what you can out of the neighbour across the landing, Mrs Church. She strikes me as being a right old busybody who's lived there a long time and it was clear she did *not* like our victim. Gossip, hearsay get what you can from her."

Again she turned to Baxter to ask, "Any suggestion the victim had a vehicle, Colin?"

"Not so far, Boss, but I'll get it checked out."

"Okay, thanks, and the last thing I want for now," she turned back to the team to again single out DC Maxwell, telling him, "Kenny, you and your neighbour, John, see Colin about the action for the victim's employer whose business address is, as I recall, in the city centre. We'll need a list of every client Bradley has visited and if there was ever any complaint about her being light-fingered, anything at all. I'm also curious to know if anyone from the company tried to contact her yesterday and, on that point," she smiled again at Baxter, "contact BT with the victim's house phone number and ask for a billing for say, the last month. Let's find out who she was in contact with, eh?"

"I'll do that myself, boss," he nodded then asked, "Who are you taking to the PM?"

"Myself, the DI and…who have you assigned to collect productions?"

"That'll be me, boss," DC Fiona McCloy raised her hand, then added, "and I'm taking Stuart McDougall with me to show him the ropes regarding production seizures."

The young man, almost five months as an aide to the CID, also raised his hand, but laughter erupted when Mary said, "It's okay, Stuart, you can put your hand down. I know what you look like."

"Right then, folks," she clapped her hands, "see Colin for your actions and let's get to it."

While the team dispersed, Mary called Fitzsimmons and DC Alan Hamilton to her and told them, "Give me ten minutes, guys. I'll need to phone the ACC to update him, so have a coffee meantime."

Returning to her room, she sat behind her desk and dialled the direct number for ACC Meadows secretary and greeted her with, "Hi, Ellen, it's Mary Wells at Govan. Is the boss available for a call?"

"He's on his second roll and bacon," Ellen's annoyed voice was almost a whisper, "but will he listen to me about his cholesterol? Not a chance. Hang on Mrs Wells, I'll put you through."

Even after the years since the divorce, for some reason it irked her to hear herself addressed as 'Mrs Wells.'

"Good morning, Mary, is this about your murder?"

"Morning, sir, and yes."

The next ten minutes were spent describing the circumstances of Elizabeth Bradley's death and the investigation that had now ensued.

"So," she could almost see him grimace, "in short, no suspect, no witnesses and you believe this woman Bradley might herself have been up to naughties in stolen property?"

"It's purely supposition at this time, sir, but once I have an update from SOCO, that they're done fingerprinting the items, I might be able to try and trace their origin. The victim has previous for theft, albeit a number of years previously, but that doesn't mean she wasn't still actively thieving, just not getting caught for it. I can't believe the items I saw were legitimately collected."

"And what do you need from me?"

"Right now, nothing. I have sufficient resources to deal with the investigation, but if I do need more troops, hopefully I can call upon you?"

"Here to help, Mary, so keep in touch."

She gathered that to be a polite dismissal and bidding him cheerio collected her thoughts before calling Fitzsimmons and her neighbour into the DCI's room.

****

"Okay, guys," she glanced from Fitzsimmons to Hamilton, "apart from the formal statement, what I need from our victim's mother is a full story about her daughter; chapter and verse. Men who were or are currently in her life, associates, her history thieving, previous addresses and if the mother knew about the ornaments and jewellery."

She stared at Fitzsimmons, then slowly smiled before she said, "I apologise Elaine."

"Boss?"

"This isn't your first time round the dance floor and here's me trying to tell you what to ask."

"Doesn't mean you can't remind me, Boss," she stared knowingly at Wells. "We all slip up sometimes."

Though Hamilton didn't catch the inference, Wells realised that her DS was referring to the DI's visit to the mother when the relevant questions should have been answered.

It was then Fitzsimmons asked, "What about the formal identification prior to the PM, Boss? Do you want me to bring the mother to the mortuary?"

Mary slowly exhaled when she replied, "I've thought about that and I'm making an uncommon decision. The daughter Sarah discovered and identified her mother to Joe Docherty and of course, for comparison purposes and as a matter of record, we have the victim's fingerprints on file; so, no. I'm satisfied our victim *is* Elizabeth Bradley and frankly, I think it's inappropriate to put her mother or her ten-year-old daughter through a formal identification." Wells could not know that her response had been exactly the correct thing to say and heartened Elaine Fitzsimmons that her DCI, quite apart from being a good manager, was also a considerate woman.

Rising to leave, Wells stopped Fitzsimmons and told Hamilton, "Give us a minute, please, Alan."

When the door closed behind the young DC, a slightly tense Mary said, "About our conversation in the car, yesterday afternoon. You were right. I saw myself in this suit," she plucked at the material of the jacket, "when I was leaving the house this morning and I look like a bag of rubbish tied in the middle."

"Boss…"

"No, Elaine," she shook her head. "I need to get myself some properly fitting underwear and a couple of outfits and frankly, it's been a while since I've been shopping for anything for myself. So," she gritted her teeth, "I was wondering if you had any ideas about…"

Fitzsimmons raised a hand to stop her speaking and quickly said, "My sister-in-law, Jill, she's a senior manager at the BHS store in the city centre, the one on the corner of Sauchiehall Street and Renfield Street. If you're okay with it, I can ask her to maybe accommodate you one evening, perhaps if you can meet her there just at closing time that I think," her face wrinkled, "is about seven in the evening?"

"Elaine that would be great if you could arrange it, yes."

"Leave it with me, Boss. I'll give Jill a call this afternoon and see what she can do," she smiled and left to join Hamilton.

Suddenly feeling a little happier, Mary exhaled with relief.

****

The post mortem went as predictably expected.

The pathologist, Mr Morgan, amicably greeted Mary and her team then proceeded with his examination.

"As you can see, DCI Wells, your victim has suffered several hard blows to the front brow and top of her head. I would suggest a sustained assault that resulted in, let me see," he peered closely at the wounds, now exposed after being thoroughly hosed with water by Charlie the mortuary assistant. "Yes, four wounds that first split open the scalp then shattered the parietal bone and the frontal bone." He turned to lift the corpses right hand then added, you will also see that her wrist and forearm are bruised and that suggests defensive wounds. That is, she has attempted to deflect the blows and been struck on the arm."

Wells watched him stoop to peer at then manipulate the forearm before telling her, "It seems that the radius and ulna bones are also fractured."

Turning to her, he asked, "Have you recovered a weapon?"

"A heavy, brass candlestick, Mr Morgan, but it's currently at the SOCO being examined. However," she turned to take an envelope from DC Fiona McCloy, "I have here a photo of the weapon we suspect was used."

"Ah, yes," he peered at the photo then nodded, "well, that looks a likely suspect for inflicting such damage."

"Right then," he smiled at her, "I have little doubt that unless the pathology arrives at a different conclusion, my decision is that the wounds suffered by this apparently healthy young woman have undoubtedly caused her premature death. In short, you are quite correct to accept she was murdered."

"Thank you, Mr Morgan," she formally nodded at him.

****

DC Kenny Maxwell parked the CID car in a bay on the road in Bath Street outside the Georgian two-storey, mid-terraced, blonde sandstone building and with his neighbour, DC John McGhee, exited the vehicle.

"This is the place," Maxwell peered at the mottled brass sign on the black painted metal railing that read, 'Sweeps 'n Dust.'

With twenty years' service as a police officer, the imposing grey haired, married forty-four-year-old, six-foot-tall, heavy-set and bullish Maxwell had come late to the CID, having been appointed just two years previously, though had spent several years of his service working within Divisional plainclothes squads.

In contrast, his thirty-two-year-old, five-foot eight inch, slightly built, slope-shouldered and prematurely balding neighbour, who wore NHS issued thin-rimmed spectacles and had served for eleven years, four as a Detective at Govan CID, was what his colleagues colloquially termed, 'a right take-on.'

The unremarkable looking, softly spoken McGhee was known and feared by the criminally minded in the G Divisional area. Mainly due to his polite and unassuming nature, many thugs and in particular, those who abused their spouses, often discovered to their cost that when pushed, McGhee's unpredictable temper came to the fore and soon found themselves dealing with an officer who to his own embarrassment, held the Divisional record for completing the most 'Use of Baton' reports.

However, what never ceased to amaze both his male and female colleagues was that the unremarkable looking, bachelor McGhee seemed to have some inner attraction to females of all ages, shape and size, unmarried as well as married; some strange charisma they found irresistible and he frequently found himself being solicited by such women. Whether McGhee ever took advantage of these many offers was known only to him for to his credit, he was not a boastful man.

And so, it was this pair who had been tasked to make inquiry about the victim's employment.

Mounting the steps to the porch entrance of the building and discovering the inner door to be locked, Maxwell pressed the bell set in the wall.

It was over a minute and a second push at the bell before the door was opened by a woman with short, grey hair cut in a bowl style who at five feet four inches tall and about fifteen stone, stared up through thick lensed glasses at Maxwell, then in a faltering voice, asked, "Can I help you?"

Guessing the woman to be about fifty years of age or perhaps older, he produced his warrant card and replied, "CID. Can we speak with someone about one of your employees?"

Inviting the Detectives to follow her, the woman, who had a visible limp to her left leg, led them to a front room that with two desks and three grey metal filing cabinets, seemed to serve as the office.

Seating herself behind the smaller of the two desks, she said in the same faltering voice, "Mr McLean isn't here at the minute, but maybe I can help you?"

"And is Mr McLean the owner?" Maxwell asked with a smile.

"Ah, yes. Alex McLean. I'm Agnes Flynn, the secretary for the company. Can I ask what this is about?"

"May we?" Maxwell smiled and pointed towards two plastic, tubular chairs, then without waiting for an invitation, the two Detectives pulled them over to sit facing Flynn across her desk.

They turned as a young woman entered the room and heard Flynn rudely snap, "Not now, Jessie!"

"Sorry," Flynn blushed as the woman fled the room, "but I'm guessing you want this to be private?"

"Ah, yes," a surprised Maxwell glanced at McGhee, then noting the absence of a ring on her left hand, continued, "We're from Govan CID, eh, is it *Miss* Flynn?"

"Yes, Miss," she blushed again.

"Right," he smiled. "We're here to ask about an employee, Elizabeth Bradley."

They saw Flynn's face turn pale when her voice almost a whisper, she replied, "Lizzie. What's she done now?"

"So, you know who we're talking about?"

Flynn scowled when she replied, "Lizzie's been a pain in the arse, pardon my French, since she started working for us and I'm surprised that Alex…Mr McLean, kept her on. Or maybe not *that* surprised," she snorted and turned her head to glance out of the window.

Seizing on her comment, Maxwell asked, "Why not surprised, then?"

She took a deep breath before she replied, "Lizzie was, how can I put this politely, a bit of a slut."

Seated beside his neighbour, McGhee tightly clamped his teeth shut before he laughed while Maxwell asked, "Are you saying they were, eh, involved?"

She leaned across the desk, then staring him in the eye, nodded when she sniffed, "Oh, aye, he was shagging her, so he was. And him married with kids, too."

Sitting back in her seat, she folded her arms then, her brow furrowed as if realising she was disclosing too much information, asked, "What exactly has she done this time?"

"What is it she's done before that's caused you trouble?" he asked.

She shrugged when she replied, "There's been complaints about her. Lazy, poor cleaning, bad timekeeping and sometimes not turning up for jobs, that sort of thing. Why?"

"Was she supposed to be working yesterday?"

Her expression mirrored her surprise when she said, "Yes, I suppose so. I mean I'd need to check her rota. We've over eighty women working here, so I don't know without checking who her clients might be for a Tuesday. Do you want me to do that now," she half rose from her chair.

"Please," he nodded and watched her walk to one of the grey metal cabinets where after a brief search she withdrew a file.

Returning to her desk, she flicked through the file then said, "Here we are. Aye, she had a client in Ibrox to visit. Didn't she turn up?"

"Miss Flynn," he took a soft breath, "I regret to inform you that yesterday afternoon, Elizabeth Bradley was discovered dead in her flat."

The Detectives watched her face turn pale, but to their surprise, she asked, "Has anyone been arrested for her murder?"

It was McGhee who quickly asked, "How did you know she'd been murdered?"

Flustered, her eyes widened in panic when she stammered, "It was on the radio! A murder in Cessnock! That's where she lives, isn't it? In Cessnock," she pointed to the file.

A tense few seconds of silence was broken when Maxwell asked, "Does her file list all of her clients?"

"Yes, it does. Well, the clients she's allocated, I mean their names and addresses. Why?"

"Well," he patiently explained, "we'll need to visit all her clients and speak with them to ask if they know who might want to have harmed Mrs Bradley."

"As a matter of interest, how many clients does the Company serve?"

"Oh, off the top of my head, over three hundred or so. Maybe three hundred and fifty?"

A sudden thought occurred to him as he picked up on her statement, the clients she was allocated, and so he asked, "I take it that it's only Mrs Bradley who visits her clients, not any other member of your cleaning staff?"

The Detectives watched her face turn red when she stammered, "That's the thing, you see. It's not that we don't *try* to keep the cleaners visiting the same clients, but with people being off sick or just not turning up or a variety of reasons for not coming to their work; well, we don't always have a record of who's visiting which clients, you know? It's a kind of *ad hoc* arrangement, like who's available at the time."

With a sickening feeling in his stomach, Maxwell held up a hand to say, "Wait a minute, are you telling me you don't have records of which staff visited your clients on what dates?"

Her face creased with embarrassment when she simpered, "I really do try to keep on top of it, but you can't imagine the paperwork that's involved. I'm mean, I'm on my own here most of the time when Mr McLean is off out, at meetings or, well, you know, elsewhere."

He didn't know what elsewhere meant, but knew it might be a good idea to find out.

Seeing she was now close to tears, he gave her sympathetic look, then seizing upon it, she added, "And I have all this paperwork to keep up with and trying to keep track of who's supposed to be where. It's just not fair on me."

He'd wisely stopped speaking until she composed herself, then gently suggested, "We'll need either the file for Mrs Bradley or a copy, whatever is easiest for you, as well as a list of all your clients." When she nodded, he added, "Can you also provide us with a note of Mrs Bradley's salary?"

"Okay," she slowly sniffed and dabbed at her eyes with a handkerchief that had mysteriously appeared in her hand, "but I'm not certain if I can give you the clients list. I think that would have to be authorised by Mr McLean and the Social Work people."

He turned to glance at McGhee before he quietly replied, "Then perhaps when you appear in court for obstructing me in my duty during a murder investigation, you can explain that to the Sheriff."

Of course, he was bluffing, but gambled that she wouldn't know that and seeing the startled expression on her face, watched as she slowly nodded. Then, her voice a mere whisper, she said, "I'll have the list photocopied for you."

"That'll do us fine," he graced her with a wide smile. "Now, did anyone from your company try to contact Mrs Bradley yesterday?"

"Not to my knowledge, no," she shook her head, unable to tear her eyes from his gaze.

"These complaints you mentioned. Were there ever complaints about Mrs Bradley removing items from her client's homes?"

"You mean stealing things?"

"Yes."

"There are *always* complaints from clients or their families about things being stolen and not just about Lizzie," she irritably sighed. "Look, you have to understand that when our staff go in to clean houses, there has to be a certain amount of trust between the company and the client."

"And are all your client's elderly?"

"Oh, no," she shook her head. "We're a cleaning company and yes," she then nodded, "we do have a contract with the City's Social Work Department for attending to the cleaning of houses where the residents are elderly, but you also have to understand some of these residents are, you know," she waved a finger in a circle around her head when she added, "a wee bit doolally?"

Maxwell, whose mother resided in a nursing home, inwardly bristled when he asked, "Do you mean the complainants are forgetful, perhaps suffering from dementia?"

"Aye, that," she unwittingly grinned at him. "I mean, sometimes they think somethings been stolen when maybe they've just mislaid it or the family have removed it for safe keeping, you know?"

"So, you have no knowledge of Mrs Bradley actually stealing from any of her clients?"

"Nothing we could prove. I mean if we thought she was nicking stuff, we'd sack her, wouldn't we?"
He took several seconds before he quietly asked, "Even if as you said, your boss was having a sexual relationship with her?"
Still unable to tear her eyes from his stare, her mouth gaped open, but she was saved from responding when the office door opened to admit a bald, bearded, rotund man in his mid-fifties of around five feet two inches tall and who striding into the office, loudly barked, "Hello, who have we here, then?"

CHAPTER FOUR

When the car stopped outside St Marnock's Primary School in Langton Crescent, DS Elaine Fitzsimmons turned to stare at the small parkland in front of the council houses across the road, then unconsciously nodding, muttered, "Seems a nice area."
"Aye. There's a few good areas in Pollok," Hamilton agreed. "I did a three months secondment up here when I was in uniform and apart from a couple of rough bits, it's not a bad place to live."
Getting out of the passenger seat, she told her neighbour, "Right, Alan, you take the lead and I'll step in if there's anything you forget to ask, okay?"
Nodding, he replied, "Okay, Elaine."
Walking together on the path around the grassed area, they stopped at an end-terraced house where Fitzsimmons saw Sarah Bradley staring at them from the downstairs front window.
Smiling at the young girl, she saw the front door being pulled open by a grey haired, older woman wearing an ill-fitting dark coloured polo shirt, navy blue coloured tracksuit bottoms and a green coloured, stained bib apron.
"Mrs Bradley?"
"That's me," she sullenly nodded then glancing behind the Detectives, added, "Come away in before they nosey neighbours of mine wonder why the CID are at my door again."
They followed her through the narrow hallway and into the sparsely furnished front room where they saw the little girl, Sarah, standing by the window that looked out over the front and unkept garden.

However, she was not alone for on either end of the three-seater couch sat two young men, both dressed in brightly coloured tracksuits with cropped hair; both in their mid to late-twenties and who stared moodily at the Detectives.

It occurred to Fitzsimmons that likely this wasn't the first time two young men had been in the company of the CID.

"These are my boys, Ricky the oldest, and he's Billy," Mrs Bradley pointed when she introduced, then indicated the Detectives sit down in the matching armchairs while she occupied a wooden chair that was placed beside the open door that led into the kitchen.

Hamilton's nose twitched at the strong smell of grease and fried food that seemed to waft through the kitchen door.

Before Fitzsimmons could explain why they were there, Mrs Bradley instructed Sarah to go upstairs and play in her bedroom.

When with some reluctance the young girl had left and closed the door behind her, she said, "I don't want her hearing anything you have to tell us and besides, I think she's had enough of a shock with her mammy being murdered."

Glancing at them in turn, she asked, "You'll not be interrogating Sarah, will you?"

Fitzsimmons stifled her smile when she replied, "We don't *interrogate* young girls, Mrs Bradley, and no, it's a bit too soon to be speaking to her. How is she, anyway?"

"I had her in with me last night," her face suddenly expressed her own grief, "and the poor wee lamb, she cried all through the night."

"You arrested anybody yet?" the young man Ricky angrily blurted out.

Neither Detective failed to see the harsh glance that his brother Billy gave him.

In a calm voice, Hamilton replied, "Inquiries are at an early stage and that's why we're here, to collect statements and your thoughts on who might have wished to harm to your sister."

Good one, Alan, Fitzsimmons thought, then watching him remove his notebook from an inner pocket of his jacket, heard him ask Mrs Bradley, "Do you know or are aware of any men that your daughter might have been seeing?"

"Men?" she stared at him then they all turned when the son called Ricky snarled, "What you suggesting, that my sister was running around? That she was some kind of a whore or something?"

Realising that the visit was turning confrontational, Fitzsimmons curtly broke in when addressing Ricky, she snapped back, "That's not what we're suggesting at all and fine you know it, pal! Look, if you want the killer caught, then you answer our questions and no matter whether you like us or hate us, I really don't care! What I *do* care about is catching the bugger that murdered that wee girl's mum! Now, do we carry on or are you going to be a petty-minded sod! Your choice!"

The tense silence saw Mrs Bradley flinch at the harsh words, while Billy sat in silence.

Whether Ricky was angry or embarrassed, Fitzsimmons didn't know and cared less when he jumped up from the couch and wordlessly stormed from the room, slamming the door behind him.

And it didn't escape Fitzsimmons attention when his brother Billy gave an audible sigh of relief.

"Alan?" she prompted Hamilton.

"Ah, yes, and again, Mrs Bradley," he calmly asked, "Do you know if Elizabeth had a boyfriend or a man she was seeing?"

To their surprise it was Billy who quietly said, "There was a guy," then holding up a hand, added, "I don't know his name or anything, but he was seeing Lizzie."

"Who is he?" Mrs Bradley sharply turned to her so.

"I don't *know* Ma," his scowled, "just that she says he was a guy she worked with. That's all I know, but I think it was just a fling, nothing else."

Her face white, his mother turned to Hamilton and in a low voice, said, "I didn't know anything about that, I swear."

"Can you tell me when your sister disclosed this?" Hamilton turned to Billy.

"Eh, months ago, I can't really remember when. Maybe at the start of the year?" he shrugged.

Glancing at Fitzsimmons, Hamilton told Mrs Bradley, "When we searched your daughter's flat…"

"You searched her flat!" Billy interrupted, his forehead knitting at what he perceived to be an outrage.

"It's a procedure, Billy," he calmly explained. "We always search the locus…I mean, the scene of the crime to try and find evidence about who killed your sister, okay? There's nothing sinister about it," he shook his head.

"Oh, right. Okay, then," Billy nodded and visibly relaxed.

"Mrs Bradley," Hamilton started again. "When we searched your daughter's flat, we found a large number of ornaments, some of them very expensive ornaments and a quantity of jewellery. Have you any idea how she might have collected such items?"

It was evident to Fitzsimmons that by her expression, Angela Bradley knew or perhaps suspected that her daughter did have such items and so she pressed her, "Do you know where she got these things, Mrs Bradley?"

It was also evident to her son that Angela Bradley probably knew more, too.

"Ma? Tell them," Billy stood up from the couch, his voice rising as he stared at his mother. "If these things, whatever they are, are what got her killed, you have to tell them!"

Clearly upset with tears forming in her eyes, his mother stared up at her son and hesitantly replied, "I don't know anything other than she said she'd got some stuff that she was holding for somebody, but I don't know who that is. Honestly, I don't, and she never said and she didn't show me the things either," her lips quivering, tears began to run down her cheeks. "All she told me was that she might make some money for holding the things."

"Billy," Fitzsimmons glanced up at him and softly said, "away and fetch your mum a glass of water, son."

Slowly nodding, he did as he was told then returning with a mug of water, handed to his mother whose hands, the Detectives saw, were shaking.

It was Billy, now returned to sit on the couch, who said, "You know that years ago, when she was a teenager, Lizzie was done for stealing; shoplifting and pinching handbags in the city centre when she was younger, but nothing, absolutely *nothing*," he waved his hands to emphasis the point, "since she had our Sarah."

"About that, Billy," Hamilton paused with his notebook in one hand and pen ready in the other. "Is Sarah's father on the scene? I mean, for our report, we'll need to know who'll be caring for her now that her mother's, eh, passed."

Billy shook his head before he said, "As far as we know it was a one-night stand, so no and as for Sarah," he glanced up at the ceiling as though seeing the young girl, "She'll live here with Ma, Ricky and me. We all love that wee lassie and she'll always have a home with one of us, stand on me about that," he vigorously nodded.

"So," Hamilton stared at him, "I'm thinking from your reaction you too had no idea either that your sister was holding stuff for somebody?"

Bill's brow knitted when he quietly responded with, "If I had known, I'd have been the first to kick her arse. Me and Ricky," he shook his head and half-smiled, "we've had our run-ins with you lot, but Lizzie?" He took a deep and angry breath. "She was supposed to be going straight and keeping away from trouble for wee Sarah's sake. I can't believe she got herself mixed up in the thieving again."

"Then you believe the stuff's stolen?" Fitzsimmons asked.

"Don't you?" he quickly retorted.

"Aye, it probably is, but we're still checking," she smiled with a soft sigh.

She caught Hamilton glancing at her and nodding, said, "Unless there's anything else, Mrs Bradley," she softly smiled at them in turn, "we'll be on our way and for what it's worth, Billy, we might never be pals, but it's good to know that we're on the same side in trying to find out who killed your sister and left that wee girl up the stairs without her mother."

He wordlessly nodded then quietly replied, "I'll see you out."

It struck Fitzsimmons as curious that when they were in the hallway, Billy should close the room door behind him, but that was explained when in a low voice, he said, "That guy I mentioned, the guy Lizzie was seeing. Trust me, I honestly don't know anything about him, but I didn't want to say in front of Ma. Lizzie told me in confidence that he *is* married, but was talking about leaving his wife."

He scowled when he added, "That old chestnut, eh? Anyway," he exhaled as if embarrassed, "she said he was the one paying the rent on her flat, that he was serious about her."

He again shook his head when he continued, "I tried to tell her the bastard was at it, that if he is married he was just wanting a bit on the side, but would she listen?"

"Billy, are they away yet?" his mother's raised voice called out.

"They're just going, Ma," he called back and opened the front door to permit them to leave.

"Anything, Billy, anything at all, give us a call," was Fitzsimmons parting comment.

In the car, Hamilton turned to her to ask, "Happy with what we learned?"

She slowly nodded before she responded with, "We know that she was seeing someone, somebody from her work and that she was supposed to be holding the ornaments and the jewellery for someone too, but is that the same person? Let's get back to the factory and let the Boss know what we've found."

****

Seated together on the worn couch, DC Philip Murray and DC Aileen Patrick, neighboured together in the door to door inquiries, declined the tea or coffee offered by Mrs Church, who seemed eager to impart her knowledge of her murdered neighbour, or as she described her, "…that woman calling herself Mrs Bradley."

"And so to continue, Mrs Church, you say she was living there for nigh on a year or so?"

"Oh, aye, and not once did she take a turn at cleaning the close," she huffed.

Choking back a snigger, Patrick asked, "And what about visitors? Can you recall ever seeing anyone visiting her?"

"Well, there was a woman that I heard the wee lassie calling her granny, so I can only assume that was her next door's mother and then there was him, a wee, short-arsed guy, if you pardon me, who used to turn up in a fancy motor; a red coloured one."

"Can you recall the make and model?"

She raised a hand when she huffily replied, "Oh, I don't know about them things, hen. A motor's just a motor to me, but it was definitely red. I think."

"You *think*?" an exasperated Patrick asked.

"Well, it was usually dark when the man was here, so I'm not positive," Church sniffed.

"Any other callers to the house?" Murray butted in.

"I think there might have been a woman, maybe a couple of women, I'm not so sure," Church hesitantly replied, her self-assured confidence dented by Patrick's disdainful attitude.

In an effort to regain some integrity, she scowled when she snapped, "Did you know that one of your officers threw up in the close right outside my door?"

His face as straight as a poker, Murray answered for them both when he lied, "Oh, no, I hadn't heard that."

"Oh, the older man that was standing guard, he asked for a bucket of water to wash it away it, but some of it was still there when I went out my door," she shivered with disgust. "I had a hell of a job cleaning it."

Poor you, you obnoxious old git, thought Patrick, but smiled sweetly when she said, "I'm certain your neighbours will appreciate your hard work. Now," she rose to her feet and glanced at Murray before Church could respond, "If that's everything?"

Taking his cue, he smiled and said, "Grateful thanks, Mrs Church for your time."

In the street outside, Murray, a single man who treated every woman he worked with as a sexual challenge, glanced at the attractive Patrick before cheerfully commenting, "That's as much as we can do for the minute, Aileen, so how's about a coffee in the café across the road?"

****

Returned to her office, Mary Wells had hardly placed her backside on her chair when the door was knocked then entered by DS Colin Baxter, who carried his notebook in one hand and the fingers of his other hand precariously hooked through the handles of two mugs of coffee.

"Thanks, Colin and sit," she nodded at the opposite chair and reached out for her mug.

"How you coping without sugar?" he teased her with a grin.

"Barely," she grimaced then asked, "What's happening?"

"SOCO have informed us that they've finished dusting the candlestick and sent the prints upstairs to the Fingerprint Department. I phoned them and asked for a quick check in their database, but as usual," he grimaced, "they asked for a name to check the prints against."

She nodded in understanding then sipping at the fiery liquid, said, "Continue."

"The blood on the candlestick is confirmed to be that of the victim and unfortunately, no trace of anyone else's blood on the candlestick or anywhere else in the flat. However, SOCO have managed to lift what they describe as a partial print in blood, from the murder weapon that is now with the Fingerprint Department. I realise this is good news, but again, without a name to compare it against," he shrugged.

She took a deep breath then slowly exhaling, replied. "Right, let's keep that little gem between us for now. Any phone calls?"

"Nothing on the murder hotline other than a couple of kids screaming abuse, but that's no surprise," he frowned.

She glanced up as Baxter turned when the door was knocked to see the Divisional Commander, Chief Superintendent Geoffrey Metcalfe standing in the doorway, who asked, "Am I interrupting? Please," he waved a hand to them both, "don't get up."

"Not at all, sir. Colin here was just giving me an updated brief upon my return from the PM."

"If you wish me to leave…" Baxter began to rise from his chair, but Metcalfe, a thinly built, grey haired, genial man who originated from London, was recently widowed and with a notable hacking smokers cough and less than a year to serve before retirement, again waved a hand and said, "Not at all, Colin. In fact, I'll be wanting a word with you when you're finished with the DCI here."

"Sir?"

"I'll explain later," he smiled, then brightly said, "Just popped up to ask if there's any help the uniform can give in your investigation, Mary?"

"Ah, nothing at the moment, sir, but I'll keep it in mind if we get overwhelmed. I'm grateful that Inspector Herdman arranged the protection of the locus overnight, but we're now finished our SOCO investigation of the flat, so I'll be able to release the locus to the owner, once he or she's identified. Oh," her brow knitted, "there is one thing. Joe Docherty. He did well as the attending officer at the locus. If you don't mind, I'd be grateful if you'd pass my own and the Department's appreciation to him."

Metcalfe smiled then waving a hand as he turned towards the door, replied, "I'll see Constable Docherty myself and thank you, Mary. Colin, pop by my office when you're free."

"Sir," he nodded, but Metcalfe had gone.

"Wonder what that's about," he pursed his lower lip.

Mary shook her head when she quietly said, "He's old school, our Geoff, and a proper gentleman, but I suspect he won't have much time left to him when he does retire. That cough of his is mighty suspicious."

"Aye," Baxter thoughtfully nodded. "You never get him in any mood other than a good one, but I heard recently from an old pal of mine who's a member of the Retired Police Officers Association, that our Geoff is having a hard time of it since he lost his missus, poor bugger."

Much as she liked Baxter and thought him a very capable Detective, there was no denying he was a right old gossip and distracting him, asked, "Right, then, anything else I should know about?"

"Not at the minute, Boss," he slurped the last of his coffee, then added, "I'm still waiting on the door to door actions coming in. Briefing at five?"

"That's the plan," she nodded and glanced up when she saw Kenny Maxwell and John McGhee at her door.

"Good news, I hope?" she greeted them.

"Maybe Colin can hear this to, Boss, him being the incident manager," Maxwell nodded.

She sat straight-backed in her chair and nodded that Maxwell continue.

Relating their visit to the victim's employer's office, he said, "Seems our victim was doing a line with the owner, an Alex McLean. Married with two kids, he was paying the rent on her flat and telling her that he intended leaving his wife for her."

"I assume he was stringing her along?"

"For the minute anyway. However, he admitted she was starting to put pressure on him to leave his wife. When he told us that, we backed off from asking him anything further."

"So," her eyebrows rose and she could feel her stomach tensing, "he's a possible suspect for dealing with his problem by killing her? Where is he now?"

Maxwell grinned widely when he replied, "Downstairs in a holding room and likely shitting himself, because we told him you're waiting to have a quiet word with him about murdering his girlfriend."

****

Arriving back at Govan Police Office, Elaine Fitzsimmons and her neighbour, Alan Hamilton, learned from Colin Baxter that a suspect was about to be interviewed by the DCI.

"Doesn't happen to work beside the victim, does he?" she asked.

Baxter's eyes narrowed when nodding, he said, "Aye, he does. How did you guess that?"

"It's not a guess, we learned from her brother that she confided in him she was having an affair with someone from her work. Does this suspect…"

"Alex McLean's his name. He owns the company she worked for." Nodding, she continued, "Is McLean married?"

"Apparently. He also paid the rent for the victims flat. A right wee love nest, eh?"

"Well," she turned to Hamilton, "I wonder if this guy McLean is the man she's been holding the ornaments and jewellery for."

Turning back to Baxter, she asked, "Any chance we can slip a note to the boss to let her know our victim was holding the stuff for someone, but we didn't get a name. It's possible that it *might* be the suspect."

"I don't think she's started the interview yet, so you might catch her in her office."

Fitzsimmons hurried from the incident room and seeing the DCI in the corridor, called out.

Mary turned as Fitzsimmons hurried towards her and recounted the information that the victim's brother, Billy, had provided.

"Thanks, I'll put that to him," she nodded.

"Oh," Fitzsimmons, lowered her voice, "if you're still interested and if you're free by seven this evening, Boss, my sister-in-law will make herself available for a bit of late evening shopping."

Smiling, Mary sighed before she replied, "Thanks for that, but let's find out first if our suspect bumped off his mistress before I make any plans for a new wardrobe."

****

DS Colin Baxter lifted the phone and after identifying himself, was greeted by the SOCO supervisor who said, "Just to let you know, Colin, we've finished dusting the items we took from the locus in Clifford Street and the prints are away up to the Fingerprint Department. If you want to send your productions officer up here to collect them ASAP, we're keen to get them away because frankly, we've little enough space here in the Department for storing stuff, particularly items of value."

"Bloody hell, that was quick," Baxter smiled, but then hastily added, "not that I'm complaining, mind. Right, I'll have Fiona McCloy and her neighbour collect them sometime today and thanks."

"Oh, one last thing, Colin. Aside from the rest of the jewellery, one of the items we found was a ruby ring. I don't know if your boss mentioned it?"

"She did," Baxter involuntarily nodded. "Said it looked expensive."

"Well," he heard the supervisor take a breath, "out of curiosity, I had one of my team look at it for me. She's right into vintage jewellery and as a hobby she attends auctions looking for bargains, that sort of thing. Anyway, and admittedly she's not an expert mind, but it's her opinion and only her *opinion*, that the ring is antique. She thinks it's possibly Edwardian and if she's right, you wouldn't get much change out of anything between sixteen or seventeen thousand pounds for it. Might be worth suggesting to your DCI Wells she has the ring and the rest of the stuff appraised by an expert, eh?"

"Good call and thanks," Baxter ended the call.

Turning to Janey McPhee, he asked her to fetch Fiona McCloy, the investigation's productions officer, and her neighbour.

CHAPTER FIVE

DI Sammy Salmon collected the suspect, Alex McLean, from the detention room in the cell corridor downstairs and with uncommon courtesy, led the extremely nervous man up to the CID suite, then into the DCI's room where Mary Wells had returned to sit behind her desk.

Ensuring the windows were closed and even though it was a warm, July day and confirming the radiators were switched on to make the room uncomfortably warm, she had removed her own suit jacket that hung on the chair behind her.

On the desk before her lay a notepad with a number of written questions she had already prepared.

When the door opened to admit the two men, she saw McLean to be older looking than his fifty-three years, around five feet two to three inches tall with a shaven head, a short trimmed beard turning grey, with a pug nose and wearing a white coloured shirt - though his tie had been removed for safety reasons by the turnkey - an expensive two-piece navy blue suit that looked far too tight for him and highly polished black brogues.

Indicating the chair that faced her on the opposite side of her desk, she calmly told McLean, "Please sit down."

Slightly behind McLean and to his left, just out of his peripheral vision, Salmon took the second chair, then almost immediately became aware of the heat in the room and noticing that the DCI had removed her jacket, wryly smiled when he also removed his jacket to hang behind his chair.

It was immediately obvious to Mary, both by his demeanour and the slight sheen of perspiration on McLean's bald head, that he was nervous and so taking advantage of this fact, she formally began in a steady voice, "Mr McLean, I am Detective Chief Inspector Mary Wells, the Senior Investigating Officer in charge of the murder investigation of Elizabeth Bradley, who I am informed is known to you. You are currently here and detained under Section Two of the Criminal Procedure (Scotland) Act of nineteen-eighty, being a person who…"

"I don't know anything about Lizzie's being murdered," he interrupted with a gasp.

Mary's hand snapped up then rudely cut him off when she hissed, "Please permit me to finish."

"Sorry," he muttered, his head bowed low.

Behind McLean, Salmon's eyes narrowed as he thought, Jesus, the boss has definitely got the bit between her teeth about this guy.

She paused for several seconds, then continued, "You, being a person who has come to our attention as a possible suspect for the murder of Elizabeth Bradley. Do you understand?"

His shoulders shaking, McLean slowly nodded.

"Now," she stared at him, "before we proceed, I understand you have waived the right to have a lawyer present or anyone informed that you are currently detained here at Govan Police Office. Is that correct?"

"Yes," he meekly replied.

"Might I assume you have waived your rights because apart from your secretary knowing you are here, you are concerned that your wife might discover that you are being questioned about the murder of your *mistress*?" she deliberately emphasised the word mistress.

Tight-lipped, he stared at her, then nodded.

"Did you kill Elizabeth Bradley?"

"For God's sake, no!" he burst out. "I loved Lizzie! I wouldn't harm her, no way!"

Her hands clasped together, Mary leaned forward onto the desk then softly asked, "So where were you on Tuesday morning between the hours eight-thirty and three in the afternoon?"

"Tuesday," his brow furrowed, "you mean just yesterday?"

When she nodded, he excitedly burst out, "Meeting a client in the lounge of the Central Hotel in the city centre! I…I mean my company, we're branching out into cleaning offices as well as residential properties and I met with a client who was interested in us taking on the office buildings in Wellington Street. He'll vouch for me because I bought him lunch, too! Then, after that, I went back to my office for a snooze, you see," he gulped, "I'd had some drinks with my lunch."

With a brief glance at Salmon, Mary felt her body involuntarily slump for if McLean was telling the truth, it was unlikely he was their murderer.

With a gentle sigh she sat back in her chair then staring at McLean, an idea occurred to her and so she softly asked, "Does your wife know about your affair?"

His eyes flickered and his mouth opened when shaking his head, he replied, "No, definitely not."

His face turned pale then nodding, fetched a handkerchief from his trouser pocket and wiped the perspiration off his face and bald head. Yet despite his emphatical denial that his wife knew nothing of the affair, she sensed rather than saw a slight hesitation and seizing upon it, softly asked, "Just when did you and Lizzie get together, Mr McLean? When did you commence paying the rent for her flat?"

"I don't remember the date," he mumbled and shrugging as though unable to exactly recall, "Maybe a year or so ago?"

Staring at him, she thought of Harry's unfaithfulness with their neighbour and though he'd never admitted when it began, wondered just how long he'd kept it hidden from her? For how long he and Beth had deceived her and probably joked about her behind her back.

"So," she stared at McLean and mindful of her own circumstances, though she knew it to be completely unprofessional, fought to keep her temper in check, "you're telling my DI and I that for a year or so, you managed to keep the affair with Mrs Bradley from your wife?

You're telling us that not *once* did she suspect you of being unfaithful?"

She watched as his pronounced Adams apple bounced like a ball in his throat and he nervously licked at his lips when eyes narrowing with suspicion, he stuttered, "Wait, you think my wife knew about Lizzie? You think that Jackie would…"

He stopped and covered his face with his hand, then shaking his head, took a deep breath when in a whispered voice, he said, "She might have suspected, I don't know. There was a time, maybe three weeks ago…it's me that does all our domestic banking," he hurriedly explained.

His shoulders slumped when tightly closing his eyes, he added, "She found a bank statement."

"A bank statement?"

"Pure and simple, I fucked up," his shoulders drooped and his face creased.

"I thought the rent from the flat was coming out of my private account, the business account I use for socialising with clients, you know; taking them to lunch, that sort of thing. Jackie, she found the statement that had come in with the junk mail and asked me what the direct debit was all about? I told her," he squeezed his eyes tight as he tried to recall what he'd said, "that I was thinking of opening a second office and that was the rental payment."

"And she believed you?"

"I thought so at the time. Now," he exhaled, "I'm not so sure."

"Okay," Mary slowly drawled then asked, "Tell me about the ornaments and the jewellery in the wardrobe in Lizzie's flat."

"Eh, what?"

She could see he seemed genuinely confused, so explained, "The large, old fashioned wardrobe that was in the small bedroom in the flat. The one containing ornaments and jewellery. Why did Lizzie have them?"

His eyes widened and shaking his head, he raised his hands defensively when he replied, "What wardrobe? I honestly have no idea what you're talking about. What? Ornaments and jewellery? What kind of ornaments and jewellery?"

"You're telling us you have no knowledge of these items?"

"No, none at all," he turned to glance at Salmon, then turning back to Wells, added, "Honestly, I don't know what you are on about."

She stared at him for several seconds before she asked, "Do you have any objection to us taking your fingerprints to check them against the items we discovered to confirm what you're telling us. That you have no knowledge of these items?"

He turned his hands palms upwards and with confidence, replied, "No problem. I have no idea what you're talking about. Ornaments and jewellery?"

Then she saw his eyes narrow when he asked, "Lizzie, why did she have these things? She didn't…oh, holy shit! She's been nicking stuff from the clients, hasn't she? The dirty cow!"

"We don't know that yet," she wouldn't reveal they'd learned the victim was supposedly holding the items for a third party, then risked a glance at Salmon before she said, "but we have her client list and we will be calling upon them."

She watched him raise his trembling hands to bury his face in them and heard him mutter, "This is just getting worse and worse. We advertise ourselves as a trustworthy company and if this gets out, it will destroy our credibility and we won't survive this, I just know it."

He paused to again wipe at his face then running a forefinger round the collar of his shirt, quietly asked, "It's awfully hot in here. Can I have a glass of water, please?"

She glanced at Salmon who taking his cue, rose from his chair and made his way to the door.

In the three or four minutes the DI was gone from the room, Mary stared pokerfaced at McLean, who with head bowed and lost in his own thoughts, stared down at his clenched hands in his lap.

She knew her dislike of him was completely irrational, that him cheating on his wife was their business, but could not help but compare it to Harry's affair with the bitch next door.

However, irrespective of her feelings about McLean, if he was innocent of the murder, then there was nothing she could do about that.

That said, she took some wilful pleasure from the thought, regardless of whether or not his wife *was* aware of the affair, that she needed to be visited and there was no way that would happen without divulging why she was being interviewed.

Then there was another thing.

"I understand you have children, Mr McLean?"
"Aye," he nodded, then sighed, "a girl, she's fifteen and my son, he's thirteen."
Old enough to learn of their father's shenanigans when we speak to the wife, she unkindly assumed, but said nothing.
The door opened to admit Salmon carrying a mug of water that he handed to McLean, then turning to her, formally said, "I've spoken with DS Baxter, Ma'am, and apprised him of the details provided by Mr McLean here, regarding his alibi."
He turned to McLean to continue, "He'll make a couple of calls to your secretary and trace the client you said you spent time with on Tuesday morning to determine the veracity of the statement."
"The very what?"
"We'll find out if you're telling the truth or trying to sell us a dummy," Mary butted in, then added, "and in the meantime, you'll remain detained here until we do verify your alibi."
"Fair enough," he shrugged, any thought of refusal overcome by the necessity to clear his name.
"Right, Mr Salmon, thank you."
Turning to McLean, she took some pleasure in her smile when she asked, "And where will we find your wife right now, sir?"
****
While DI Salmon escorted a shaken McLean back downstairs to the detention room and with the promise of a coffee, DCI Wells attended at the incident room where sitting at his desk with Colin Baxter, she related the sum of the interview with McLean and the probability he was telling the truth, that he was alibied for the murder. However, it left the possibility that if his wife was aware of the affair, she herself might now be considered a suspect then she asked, "Anything happening?"
"That's some of the door to door actions coming back in, Boss, and one in particular is of interest; the interview with the neighbour, Mrs Church. She says a man who drove a red car that she described as a short arse," he smiled, "or so she thinks, frequently visited the victim, but no make or model of the motor. There were women who also visited, but regretfully no description of the women either."
Mary glanced at her wristwatch when she said, "Have someone pop downstairs to confirm what colour of car McLean drives. I've a feeling that he's the frequent visitor."

"Will do and the SOCO phoned regarding the productions in the flat. They're all dusted and ready for collection, so Fiona McCloy and the aide are on their way now to collect them," then related the conversation about the ruby ring and it's possible value.

"Don't get many of them in a lucky bag, do you?" retorted a surprised Mary.

Her brow knitting, she continued, "Might be an idea to have all the jewellery and the ornaments valued to determine just how much the collection is worth. Don't happen to know any jewellers, do you?" she grinned at Baxter.

His brow narrowed in thought before he replied, "There's the guy that works in an auction house just off the Great Western Road that I had dealings with in the past that always does a good turn for the polis, Boss. I could give him a phone and see if he's available. Might cost us a bottle of the good stuff, but could be worth it."

"Okay then, Colin, chance your arm and give him a call."

Seeing she was wearing her suit jacket, he asked, "You off out, boss?"

"If McLean is telling the truth and in all probability *is* alibied, then if his wife knew of the affair it makes her a possible suspect for killing her husband's lover, so the DI and I are taking a wee turn out to his house to interview her."

Baxter thought it a little odd that the DCI would want to go out herself to conduct an interview when she had not only the DI, but DS's who could do that job, but guessed she must have her reason.

"Roger, so if anything comes in, I'll get you on the car radio?"

"Yes," she turned her head to glance around the room, then asked, "Where's Elaine Fitzsimmons?"

"Ah, she's away with her neighbour tracking down the client who is McLean's alibi for the murder. You want me to have her fetched back?"

"No, you're okay, but tell her that if I'm not returned by six-thirty, just to cancel this evening. She'll know what I mean."

"Okay, Boss," Baxter thoughtfully nodded, yet could not imagine what the pair were up to.

****

Driving to Barrhead, Sammy Salmon risked a glance at his DCI when he said, "Can I ask you something without you going off on one?"

Taken aback, she turned to stare at him when she replied, "Why would I go off on one?"

He hesitated for a few seconds then as though committed, softly exhaled before he asked, "Why are you really coming with me to interview McLean's wife?"

She involuntarily arched her back as though in defence of his question and her eyes narrowed with curiosity when she said, "I don't know what you mean."

"Look, boss, we don't need the SIO to come out for an interview. Your job is to manage the team and me, not run around interviewing witnesses or suspects. Aside from me, we've DS's and DC's to do that, so what's the real reason you're coming with me today?"

He risked another glance at her then nervously asked, "Is it anything to do with McLean cheating on his wife?"

She was about to snap back at him, but in that heartbeat, realised that he was exactly correct, that's why she was with him, to break the news to Jaqueline McLean that her husband, just like Harry, was a cheating bastard.

And to her inward shame, admitted that she had been looking forward to it, too.

Suddenly feeling deflated, she quietly said, "Is it that obvious, Sammy? Am I turning into some sort of cantankerous old git who takes delight in other people's misery?"

"Look, Mary," he softly replied with the unaccustomed use of her forename, "I can't imagine what that bastard of a husband of yours put you through and when you'd just delivered your daughter, but you're a strong woman and heavens, don't I know that," he smiled.

"But there comes a point when even I know, you need to move on. Yes," she watched him nod, "you've come a long way since he upped and left you, but do *not* be sliding backwards, not now that you're achieving so much."

She stared at him with a new-found regard, for never before had she and Salmon had such an intimate conversation.

Why, she inwardly smiled, he's even called me Mary.

At last she replied with a sigh and some inward remorse, "You're right, of course, and God forgive me, but I was looking forward to telling that poor woman her husband was having an affair. I was thinking more about how it would probably destroy him, rather than what it might do to her."

She took a deep breath then slowly exhaled and said, "Sammy, thank you and I do mean that. It's about time that I took a good hard look at myself and…"

Seizing upon this new intimacy with her, he took his left hand off the steering wheel and raising it, interrupted with a smile when he told her, "If you don't mind me saying it too, since you've lost all that weight, maybe get yourself a couple of new outfits and some, eh," he grimaced, "better fitting undergarments?"

Her face first registered her shock at his boldness, but then to her own surprise found herself laughing uproariously and was joined by Salmon who to his own astonishment, couldn't believe he had been so forward.

Still giggling and wiping tears of laughter from her eyes, she shook her head before she asked, "Is it that obvious that I'm turning up for work in a right dishevelled state?"

"Not at all," he smiled, "but our lot wouldn't be Detectives if they haven't noticed you're looking *physically* better and, well," his eyes narrowed when he glanced at her, "maybe you could lose some of that grey hair. I mean you're not *that* old."

"What," she teased him, "now you're my fashion consultant?"

Mary couldn't believe that this conversation was taking place and even less so with Sammy Salmon, who she had always considered to be a bit of an airhead.

Then to her own surprise, she shared her own innermost secret when she told Salmon, "After Harry left, I really fell apart. I doubted everything about myself, completely lost my confidence and really, it was all about the kids needing me that kept me going. At one point, I considered resigning, just locking the door and staying at home for the rest of my life."

Several seconds passed until he said, "I'm sorry Mary, as your DI I should have been more supportive, visited you at least. A couple of phone calls doesn't really cut it, does it?"

"Don't blame yourself, Sammy, I probably wouldn't have wanted to see you anyway. I mean, anyone from the Department. As it was, I barely had the courage to open the door to Keith Meadows."

He smiled and decided now they were bonding, was the time to break the news.

In a soft voice, he told her, "Since I've been working for you, you've been good to me and whether you know it or not, I've learned a lot from you. However," he drew in his breath, "I don't think I'm cut out for the CID and once we've concluded this murder investigation, I'd like to apply for a return to uniformed duties. Would you be okay with that; I mean, endorsing my application?"

"Well, firstly," she cautiously replied, "I'd like us to have a longer discussion about what you intend, but whatever you decide, Sammy, you *will* have my backing."

"Thanks," he slowly nodded, then said, "Now, if my memory serves me correctly from reading the A to Z, Carlibar Road should be just around this corner."

CHAPTER SIX

Carlibar Road proved to be a long winding road and it took them a couple of minutes to travel the length where they found McLean's semi-detached villa hidden behind a high hedgerow and near to a bowling club.

Getting out of the vehicle, they saw a new, four-door black coloured Mazda saloon car parked in the driveway and making their way to the front door, saw it pulled open by a tall, slim and extremely attractive blonde-haired woman who Mary thought to be no more than in her mid-thirties. Her shoulder length hair lying on her bare, suntanned shoulders, the woman wore a tight, hip-hugging, short yellow coloured summer dress that barely covered her thighs. She saw too her legs were bare and she was shoeless.

As they neared, she could see the two top white buttons of the ruffled bosom of the dress were undone and it was clearly obvious that the well-endowed woman was not wearing a bra.

As she later intimated to Salmon, I thought of her husband and couldn't believe this gorgeous woman was his wife.

However, when the woman, who indeed proved to be Jaqueline McLean, opened her mouth, her strong, throaty Glasgow accent seemed to be a complete contrast to the beauty that she was, when she rudely asked, "You pair must be the polis come about that wee fat *bastard* of a husband of mine."

"Ah, yes, DCI Wells" she confirmed, then nodding at her neighbour, introduced Salmon.

To their mutual surprise, Mrs McLean stared with wide eyes at Salmon and replied, "Pity you hadn't come alone, sweet thing." Inviting them in, a blushing Salmon followed Mary as they were led through the expensively furnished house to a large conservatory at the rear, where inviting them to sit in the luxury chairs with the padded arms, she said, "Call me Jackie. Now, can I get you a drink?"
"We're fine, thank you," Mary answered for them both, then stifled her grin when Jackie sat down on the arm of Salmon's chair with her thigh against his shoulder and stared down at him.
But then she gulped for she thought that Jackie was about to stroke Salmon's hair and to distract her, quickly asked, "You were expecting us, then and eh, can you oblige me by sitting on that chair there," she pointed, "so we can both see you?"
"Oh, okay," with obvious reluctance and a last longing stare at Salmon, Jackie moved to sit on the chair opposite him, then slowly crossed her legs and subtly pulled the hem up to reveal her firm, tanned thighs.
"Agnes, that wee fat secretary of his, she phoned earlier this morning to say the cops had lifted him. Told me that his bit of stuff had been murdered, too. I take it that's right then, and you think he did it?"
"Our inquiries are at an early stage," Mary formally replied then almost relieved, she added, "So, you already knew your husband was seeing another woman?"
Jackie grinned widely and shook her head before she replied, "The wee sod thought he was so smart that I wouldn't cotton on to him shagging Lizzie Bradley. He'd been at it with her for almost a year, maybe more," her brow furrowed, "and I found out he was paying the rent on her flat, too."
"You knew her?"
"No, I didn't *know* her," Jackie waved a hand, "I knew *about* her, tart that she is…or should I say was," she evilly grinned.
Pot, kettle, pot, kettle, thought Salmon as he tried in vain to ignore her lovely, shapely legs as well as the deep cleavage that seemed to beckon his eyes.
"Have you ever met or visited her at home?" Mary took point in the questioning.
"No, why would I?" then Jackie's expression changed as she sneered, "Oh, you think it was me that maybe done her in, is that it?"

"It did occur to me, yes," she decided then she most definitely did not like this younger woman.

The smile on Jackie's face was, she decided, more devious than pleasant, then when her eyes narrowed and her teeth gritted, she said, "The wee shit doesn't know it, but I'm divorcing him, so I am. I've contracted a lawyer to act for me and I've given the lawyer all the information about Alex and his tart *and* I'm going to take him for every penny he has, so why the *fuck* would I risk that by killing her?"

And she has a point, Mary inwardly conceded, but had to ask anyway.

"Can you confirm your whereabouts on Tuesday, yesterday that is, between nine o'clock and three in the afternoon?"

Theatrically raising a manicured forefinger to her lips and raising her eyes to the roof, she replied, "Now let me see? Tuesday is always the day when the grass gets cut and when ba'jaws had left for work and the kids were away to school, the gardener comes by for the *whole* day and well," she shrugged and giggled like a schoolgirl, "let's just say he's a right young, athletic and good looking guy and he attends to my bush as well as mowing the lawn, if you get my meaning."

The few seconds of stunned silence was broken when Mary abruptly said, "Then perhaps you can provide us with his details; his name and contact address if you wish to be alibied for the murder."

"No problem. I'll just get it for you now," she smiled at them in turn.

It was when they were about to depart the house that Jackie, almost proprietorially, lightly touched Salmon's arm to say, "If you have any more questions or anything I can do for you, Detective, *anything* at all," she suggestively run her pink tongue round her lips, "you know where to find me."

It was when they were in the car that Salmon slowly exhaled and turning to her, humourlessly smiled when he said, "On hindsight, Boss, regardless of the reason, that *was* a good call, accompanying me here today."

****

Returning to Govan Police Office and while Sammy Salmon went to fetch two coffee's, Mary visited the incident room where Colin Baxter informed her that Elaine Fitzsimmons had phoned in to confirm she and her neighbour had traced the businessman McLean had lunch with and who, Fitzsimmons said, appeared to be a reputable alibi.

"According to Elaine," Baxter checked his written notes and continued, "The guy said he and McLean met at The Central Hotel Champagne Bar just after nine o'clock, they had a few drinks, then moved on to a restaurant where McLean treated him to an early lunch. He says he and McLean are big Rangers fans, so they had a long chat about the 'Gers."

Glancing at his note, Baxter continued, "It was a little after one when they parted at which time, McLean wasn't fit to drive. The witness says he saw McLean catch a taxi to his office and heard him tell the driver, Bath Street. Elaine's noted his statement and is attending at McLean's office to firm up on his arrival there and if indeed he did kip down for a few hours. She should be arriving back here any time, Boss."

"So," he asked, "how did it go with Mrs McLean? Suspect or what?"

"First of all, she's a right piece of work that woman," with a scowl, she shook her head.

"If for any reason you have to send anyone to speak with her again about anything, send two female officers. She's a bloody man-eater and I was lucky to get away with the DI in one piece. If her alibi checks out as I suspect it will," she dryly replied, "it will eliminate both her and her husband from our investigation. DI Salmon has the details of her alibi, so I'll let him provide them. Anything else doing?"

"Two things. Firstly, the result of the SOCO fingerprint examination and the photos of the items from the wardrobe are on your desk for you to peruse and secondly, the Media Department from Pitt Street were on the phone, asking for information about the murder and wanting to know if there is anything specific you want included in an appeal for information."

"Right, let me think about that," her mind cast back to the ornaments and jewellery.

She glanced at her wristwatch and said, "If nothing critical comes in this afternoon, organise the debriefing for, say, five-thirty."

"On it, boss."

"Right," she glanced back to see Salmon enter the room, a mug of coffee in each hand and walk towards her.

"The DI and I will go downstairs and give Mr McLean the good news that he's free to leave."
****

On their way downstairs, Salmon asked, "You going to tell him about his wife divorcing him?"

"No," she smiled, "I'll leave that good news for her to disclose. I've another idea, though."

While the turnkey went to fetch McLean from the detention room, she and her DI stood with Inspector Herdman at the charge bar, the detention forms in front of the Inspector waiting to be concluded.

"Ah, Mr McLean," she smiled amiably at him, "I'm pleased to inform you that after some sterling effort by my officers, they have confirmed your alibi on the day of your mistress's murder."

"That mean I'm no longer a suspect for killing her?" his eyes widened.

"Not unless you've something to admit," she continued to smile at him.

"Aye, very good," he frowned at her, then handed a pen by the Inspector, signed the form to enable his release.

"My wife, did you happen to say…" he anxiously asked, but expecting the question, Mary politely replied, "Regretfully, it was your wife who informed us of your extramarital activities, Mr McLean."

"Oh, shit," his shoulders slumped.

Glancing over the top of him to Salmon, Mary then thought, what's good for the goose, etcetera, but asked, "Do you ever travel home on a Tuesday for lunch, Mr McLean?"

"Eh? No, why?"

"No reason," she stared meaningfully at him, "but perhaps you might consider it in the future."

He in turn stared at her with curiosity written all over his face.

With the seed of suspicion planted, she smiled when she nodded to the turnkey then added, "Now, this gentleman will show you out and thank you for helping with our inquiries. If there's anything else that you might think of that could assist us, please don't hesitate to call us."

When McLean had left through the rear door then through the courtyard that would take him out to Orkney Street, she turned to see

Salmon grinning at her and hear him say, "You're a fly one, Boss. I'd like to be a fly on the wall if he does go home next Tuesday."
****

They returned to Wells office where handing him the photographs from her desk, she read the SOCO report that discovered where possible, most of the ornaments had fingerprints lifted from them, but it would be down to the Fingerprint Department to identify if any of the prints were currently on record. That, she knew from experience, would be a long and laborious process.

Finished viewing the photos, Salmon thoughtfully asked, "Does the Stolen Property Index on the PNC have the facility to display photos, boss?"

"No, a description only. That said," she slouched back in her chair, then laying the report down, sighed before she continued, "it would make life a lot easier if there were that facility, but who knows that with the development of technology, it could be in the pipeline within a year or two."

"Okay," she glanced at her wristwatch then suddenly sat upright, "time to brief the troops."
****

The team were all assembled when Mary and Salmon entered the incident room.

The day's debriefing didn't last any longer than twenty minutes during which she learned the door to door inquiries disclosed nothing new and so she decided to extend the inquires to include the tenements on Paisley Road West that backed onto Clifford Street. As she explained, "We have no idea if our killer entered the close from the front or the rear door, so if there *is* a possibility that access to the close was from the rear court, I want tenants of the flats on Paisley Road West with windows that overlook the rear courts interviewed. Yes, guys," she shook her head, "it's a small possibility, but we all know, no stone unturned, okay?"

A chorus of, "Yes, Boss," and nodding of heads followed.

Sammy Salmon thereafter related the interview with Alex McLean, the victim's boss, and subsequent interview with McLean's wife, though prudently omitted her overtly sexual advances towards him, then confirmed that while the husband had been eliminated as a suspect, it was likely the wife too would be eliminated, though that was an action for the following day.

However, when he had concluded his debrief, to the teams surprise Mary raised her hand and when she had the attention of the room, loudly called out, "What the DI failed to tell you, handsome devil that he is," she outrageously winked at Salmon whose face was about to explode, "was that Mrs McLean, who admittedly is a right looker, was all over him like a bad rash, even asking if he would be coming back to see her."

"Aw, Boss," to loud laughter and good-natured jeers, an embarrassed Salmon shook his head, yet though he was the butt of her humour, he realised that she had recognised their heads were down a little and was sending them home in good humour.

"Right," a still grinning Mary called for calm, then loudly said, "Tomorrow morning, eight-thirty sharp, guys."

As the team dispersed, she caught the eye of Elaine Fitzsimmons and gave her a thumbs up, then phoning home, advised her child-minder Eileen, that she might be a little later than expected.

Her last act before she left to go shopping was to corner Colin Baxter, where in the privacy of her room, she asked, "You met with the Div Comm?"

"I did, Boss," he sighed.

"I don't want to pry, Colin, but is everything okay?"

His face contorted when he replied, "Yes and no. You know that Mr Metcalfe is due to retire in less than a year?"

"Aye, I'm aware of that."

"Well," he took a breath, "our Geoff called me in to his office to tell me that there's a promotion parade due in the next four weeks and has offered to submit my name to be promoted to uniformed Inspector."

"Well, that's good news," she grinned, "and I can disclose I've been pushing for it too, but with his backing and while it's long overdue, hopefully it will now happen."

"Well, here's the thing," he grimaced, "I've just under two years left to serve and I was hoping to see my time out in the CID, rather than return to uniform and the shift pattern those poor buggers work. That and to be honest, I've been a Detective now for just gone twenty years and while I'm privileged that I'm being offered the opportunity, I don't know that I want to leave the CID."

"You do know that the pay increase to Inspector will not only enhance your salary, but also your commutation when you retire?"

"The money will be useful," he nodded, "but I do love what I'm doing, Boss. Balance that against almost two years of misery," he shrugged.

"Has Mr Metcalfe given you some time to come to a decision?"

"His Divisional submissions have to be forwarded to the Personnel Department by this coming Monday, so till then."

"Okay, Colin," she softly smiled, "discuss it with your wife, but I'm certain whatever decision you make will be the right one for you."

****

As they'd agreed and after parking her car in a bay in Bath Street, Mary met with Fitzsimmons at the Sauchiehall Street door into the BHS store. There she was introduced to Fitzsimmons sister-in-law, Jill McGillivery, a friendly, dark-haired woman of forty with a models' figure, who wearing a black coloured trouser suit, stood with her hands on her hips and casting a critical eye over her, with a frown, surprised her when she said, "If I can just say without offending you, Mary, for an attractive woman you're dressed like a bag lady. Now, anything you buy will be on my staff card, so there's a saving right away. Right, let's get you sorted with something more appropriate to your shape."

When she turned away, Mary stared with upraised eyebrows at Fitzsimmons who choked back a snort then both women followed Jill to the Women's Section of the store.

Fitzsimmons hesitantly whispered to her, "Jill tends to tell it how it is, Boss, but she means no offence."

"Just as well then that I'm thick-skinned, eh," she wryly whispered back.

"Now, then," Jill turned on her heel and with a hand raised and her chin resting on her hand, staring at thoughtfully at Mary then smiled widely when she said, "Let's spend some money."

It was almost an hour and a half later, the store now closed to the public with only the staff within who were re-stocking the departments.

Examining herself in a full-length mirror and lightly fingering the material of the light green, skirted business suit, Mary almost gasped at her reflection, then in a low voice, said, "It's lovely."

To her own surprise, she fought back tears for not in a very long time had she admired her own body and faking a cough to hide her embarrassment, nodded when she asked Fitzsimmons, "What do you think?"

"Of course, I'm only saying this because you're the Boss that does my annual appraisal," she teased with a smile, "but with your new figure and wearing that tomorrow at the office, you're going to turn a lot of heads."

"So, you'll take it," Jill asked.

"Damn right I'll take it," she softly laughed, her eyes on the mirror as she twisted and turned.

"Then," Jill's face creased as she mentally ticked off the purchases, "that's the two trouser suits, two skirted suits, four, no, five blouses including the one you're wearing, the brassieres and the knickers and that cute floral dress and the two skirts," she smiled, then added, "Oh and the Kimono."

Suddenly her expression changed to a questioning frown when she asked, "My God, Mary, when was the last time you treated yourself to a new outfit?"

"You don't want to know," she sighed with a shake of her head.

It took another five minutes for the clothes to be bagged then handing over her cheque, she said, "I really am grateful for all your help, Jill. You've no idea how much it means to me."

She didn't fail to notice the glance that Jill gave her sister-in-law before she replied, "I don't want to overstep the mark, Mary, but when Elaine asked me to hold open the store for you, I was naturally curious so I asked why. Don't get annoyed with her, but she shared a few things with me and for what it's worth, I do know how you feel."

She watched as the Jill's face distorted with anger when she continued, "I was married to a man, rotten bastard that he is, who cheated on me when I too was pregnant. Like you, I had to take time off work, but like you, I'm back on my feet again," she brightly smiled, then added, "Let me assure you, there is a light at the end of the tunnel after all. Now, you need anything else, you come directly to me, okay?"

Before she could respond, Jill took her aback when without warning, she reached out a hand and gently stroking at Mary's hair, added, "Don't forget to spoil yourself at the hairdressers and maybe a beauty parlour too, Mary. You've good, clear skin and you certainly don't look your age, but even with those attributes, us girls do need a

little help now and then, eh?"
They parted with a warm hug, then helping Mary with the bags and walking her to her car, Fitzsimmons said, "I hope you're all right with it, Boss, that I told Jill a couple of things, it's just that I knew she'd be understanding and…"
She stopped walking and turning to her, said, "Here's the thing, Elaine. The last wee while my life's been a kind of open book, but you and some others have stood by me and if nothing else, made me look at myself and to be honest, I didn't really like what I was seeing. Now two things. First, when it's me and you together, it's Mary and Elaine and second, don't be apologising for being my friend, okay?"
Fitzsimmons, slowly nodded, then with curiosity written all over her face, replied, "Okay, Mary; so, what outfit do you think you'll be wearing tomorrow?"

CHAPTER SEVEN – Thursday morning

When Eileen McAulay arrived at the house early the next morning wearing her brand-new BHS Kimono, she literally gushed with pleasure when she saw Mary making her way down stairs, her hair lying loosely on her shoulders and wearing not just a new white blouse, but a navy-blue skirt that hugged her shapely figure and the matching jacket carried over one arm.
"My heavens, missus," she greeted Mary with a slow nod, "you look like the proverbial million dollars. How do you feel?"
Her face flushed, she replied, "I can't explain it, Eileen, but just putting on these new things makes me feel better and believe it or not," she plumped both hands around her breasts, "just having a bra that actually fits makes all the difference too. That and last night, I took myself a long bath and," patting at her hair, confided, "I used one of those wash the grey away shampoos. I think it needs a few treatments before it really works, though. However," she sighed, "I'm determined to get myself together, so this is the start of it. Oh, and you suit your Kimono."
"Love it," Eileen enthused then after a twirl, waved a hand at Mary and told her, "Put the jacket on and let's see the whole outfit, then."

A little self-consciously, she donned the jacket then at Eileen's insistence, turned about.

"Mummy looks different," her daughter Morven cried out from the breakfast table, only to be hushed by her brother Jamie, who seated beside her, frowned and with the wisdom of a five-year-old, told her, "Mummy's not fat anymore and that's why she needs new clothes."

"From the mouth of babes," his mother sighed, then warily kissing both her children on top of their heads to avoid their toast encrusted fingers, was hugged by Eileen who told her, "Knock them dead, sweetheart, and don't be worrying about this pair. I'm not going anywhere in a hurry tonight and as it's the makings of a fine day out there," she pretended to grab at the squealing Morven, "I think I'll be taking this pair of scallywags and a picnic lunch to the park."

Grabbing her handbag and overcoat from the hall stand, Mary hurried to the door then stepping out into the short path, was again surprised to see the new neighbour exiting his house at the same time.

"Morning," the tall man cheerfully called out.

She half-turned as he spoke and with a fixed smile, nodded, but though she couldn't explain why, she didn't verbally respond and without turning, headed across to her car that again she had been obliged to park on the opposite of the road.

Opening the door, she was aware he had followed her across the narrow road then heard him say, "I'm sorry, have I been stealing your car space?"

Getting into the driver's seat she was suddenly aware that her skirt had risen up to her thigh and embarrassed, abruptly replied, "It's a free road. Now, if you'll excuse me."

Closing the car door, she fixed her eyes on the road ahead, acutely conscious the man was staring down at her, then as she started the engine, he walked off to return to his own vehicle.

Driving off, she thought, bugger it; I made a right hash of that and again was acutely aware that the man must think her to be an ignorant cow.

Well, she shook her head, he's only a neighbour not someone I have to get to know, then at the junction, waited for a space in the traffic to turn out onto the parallel road that led to the busy Crow Road.

****

Climbing the stairs to the CID suite, she was met at the top of the stairs by DI Salmon who smiling, watched his eyes narrow when slowing nodding his approval, he appreciatively greeted her with, "Looking good there, Boss," then in a lower voice as they walked together along the corridor, asked, "How do you feel?"

"Like I'm wearing something that fits," she grinned at him, then asked, "Any developments this morning?"

"I got here about ten minutes ago and as usual, Colin Baxter was first through the door, but he does have something to tell us."

She pushed open the door to the incident room to see Baxter at his desk and several of the team already arrived.

Fixing her gaze on Baxter as she approached him, she was conscious of the stares and the nudges and found herself flushing that the team had obviously noticed her new appearance.

"Morning, boss," Baxter stared at her with unconcealed admiration, then said, "First, I've that guy from the auction house coming in this morning as a favour to us to examine the productions seized from the locus. Secondly, DI Reilly called from Pollok. Wants you to phone him back."

Lowering his voice, he quietly added, "He sounded pissed and I don't mean literally. Probably another whining complaint of his."

"Okay," she nodded, then said, "And as you've not mentioned it, I take it no new information about the murder and nothing on the hotline?"

"Nothing," then lips compressed, he shook his head.

"Right, briefing in fifteen minutes, once I've phoned Pollok."

With a knowing look, she passed by Salmon who having overheard the conversation raised his eyes to the ceiling in understanding of what awaited her telephone call.

Making her way in the corridor to her office, she passed by two male uniformed Constables who politely greeted her, though could not help but notice the senior cop's eyes widen.

Mary, she thought to herself, you're knocking them dead today, hen, yet the cop's surprised stare pleased her no end and if she were to admit it, boosted her morale.

Thinking of morale, she sighed then seating herself at her desk, prepared for the telephone call with Martin Reilly.

Reilly was her Senior Detective Officer in charge of the sub-Divisional CID stationed at Pollok Police Office. A third DI, Gerry

Turney, a capable and cheery man she got on well with, looked after the CID at the Giffnock sub-Divisional office.

However, it was Reilly who during her tenure as the DCI at Govan, that had caused Mary the most problems and if what she heard while she was those months off on compassionate leave, caused Sammy Salmon no end of grief too.

Three years over his obligatory thirty years at which point he could and should have retired, Pollok's Detective Inspector was, in her own opinion, the major pain in her arse and the one officer she was keen to see depart her Divisional CID.

How he managed to remain in situ had in itself been a headache and though she had made some subtle inquiries, it had come to nothing; however, she suspected Reilly must have someone in the police upper management by the short and curlies who was looking out for him and that, she knew from experience, made him dangerous.

A former City of Glasgow Detective, the DI was a boastful chauvinist and intolerant of anyone who did not share his views on women in general, Glasgow Celtic Football Club and particularly of female officers senior to him. Many of his sexist comments reached her ears, but there was never anyone with enough nerve to stick their head above the parapet and make an official complaint that she could follow up.

Quick to criticise and slow to praise; slow to praise, her brow furrowed.

What was she thinking; the bugger *never* praised his staff and likely that was why the detection statistics for the Pollok office were invariably the worst of the city's Divisions.

A divisive leader, Reilly's three Pollok based Detective Sergeants were themselves usually at odds and the only thing they had in common was that all three disliked their DI, though to be frank, Mary wasn't certain about DS Hugh Donnelly, himself a misogynist and as nasty as his boss, Reilly.

However, such was the bad atmosphere that existed within the sub-Divisional CID officers that Mary frequently received requests from the eight DC's based there, for a transfer within the Division.

Exhaling through pursed lips, she prepared herself then dialled the direct line for the DI's office at Pollok.

When Reilly answered, she brightly said, "Good morning, Martin. What can I do for you today?"

There was no cheery return greeting, just Reilly's dull growl when he replied, "You can tell me why you're taking one of my DS's and two DC's down to Govan."

She bristled at his harsh response and smoothly replied, "As you know, we have a who-dunnit murder investigation going on and I need extra bodies to assist with the inquiries and *that's* why I'm taking your staff down to supplement my team. Now, I know that you have the experienced staff and the overtime budget to work with what you've got, so of course once the investigation is completed, you'll have them returned immediately."

A few seconds silence was broken when he replied, "If you feel you can't deal with the murder investigation, *Detective Chief Inspector*, perhaps you should let me take it over."

She knew his addressing her as Detective Chief Inspector was as near as he could get to being rude, but while she could ignore that slight, she wasn't having him suggest she was inept, so harshly replied, "I'll let that slide, DI Reilly, because the day that some old fart like *you* could do my job is the day I'll retire, like you should have fucking done years ago!"

Slamming the phone down, she shook with rage yet was annoyed with herself for permitting him to bait her.

Taking a deep breath to compose herself, she imagined him seated at his desk and laughing at her.

Bastard!

When the door was knocked, still red-faced, she angrily called out, "Come in," then almost immediately regretted it when the door was opened by Colin Baxter, who a little taken aback at her response, told her, "That's the guy from the auction house arrived, boss."

As if sensing the phone call with DI Reilly had not gone well, he tentatively asked, "That old sod up in Pollok trying to wind you up?"

"That old sod *did* wind me up," she admitted with a grimace, then added, "Let's go meet your man."

****

If nothing else, Stephen Urquhart certainly looked the part of an auctioneer.

Mary guessed him to be in his late fifties with slicked back silvery grey hair, clean shaven and wearing a dark grey shirt with a scarlet coloured tie and a light grey three-piece suit with, she was certain, a fresh red carnation in the button hole.

Had Urquhart been of relatively medium build, the outfit might have worked, but with his stomach hanging over his waistline, to her he just looked like a tubby little man.

She didn't fail to notice the amusement in DI Sammy Salmon's eyes when Urquhart shook her hand and smiled, his dazzling professionally whitened teeth almost blinding her and his deep, bass voice, she also guessed, was probably practised to impress clients. Staring at her, she saw his eyes widen as like one of his auction items, his eyes appraised her, then held her hand a fraction longer than was polite that to her irritation, caused her to blush.

"Eh, I've set up all the productions in the FACU room, Ma'am," Baxter broke the spell, "so if you, the DI and Mr Urquhart would like to follow me?"

The FACU room, a long and narrow room that had once been utilised as a filing room, had been turned over to the Female and Child Unit at their formation just several months before, the room being all that was available in the old Victorian office where space was at a premium. In fact, such was the demand for workplaces, the room requisitioned as the CID general office had at one time served as the local District Court and still bore the large, royal seal upon the wall where the local JP's had sat in judgement.

Entering the room, Mary saw that Baxter, who carried a clipboard with fresh A4 sheets upon it for notetaking, had collected several trestle tables from somewhere and set up the productions on the tables with each item sporting a brown production label attached by string.

"Good job," she smiled at Baxter, then turning to Urquhart, added, "I'll have DI Salmon remain with you and when you're done, he'll bring you to my office."

"I look forward to it, dear lady," he dazzled her again with a broad smile.

Handing Salmon the clipboard and behind her back, Baxter barely contained his grin when he followed her back to the incident room.

****

Entering the incident room where the team had assembled and awaited her morning briefing, Baxter resumed his desk, his notebook in his hand.

"Not much more to tell you guys," she began, "other than as you already know, the victim's brother relates being told by her that she was holding the ornaments and jewellery discovered in the wardrobe of the locus for a third party. Now, that begs the question; had there been a falling out among thieves and the third party is our killer?" She shook her head, then added, "Speculation only. However, it *is* vital we identify this third party for unless any of you have a different idea and by that, I'd be all ears, then I'm of the opinion that the items discovered have all been stolen from clients of the victim's company. Now," she continued with a glance at them, "Tommy Maxwell and John McGhee were told at the company's office that unfortunately, they did not keep strict records of what staff visited which client at any particular time. Therefore that, ladies and gentlemen, leaves us with a huge headache. With a staff in excess of eighty cleaners and over three hundred clients, there's a lot of interviewing to be done."

She cast a glance around the room, then said, "Now, the productions have all been fingerprinted, but with no names to compare them against, they're just sitting waiting to be identified. It's also more than likely that many of the fingerprints lifted will belong to the owners of the items."

She paused for breath before she continued, "We have the staff's company records, so I intend that DS Baxter will have two of you issued an action to conduct background checks on the staff. PNC as well as local Divisional Collator's, who sometimes have information that isn't worthy of being recorded on the PNC. If any of the staff have come to our attention in the past and been fingerprinted, then ensure they are quoted for comparison to the Fingerprint Department."

"Tommy and John," she turned to Maxwell and McGhee, "the SOCO will have the negatives of the photos they took of the productions. Have them make up a couple or three photobooks and I want you guys," she stopped, then turning to Baxter, said, "as well as two other sets of neighbours, please Colin, that will do the rounds of the clients and show them the photos to determine if they recognise any of the property as theirs."

She softly smiled when she again continued, "I know it's a long and tedious process, ladies and gentlemen, but with the lack of any witnesses or forensic evidence, it's the best we've got for the minute. Any questions?"

It was Maxwell who said, "The photobooks, Ma'am. The SOCO boss might complain about the cost coming off their budget, what will I tell them if they kick off about it?"

"I'll speak with ACC Meadows, so tell them to send their complaint to him. Anything else?"

"Just one more thing, Ma'am," Baxter piped up. "We carried out door to door on the Paisley Road West flats overlooking the rear courts, but all negative."

"Thanks, Colin," she sighed, then clapping her hands together, addressed the team as a whole when she said, "Right, let's get out there, eh?"

****

Standing at the front bedroom window of the three bedroom, detached house in Meadowhill in the Newton Mearns area of the city, Mary Wells father, Michael MacDonald, glanced out from behind the curtain and smiled with satisfaction when he saw his wife Natalie getting into the year-old, silver coloured, two door BMW sedan, then watched as she drove off for her morning meeting with the ladies of the parish committee. He reckoned that the meeting might last an hour then Natalie would gather with some of her cronies to hold court at a coffee shop in the local Avenue Shopping Centre and that would invariably take up another two hours, giving him plenty of time to make the rendeavous before having to return home.

Just as he stepped away from the window, he turned to stare out as his own car, an insipid looking grey coloured eight-year-old, four door Ford Escort.

Not for the first time he shook his head and wondered; did I work all those long hours, all those years for that?

Now approaching his sixty-sixth year, Michael made his way downstairs, pausing to grab at his jacket as he made for the front door.

A mild-mannered man, more than a few times Michael had regretted marrying Natalie and it was only when their son Alan was born did the truth strike him like a hammer blow.

The manipulative and he was soon to learn, deceitful Natalie, three years his senior, had been his first sexual encounter, though even at the tender age of twenty-one, he had realised he certainly wasn't *her* first encounter.

Then, a few weeks later, the devastating news that she was pregnant. Of course, his parents had wisely cautioned him to question if he was the father, but being the honest and naive individual he had been then, he had thrown all caution to the wind and proposed marriage. When Alan had arrived two months prematurely, it was Michael's mother who learned from the midwife the baby seemed to be full term, but by that time there was no going back.

He had been unprepared for the unconditional love he had for the baby, a love that swelled when Mary, then William, arrived.

However, growing up in a loving and close-knit family, nothing had prepared him for the hard-nosed and ambitious Natalie, who through the years was the cause of William's estrangement from friends and even some of his family.

As for Natalie's own family, rough and ready though they were, they had been welcoming of their new son-in-law, but his new wife believed by marrying Michael she had moved up in the world and soon dissociated them from her working-class parents and siblings who were, as she later described them to her new friends, of a different class.

Locking the front door and making his way to the Ford Escort, he smiled at the neighbour next door who was passing by the driveway and though Michael would never know it, the neighbour felt sympathy for the poor man married to that bloody snobbish, hussy. Getting into the car, Michael tilted the rear-view mirror and run a hand around his shaven face, then with a happy smile and eager to be gone, started the engine.

****

As the day wore on and the teams returned in the late afternoon to the incident room, Colin Baxter became increasingly frustrated that not one action provided any further information that might identify a break in the investigation.

When Mary Wells arrived in the room to request an update, he glumly informed her that there was none.

With a sigh she slumped down into the chair adjacent to his desk then asked, "What are we doing wrong, Colin? What questions are we *not* asking?"

He slowly shook his head then glancing at the paperwork on his desk, slowly said, "We've teams out with the photobooks doing the rounds of the clients, we've teams out interviewing the victims co-

workers, we've completed the door to door with negative results, we've an appeal out in the media, the stuff discovered in her flat has all been fingerprinted and all we need is a name to compare against the prints lifted and particularly on the candlestick. So, you tell me, Boss, what are we missing?"
She didn't immediately respond, but glancing at her wristwatch, then asked, "How's the team's morale?"
He frowned when he replied, "You know yourself, they're a wee bit down because of the lack of information coming in, but there's always the expectation that the interviews with the company's clients or the staff will turn up something."
"In that case," her eyes narrowed, "can we supplement the teams by an extra couple of bodies each? That way we'll get through the number so much quicker."
"I'll make it happen," he nodded.
"Right then, gather the team, Colin, and we'll have a short debrief and give then an early night. No point in them hanging around and perhaps an early knock-off will improve their morale for tomorrow morning."

CHAPTER EIGHT

Friday morning dawned bright and sunny and when she arrived, Eileen McAulay as usual had the children excited at the prospect of a day in the children's play area within the Kelvingrove Park.
"Sorry, Eileen, if I had thought about it, I'd have prepared sandwiches for you guys," Mary's face creased.
"Not to worry, I've already got all that planned," Eileen smiled then taking a step backwards, stared critically at Mary before she asked, "I take it that's one of the new trouser suits?"
"You like it?"
"Fits you like a glove and by that, it lets people know you've got a fine figure, my lady," she winked outrageously and made Mary blush.
"Right, scallywags, mummy's away to work, so I'll see you when I get home and be really good for Eileen, okay?"

Smothering their heads with kisses, she made her way outside to her car and to her surprise, wondered if her neighbour would again be leaving for whatever job he did. However, there was no sign of him nor of his car which when she arrived home the previous evening, had been parked across the road, leaving her usual space free for her Toyota Corolla.

Drawing up to the junction with Crow Road, she was behind a delivery van when she saw the black coloured Ford Capri stopped in the middle of the road and signalling to turn right into Ancaster Drive. Taking advantage of a break in the traffic, the Capri finally turned just as the delivery van in front of Mary's car also moved into the line of traffic. As the Capri passed her, she smiled at the driver, but whether her new neighbour didn't see her or simply ignored her, she wasn't certain.

Maybe he's decided I'm just an ignorant cow and won't bother trying to be friendly, she told herself.

Arriving at Govan Police Office rear yard, she locked her car and made her way through the back yard into the uniform bar to collect her mail.

"Morning, Ma'am," Inspector Kenny Herdman formally greeted her at the public bar as he handed her the correspondence.

Smiling at him, she asked, "Back indoors again, Kenny, or is this a permanent move?"

"I hope not," he sighed, then leaning forward with his hands flat on the counter, said in a low voice, "My opposite numbers apparently got the flu; the man-flu that I believe is associated with too many drams."

She grinned and was about to turn away when he added, "I thought you might have been out earlier, what with the murder."

"Eh, no, that's ongoing."

"No, I mean the new murder, the one last night from up in Pollok. A domestic I'm told."

She could feel the blood drain from her face when she replied, "Last night?"

"Aye, I've a man in the cells locked up for stabbing his wife," then realising that perhaps he had spoken out of turn, added, "Sorry, Ma'am, I thought you were aware."

"I am now, Kenny, so excuse me, please."

Hurrying up the wide stairs, her mind in a whirl, all she could think was, that bastard Reilly!

Protocol whether or not the DCI chose to attend such an incident was the decision of the DCI. Regardless of that decision, the senior CID officer must *always* be informed of any major incident that occurred within the Divisional area and murder most certainly did count as a serious incident!

Whether it was a straightforward domestic spousal murder that needed little investigation or a whodunnit, the practice was in place for a reason, for the DCI was ultimately responsible for the investigations of all such serious incidents.

Reaching the top landing, she was met by Sammy Salmon who holding up both hands, said, "Your office, boss, if you please and can I suggest you take a breath before you go off on one."

Nodding sharply, she strode towards her office closely followed by Salmon, then after he entered behind her, quickly shut the door and her arms tightly folded, hissed at him, "Okay, what do you know?"

He took a deep breath before he began, "Uniformed officers were summoned along with an ambulance about eight o'clock last night…"

"Eight o'clock!" her eyes widened in shock.

He nervously licked at his lips then continued, "Yes, eight o'clock or thereabouts, to an address in Brock Road. A ground flat in a block of four. A woman lying in the kitchen with a single knife wound to the abdomen, or so it seemed, and who was later pronounced dead at the locus. The uniformed cops called the Pollok CID out, who in turn called out DI Reilly."

"Reilly," she vehemently muttered and felt her body go cold.

"The husband admitted it was he who had stabbed his wife and he was arrested at the locus. The body was removed to the mortuary and a PM organised for," his face creased, "I think it's booked for about eleven this morning."

"You said the knife wound to the abdomen, something about or so it seemed?"

"The duty Casualty Surgeon is of the opinion that a wound where she was stabbed might not have itself proved fatal; however, she suspects the knife was thrust up under the victim's ribs and it has entered the heart causing an immediate fatality."

Shaking her head, she stepped back and sat with her backside on the edge of her desk, trying to control her anger.

"There were two children in the house at that time, a son and a daughter, aged, as I recall, eleven and thirteen years respectively."

"What about the Govan CID late shift and night shift? Didn't *anyone* think to phone me and let me know about it?"

"In fairness, Boss," he shook his head, "they've probably assumed that Reilly had done that. I mean we all know that's a must. I haven't spoken with the night shift because they were away before I got in, but I can't imagine them thinking anything other than you must have been informed. I mean, horrible git that Reilly is, even he knows he has to contact the DCI regarding a murder, so I can only speculate his own late shift and the guys here must have believed he did that."

Her body shaking with anger, she finally sighed and said, "Thanks, Sammy, but this time that sod's gone too far. Him and I will be having words later today."

"Oh, one more thing, I asked for a copy of the report to the Fiscal, so it's on the desk behind you."

"Okay," she turned to glance down at the report then said, "I'm too angry to brief the team right now, so perhaps you can do that and if there's anything I should know, come and tell me later."

"Will do, Boss," he solemnly nodded then left the room.

What a bloody start to the day, she inwardly fumed, then seating herself at her desk, raised her head when her door was knocked and flung open by the young FACU officer, Constable Janey McPhee, who without waiting for an invitation, stormed in.

"Oh, you're here," she began, then stunned Mary when her face contorted, she angrily began, "Ma'am, that man that's locked up for murder downstairs, Mr Auld. It's not right, Ma'am! I tried to tell DI Reilly, but would he listen? Would he fuck! Ma'am you have to…"

Raising her hand, she loudly called out, "Stop right there, Constable McPhee!"

Pale faced, the younger woman stared at her DCI, who then told her, "Now, you will leave my office, you will compose yourself and calm down, then return in five minutes with two mugs of coffee and you will make sure mine isn't sugared. Then you *will* sit here like a sane person and tell me what the problem is. Is *that* understood?"

Red-faced now, McPhee nodded and wordlessly, turned and left the room.

When the door had closed behind McPhee, she took a deep breath and began to read Reilly's report to the Fiscal.

In fairness, she thought, it was a clear and concise report, if a little brief.

As Salmon had verbally reported, Mary read the police attended the house in Brock Road after a nine-nine-nine call from the occupant, Alistair Auld, who told the emergency operator he had stabbed his wife.

The summoned ambulance crew, who according to the report arrived within minutes of the uniformed officers, could do nothing for the wife, Patricia Auld, who was pronounced dead at the locus by the duty Casualty Surgeon. The Scene of Crimes Officers were at the time of the compilation of the report, in the process of examining the locus. The murder weapon, a black handled nine-inch boning knife that was identified as part of a set from a wooden block located on the worktop in the kitchen, was bloodstained and lying on the floor by the deceased.

Detective Inspector Martin Reilly was called out by the attending officers and arrived at the locus within forty minutes of the emergency phone call and learned that the now accused, Alistair Auld, had admitted to the crime.

It was DI Reilly's decision that the children were removed to their aunt's house, Mrs Fiona Blackley, who resided in the nearby Priesthill Crescent.

Auld was removed to Pollok Police Office where he was cautioned by DI Reilly under common law, then charged with the murder of his wife, Patricia Auld.

The report concluded that Auld would be brought before the Sheriff Court later that afternoon for a two o'clock hearing.

Attached to the report were a list of witnesses and productions, but with the report now read, Mary had no need to read on.

She sighed then closing the report, glanced up as the door was nudged open by Janey McPhee's shoulder and who carried a mug in each hand.

Using her foot, McPhee kicked the door closed then approaching the desk, shamefacedly said, "I'm sorry, Ma'am. I was right out of order."

"Aye, you were, Janey," she nodded her thanks when she reached for the mug, then softly asked, "Do you have a personal interest in this case?"

"Personal interest?" her face creased, then vigorously shaking her head, replied, "No, Ma'am. But I have had dealings with the family through my time in the FACU."

She sighed when she continued, "That's why I tried to speak this morning with DI Reilly when I heard about Mr Auld being locked up, but he just..." she hesitated, then stony-faced added, "he just hung up on me."

And likely with an expletive if I know that foul-mouthed git, she thought, then said, "Start at the beginning and tell me how you came to know the family."

Mary watched the younger woman take a deep breath, then she began, "Before I came to see you, I dug out the paperwork to refresh my memory. It was in March this year, I received a phone call from Mr Auld's sister, a woman called Fiona Blakely."

"Yes, she's mentioned in the report," Mary pointed to the file. "I understand she has the two children in her care now."

"Nice wee woman widowed with a grown-up family and now lives alone. Anyway," McPhee leaned forward, "she often has her niece and nephew staying over and particularly at weekends. In March, when she contacted me, I went to visit her about concerns over the children; bruising on their arms and legs."

"And did you see these bruises?"

"I visited again the next Saturday when Mrs Blakely, Fiona," she briefly smiled, "had the kids overnight and yes, there was a clear indication that the kids had what looked to me like bruising that must have occurred both historically and recently, given that some were still red while others bruises had turned that yellowish colour, you know?"

She nodded, then her eyes narrowed when she asked, "The father?"

"No, Ma'am," McPhee shook her head. "The mother."

"And can you be certain about that?"

"The children completely denied being hit and even come up with such excuses as, 'I fell down the stairs' then telling me, 'We like to wrestle,' that sort of thing, but I know from my experience with the FACU, more than likely they were protecting their abuser."

"Anyway, a couple of days after my initial visit to Fiona, she arranged for her brother to meet me at her house and if I'm honest, I was a bit sceptical because I wrongly assumed he must be a party to the weans being beaten like they had been."

She paused and glanced at the floor, as though remembering the meeting and how awful it must have been.

"The sad fact is he knew about his wife's conduct, but at his sister's insistence and believe me, he wasn't for it, he showed me his arms and his upper torso. He's taken some hidings from his wife, too."

In her time in the police and in particular, the CID, Mary had met with all types of abusers and while in general most abusers *were* men, there were also a number of women who took out their anger, frustrations or simply didn't need a reason to hurt their spouses or partners. These individuals who exercised such coercive behaviour towards others of weaker character, whether that power be physical or verbal, were in the main cowardly bullies, but that didn't stop it going on, she inwardly sighed.

After all, isn't my father as much a victim as anyone, she inwardly thought with a start?

"Did he say why he didn't report this to the police?" she heard herself ask.

McPhee bit at her lower lip for a brief second before she replied, "He told me that if he tried to take the children away, if he told anyone about his wife hitting them or hitting him, she'd kill him, kill the weans, then kill herself."

"Fuck," a stunned Mary involuntarily gasped, then her brow knitting, asked, "He obviously believed her?"

"Yes, Ma'am, sadly he did."

They sat in silence for several seconds before she asked, "You have your suspicions, Janey, about the murder?"

"I do, Ma'am, yes," she vigorously nodded.

"And from your earlier outburst, you tried to inform DI Reilly about these suspicions?"

"I did, aye," she stared stony-faced at Wells, then sourly said, "but I'm a uniformed Constable in plain clothes working in a Female and Child Unit, so stepping out of my remit and trying to advise a Detective Inspector is beyond my scope," she almost spat the words put.

"No offence meant, Ma'am."

To McPhee's surprise, Mary softly replied, "Actually, offence *is* taken Janey. First and foremost, you are a police officer and bound by your oath to guard, watch and patrol and without fear or favour so whether you are listened to or not, it is your duty to speak out when you believe a wrong is being committed."

She paused for a second, then continued, "That said, you have quite obviously identified an issue with the case against Mr Auld, that issue being information that you believe is relative to the circumstances of the death of his wife and as I said, you are duty bound to bring it to the attention of a senior officer, which you so correctly did. The fact that the senior officer refused to listen to you says more about him than it does you and because you believe what information you have should be heard, you came to me."

She smiled when she added, "Admittedly, a bit on the pushy side, but like they say, every day is a school day, yes? So, no matter what the outcome of this is, you *have* done your duty as a police officer."

Wells took a deep breath before she said, "Right, Janey, here's what's going to happen. I want you to go and see Colin Baxter, have him give you a set of keys and you are to go now and bring Mrs Blakely and the children here to Govan. I think we should have a wee word with them."

"Okay, Ma'am, but what about DI Reilly? Shouldn't we tell him we're going to speak with his witnesses?"

"Oh, trust me," she replied with some feeling, "you can leave DI Reilly for me to deal with." When McPhee had left the room, her eyes narrowed in thought.

****

Watching the children play, Eileen McAulay, seated on a bench table by the sandpit, munched at the sandwich before taking a slurp of her tea.

Smiling at Morven's attempts to follow her big brother up the chute, she watched as Jamie reached down to grab at his sister's arm before helping her onto the platform where with a wild shriek, she followed him down the metal slide.

Crazy kids, she stared adoringly at them.

Her thoughts turned to the last nine months and couldn't believe how much her life had changed in such a short time.

Widowed almost ten years previously at the age of forty-seven, she had sunk into a deep depression that neither alcohol nor prescribed medication could help. With no close family and what few friends remained after cutting herself off from the world and believing herself unable to cope with life itself, then came that fateful evening when she had decided to end it all.

Her brow creased at the memory and in her mind, could almost taste the awful bile that forced her to vomit the contents of her stomach onto the lounge carpet, the vomit that in turn discharged the drugs and alcohol from her system. And there she had lain for God alone knows how many hours before dragging herself to the bathroom, her hair, face and clothes reeking with the sour smell of puke.

In her hand, the mug of tea from the Thermos flask grew cold as her thoughts continued.

She had loved her Jack with a passion, though, she involuntarily smiled, he could sometimes be a bit of a handful. Sadly, she never bore him any children though never once did he complain, telling her that it left him with time to spend with her.

And spend it together, they did.

My God, she found herself grinning widely; the things we saw and did.

Her extremely lucrative job as a corporate lawyer with her business suits, regular visits to the expensive salons, the fancy sports cars and the foreign trips had taken her to some faraway places while Jack's business ventures, though not always successful, allowed him time to travel with her. And what times we had, she smiled at the fleeting memories.

Then the sudden and unexpected heart attack that took her outwardly healthy husband had devasted her, so much so that life just didn't seem worth it anymore.

She hadn't known about his secret appointments with the cardiologist and when she'd later challenged their GP who had made the arrangements, he apologetically explained to Eileen that Jack had forbidden him from disclosing any details of the visits.

Her reaction had surprised even Eileen, for after he died she was so very, very angry with Jack, angry enough to almost hate him for keeping his condition from her and leaving her alone.

It was then she realised he had known that he would not have a full life and in expectation of his death, took out a number of insurance policies that more than guaranteed Eileen would neither have to work nor ever want for anything again.

At first, she had tried to continue her life, but her lacklustre performance at her firm left her bosses with little option but to sack her, albeit with an extremely rewarding pay-off and pension.
But that was then and this is now, she told herself and inwardly smiled at the woman she had become.
Gone was the perfectly coiffured, smartly suited lawyer who carried an expensive three-figure leather briefcase, who wore top of the range clothes and drove the Mercedes-Benz 450SL Roadster.
Gone were the regular visits to the fashionable hair and beauty salons.
Gone too after Jack's death, was the later addiction to alcohol and prescribed medication, all to be replaced by a happy hippy, as she often referred to herself, who drove a second-hand Beetle and now preferred soft furnishings and comfortable clothes and who now no longer gave a fig about what people saw or thought of her.
But it hadn't been easy.
The months of denial had been more difficult than she'd ever imagined, but once she was over that and took a good look at herself in her mirror, she saw the woman she was to become.
And of course, the counselling had been a significant help.
It had been the best day of her new life when the counsellor had introduced her to Mary who in turn, some months later introduced her to the children; a ready-made family she could be part of and though never having had children of her own, almost immediately settled into the role of childminder.
With the insurance money and her pension and though Mary would never know that the stipend she paid Eileen was valued, she had no need of the money, for Jack had left her independently wealthy, though of course she would have given it all up just to have her husband back.
But again, that was then and, she inwardly smiled, times had moved on.
She had moved on.
She glanced up then grinned as the children run to her, Morven throwing her arms around Eileen's legs while Jamie turned to sit on the bench, ensuring he snuggled tightly up against her, then stared up at her when he asked, "Can I have another drink of juice please, granny?"
She startled and thought she had misheard, but then Morven, with

the cheeky grin that always touched her heart, began chanting, "Granny, granny, granny."

Catching her breath and with a lump in her throat, she slowly asked Jamie, "What brought this on then, calling me granny?"

He pointed across the playground to a tousled-haired boy of about his own age and replied, "That's my new friend; his name's Joshua. He asked if you were my granny and I said, yes. Is that okay? Will you be me and Morven's granny now? Granny Eileen?"

She felt herself well up and unable to trust herself to speak, simply nodded.

"Good," Jamie's face lit up, then handing back the juice bottle, turned and screamed, "Morven! Let's go!"

Like the obedient and adoring little sister she was, she chased after him, stumbling and falling flat, then up in a second and running towards the climbing frame.

Eileen wasn't aware of the tears running down her cheeks then minutes later, dabbing at her face with a handkerchief, became suspicious of the clouds overhead.

Throwing the cold tea onto the grass, she packed the sandwich boxes, flask and the juice bottles in the bag beside the two mugs then called for the children.

****

Constable Janey McPhee was invited into the house by Fiona Blakely, who standing with her in the hallway, cast a glance towards the closed door of the lounge, then said in a low voice, "But why do you need to speak with the children? To be honest, hen," she shook her head, "I don't really know if they're up to be spoken to. Do you know they've hardly opened their mouths since they got here? That can't be right, can it?"

"It's my boss, Fiona. DCI Wells. She's a good woman and she's got kids herself. I promise you," she held her palm raised, "If anyone can do anything to help your brother, it's Mary Wells. Stand on me about that."

She watched as the older woman seemed to deliberate on whether to agree to take the children to Govan, then with a resigned sigh, asked, "Can I sit with them when they're being spoken to? I mean I'm not having them being on their own. They've been through enough in the last twenty-four hour."

"Course you can," a relieved McPhee replied, then added, "You get their coats on and I'll wait in the motor."
****

Popping along to the incident room, Mary asked Sammy Salmon, "How did the briefing go?"
"Nothing to report, boss."
His eyes narrowed when he lowered his voice to ask, "You spoke with Martin Reilly yet?"
"Not yet, I've a few things to clear up first. In the meantime," she handed him two five-pound notes, then said, "Can you use your charm to persuade that young lassie from the typing pool to nip out to the shops and fetch me in two cans of Coke, two big bars of chocolate and a couple of magazines, one suitable for a boy of eleven and one for a girl of thirteen."
He grinned, then stared suspiciously at her when he asked, "You can't ask her yourself because you've forgotten her name, haven't you?"
"Aye, very good, smart arse," she pretended to growl, then sheepishly added, "It's Lisa, isn't it?"
"Laura," poker-faced, he corrected her.
****

She was watching from behind the curtain when Michael arrived home, still bristling that he had been gone without telling her where. She stood back a little and saw him getting out of that old Escort of his and quickly moved to the armchair where sitting down, she positioned herself with her legs neatly under her and pretended to read a magazine.
Shit, she thought. The curtain from where she'd watched him was out of alignment with the other curtain, but hearing him call out, "I'm home," from the hallway, knew she didn't have time to cross the room to fix it.
The door opened to admit him and he asked, "Have a nice time with your friends?"
"Where have you been?" she snapped.
He audibly sighed when remaining stood at the door, he replied, "I told you, I was meeting with some of my old colleagues for coffee in the city centre."
"You never *did* tell me that," she growled at him.

"I *did* tell you. The problem is, Natalie, you never listen to me. Now, how was your day," he politely asked again.

"Are you telling me that you went out dressed like that? My heavens, Michael MacDonald! What will people think?"

"Frankly," he sighed, "I don't care what people think. I'm a retired man and besides, you needn't worry what people think. It's not as if we're ever seen together, is it?"

"And whose fault is that!"

"Yours, actually, but don't be worrying. I'll not embarrass you in front of your snooty friends. Now, if you'll excuse me, I'll go and prepare lunch."

When the door had closed behind her husband, an irate Natalie wondered how she had ever managed to land herself such a useless man like him and not for the first time, her thoughts turned to all those decades ago, to the Spanish salesman who had promised so much, yet delivered nothing.

****

Mary Wells door was knocked then opened by the young woman from the typing pool who holding a plastic bag, said, "Your shopping, Ma'am."

"Oh, great, thanks," she graced her with a smile, then said, "It's not for me. I've a couple of young witnesses coming in and it's to settle their nerves."

"Oh, right, and here's your change."

"Stick it in the tea fund, Laura."

"Oh, it's actually Lisa, Ma'am."

"Ah, right, sorry. Lisa," she nodded, yet when the girl had gone, could not but help grin that Sammy Salmon had so easily set her up.

Minutes later Janey McPhee popped her head into the room and said, "That's Fiona Blakely with Mr Auld's children, Ma'am. I've got them sitting in the FACU room with one of the girls."

"Okay," she handed McPhee the plastic bag, "dish those out to the kids and bring Mrs Blakely here to see me."

Less than two minutes later, McPhee escorted a woman who stood no taller than five feet two inches, with a rotund figure, short dark hair and black-framed spectacles. Wearing a blue coloured, knee length woollen coat, she held a black coloured handbag in both hands clutched close to her chest and it was immediately obvious she was extremely nervous.

Standing up from her desk, she moved around to the side and extending her hand to greet her, said, "Hello, Mrs Blakely, I'm DCI Mary Wells. I regret we're meeting under these awful circumstances."

Indicating she sit down in one of the two chairs in front of the desk, Mary nodded that McPhee could leave, then occupied the second chair and continued, "Now, I'm very grateful to you for coming down with the children. If I may, can I call you Fiona?"

Her voice almost a squeak, she nodded and replied, "Yes."

"Well, I'm Mary, so that makes it much easier, eh?" she encouragingly smiled.

"What is it that you want, eh, Mary?"

"Janey has brought it to my attention that she isn't happy about your brother Alistair being charged with murder, Fiona. It seems there might be some unanswered questions, so I'd like your permission to speak with the children. With you present, of course," she added.

"Will it help our Ali?"

"To be honest, I don't really know, but one thing is for certain. It won't make things any worse for him."

Softly, she asked, "Tell me about your brother's wife."

Blakely's eyes danced in her head, then taking a breath before exhaling, she replied, "Patricia, she wasn't a nice a nice woman and an even worse wife and mother."

Her head dipped slightly as she stared at the desktop, then licked at her lips before she continued, "I shouldn't be speaking ill of the dead, Mary, but some things need to be said. That woman gave my brother a hell of a life, with her drinking and her chasing after the men."

Mary decided not to speak, to let her continue her story in her own time.

"Patricia, she was brought up like us in Priesthill. Her parents, God rest them, were a lovely couple, but she was spoiled rotten. She had two brothers who were a wee bit older than her and they left on that Government scheme they had back in the sixties, the ten-pound passage to Australia."

She turned to ask Mary, "Do you remember they days?"

Mary Wells nodded with a smile, then said, "Please, go on."

"Anyway, with the boys away to their new life, Patricia's parents more or less let her do what she wanted and by Christ, did she take advantage of that. Drink and wild parties, she was the talk of the area so she was," she sniffed to show her disapproval.

With a resigned sigh, she shook her head and frowned when she said, "Why she got her claws into our Ali I will never know, but he was, what's the word," her brow furrowed, "bewitched?"

Mary smiled when nodding, she said, "It's as good a word as any."

"Anyway, the next thing we know she's pregnant and tells our Ali it's his, so he does the right thing and marries her."

Mary took an inward breath as her father's face jumped into her thoughts.

"She had the baby and our Peter, he arrived just over a year and a bit later. Ali, he had a right good job in the shipyards in the architect's office down here in Govan, but that still wasn't good enough for her, oh no," a bitterness infected her voice.

"She had him doing *two* jobs so that she could keep up her lifestyle and," she turned to stare at Wells, "I love my brother, but he's such a weak man and he just went along with whatever she needed. Many's the day she would leave the weans with me then head into the city centre on a shopping spree and be away most of the day and the night, usually returning with a drink in her and," her eyes angrily narrowed, "sometimes with her knickers in her handbag, if you know what I mean. As for Ali, for the sake of peace he'd turn a blind eye and between you and me, Mary, it was him that raised those two kids. He's the one who saw them washed them and fed them while she was out galivanting with other men."

"Janey, she told me that you contacted her because of the bruising on the children?"

Blakely's shoulder's slumped when she nodded, then said, "It had been going on for a while, now. I tried to get Ali to do something about it, but he was worried that the kids would be taken away by the Social, so he didn't know I'd contacted Janey. In all honesty, I think he was relieved when I told you, the polis I mean."

"Did you have any recent contact with your sister-in-law?"

"No," she shook her head. "She never really liked me or my husband and believe me, the feeling was mutual, so she banned me from her house, but that didn't stop her sending me her kids for overnighters when Ali was out working, so that she could go out on the town."

She watched the older woman's eyes glisten with unshed tears, then quickly asked, "Who would be the best to speak with first? Gillian or

Peter?"

Buckley's brow furrowed in thought before she hesitantly replied, "Gillian's a good girl, but she withdraws into herself, so she does. Peter, he's a quiet lad, a bit like his dad when Ali was young. Very thoughtful," she smiled at the memory of her brother as a young boy. "But he's the sort of wee boy who sees things and hears things that me and you might miss, you know?"

"I've got two kids, younger than Peter and Gillian, but both as wide as the Clyde," Mary smiled, "so yes, I've an idea what you're talking about."

Blakely took a deep breath then in a firm voice, said, "Then it's Peter. Speak to Peter first."

CHAPTER NINE

Stopping the car outside the end terraced house in Sandgate Avenue in the Sandyhills area of the city, DC Hamilton turned to his neighbour before he asked, "Here goes number four."

DS Elaine Fitzsimmons opened her eyes then wearily replied, "Sorry, I was dozing there. Sleepless night. Right," she yawned and stretched as far as the confines of the front passenger seat would permit, "Who have we got here?"

Hamilton reached behind him to lift the folder from the rear seat, then checking the Action form, replied, "Katherine Carmichael, aged forty-eight. Nothing on the PNC and been with the company for four years."

"Here's hoping she's in and not out visiting a client, then," Fitzsimmons opened the car door and got out.

As it happened, the door was opened by the bespectacled Carmichael who almost as tall as Fitzsimmons and with her fair tied back into a ponytail, wore a polo shirt with the company log on the left breast and jogging bottoms, then staring apprehensively at them, immediately suspected them of being one of the fancy Christian faiths that pedalled their religion round the doors.

However, when Fitzsimmons identified them as CID, they were ushered straight into the front room where almost immediately the thinly built woman disappeared through the kitchen door, calling behind her, "I'll just get the kettle on and you're in luck. My man was at the bakers earlier on and he's brought in some cakes, before he went out to the bookies."

Hamilton suppressed his grin when he heard his neighbour mutter, "Hope they're low calorie."

While they waited, Fitzsimmons glanced around the room, seeing the framed print of 'Christ On The Cross' on one wall and several religious articles on both shelving and the mantlepiece.

"I'm suspecting that this is definitely a waste of time," she muttered to Hamilton, who staring curiously at her, then turned when she pointed out the artefacts scattered around.

"How so?" he whispered.

"Strict Catholic," she sighed, "Can't see her being into the thievery."

"Have you found out who killed Lizzie, yet?"

They turned to see Carmichael carrying a tray with cups, saucers, sugar bowl and milk jug, but it was the plate of strawberry and cream doughnuts that lit up Hamilton's eyes.

"It's an ongoing investigation, Mrs Carmichael," Fitzsimmons accepted the cup and saucer, then quickly asked, "Did you know Mrs Bradley?"

"Lizzie? Oh, aye, I knew her well. A nice young lassie, but kept herself to herself quite a lot. Saying that, because we usually just work alone at a client, you don't really get to know your co-workers too well, so she might have been a bit of a live wire outside work, you know?"

Out of politeness, Carmichael offered the doughnuts first to Fitzsimmons, who to Hamilton's disappointment chose the biggest one.

"So, you didn't know her outside work?"

"No," she shook her head "I did work with her *sometimes* when the job required two cleaners to be present. Two for self-protection. You know, when it was a touchy-feely job."

"Sorry," Fitzsimmons eyes narrowed, "what is that, a touchy-feely job?"

"Oh," Carmichael blushed, then glanced towards Hamilton, "I don't know if I can explain it in front of a young guy like him."

"Oh, don't worry," Fitzsimmons, already guessing where this was going, smiled when she added, "Alan here is older than he looks and I assure you, he has seen and been involved in some things that you would *not* believe."

Hamilton stared curiously at them in turn then Carmichael began. "Most if not all our clients are pretty old or have what they call a debilitating physical issue or might sometimes be suffering from dementia, you know?"

"Go on," pokerfaced, Fitzsimmons could see that Carmichael was clearly uncomfortable, but wanted to also see how Hamilton would react to her explanation.

"The touchy-feely clients, mostly men of course though," she pursed her lips as she stared in space, "there are a couple of old women who are like that and being pensioners, they don't get out much so they've not a lot of opportunities to spend their money on. Well, the short version is that they like a wee bit of relief, you know?"

"Relief?"

It was unfortunate that Hamilton had just taken a large bite of his creamy doughnut when Carmichael casually replied, "Aye, you know. A wank or a blowjob, though it's usually just a wank," she shrugged.

His face purple, Hamilton exhaled a great goblet of doughnut that flew across the room like a projectile to squarely hit the fireplace and splatter cream on the tiles.

Watching him choke, Fitzsimmons jumped to her feet to thump him on the back and watched as a piece of doughnut covered in phlegm landed on his suit trousers.

Still spluttering, he got to his feet and managed to gasp, "Bathroom!"

"Up the top of the stairs, son," a worried looking Carmichael pointed to the hallway door.

Turning to Fitzsimmons, she asked, "You think he'll be okay? Should I go up?"

"Oh, he'll be fine," she reassured her, then added, "I think if you follow him up there he'll just panic."

"Ah, okay," Carmichael didn't get the inference, but simply stared at the mess on her fireplace before she muttered. "I'll get that when you're away."

"Now," she fought to keep her face straight, "I assume that providing, eh, sexual *relief* to the clients is not condoned by the management?"

"Oh, no, not at all," she waved a hand as if the idea was preposterous.

Then her face contorted, she shrugged when she added in a conspiratorial voice, "Me, I have had a few of the old guys asking me to do them, you know?" she blushed, "but I'm not into that sort of thing. Not like some of them, anyway," she haughtily sniffed.

"So, some of your co-workers do make their own arrangements with the clients?"

"Well, I heard over the years that some of the women, but mind, I don't know any names," she discreetly added, "might have earned some extra cash by wanking some of the old guys off."

"Have you ever heard that instead of cash, these women might have been paid with jewellery or ornaments?"

Clearly taken aback, Carmichael's eyes narrowed in thought when slowly shaking her head, she replied, "Never heard of that in *my* time there, no."

"One last question," but before she could ask, they heard the loo being flushed then the sound of Hamilton tramping down the stairs.

Re-entering the room, he grimaced then addressing Carmichael, said, "I am *so* sorry."

Pointing to the fireplace, he said, "Can you get me a cloth and I'll clean that up?"

"Forget it, son, I'll get it when you and your friend are away. I mean, that's my job, isn't it? Cleaning?"

Laughing at her own joke, she turned when Fitzsimmons asked,

"Last question Mrs Carmichael. Are you aware of Lizzie being close to any of her co-workers?"

"What," her lip curled, "you mean apart from the boss, Alex McLean?"

"So, you knew of an affair between them?"

"Oh, aye, it was the talk of the place, so it was. Him with a wife and weans, taking advantage of a young lassie like her," she sniffed to show her disgust at McLean's extramarital affair, yet wryly forgiving Elizabeth Bradley for her part in the cheating.

"What about Lizzie being closed to any of her co-workers? Friends, I mean?"

Carmichael gave it some seconds of thought, but then shook her head when she replied, "I can't say for certain I took any notice. Sorry."

"Oh, one last thing," Fitzsimmons held up her hand. "I should have asked you earlier. We know from speaking with the staff that company's like yours are forever receiving unfounded allegations of the cleaners stealing property from their clients. Do you know of or have your suspicions about any individuals who *might* have taken advantage of their position, visiting client's homes?"

"Truthfully, no, but I don't know if this is of any use to you. I did hear a couple of weeks ago from one of my pals, a lassie that's been there longer than me, that there has been an increase in complaints of theft from clients, but to be honest, I don't know if it's true or just a rumour."

"Thank you, you've been very helpful," Fitzsimmons forced a smile when they left.

Back in the car, Hamilton stared miserably down at the damp patches on his suit trousers when he said, "I will never again look at *any* doughnut without remembering this day."

****

While Gillian Auld remained with the FACU officer in the room with her Coke, chocolate bar and magazine, Janey McPhee brought eleven-year-old Peter down to the small, cupboard like room that had been converted to an interview room.

There they met with Fiona Blakely and Mary Wells, who explained the working of the tape-recording machine. When all four were comfortably seated, Mary smiled encouragingly at the nervous wee boy then began.

A little over twenty minutes later, McPhee left with Peter to fetch Gillian, where upon the young girl's arrival, the procedure was repeated.

Twenty-five minutes later, satisfied that she had as much information as she needed, Mary terminated the interview and leaving Blakely and the young girl with McPhee, dropped the tapes into the typist room before returning to her office.

At her desk she lifted the copy of Martin Reilly's case to the Fiscal and thumbed through it once more. Having reported more than a few murders, Wells knew that the case papers should also include a report from the police Casualty Surgeon, who would have been brought in to examine the accused to ensure there was neither a physical nor any mental health reasons why an accused could not face a pleading diet at court.

Mentally kicking herself for not previously having considered it, she scanned the doctor's written report and without realising it involuntarily nodded, for it was as she suspected.

Gathering her thoughts, she took a few moments to compose herself then reaching for her desk phone, began to make the first of two difficult calls.

****

Sammy Salmon, sitting in the incident room checking through the completed actions, glanced up when DS Donald Corbett breezed through the door and made his way towards the DI.

"Morning, Boss, what's doing?" he stared down at Salmon.

A bear of a man and one of the stalwart props of the Strathclyde Police rugby team, the shaven headed, red-bearded and much-experienced Corbett had been designated by Mary Wells to be in charge of the CID general office, now manned by a handful of Detectives who with Corbett and a team of plainclothes officers from the shifts, continued to carry out general inquiries. However, just in case there was any kind of overlap between the murder investigation and the general duties being carried out, Corbett also attended the murder investigation briefings to be updated with information that his officers might need to know or could assist with when carrying out their general duties.

"The boss is interviewing a couple of kids, the children of the man arrested by Martin Reilly for murdering his wife. As for this," he waved a hand around the room, "nothing coming in that's leading us anywhere."

Corbett's eyes narrowed in curiosity when he asked, "Why is Mary interviewing the children? Surely Pollok CID should have done that?"

A thoughtful Salmon slowly shook his head then frowned when he replied, "She hasn't shared that, Donnie. All I know is that she spoke with Janey McPhee earlier on today, so it might be something Janey's told her."

"So," he continued, "anything doing on your side of the fence?"

"No, just the usual," Corbett sighed. "Same old story when there's a murder. The place quietens down for a while because the local worthies are shit scared they'll get a pull and it'll interfere with their nefarious businesses," he widely grinned, showing gaps in his mouth where at various times his teeth had been left in the muddy rugby fields.

A thought occurred to Salmon, who asked, "Am I correct in thinking that about a year ago, though it might be longer to be honest, you put in a case against an old guy, a resetter who lives over in F Division?" Corbett's eyes narrowed in thought, then he slowly nodded and said, "You mean Max Pettigrew?"

"That's the name," a grinning Salmon replied. "You said at the time he looked like Santa Claus."

"Oh, aye, that's Max. Old bugger got a Not Proven, even though we found the stolen property in his flat. An extremely rare Japanese seventeenth century writing set in a carved walnut box and worth five figures, as I recall. His defence was that the seller had produced a letter of provenance even though he also claimed the seller must have stolen that from *him*. Fly old sod, so he is," he shook his head, then with an amused grin, he added, "That all said, you can't help but like the old duffer. So, why do you ask?"

"I was just wondering with our investigation being a murder and if we can convince him we're not there to turn his place over, he might be able to tell us if he's got any knowledge of property similar to what we discovered in the victims flat being offered to him."

"You can but ask," Corbett shrugged.

****

Wells had just completed her second phone call when the door was pushed open by Inspector Kenny Herdman, who remained standing at the open door and, his face flushed and frowning, angrily said, "Ma'am, I've just had that *bloody* muppet Martin Reilly on the phone from Pollok barking in my ear as to why his murder suspect hasn't yet arrived at the Sheriff Court! When I tried to explain that you had instructed Mr Auld to be detained here until you'd spoken with the ACC, I regret to say your DI became very abusive and to be frank, I will *not* be spoken to like that!"

"Okay, Kenny," she raised a hand to soothe him, "I'll phone him and make my explanation and I regret that you got the brunt of his anger."

"Oh, there's no need for you to phone him," Herdman vigorously shook his head when he replied through gritted teeth.

"He said before he hung up on me he'll be on his way here now and, may I quote him, also said it's his intention to kick arses!"

"Really?" Wells supressed a smile, then carefully said, "Inspector Herdman, if DI Reilly arrives at your uniform bar and decides to kick off with his abusive behaviour, I'm certain there is sufficient officers within the bar to restrain him and well," she shrugged with complete indifference, "the decision whether to arrest him or not lies with you."

Herdman's eyes widened as he stared unbelievingly at her before his face broke out into a wide smile when nodding, he calmly replied, "There's always that option, Ma'am. Good luck and I'll be downstairs if you should need me."

He turned to find Sammy Salmon at his back, who stepping into the room, said, "I heard all that, Boss. What's going on?"

"DI Reilly is not at all happy with a decision I've made," she carefully replied, "so you'll know he's on his way here and likely we'll be having words. Anything doing through in the incident room?"

"No," he shook his head, then turned to closed the door.

"What you doing, Sammy?"

She watched as he strode towards her desk then picking up one of the two chairs there, lifted it and moving it towards the side wall, then sat down.

"Sammy?" she stared curiously at him.

He held up a hand in defence then replied, "Look, Boss, I know you are more than capable of dealing with that," he smiled and took a deep breath, "what did Kenny Herdman call him? Oh, aye a muppet. But Reilly is a smarmy old bastard and if there's going to be words exchanged, it'll be down to credibility if your meeting goes apeshit, as I fully expect it will. He says, she says, that sort of thing, so I'm staying. I won't say a word, I promise," he held up his hand, "but I will be here to corroborate anything that *is* said. Don't forget, too, that he's got a wire somewhere in headquarters who has been looking out for him, so you'll want someone to watch *your* back and that's me."

"And, Detective Inspector," she stared meaningfully at him, "if I tell you to leave the room?"

"Nope," he shook his head then folded his arms. "I'm going nowhere, Boss, and even if I did leave the room, there would be one of your team out there who would in here in a flash to replace me because it wasn't just me that heard Kenny Herdman ranting about

Reilly, so the word will have got out that he's on his way."
She felt her chest tighten at the loyalty being displayed by Salmon and tried with difficulty not to respond.
Of course, he was correct.
Martin Reilly had been in the CID for almost as long, if not longer than she had been a police officer and notoriously was a cunning and nasty individual who, to use the old Glasgow vernacular, was always worth the watching; a man who had ruined more than one young officer's career in his time as a supervisor.
However, depending on how this meeting went, it was just possible that he had overstepped the mark this time and if she was careful, she might finally be rid of him.
She?
The CID *and* the police service in general, she corrected herself.
"So," Salmon cheerfully smiled, "how's life in general, then?"
****
The young DC who had been instructed by Reilly to drive him to Govan Office, was a little afraid of the cantankerous old sod and throughout the journey, had to suffer in silence his bad-tempered whining and foul language for the full thirteen minutes it took the DC to arrive at Orkney Street.
Stopping the car outside the main entrance, Reilly turned to the DC to rudely snap at him, "You drive like a schoolgirl. Now, wait here till I get back."
Awkwardly pulling himself out of the car, he slammed the door behind him.
Watching Reilly push open the doors into the entrance, the DC thought, I hope Mary Wells tears you a new one, you arsehole.
Seated at his desk, Inspector Kenny Herdman turned to watch Reilly stride past the public counter and breathed a sigh of relief. He was acutely aware that his bar staff of three uniformed Constables were watching their Inspector and were standing ready at Herdman's nod, for if Reilly had dared to enter the uniform bar and kicked off, fellow police officer or not, the unpopular DI would have been arrested for a breach of the peace.
Striding up the wide stairs like a man possessed, Reilly stopped at the top to catch his breath, his face flushed and his legs shaking, for not only was he extremely unfit, but the diagnosis just the previous month had disclosed stage three emphysema.

But of course, the doctor was wrong, he had later told his wife; the shortness of breath and coughing was probably just a heavy bout of a summer cold or the onset of flu and after all, he had shaken his head at her nagging, it couldn't be the fags. For most of his life, hadn't he always been a forty a day man?

Wheezing now, he righted himself and strode towards the DCI's room.

The room that by rights, he inwardly snarled, should have been mine.

****

There was no courtesy knock.

The door was flung open then Reilly, wearing his usual, outdated and cigarette reeking three-piece plaid suit, his face so flushed it resembled a baby's spanked arse stepped into the room then turned to slam the door closed behind him.

When he turned back, Mary, her hands clasped on the desk before her, saw his eyes narrow before he snapped, "What's he doing in here?"

She glanced at Salmon, then calmly said, "The DI is here to ensure that what I tell you is clear and concise and you do not wrongly interpret anything I tell you."

"What's *that* supposed to mean?"

"Please sit down, DI Reilly."

His eyes betraying his suspicion, he slumped down into the chair in front of her desk and struggling to control his breathing, with another glance towards Salmon, said, "I hear you refused to send my murder suspect to the court. Why?"

"Because he did not murder his wife."

The pregnant pause as wide-eyed, he stared at her was broken when he sneered, "Oh, and you know this how?"

"Unlike you, DI Reilly, I conducted some basic investigative techniques."

"Like what!"

"Firstly, I asked questions."

"Are you aware, *Detective Chief Inspector*, that the man *confessed*?" he leaned forward to stare with clenched fists and beady eyes at her, his voice literally dripping with sarcasm.

Wells found herself clenching her own hands that little bit tighter and fighting to control her rage, she replied, "Let's begin with the case in question. Now," she glanced down at her notes, "after you assumed charge of the murder investigation as the SIO, you had Alistair Auld conveyed to Pollok Police Office. Correct?"

"Are we really going to play this game," he sneered once again, then slowly folded his arms.

"Bear with me," she favoured him with a fixed smile. "Correct?"

"Correct," he nodded with a bored sigh.

"Did you interview him?"

"For what purpose? He phoned the polis, we arrive, she's dead he's greeting and wailing and admits the murder *and* he's covered in her blood. What else do you need?"

"Did you interview his children?"

"They were in a right state, so no and besides," he shrugged, "that's a job for you women."

"Us…women," she slowly repeated in disbelief, then added, "In this case, you are absolutely correct."

His brow furrowed in suspicion when he thought, what's that supposed to mean?

"So, given the evidence you *believe* you had at that time, you *believed* you had solved the murder and so transcribed the notes to be typed the next morning and the case submitted to the Fiscal's Office. Is that correct?"

"Yes," he cautiously replied, the first suspicion entering his head that this bitch might be trying to outmanoeuvre him in some way.

"A question, if you please," she stared at him. "Did you at any time ask Mr Auld why he killed his wife?"

"What was the point? It was a domestic, pure and simple. My God, do you know how many of these *fucking* domestics I've dealt with through the years? Do you!" his voice rose and to one side, Salmon, on edge, prepared himself if the mean bastard decided to have a go at Mary Wells.

To both men's surprise, she quietly replied, "More's the pity, DI Reilly, no, I can't imagine how many of these domestics you have dealt with. Now, moving on. I gather you arranged for Mr Auld to be medically examined after he had been removed to Govan Police Office, here. Have you…"

"That's what proper SIO's do," he openly sneered once more.

"Okay, but have you actually read the Casualty Surgeon's report of that examination."

"No, of course not. The doc's report goes with the case. Any *competent* SIO knows that. If there was anything to know, I'd have heard about it. After I locked up the murderer, I went home to my bed. Why?"

She lifted the case and handing it across the desk, told him. "This is a copy report of your case. I've left it open at the doctor's report. You might want to read it now."

She watched him irritably sigh when he withdrew a pair of spectacles from an inside pocket of his jacket, then slipping them on, began to read.

Staring at him she saw his normal ruddy complexion pale as he scowled, then he stuttered, "Why wasn't I told about this?"

Watching and listening, Salmon, his face blank, inwardly thought, go for the jugular, Mary.

"Well, in my *own* experience, DI Reilly," she permitted him a soft smile, "after having arrested a murder suspect, most SIO's remain at the office until such times the medical examination is completed, the case fully written up and all avenues indicating the suspects guilt that include witnesses to the incident, have been explored. That's why SIO's get paid the big bucks, as the Americans say."

"I should have been told about his injuries."

She casually shrugged when she replied, "I suppose if you were at your desk you *would* have been told. And by his injuries," she picked up the report from where he had slapped it back down onto her desk, "I assume that aside from the multiple bruising, you refer to the old puncture wounds on his arms and hands that the doctor opined are probably defensive wounds, as well as the numerous cigarette burns on his torso?"

Salmon could almost feel the tension and the hate coming from Reilly.

"Did you have the deceased and her husband PNC'd?"

"Why? I didn't see any need to. As far as I was concerned, the case was all wrapped up," he shrugged.

"Perhaps if you had PNC'd the couple, you would have discovered Mr Auld has never been known to us, but his wife? There's a story. Patricia Auld had a number of convictions for assault, a couple for theft, three for minor possession of drugs, some for breach of the peace and even one when she was younger, for being in possession of a bladed weapon. Now, if you had PNC'd them, what do you think that information might have caused you to think?"

His mind in a whirl, he didn't respond, but simply stared at the closed window behind her head, then his brow creased when he quickly said, "Wait, you said witnesses? What witnesses?"

"The children. You never had the children interviewed. You simply accepted Mr Auld's explanation that they were in another room, watching television."

His pale face had now turned crimson, causing her to panickily think, oh, my God! Is he having a stroke or a heart attack?

Reilly's body bent double as he was overtaken with a coughing fit. Turning to Salmon, she nodded that he fetch the DI a glass of water. Less than a minute later, he turned and handing the glass to Reilly, watched as his hands shaking, the older man gulped down the water then to both his and Mary's amazement, reached into a side pocket of his jacket and drew out an opened packet of Capstan cigarettes.

"No, DI Reilly, but I do not permit smoking in my office," she curtly told him, then added, "Shall we cut to the chase and I will tell you where you went wrong?"

He pushed himself to his feet and shouted at her, "Where I went wrong!"

Aware from her peripheral vision that Salmon too was on his feet, Mary quickly stood up and both hands flat on her desk, screamed back, "Yes, where *you* went fucking wrong and arrested an innocent man! Now, sit your arse back in that chair! Now!'

His body shaking and unable to tear his gaze from her, Reilly slumped back down and clamped his mouth shut.

Glancing at Salmon, she watched him sink into his chair then resumed her seat.

Seconds went by, precious seconds that allowed her to compose herself, then clearing her throat, she said, "You will recall that this morning, Constable Janey McPhee of the FACU unit tried to speak with you?"

"And what would a wee split-arse like her have to tell a man with my experience," he muttered, yet in his mind he was beginning to realise not taking her call might just have been an error of judgement.

"Firstly, I'll ignore that offensive remark about our colleague and put it down to you being a narrow-minded dinosaur who has absolutely no regard for the abilities of any of your female colleagues."

She took a soft breath and continued, "Secondly, had you taken that call you would have learned that Mr Auld and his children had for many years been subjected to domestic abuse by the deceased and it might have provoked even a *rookie* Detective, let alone a man with your supposed experience, to consider making further inquiry before sending an innocent man to the court!"

"You keep harping on about him being an innocent man," he jeered with a shake of his head.

"Don't you get it, you idiot? He confessed!"

"He might have confessed, yes," she almost screamed at him, "but it wasn't murder! It was an accident!"

A tense few seconds followed during which she saw the blood drain from Reilly's face as he muttered, "What? No, it was murder," he added, his lips quivering and his voice now almost a whisper, his belligerence slowly ebbing from him.

She exhaled then softly repeated, "It was an accident, Martin, but you were too blinkered and sure of yourself that you couldn't see the wood for the trees. If you had just made the most basic investigation, you wouldn't be in this situation now."

It was as if he had been given a lifeline when his eyes narrowing, he summoned the strength to ask, "How do you know for certain it wasn't murder, then?"

"When you ignored Janey McPhee, she spoke with me. I had the children brought in and independently interviewed them. Mr Auld works two jobs and so is out for most of the day to sometimes late in the evening. Anyway," she exhaled again, "the true story is that Mrs Auld, who was a heavy drinker and quite liberal with her charms, was out in the city centre most nights, drinking and chasing men. Last night when she returned home, she was her usual drunken self and dragged her daughter, Gillian, by the hair into the kitchen and ordered the girl to make her a fry-up. Did I *mention* the children were terrified of their mother?"

He continued to wordlessly stare at her, though his mouth opened and closed like a gaping fish.

"Anyway, Mr Auld returned home, entered the kitchen to find his daughter distraught and his wife screaming at her. He tried to intervene and that's when his wife lifted the boning knife, then pointing it at him, told him to," she glanced at her notes, "and I quote, *get the fuck out of the kitchen*. At this point the son, William, entered the kitchen and having on numerous occasions witnessed his mother," he paused and read her notes, "and once more I quote, *poking the knife into my daddy*, for some unknown reason tried to grab the knife from her. In that short heartbeat, Mrs Auld, drunk as she was as evidenced by the blood count from her PM, stumbled forward against William and with her still holding the knife, the blade reversed and she fell upon it."

She paused to take a breath, then in a room filled with tension, quietly continued, "Fortunately for the wee boy, he wasn't injured; however, *unfortunately* for her, she was holding the knife at waist height, so it entered her abdomen at the bottom of her ribs, then falling against her son, she inadvertently killed herself, for the blade travelled up inside her ribs and punctured her heart. A killing blow." Further seconds of silence followed, then Mary again continued, "Of course, as you can imagine, both children were hysterical and neither more than Mr Auld, who sick with worry feared that his son might be blamed for his mother's death. That's when he decided that believing he had failed them their whole lives, he made them swear that they had been together in the front room watching the TV and it was he who had killed his wife."

"I...I couldn't have known."

"But if you had conducted a more thorough investigation," she sombrely replied, "You would have."

Sat watching the now wretched DI, if Mary Wells and Sammy Salmon had even the slightest modicum of respect for Martin Reilly's thirty-three years of service as a police officer, then they immediately dismissed such thoughts when the next words out of his mouth were not of concern for the man he had unjustly accused nor of the children who had undergone such a traumatic incident, nor was it to offer any kind of apology for his complete and utter lack of professionalism as a senior Detective Officer of the CID.

No, Reilly sat squarely in his chair then abruptly barked at Mary, "So, where do I go from here, then?"

Snapping a glance at Salmon and seeing him subtly shaking his head at Reilly's apparent indifference to the hurt and anxiety he had caused, she coolly told him, "Having been informed to expect an accused this morning to appear for a pleading diet at the Sheriff

Court on a charge of murder, I had to contact the Fiscal's Office where I spent some time on the phone with an Assistant Procurator Fiscal, who not only lambasted me as an individual for being in charge of the Divisional CID and permitting it to happen, but will ensure a formal complaint will be made to the ACC (Crime), Mr Meadows."

She paused then continued, "Following *that* call, I then had to contact Mr Meadows office to inform *him* to expect to receive the formal complaint. Needless to say, Mr Meadows is not best pleased and already envisions another formal complaint from Mr Auld's legal representatives as to why a more thorough investigation had *not* been carried out left him hanging under a charge of murdering his wife."

"Yes," she slowly nodded, "you might say he was part and parcel of him being charged; however, it doesn't take away from the fact had you done your job and the proper interviews conducted, he would not have been locked up with a charge of murder hanging over his head. As for me, as the DCI, I am to be called to a meeting with the ACC to explain why I permitted such a report to be sent to the Fiscal's Office and might I remind you," she almost snarled, "if *you* had followed protocol, I might not find myself in this position."

"But me," he stammered. "What's happening to me?"

"Did you travel down to Govan in a CID car?"

"Aye," he nodded.

"Then, DI Reilly, I suggest you make your way to Pitt Street where Mr Meadows awaits you. I believe from the way he spoke with me on the phone, he is considering bringing in the Complaints and Discipline Department to review the sloppy manner in which you brought a case against Mr Auld that might possibly result in our Chief Constable being exposed to a formal complaint, that quite *likely* might reach the media."

She watched his face turn a ghastly shade of pale, then making a show of tidying the paperwork on her desk; she curtly dismissed him with "That's all DI Reilly. You may go."

****

When the door had closed behind a subdued Reilly, Salmon stood up from his chair then staring with narrow eyes down at her, suspiciously asked, "How much of that is true?"

"What bit?" she grinned up at him.

"You sneaky bugger, Boss. You and the ACC. You're setting him up to immediately resign, aren't you?"

She glanced behind him to ensure the door was definitely closed before she replied, "I did get a bollocking from some snotty-nosed Fiscal Depute who sounded about ten years of age," she fumed. "Bloody torn faced cow whoever she is, but there was no way round that. As for Keith Meadows, when I explained what Reilly had done, he was livid and wanted him brought up on charges of negligence and incompetence. However, I persuaded him that would only prolong Reilly's time as a serving officer and what occurred with that poor family might become public. Anyway, whatever Mr Meadows decides, I think we've finally seen the last of that serial sexist, bigot. Which brings me round to another topic," she grinned at Salmon whose face creased and shoulders slumping, defensively raised his hands and suspiciously said, "Please don't say it, Boss."

"Sorry, Sammy," her grin turned into an apologetic grimace. "You're going to Pollok CID until we get a replacement DI, but don't worry, I've something in mind for that. Now," she rose to her feet, "let's go downstairs and give Mr Auld the good news."

CHAPTER TEN

That evenings de-briefing and not only because it was Friday, but more to do with the fact that no new information had come in, was literally over within ten minutes.

Mary sensed that the team were desperate for information about what had gone on in her closed office with DI Martin Reilly and she suspected that in time, that story would leak, but for now she was too tired to get into it again.

"Right, folks, as it's a murder investigation, you all know the drill. No weekends until we find Elizabeth Bradley's killer. So, who has what? Let's start with Tommy and John," she nodded to them. "Tommy?"

"Still making our way through the client list, Boss," Maxwell shook his head, "but half the old duffers we're meeting hardly recognise their own names, let alone anything from the photobooks."

"The thing is," McGhee followed on, there's a lot of the clients are men and to be honest, not a lot of them can recall what jewellery their wives wore or what kind of ornaments they had on their mantlepieces. "Us guys are not the ones that wear necklaces or dust the mantelpieces," he turned to smile at some heckling from the female officers' present.

"Ah, speaking of old duffers, boss," a grinning Elaine Fitzsimmons held up her hand at which point her neighbour lowered his head and covered his face. "We're still working our way through the staff list," then recounted their visit to the home of one of the cleaners, Katherine Carmichael.

To Alan Hamilton's relief, she did not disclose his vomiting, but had the room laughing uproariously when she related Carmichael's disclosure about the elderly clients who paid for some sexual relief. When the room had again quietened, Mary, still smiling, asked, "No names or whether payments were made for anything we discovered at the locus?"

"We did ask, but Carmichael had no knowledge of that, Boss," Fitzsimmons shook her head.

"Yet it seems to be common knowledge among the staff about these clients who are willing to pay for, eh, their extracurricular services?" she grimaced, but that only set the team off again.

"Okay, calm down you lot," Mary waved her hands and grinned before she asked, "But no names?"

Fitzsimmons shook her head, "Apparently not, no."

"Right," she turned to Colin Baxter, "create an action to have someone to speak with that company secretary…"

"Agnes Flynn."

"…and have her interviewed to find out if she knows who might be up to, eh…"

"Wanking off old guys?" he stared pokerfaced at her.

Even Mary lost it at that, then when the room calmed down, said, "Aye, that. It just might be there's a wee clique among the staff and if they have no scruples about earning some cash doing that, what else might they be up to?"

"I'm guessing the office will be closed over the weekend, so we're looking at Monday?"

"That'll be fine," she agreed, then turning back to Baxter, asked, "Colin? Anything else?"

"The DI has suggested we visit that old resetter, Max Pettigrew, who works out of F Division, and find out if he's heard anything about the items we seized as productions, so I'll create an action for him to be visited tomorrow."

She turned to Salmon and said, "Good one, Sammy," and smiled at him.

It was then she thought perhaps she should mention something of what went on in her office with Martin Reilly and so said, "Now, I know it's Friday and you're keen to get away, so just for information and no questions, please," she held up her hand to emphasise the point. "As of this forthcoming Monday, DI Salmon will be moving briefly to take over the running of the CID office at Pollok. With Colin continuing to act as the incident manager and Donnie Corbett running the general office; Elaine," she turned to nod at her, "you'll step up as deputy SIO."

"Boss," a stunned Fitzsimmons returned her nod.

"Right then," she loudly clapped her hands, "away home and spend time with your wives or your sweethearts or whoever you're seeing at the minute."

****

Though there had been no requirement or suggestion that she assist Fiona Blakely, Constable Janey McPhee had a quiet word with the older woman and persuaded her that they should first drop off Blakely's brother, Alistair Auld, and his two children at Blakely's house. Thereafter accompanied by the older woman, she drove to the house in Brock Road to thoroughly clean the kitchen of bloodstains to ensure there was nothing to remind the children of the horrific memory of their mother lying dead on the floor.

While they toiled at their task and still a little emotional and overwhelmed that her brother had been released from custody, Blakely enthused that the Chief Detective, Mrs Wells, had been so compassionate and after listening to what young Janey had told her, found out the truth of what really had occurred in the house. Patiently listening to the older woman with the realisation that Blakely needed to get if off her chest and while she twisted the mop head in the pail to drain the last of the water, McPhee smiled then pulling off her nitrile gloves, critically examined the mopped floor.

"We're lucky right enough to have a boss like her, Fiona. I mean, she's not just a good boss, but being a woman, she's a good listener too."

"Aye," Blakely nodded, "if it had been a man like that other one, him that charged our Ali, what's his name…?"

"DI Reilly."

"Aye, him," she scowled, "our Ali, he might still be in the jail."

"In fairness, Fiona," though it grated on McPhee to defend Reilly, "though he thought he was doing the right thing by confessing to killing your sister-in-law, he should have told the DI the truth straight away and we might not have ended up with the situation he found himself in. Anyway," she shrugged, "in the end, it all worked out, so Ali can get on with his life with the kids, eh?" McPhee smiled then hauling the bucket to the back door, threw out the waste water.

Blakely stopped and staring at McPhee, her eyes glistened with unshed tears when she stammered, "But it was you, hen, you're the one that started it all. You're the one who made it right, so you were."

Taking a few steps across the kitchen McPhee opened her arms and hugged the older woman to her then seconds later, brightly said, "You hang fire here and get the kettle boiled while I'll away and fetch your brother and the kids round."

A little over fifteen minutes later, the Auld family returned home, McPhee bid them farewell and set out to return to Govan Police Office.

On the way there, her thoughts turned to her own family.

Her husband Neil, at thirty-three, four years her senior and a ward Charge Nurse at the Royal Infirmary and her daughter Stella, aged three, the double of her fair-haired father.

McPhee hadn't thought anything of her contribution to freeing Alistair Auld from the murder charge; at least not till Fiona had thanked her, "…for making it right."

A smart young woman and to the disappointment of her parents, McPhee had dropped out of university in her second year to join the police and now with eight years' service under her belt and with both her elementary and advanced exams passed within her first four years, originally set her sights on promotion.

However, she hadn't reckoned on meeting the outgoing Neil and after a whirlwind romance, was married and pregnant just a year later.

Unlike most happy beginnings, the pregnancy and delivery had been a torturous affair, yet when Stella arrived all previous pre-natal issues and career ambitions flew out the window when holding her new born baby. In those first brief moments, her outlook and ambitions about her life completely changed too.

Returning to work and for the first time since she'd been born, leaving Stella had been difficult, but within months she found herself transferred to the FACU where she believed she had finally found her niche.

Turning into the rear yard of the office, she switched off the engine and sat for a few moments, collecting her thoughts.

Yet though she could not put her finger on it, she still thought there was something lacking in her day-to-day job, something that eluded her.

Once more her thoughts turned to the day's events and like most of the staff on the door of the CID suite, she too had heard the shouting going on behind the DCI's door.

God, she grinned and thought as she turned into Orkney Street, I wish I'd been a fly on the wall when *that* was going on.

Not a woman who would normally hold a grudge, nevertheless when she'd phoned the DI with her suspicions that morning, the vile names he had shouted down the phone at her had been beyond the pale, leaving her shaking and more than just angry.

It was therefore very satisfying when standing in the corridor outside the FACU room, she had seen him leave the DCI's room, his face pale and strained and so obviously upset.

Fortunately, he had barely given her a glance when he passed her by. And though she could not deny it, she had sensed a feeling of elation that she had been proven correct.

All in a day's work, she smiled and opened the driver's door.

****

Though he could not possibly know or suspect it, earlier that day Michael MacDonald's wife Natalie had followed him from the Kelvingrove Park and now as the evening drew near, she was returned home and she saw his car parked in the driveway of their home.

There had been something odd in his recent behaviour that had sparked her suspicion, something that had caused her to wonder why he was suddenly speaking back to her, even on the odd occasion arguing against her.

At first, she had assumed he was losing his mind, maybe the onset of one of those forgetful brain diseases, whatever they were called. He had even taking to going out more frequently, meeting his so-called friends from his past. Of course, she knew he regularly visited their sons and daughter, something in which she really had no interest and which she permitted, but this new, what would she call it; this new *vibrant* behaviour was extremely curious.

Yes, he was definitely up to something.

When she had left the house that morning, and though he hadn't actually *said* he would visit Mary's children, she had waited in a street off the nearby Crookfur Road for his car to pass by, rightly guessing he would take his usual route to their daughter Mary's house and with some relief, was proved correct when fifteen minutes after parking up, he passed her by. She knew he would never suspect nor have any reason to believe that she would follow him and so had no fear of keeping just a few cars behind the old and rusting Ford Escort.

She would never understand why he had such affection for Mary and their sons. She'd delivered the three of them and as far as she was concerned, her job was then done.

She had no qualms in admitting it was Michael who had raised them and now that they were old enough to make their own decisions, she could not understand why he chose to remain in their lives. In fact, if she were brutally honest, since their youngest, William, left home, what little relationship she and Michael might have had completely dissolved for while she still liked to go out and have a good time, he on the other hand was a right fuddy-duddy; old before his years and who hardly got his backside off the chair in the lounge.

Determined she would continue to have a social life of her own she beamed at the recent memory of the silver haired and recently widowed male church elder who insisted on paying her so much attention. And what a beautiful home he had too, her eyes narrowed with the thought of what refurbishments she already envisaged.

Her thoughts returned to her children and *their* children.

As for her oldest son Alan's children and Mary's too; yes, she was their grandmother, but she had absolutely no affinity with them at all. They certainly weren't *her* children to raise; she'd already been through that phase of her life watching Michael raise their children and *that* had been difficult enough, having snotty nosed kids that became awkward teenagers, living in her house.

Yes, there was the very odd occasion when Mary, now a single parent since that good-for-nothing husband of hers had buggered off, almost begged her to mind the children because that weird woman, that shiftless childminder of hers, was unavailable.

Natalie wasn't naive and knew fine well that she must be the last resort if her daughter needed her for, as she frequently told her friends at the church group, Mary and she were *not* at all close.

Even when Mary was going through her *supposed* mental health issues and depression, if that's what they really were, she inwardly sighed, she'd never understood how any woman would embarrass herself by admitting to such a thing. Then when she'd poo-pah'd the whole issue, to her surprise and unusually for him, even Michael had lost his temper with his wife for what he called her lack of empathy and understanding.

Course her friends all agreed with her that it was all stuff and nonsense and just an attention-seeking thing.

Her eyes glued to the Ford Escort two cars ahead, it was fortunate and if she were honest, a little exciting too that Michael had never been a speedy driver, unlike her; he was far too cautious she had always complained, so keeping sight of his old Escort had not been too difficult.

The only hiccup was when he had turned onto the M8 then taken the Clyde Tunnel, but to her surprise, instead of continuing onto Crow Road as she expected, he had taken the Clydeside Expressway before making his way off that and towards the Kelvingrove Park, where she watched him slow, then park in Kelvin Way. His sudden change of direction had taken her by surprise and when she dodged across a lane, it was only the quick reaction of the van driver in that lane that prevented them colliding.

Shouldn't have been travelling at that speed anyway, she turned her head to scream at the van while ignoring the angry sounding of his horn.

Now here she was, stopped in Kelvin Way, her BMW some twenty or thirty yards behind the old Escort, watching through slitted eyes as he got out of the driver's door, then crossed the road to a gate leading into the park and disappeared from her view.

She grabbed her handbag from the passenger seat beside her then quickly getting out of the car, hurried after him.

What the hell is he doing, she wondered, but excitedly realised that as she had suspected for some time, he was definitely up to something.

He could not know it and wouldn't till the papers were served, but some weeks ago she had spoken with a lawyer and set in motion the papers for divorce, citing irreconcilable differences and, if her lawyer were correct, she would walk away with the house and most of their savings.

Then she would be free to lead the life she truly deserved.

Reaching the opposite pavement, she watched as some forty yards in front of her, Michael entered the children's play area and her heart sank, for it was then she guessed who he might be meeting.

It was not as sinister as she had suspected.

Hidden behind a large rhododendron bush and just as she thought, she watched when seconds later he was bending to lift Mary's daughter, Morven, up into the air while his grandson Jamie came running to wrap his arms around his grandfather's legs.

Curious that she always thought of them as Michael's grandchildren rather than *their* grandchildren.

Even from where she stood she could hear the children's squeals of joy.

Stopped by a large bush, Natalie experienced a sense of deflation and watched as Mary's childminder, the woman with the crazy red hair piled on top of her head and the outrageous dress fashion, approached Michael and the children.

It was then that her eyes widened, for Michael placed Morven back down on the ground and as the children returned to the playground, he took the childminder in his arms and as Natalie continued to watch, they embraced and shared a long and passionate kiss.

Stunned, it had never once occurred to her that though she'd suspected him of being up to *something*, had anyone suggested him seeing another woman she'd had laughed outrageously and said, not boring, pathetic Michael, for after all, what could any woman possibly see in him?

But there he was, smothering the bloody woman in kisses.

Angry now, her own indiscretions with other men through the years forgotten, she felt a curious sense of betrayal and was about to step out from the bush and scream at them, but then stopped.

With a smug smile, she knew she'd seen enough, but now was not the time to confront them.

No, that she'd keep for a more opportune moment.

****

After dismissing her team, Mary Wells collected herself a coffee then made her way back to her office, deciding to complete a half hour catching up with some correspondence that needed her attention.

Some twenty minutes later, some of the pile of paperwork dealt with and the rest decided to be of no immediate urgency, she sat straight in her chair and arched her back, then slowly twisting her neck to ease the ache, concluded she had done enough for the day.

If she were honest, she was a little annoyed that instead of attending to her immediate priority, the murder investigation, she had instead been too occupied clearing up the mess caused by Martin Reilly's shoddy investigation.

She was surprised then when her door was knocked and opened by her boss, ACC Keith Meadows, who greeted her with, "Heard you were still here. I didn't phone because I was on my way home to the Mearns anyway, so took a chance that you'd still be at your desk."

He strode across the room then pointing to her empty mug, sat down in the chair in front of her desk and said, "How's about you grab a couple of those and we can have a chat?"

"Two minutes," she smiled.

Making the coffee gave her the opportunity to consider why Meadows might have dropped in and guessed it was something to do with the complaint from the Fiscal's Office.

Ah, well, and preparing herself for a rebuke, she inwardly sighed it goes with the rank and the salary.

Returning to her room, she handed Meadows his coffee before sitting herself back down, then asked, "What can I do for you, sir?"

"First, how's your murder investigation progressing?"

"The short answer is, it isn't. Unfortunately, I spent most of the day dealing with DI Reilly's handling of the domestic, so I had to let my team get on with it themselves."

She watched him nod then sip at his mug before he replied, "Can't always be in two places at once, Mary. Are you aware I once worked with Martin Reilly?" he thoughtfully asked.

Her brow furrowed, she pursed her lips when she shook her head.

"Aye, back in the day," he sighed, "when we were both DS's in the old City of Glasgow Force. Hard to believe, but he was a very competent Detective back then. Like most of the CID, smoked like a chimney and took a fair swally too, but that wasn't unusual in those days," he gave her a wry smile.

She didn't respond, content to let Meadows continue.

"I recall that he made DI before I did, though I'm not certain why he stayed at that rank," his face creased in thought, "but something obviously blighted his career. As I recall, he was part of an internal investigation, but when the Forces merged back in seventy-five to become Strathclyde Police, a lot of the files," he used his forefingers as italics in the air, "disappeared, so whatever the matter was, it'll be down to people's recollections now and probably most of those involved are likely now retired."

"If as you recall he had been a decent enough Detective, sir, why then do you think he made such an arse of the murder?"

"Who really knows," he shook his head. "I might suggest complacency combined with arrogance; a belief that he knew the job inside out, that he didn't need anyone telling him what *he* believed to be true. A kind of black and white view of the circumstances with no grey areas, if you see what I mean. And after all, as I understand it, the man that Reilly accused *did* confess to killing his wife."

"What about the Fiscal, sir? Will there be some sort of backlash from Clyde Street?"

He softly smiled as he replied "I had some young woman on the phone to me. Sorry, her name escapes me" his mouth twisted and he frowned.

"It seems that she believed because we as the police act on behalf of the Procurator Fiscal Service that she was owed…no, let me rephrase that, *demanded* some sort of explanation." He smiled when he continued, "Not that I am normally a forthright individual, Mary, but I had to remind her she was speaking with the Assistant Chief Constable in charge of crime throughout the Strathclyde Police area and let's just say, after that I accepted her rather grovelling apology."

Mary, guessing it was the same individual she had spoken with, bit her tongue for she really would like to have learned just how grovelling the woman had been.

"So, to answer your question, no; there will be no fall-out regarding DI Reilly's blundering handling of the whole sorry mess."

"Can I ask, sir," she said instead, "did Reilly have any kind of explanation for his behaviour?"

He slowly exhaled before he replied, "Let's just say that Martin Reilly is the sort of man who will never really change. The world round about him will move on, but he's stuck in the sixties with the attitude that Detective work is a man's job."

He held up a hand and quickly said, "Can I ask we don't make *that* an issue, because that is not how *I* feel about my female Detectives. Some of my best Detectives are women, so this is one old guy who *is* moving on," he smiled.

"Anyway," he continued, "as for Reilly, perhaps the best way to explain him is he belongs to that dwindling cadre of men who believe 'this is how we always did it and that's good enough for me.' If he had any sense, he would have gone when his thirty was in, but in my experience, Mary, there's a lot of men and women who achieve a rank that provides them with a certain status and simply can't face returning to simply being Mr or Mrs."

"Can I ask how your meeting concluded?"

She knew she might be stepping on Meadows toes, but also knew it had to be said.

"The reason I ask is I have to be upfront, sir, I don't want him back in my Divisional CID."

He sighed when to her relief, he added, "Well, the short story is he's now a retired man or rather, he will be effective as of midnight on Sunday."

Staring at him she quietly said, "There is a rumour that he has a wire at Pitt Street," then took a short breath when she asked, "I'm guessing it isn't you?"

He smiled when he replied, "I said I worked with him, Mary, I didn't say I liked him and no, though I knew about the rumour, it wasn't me nor do I know who it is…or was."

He stared for several seconds at her, then as if to confirm his statement, said, "After we had words, Reilly completed a retirement form in front of me that I immediately sent to the Personnel

Department; so no, he won't be back. But that leaves you with a problem, doesn't it? You're now a DI down. So, what's your thoughts on that?"

"I already have an idea about that, sir, but for the minute, I've transferred DI Sammy Salmon to Pollok to temporarily take over the CID there and my first inclination would have been to place DS Colin Baxter in the role of deputy SIO. However, Colin's so good at the incident manager job and with his finger on the pulse of the investigation, I've no option but to leave him in situ. My second choice would have been my other senior DS, Donald Corbett, but…"

"The rugby player?"

"That's him, sir," she smiled.

"Seen him play a few times and he is one rough man. Wouldn't like to arrest that big guy for a fighting breach," he muttered with a smile.

"Anyway," she smiled, "I'm leaving him with the day to day running of the office so my junior DS, Elaine Fitzsimmons, is stepping up as the deputy SIO."

"I know Elaine," his brow creased as he thoughtfully nodded. "She's a good one and worth watching for advancement. Anyway, half the reason I called by was to inquire if you needed a temporary DI while your vacancy is filled, but you seemed to have it sorted. Right then," he emptied his mug, "tell me about this idea for replacing your DI?"

****

Getting to his feet, Meadows smiled down at her then said, "I'll let you get on, but don't forget it's Friday and you have a family at home."

It was when he was almost at the door that he tentatively asked, "Am I missing something about you, Mary? You seem a little, eh, smaller?"

She laughed then replied, "I'm watching my weight, lost a couple of stone and thinned down, plus I've bought myself a few new outfits."

"Oh, right, okay," he nodded, then Mary had the unique pleasure of seeing her Assistant Chief Constable blush, who waving cheerio, added, "I'll let my Mattie know how you're getting on. She always asks fondly after you, you know."

When he had gone, Mary was still smiling and a little touched that Mattie Meadows still remembered her from the happy days.

Or more correctly, days she thought she had been happy.

Glancing at her wristwatch, she thought, might as well take my boss's advice and go home.

CHAPTER ELEVEN

On his way to work early that Saturday morning, DS Colin Baxter yawned and regretted he was about to miss out on what seemed likely to be a glorious July morning.
The murder investigation had disrupted the CID's usual shift pattern and though some of the younger guys who like Baxter should have been off duty that day, were more than happy working overtime on their rest days, his hobby was coarse water fishing and on such a glorious, sunny day, would have been ideal for travelling to the Border Esk region with a picnic and his rod.
Travelling from his home in Johnstone, Baxter, a former Renfrew & Bute Constabulary officer prior to the amalgamation, reflected on his late-night conversation with his wife about the decision that he had to make prior to this forthcoming Monday.
Dinner over and though it had started out reasonably genial, it had grown more heated with his wife stressing the point that while she was aware he enjoyed his time in the CID, when he finally did retire she would prefer him to do so on the salary of an Inspector, with a few more thousand pounds the new rank would have brought in, and the increase in the pension pot to make their lives that little bit easier.
His plea that he loved being a Detective cut little ice with her and her voice raised, though probably more to do with the two gin and tonics she'd put away, she had sharply reminded him that through the years it was she who had struggled with poor salaries to keep the house and him and their three children, properly fed and clothed.
"So, don't *bloody* tell me, Colin Baxter, that *you* have a decision to make! This is a joint decision because we're either a partnership or we're not!"
The slamming of the lounge door had ended the discussion and it was with some trepidation that he finally ventured upstairs to find his pyjamas, clean shirt, matching tie, underwear and socks neatly folded on a chair in the hallway outside their closed bedroom door.

Taking the hint, Baxter collected the clothes then tip-toed to the spare bedroom, vacated a year previously when their eldest daughter was married, and began a sleepless night.

Now arriving at Govan Police Office, he switched off the engine and sighing, decided that with push now having come to shove, his wife was correct. The extra money would be very useful and so with some reluctance, agreed with her decision.

Well, he inwardly grinned, I can't be spending the rest of my marriage in a single bed now, can I?

Making his way upstairs and a little relieved that the difficult decision had in fact been taken out of his hands, he met in the corridor with Elaine Fitzsimmons who greeting him in a low voice, asked, "Do you not think the boss was a little premature, Colin, sending the DI to Pollok? I mean, we can't be sure that Reilly won't turn up there this morning, can we?"

"Stand on me, Elaine, after the balls-up he made yesterday charging that poor sod, he won't be able to hold his head up. I'm betting every city Divisional CID will have heard the story by now and besides, the DCI sent him to Pitt Street to see the ACC and I'll bet you a pound to a penny that Keith Meadows won't just have torn him a new one, he'll have given him his matching orders. Reilly's balls-up has probably embarrassed the Chief Constable and sending a *murder* report to the Fiscal without there being a murder? Do you think those plonkers along in Clyde Street are going to miss the opportunity to stick it to the polis? Not likely," he shook his head.

"The Procurator Fiscal himself," he continued, "will be on to Meadows and using Reilly's balls-up as leverage to use the next time he's needing a favour from us. Politics, hen, politics," he grimly shook his head again.

"What you two conniving about?"

They turned together to see Mary Wells staring at them with mock suspicion.

Her hair up in a bun and wearing a fitted plaid jacket and a black pencil skirt, she was beginning to feel more comfortable in her new outfits, but didn't miss Fitzsimmon's glance of approval.

"Take it you guys have just arrived?" she asked.

"Minutes before you, Boss," Baxter answered for them both.

"Right, grab some coffees then my office in two minutes where we'll plan the day."

****
Michael MacDonald, rising at his usual time, was showered and dressed then quietly closing his bedroom door, was heading downstairs when to his surprise, his wife Natalie popped her head out of the master bedroom to ask, "Where are you off to, today?"
"And good morning to you too, dear," he forced a smile.
"Yes, very good," she sarcastically replied then waved a hand.
"Well, I'm thinking of going over to see Jamie and Morven, maybe take the wee guy out of a kick-about in the Victoria Park. You know how he's right into football these days," he continued to smile.
"Oh, is he?" her voice betrayed her disinterest in anything her grandchildren were doing.
She stared at him when she said, "And I suppose you'll have dinner with Mary then, that there's no need for me to make you something?"
His brow furrowed at the odd comment, for Michael couldn't remember the last time that Natalie had stepped foot in their kitchen, other than to make herself something or fetch ice for her gin or vodka, but certainly not to cook for him.
"Eh, yes, I suppose so," he shrugged. "Anyway, can I get you some breakfast before I leave?"
She stared through him when she replied, "A coffee before you go and bring it up to my room."
He watched as she closed the door, then shaking his head thought, it's a long time since I've thought of it as anything other than *your* room, then made his way downstairs.
In the bedroom, Natalie humourlessly smiled.
Today was the day, she decided. Why prolong it when she could have things underway this coming Monday and returned to bed smiling, with thoughts of the silver haired church elder and his lovely home foremost in her mind.
****
The team now gathered in the incident room, Mary Wells, standing with her back to Colin Baxter's desk and her arms folded, cast an eye around then began with, "By now you'll all be wondering about DI Reilly and I'm absolutely certain you'll have heard or been told about the shouting match coming from my room yesterday. I won't go into specifics, but suffice to say that information that was not initially available to DI Reilly at the time a man was arrested for

murder later came to light. That information not only exonerated the individual, Mr Auld, but revealed that the deceased had not in fact been murdered, but died due to an unfortunate accident."

She paused to permit this information to sink in, then continued, "I do not want anyone here to speculate about the circumstances of what occurred; however, I would ask that you simply accept DI Reilly was mortified that he had accused an innocent man and so I learned last evening that he not only accepted full responsibility for the issue, but as of tomorrow evening, has decided to retire."

A hubbub of noise run through the room, but quietened when she raised a hand, then added, "Needless to say the CID is losing a much-experienced Detective officer and I'm sure with me, you will wish Martin Reilly a long and happy retirement."

Staring around the room, she saw the bland faces and knew that her good wishes for Reilly was falling on deaf ears, that not one man or woman staring back at her liked or had any kind of good word for the foul-mouthed DI, who through the years had done so much damage to so many careers.

With a sigh, she continued, "Right, DS Baxter has some new actions to issue, so I'll let you guys get on with it."

Catching Janey McPhee's eye, she beckoned the younger woman to follow her from the room.

Leading McPhee back to her office, Mary closed the door behind her then bidding McPhee sit, said, "Of course, Janey, in confidence we both know that what I said in the incident room is a right load of old tosh. Reilly gone is the best thing that's happened to this Division's CID for some time."

"But has he *really* retired, Ma'am?"

"Oh, aye, he's retired," she smiled, "and likely looking for a small telephone kiosk somewhere to host his retirement party. But I don't want to talk about him."

"Ma'am?"

She stared at the younger woman and took a deep breath before she said, "What you did by picking up on the arrest of Mr Auld and knowing the circumstances behind the family's domestic issues, then trying to apprise DI Reilly of your knowledge was a good bit of police work. However, when Reilly refused to listen, you tenaciously followed your instinct and that resulted in an innocent man being freed from facing a possible conviction for murder. Not only have you prevented a grave miscarriage of justice by saving Mr Auld from the possibility of a lengthy prison service, Janey, but if the truth had come out at a later date, also prevented Strathclyde Police's Chief Constable from facing an official inquiry as to why his Force conducted a ship-shoddy investigation, then prosecuted an innocent man."

"It was just me doing my job, Ma'am," a red-faced McPhee quietly replied.

"No, Janey," Wells shook her head, "you did more than your job and that is why in consultation with and the approval of ACC Meadows, I am recommending you for a Chief Constable's commendation."

"Ma'am?"

"You'll hear word in due course, Janey, but I believe it will be a done deal, so congratulations."

Stunned, McPhee could only stare, but seconds later, broke into a huge smile then rising from her chair, left the room.

****

Making their way down to the yard to collect their CID car, DC's Kenny Maxwell and John McGhee were keenly eager to meet their interviewee, Max Pettigrew, a licensed pawnbroker who was also known locally in the south side of the city as an unlicensed moneylender, but known by most of the city's Divisional CID as a resetter of stolen property.

What baffled most of the CID, however, was that the sixty-eight-years old Pettigrew, who had been involved in the activities for most of his working life, had accrued so few convictions for it was commonly believed that he was either very good at evading arrest or what was more likely, touting to some senior Detective who kept him one step ahead of the law that sought to imprison him.

A little over ten minutes later, McGhee parked their car in the dead-end of Balvicar Street at its junction with Pollokshaws Road, next to the tenement building that stared out across the nearby Queens Park.

"According to the PNC, he's got a corner flat up there," Maxwell pointed to the tenement.

The man who answered the door to their knock looked, as McGhee later related, like someone from a Santa Claus movie.

A shoulder length mane of white hair and full white beard and wearing an old, stained boiler suit, Max Pettigrew eyed them suspiciously until they produced their warrant cards.

Inviting them into the flat, he led the Detectives through narrow lanes of boxes that seemed to Maxwell and McGhee to be filled with every type of object that came to mind.

Everything from kitchen utensils to sewing machines, cassette players to stacks of LP records.

Leading them into what at what time must have been a large sitting room, he bid them sit at two rickety cane chairs in front of an antique desk, then asked, "Tea or coffee, gentlemen?"

When both opted for tea, he left the Detectives in the room, their heads swivelling at the extraordinary amount of property surrounded them that was stacked from floor to ceiling. Rolls of carpets, wooden cases of ornaments, large china vases, empty bird cages, shelves filled with books, tennis racquets, shinty sticks and suitcases filled with God alone knew as well as numerous other items, far too many for them to take in.

Glancing around him, Maxwell idly wondered how the floorboards could cope with such a weight.

"Have you ever seen anything like this, Tommy?" gasped McGhee.

"Phew, first for me," Maxwell shook his head.

In the kitchen and while the kettle boiled, Pettigrew lifted the phone from its wall cradle then dialling the direct number, quietly identified himself to the woman who answered. When her husband came on the line, he anxiously said, "It's Max. I have two Detectives here seeking information about property that is related to a murder in Govan somewhere. Are they genuine or here for me?"

The voice on the phone paused before he replied, "They're genuine. They're not interested in you, Max, so just tell them what they want to know."

Pettigrew didn't respond, but simply ended the call and returning the phone to its cradle, turned to brew the tea.

Minutes later, each with a mug of tea, Pettigrew resumed his chair behind his desk then asked, "How may I be of assistance to you gentlemen?"

Handing him the photobook of productions, Maxwell explained they were seeking to inquire if any of the items had ever been offered to Pettigrew for sale or any attempt made to pawn them.

Using an old fashioned, bone-handled magnifying glass, Pettigrew took his time poring over each item, but to the disappointment of the Detectives, finally shook his head, then said, "I regret I cannot identify one single item as having been offered or having passed through my hands, gentlemen."

They watched his forehead knit when he asked, "I appreciate you can only give me the barest details of how these items came into the possession of the police, but might I ask some questions of you?"

With a glance at McGee, Maxwell replied, "Aye, go ahead."

His expression thoughtful, he asked, "Are all these items from the one location?"

"We don't think so, no," Maxwell shook his head.

Slowly nodding, Pettigrew then asked, "Were they discovered in the possession of one person?"

"Yes."

"I assume you believe them to be stolen?"

"Yes."

"Do you know if they were stolen by this one person or a number of persons?"

"Eh," Maxwell glanced again at McGhee, "we think it might have been more than one person, but we can't be certain. What makes you ask that?"

"Some of these items are very valuable," he waved a hand at the photobook, "and I use as an example, the ruby ring pictured on page twenty-three. Others, *not* so valuable," he smiled and turned to the photo of a ten-inch high, garishly painted figure of a naked woman stood holding a water jug on her shoulder.

"In fact some of the ornaments I wouldn't give house room, if you get my meaning. That would suggest to me that among the valuable items stolen, there is also the opportunistic thefts; by that I mean the thief has stolen the cheaper items because he or she *believes* it to be of some value, something that they *like* rather than see as valuable and that would suggest to me someone who is neither very bright nor aware of the value of what they stole."

"The other thing about most if not all of these items," he slowly continued, "is the jewellery and ornaments. They are not the sort of things one would see in a young person's home or the jewellery worn by a young woman."

He paused to let this information sink in, then continued.

"As for the ruby ring?" he raised his eyebrows, "Perhaps, but it certainly seems to me to be antique and if it were stolen and *discovered* stolen, there would be a hue and cry, for it is far too valuable *not* to be reported, so I must again assume; stolen from an elderly persons home who is either dead or perhaps suffering some form of memory loss and is unaware the ring is gone? I think so, yes," he slowly nodded as though convincing himself.

After a few seconds pause, he drew a breath then said, "However, the thief's difficulty with the ruby ring is, how to sell it. I say this because if it were offered to me," he pointed a fat finger at his chest," I would immediately be suspicious and I am certain too that no reputable jeweller would buy it without some form of provenance. Therefore it has been too difficult to get rid of, you see?"

He paused again then continued, "You have not mentioned if these items are the result of housebreakings, so I'm thinking, these items have been stolen by someone or some persons who has access to a number of homes. Access that is legitimate, maybe. A cleaner, a carer or a gardener perhaps?"

Pettigrew glanced from one to the other and saw by their expressions he was correct.

Before they could react, he continued, "If you are looking for a thief who is part of a team, perhaps, then I suggest you start with those of low esteem, someone who is probably being manipulated into stealing from the homes of their employer. Someone easily influenced and," he shrugged, "my guess is they might be young, too. Certainly not as bright as the individual who is orchestrating the thefts."

"You seem pretty certain of what you're telling us, Mr Pettigrew," McGhee stared curiously at him.

Pettigrew smiled when he replied, "With forty-five years in the business, young man, let's just say I have accrued a modicum of experience."

"We actually had an expert visit the office," Maxwell interjected, "a man from an auction house over in the north side of the city, a Mr…"

"Stephen Urquhart?"

"Aye, that's him," Maxwell nodded. "You know him?"

Pettigrew slowly smiled before he replied, "Stephen is good at what he does; selling to naive old ladies. But, if you choose to go with what he tells you, your choice," he shrugged.

Maxwell glanced at McGhee who pursed his lips, then replied, "No,

I think we'll stick with your advice, Mr Pettigrew, so I have a couple of questions that I'd like clarified and while we're doing that," he smiled, "maybe John here can stick on the kettle for another cuppa, eh?"
****

Twenty minutes later, when the Detectives had finished taking their notes, Pettigrew smiled and with a glance from the window to ensure that they had driven off, lifted the phone and dialled the number that he knew, but had never written down.

When the call was answered, he said, "Your lads have gone and I believe I have been some help to them."

"Thank you, Max, if your information pans out, then that's one I owe you."

"Always happy to help an old friend," Pettigrew smiled, "and as for you owing me one, let's just call this *quid pro* for all the help you have given me in the past."

"And long may this exchange continue," the man replied with some feeling.

When the call ended, the man stared down at the phone, then turned when his wife said, "Really, Keith, this is supposed to be your day off and on that point, who *is* this mysterious Max who occasionally phones you?"

Smiling, Meadows replied, "Probably the best eyes and ears in the city and the source of much needed intelligence that over the year's helped convict more than a few bad people, dear, but *never* a name we'll ever discuss in company."

Taking the hint, his wife Mattie, curtly said, "As you wish. Now, about lunch?"
****

Mary Wells was at her desk once more trying to catch up with overdue paperwork and wondering if a Divisional DCI could be assigned a secretary to help with the administration of a large department, when the door was knocked then pushed open.

She glanced up to see Inspector Kenny Herdman enter, who strode to her desk then breathlessly said, "Sorry for the intrusion, but I've just had the indoor Inspector from Partick Police Office on the phone." He held up his hand then continued, "First of all, your kids are okay."

"What!" her eyes lit up and she felt a cold hand clutch at her heart.

"There was a disturbance call for your home address and though I don't have all the details, there's a unit there the now; a sergeant and a cop as I understand, but the Inspector at Partick suggested you might want to return home right away."

"Did he say what kind of disturbance?" she was already on her feet and grabbing at her jacket and handbag.

"Only that a neighbour phoned the polis and whatever's happened, it's all calmed down now, but the sergeant at the locus learned you're a DCI and as a courtesy, it was him who suggested you should go home."

Nodding, she stuttered, "Thanks, Kenny, can you have a quiet word with Colin Baxter in the incident room, tell him what you told me and that if I'm needed, he can contact me at the house."

"Of course," Herdman held open the door for her then holding up a cautionary hand, he warned her, "Listen to me, Mary, I know you'll be anxious, but like I said it's all quiet now, so getting yourself killed on the way home won't do anyone any good."

"Okay, and thanks, Kenny," she squeezed his arm as she hurriedly passed him by.

CHAPTER TWELVE

Conscious of Kenny Herdman's advice, Mary slackened off her speed, though her instinct was to push down on the accelerator.

A disturbance?

What kind of disturbance?

When she'd left the house that morning, Eileen had arrived in a good mood and intimated her plans for taking the children out to one of the parks, getting them fresh air so they'll sleep tonight, she had grinned as they'd danced around her.

Who the hell would create a disturbance?

Her first thought was that her ex-husband Harry had arrived and perhaps tried to take the children, but just as quickly dismissed the thought because for all his faults, him being a lying, cheating bastard, he wasn't stupid and no way would he try to abduct his own children.

No, with a sense of foreboding, she realised whatever happened she'd find out soon enough.

****

Turning into Ancaster Drive, she slowed the Toyota and saw two marked police vehicles parked outside her house; a Transit van that she correctly assumed was the emergency response vehicle and a Ford Escort beside which stood three male officers, a sergeant and two constables who she assumed were the emergency response crew. Stopping her car behind the Transit van, the cops both turned as she exited the vehicle, then the sergeant walked towards her.

"DCI Wells?"

"That's me,' she nodded.

Pokerfaced, he said, "I'm Sergeant Iain Cowan, Ma'am. First, your son and daughter are fine, though your father has taken a bump to the side of his head."

"My father," her face must have expressed her confusion, because Cowan then said, "I take it you've not been told what occurred?"

"No, just a suggestion that I get home quickly, so Sergeant…can I call you Iain?"

For a brief second she saw indecision in his eyes, but then he slowly nodded before he replied, "Iain is fine, Ma'am."

"Then, Iain, as this affects me as a civilian and a possible witness, I'm Mary. So, my dad, is he okay?"

Cowan visibly relaxed at her courteous informality before he replied, "Aye, he'll be fine. Your neighbour is attending to him in your kitchen and don't be worrying about the weans eh, I mean your children. They're watching a cartoon on the telly."

Again he saw she was confused, so raising his hand, he took a breath then quietly said, "Let me start at the beginning. We received a call from a woman, a Mrs McAulay, who said that she and your father were being attacked by another woman. When my guys got here," he thumbed back towards his officers still stood by the Transit van, "They discovered your neighbour from that house there," he pointed across the path to the new guys house, "restraining a woman to prevent her entering your home. He was having a right time of it to, and I'm thinking his shins took a bit of a beating."

He then added, "As you might have guessed, Mrs McAulay and your father had by then taken refuge in your house."

"The assailant, if you want to call her that, is sitting with my other cop in the back of the van," he pointed across the road towards the Transit.

"Who is she, did you get a name?"

He hesitated for a few seconds, but before he replied, she had already seen the parked silver coloured BMW and with a hollow feeling in the pit of her stomach, heard him say, "That's why I asked you to return home. She says she is your mother and that when you got here, *you* will ensure that *I* will lose my job."

****

Assuring Sergeant Cowan that regardless of her mother's comment, she was grateful he had called her then accompanied by him entered her house.

First checking the lounge to see for herself the children were fine, she moved through to the kitchen where to her surprise, her father sat at the kitchen table, patiently being attended to by her new, next-door neighbour, who wearing blue coloured surgical gloves, was dabbing with a moistened dishcloth at a bloodied bruise on the left side of her father's head.

Sat beside Michael, Eileen McAulay, her face tear-stained, comfortingly held his hand, but upon seeing Mary, quickly released his hand to clench her own hands together in her lap.

"Dad," Mary felt tears bite at her eyes as she moved towards him.

"Hello, sweetheart, sorry you had to be dragged away from work for this," he waved a hand at his head.

"Mum did that?"

"Afraid so," he sighed as he stared guiltily at her. "Walloped me with that fancy handbag of hers, right on the napper. I think there must have been a half brick in it," he tried to joke.

"But why?"

It was then she caught the glance from Michael to Eileen and startled at the sudden realisation that maybe there were things going on that she had previously not noticed.

Her neighbour, who had moved his chair back to permit her to hug her father, then interrupted with, "He's taken quite a bang on the side left of his head, so I think I'll get him along to the casualty at the Western Infirmary just to get it properly dressed and to check there's no internal fracture here," he pointed to Michaels wound.

"Thank you," she turned and a little more curtly than she intended, replied, "but if my father is to be seen by a doctor, then *I'll* make an arrangement to transport him to hospital."

The tense silence was broken when the neighbour calmly replied, "Mrs Wells, I *am* a doctor and I happen to be in charge of the Casualty Department at the Western, so unless you want your father hanging around for a couple of hours waiting to be seen, I suggest you permit me to take him there myself where he will receive immediate treatment."

Taken aback, her face turning red, the silence was broken when Michael said, "Mary, your mother, you're not going to arrest her, are you?"

Seizing the opportunity to tear her eyes away from those of her expressionless neighbour, she stuttered, "That's not down to me, dad. Sergeant Cowan is the man in charge, so it's his call," she turned to nod at him.

"I can't interfere with an ongoing police incident that I'm not involved with *as* a police officer," she explained. "However, if you choose not to make a complaint of assault, then you need to tell the Sergeant, not me. Eileen," she turned with furrowed brow towards her, "did Natalie assault you too?"

"Nothing serious, hen, just a push and wee bit of a shove and, well, a few choice names too."

Mary stood back from her father who getting to his feet, then forced a smile when he said, "I'll let Bill here get me along to the hospital and we'll maybe speak when I get back?"

"Bill?"

It was her neighbour, who replied with a touch of humour in his voice, "Bill Howie. So pleased to meet you Mrs Wells. Right then, Michael," he took the older man by the arm, you and I are off on a jolly to my place of work, but hopefully we'll be back within a couple of hours."

Turning to Mary, pokerfaced he added, "If there *are* any issues, I'll get in touch."

When they'd left the kitchen, Sergeant Cowan said, "Ma'am, eh, Mary, I mean. Can I have a word, please?"

In the hallway, he shrugged when he said, "How do you want this handled?"

Her forehead creased, she leaned with her back against the wall, her arms folded and suddenly feeling completely drained, then replied, "You heard my dad, Iain, he's not wanting to make a complaint. As for Eileen, it's unlikely she'll want to provide a statement either."

"Can I ask a personal question?"

"Yes, of course, go ahead."

"Were you aware your father and Mrs McAulay were having an affair?"

Shaking her head, unaccountably, she found herself smiling when she sighed, "Not at all. It's been a complete revelation," then added, "Saying that, I don't blame the old bugger. My mother is an absolute arse of a woman and treated him like shit for most if not all of their married life. You know the old saying, you can pick your friends, but not your family."

A little more relaxed, he returned her smile when he replied, "What's the relationship of Mrs McAulay to you, then?"

"Eileen? She's my childminder and what a wonderful woman she is. The kids adore her, she's completely trustworthy and as you likely know, with the hours that I keep in my job, she's there ninety-nine percent of the time without fail or complaint."

Her eyes narrowed when she added, "In fact, I don't know why I never saw it before. Anytime he's been visiting here in her company, he's been so much happier than I've seen him in a very long time."

He softly smiled when he said "I'm guessing you'll give up your mother before you'll give up your childminder?"

She stared curiously at him for several seconds before nodding, she replied, "You know, Iain, I'd never have given that any thought, but you've never said a truer word. I owe my mother nothing, *nothing* at all, so if it's coming down to choosing a side, I've already voted. Now," she stood upright then formally said, "how you wish to deal with her, Sergeant Cowan, is your prerogative, but let me assure you, whatever decision you make, you have my full and unequivocal support and one more thing. The very fact she should invoke my name to try and influence your decision absolutely appals me and for that I unreservedly apologise."

"No need to apologise, Mary," he smiled as he held up his hand, "I believe I'm long enough in the tooth to ignore such threats, but still, it's nice to hear you're leaving the decision in my hands."

His face creased when he said, "What I'll do is formally take her details, charge her with a minor assault and a breach of the peace, but when I report the case I'll request that in the meantime, no action be taken other than perhaps a warning letter. That way she's not only recorded in the system, but if she should again threaten your father or Mrs McAulay, today's circumstances can be included in any subsequent report against her. Also, if I were to let her go without charging her, it would provide her the opportunity of making a false arrest allegation. Charging her will protect me and my guys from any complaint if she should consider such an allegation."

"When you've dealt with her, Iain, can I have a quick word before she's released?"

"I'll knock the door to let you now we're done with her," he nodded, then left the house.

****

Checking once more Jamie and Morven were still enthralled in the cartoons, Mary returned to the kitchen to find Eileen still seated at the kitchen table and sobbing into a handkerchief.

Wordlessly, Mary filled the kettle then prepared two mugs of coffee. When the kettle was boiled, she placed a mug before Eileen then sitting opposite her at the table, softly asked, "Are you really okay? You're not hurt, are you?"

"No," she sobbed, "I got more of a fright than anything. She just arrived when your dad and me and the kids were heading out to the park. Just came at us, swinging that handbag and clouted Michael on the head with it. The look on her face, Mary, I was too scared to tackle her," she sniffed, "so I got the kids into the house and dialled nine-nine-nine. Then your dad came stumbling into the house, a bit dazed too he was. Then the man next door, Bill's his name, Michael said he shoved your dad into the house and wouldn't let her into the house, otherwise I can't imagine what she might have done."

Eileen, her head bowed and her body shaking with emotion, sniffed before she replied, "I'm not hurt Mary, but I'm so ashamed and feel I've let you down. I'm really, really sorry. When Michael comes back and I know he's okay, I'll leave."

"Eileen...*Eileen*, look at me, please."

The older woman turned her head to stare at Mary, who told her, "You and dad. Tell me what happened from start to finish. Begin when you and dad started having feelings for each other."

Eileen took a huge gulp of air, then quietly said, "It was about four, maybe five months ago. I mean, we'd met here long before that, but

I didn't think of your father as being anything other than a really nice man. If I'm honest, I felt a bit sorry for him, the way your mother spoke to him and treated him and…"

"Sorry," her eyes widened in embarrassment, "I don't mean to badmouth your mum or anything," but she got no further for with a wry smile, Mary held up her hand then interjected with, "Eileen, I know exactly what my mother's like, so you'll not offend me when you describe her for what she is; an out and out bully."

Almost with relief, Eileen sighed when she said, "Well, when your dad would come here on his own to maybe take Jamie out for a kick about or he'd meet us in one of the parks, we got to talking and, well," she slowly exhaled, "on your days off when you had the children, Michael and I would sometimes meet for coffee or lunch."

"And that's how it started?"

"Yes," Eileen, her bottom lip trembling, breathed out, "that's how it started."

"And did you ever, I mean…"

"What?" Eileen face first expressed her surprise, then shock when she realised what Mary was inferring and stammered, "No, never, not like that! I swear it, Mary! No! We didn't!"

If shocked when Mary asked the question, then Eileen was more than stunned when she offhandedly remarked, "Pity, I think it might have done you both some good to have a bit of romance in your lives."

"Mary Wells!" Eileen stared wide-eyed at her, then to both their surprise, they began to laugh outrageously.

Still laughing, Mary turned when the front door was knocked. Preparing herself, she told Eileen, "Be back in ten minutes."

****

Walking with Sergeant Cowan to the rear of the police Transit van, she saw him open the door then beckon to his constable to leave the back. When the young officer had done so, Mary stepped towards the rear door and at her mother.

A dour faced Natalie, her lips tightly pressed together and her normally pristine hair in disarray, in turn stared at her daughter and moved to exit the vehicle; however, Mary raised her hand to stop her and said, "As I understand it, mother, you are still under arrest, so sit where you are."

Stunned, Natalie hissed, "You're supposed to be a Chief Detective, do something about this and deal with that pasty-faced sergeant who was so rude to me!"

It was typical of her mother, Mary thought, that even after wounding her husband, Natalie had no interest in asking after him, for it was she who in her own mind was the person of importance; she who was the injured party.

Mary didn't immediately respond, but deciding to ruin her mother's day even more so and mindful that Sergeant Cowan was standing behind her, listening, calmly replied, "That *pasty-faced* sergeant has charged you with assault and a breach of the peace. He is currently deciding whether or not to release you for report or take you to Partick Police Office to be detained till your appearance on Monday at the District Court, so I *suggest* you watch your mouth!"

Her face turning from pale to a rosy red, Natalie stared angrily at her daughter when she hissed, "Then deal with it! *Must* I remind you, Mary MacDonald, I am your mother?"

Mary slowly smiled when she replied, "I haven't been Mary MacDonald for a very long time and as for you being my mother?" her face betrayed her scorn. "Do you even have any idea what a mother *is*?"

She drew a deep breath then continued, "I am Detective Chief Inspector Mary Wells, as fine you know, and if you ever have any hope or even a *desire* to see me or my children again, then you will refrain from ever again using my name and rank to threaten my colleagues or anyone. *And*, as I have no jurisdiction over the sergeant who has charged you, my advice to you is that you find some manners and when the sergeant speaks with you, try at least to show some remorse for your actions."

"My actions? You do realise your father is having an affair with that…that *slut* you have watching my grandchildren!"

Mary thought it curious that Jamie and Morven were her mother's grandchildren, but only when it suited her, then replied, "Actually, an affair suggests an intimate relationship, but unfortunately, you got *that* wrong. Yes," she nodded, "they're close friends, but they are not having an affair."

"I saw them yesterday with my own eyes," she snarled, "in Kelvingrove Park. Kissing!"

"You may have done," taken aback at the revelation, though she would never admit it to Natalie, Mary shrugged, then said, "but a kiss isn't an affair, mother."

"And let's face it," no matter the sergeant was standing listening and even though Mary knew she was being baited, she couldn't help herself when she continued, "when the boys and I were young, how many weekends did you leave my dad and us to have your girly days and nights away?"

She made italics in the air, her teeth clenched in anger when she hissed, "Girly days? You must have thought we were stupid! You were off banging some guy and now you're sitting here pretending to be the cheated wife, taking the moral high ground when you're really nothing but a…"

She stopped, feeling her chest tighten for even she couldn't believe the vehemence in her voice, the loathing coursing through her body for this woman who had through the years cheated on not just her father, but her children too.

But in that heartbeat, she could not anticipate Natalie's reaction who jumping to her feet and with a speed that surprised both Mary and Sergeant Cowan, leapt towards her then viciously slapped her daughter across the face.

It was then that Cowan pushed past Mary to manhandle Natalie back down onto the wooden bench seat, then with a glance at Mary, asked, "You okay, Ma'am?"

However, if there were ever a last straw, then that was it, for Mary's instinct was to take her mother by the hair, pull her from the van then and cast her down to the ground, but in those few seconds before she replied, a sudden calm overwhelmed her as she stared at Natalie and saw her now for what she really was. An old woman living in a past where she believed herself to be a cut above everyone else, where with a liberal use of her hands she bullied not just her husband, but her children too.

And it had always been so, Mary now realised.

"Ma'am?"

Mary turned to see Sergeant Cowan staring at her, acutely aware he had witnessed Natalie assault her, then heard herself soberly respond, "I'm fine, but I'll give her that one, Iain, because it's the last time I'll ever see her, so no need to take a statement from me."

He nodded in understanding then quietly, but forcefully told Mary, "I think *we'll* deal with Mrs MacDonald from here, so if you don't mind, Ma'am?"
Swallowing her bile, she nodded, then walked off without a backward glance and made her way indoors.
****
She couldn't help herself and while Eileen tidied up in the kitchen, she watched from behind the curtain in her first-floor bedroom as her mother was helped from the Transit van, then make her way to her own car where a minute later, she drove off at speed.
When the police vehicles too had gone, though not before Cowan had intimated he'd decided to libel a further charge against Natalie for her assault upon Mary, she used her bedside phone to call the incident room where she informed Colin Baxter that yes, everything was okay, but she wouldn't be returning this afternoon to work, that she'd catch up with him tomorrow.
In the meantime, Elaine Fitzsimmons, as deputy SIO, was to take the evenings de-brief and if anything of note occurred during the day, to call her at home.
Ending the call and feeling as though the energy had been sapped from her, she sat on the edge of the bed, unconsciously rubbing at her cheek that still stung a little, and listening to the children squealing downstairs as Eileen ushered them through to the kitchen for their early evening supper.
It couldn't have been any more than a couple of hours, but whatever time had passed, Mary startled awake at the sound of the front door closing.
Her eyes flickering, she realised she was staring at the ceiling, that somehow or other she had lain back on the bed with her legs dangling over the side then fell asleep.
Her body shaking and aching, she stumbled to her feet and into the en-suite where splashing water on her face, she dragged a brush through her hair and hurried downstairs.
Passing the lounge, she saw the children were now in their pyjamas and again watching the television.
Making her way into the kitchen, she saw her father, now a sporting a large sticking plaster on the left side of his head, seated at the table while Eileen was at the kitchen cupboard and drawer, fetching out dishes and cutlery.

She raised her eyebrows at Eileen who already prewarned, subtly shook her head to confirm she had not mentioned Natalie slapping Mary on the face.

Bill Howie, as she now knew her neighbour, was standing to one side as if about to leave.

On the table sat a plastic carrier bag from which wafted the appetising smell of fish and chips.

"I'm fine," Michael smiled at her when she moved towards him to hug him tightly against her, then turning, a little sheepishly she told Bill, "Thank you, for seeing to my father and sorry for being such a pain."

Bill tightly replied, "Not a problem."

Addressing Michael, he said, "I realise that though your X-ray showed no issues and while I don't believe there's any risk of concussion and what you really need is a good night's sleep and if needed, a couple of paracetamol should sort out any headache. However," he paused to let his next statement to sink in, "that all said, if you do feel dizzy or disorientated, get yourself to a casualty, okay?"

"Okay, doctor," Michael smiled and returned a mock salute.

Pointing to the bag, Bill continued, "Fish and chips, the doctor's prescription for shock after a stressful incident."

When he turned towards the door, Mary said, "Aren't you sharing this with us? Oh, sorry, you have someone at home?"

"No," he smiled, "it's not that. I thought you guys might want a bit of family time to talk over what happened and besides, I only bought three suppers and two bags of chips for your children."

"Oh, the kids have been fed," Eileen stepped forward with the plates and cutlery, then began setting the table for four, "so I'm certain there's enough for a full meal for everyone. Mary?" she turned to stare meaningfully at her.

"Absolutely," Mary, her face reddening even more at Eileen's subtle eye contact, then added, "I'll organise the tea."

While Eileen shared out the suppers and Michael called the children through to the table, Mary glanced sideways at Bill.

Her age she thought, if perhaps a year or two either way, and around six feet one or two inches tall. Not overly handsome, though not at all unpleasant to look at either, though she saw he sported a two-inch scar to the left side of his forehead that showed up lighter against his complexion. Muscular with short brown hair, his swarthy appearance seemed to indicate he had recently been abroad for some time.

When the food had been served, it was Eileen who asked, "How long have you been working at the Western Infirmary, Bill?"

"Just three weeks, Eileen," he smiled at her, showing a full set of gleaming white teeth. "They put me up in a hotel for a couple of weeks, then rented the property next door for me. Truth is, it's far too large for me on my own, but it will serve my purpose for the time being, at least until I can find a more moderately sized flat somewhere."

And that, Mary thought, explains the absence of a wedding ring.

"I'm guessing you've recently been abroad," Michael asked.

"For a number of years, yes, but you can tell from my accent that I'm a Weegie, so I thought it was time to return home. That and I have family in Glasgow who I want to reconnect with. Oh, through the years I *have* kept in touch," he grimaced, "but a letter or occasional phone call isn't the same as being there and able to attend weddings, funerals or even family get-togethers."

She couldn't resist herself and asked, "Where abroad were you working?"

"Have you heard of Médecins Sans Frontières?"

Mary's brow furrowed when she asked, "Isn't that the French charity? It translates as doctors eh, something? I'm not certain. French was never my best subject at school," she blushed.

"Doctors without borders," he smiled at her. "It's a humanitarian organisation that provides emergency medical aid to underdeveloped countries."

He humourlessly smiled, then continued, "A little over eight years ago, I left Glasgow full of enthusiastic zeal to save the world, but soon realised that my contribution was not even a drop in the ocean. Yes, I like to think that with my colleagues, we did some good, but after eight years living amongst some of the poorer nations in the world, I'm afraid I have lost my commitment and decided to return home. It's the little things you miss," he smiled, "like flushing toilets, cold beer and this," he pointed to the remains of their suppers, "fish and chips with brown sauce. Fortunately, the Western was looking for someone to run their Casualty Department with extensive experience working not only with the minimum of resources," he smiled again, "but also with varied experience in general medicine, disease control, paediatrics, orthopaedics, emergency surgery and surprisingly, even gunshot and blast wounds *and* with the experience in training junior doctors. And so here I am," he smiled.

"Gunshots and blast wounds?" Eileen stared wide-eyed at him. "In Glasgow? Just where exactly *where* you working, Bill?"

"Oh, Eileen," he smiled as he ruefully shook his head, "some of the places I worked didn't even have names, let alone being recorded on any maps."

With a sudden and unexplained new-found respect Mary thoughtfully asked, "Tell me, Bill, are you partial to a glass of red wine?"

****

It was Michael who suggested that he and Eileen put Jamie and Morven to bed, then half an hour later, the children settled, they returned downstairs to inform Mary that they were leaving.

"Oh," a little taken aback, she stared at her father when she said, "I'm sorry, dad, I thought I was putting you up here for tonight?"

"Don't be reading into it, sweetheart, but Eileen has the spare room and to be honest," he glanced at Eileen, "we've a bit of talking to do after what happened today."

"Don't worry, though," Eileen interrupted, "we'll both be here sharp tomorrow morning to let you get to work and as for your dad," she turned to smile at him, "again don't be worrying, Mary. He's in safe hands with me."

And I have no doubt about that, she thought as she glanced from one to the other.

****

Their farewells made, Mary saw her father and Eileen to the door and watched as he left with her in the yellow Beetle.

Returning to the kitchen Bill had risen to his feet and said, "If you're working tomorrow, I'd better be off and let you get to your bed."

"You've still half a glass of wine to finish," she observed, then suggested, "Why don't we move through to the comfortable seats in the lounge."

Carrying their glasses, Mary led the way and slumping down into the couch, kicked off her shoes and slipped her legs beneath her.

"Been quite a day," he said as he occupied an opposite armchair.

She tiredly run her hand through her hair when she replied, "If you had asked me this morning what today would bring, I couldn't in a million years have guessed that I'd learn my father is having a relationship with my childminder or that my mother would be arrested, so yes," she frowned, "as you say, quite a day."

They sat for several moments in comfortable silence, sipping at their wine, when he said, "I'm probably overstepping the mark, but no Mr Wells?"

"There was," she cautiously replied, "but he took off with one of the previous tenants from your place."

Keen to change the subject, she quickly asked, "And you? No one special?"

There was just the hint of a pause before he wryly smiled, then said, "No, no one in quite a while."

Again, there was the silence, though perhaps, Mary thought, a little awkward this time, but broken when he said, "I gather from your reaction to your father being assaulted by your mother, there's no love lost between you?"

"Mum? No," she sighed with a shake of her head.

"Bill, I say this without meanness, but my mother is probably the most conceited, self-centred woman I know. Woman? Individual I *should* say. She's given my father one hell of a bad life and frankly, treated both my brothers and I as *his* children, rather than *their* children, if you see what I mean. Sadly, I can't say I have ever had any feelings of love or even a liking for my mum."

Her face creased when she stared at him, then sighed, "How sad it that?"

He didn't immediately respond, but thoughtfully staring back at her, he said, "You know, Mary, there is a belief and an ongoing discourse among academics, social workers and a number of those in the medical profession that the maternal instinct is in fact a complete fabrication. There are those professionals who theorise the notion of mothers having a maternal instinct is rooted in the religious perception that it is the duty of a mother to be selfless and entirely committed to that role," he slowly drawled.

"Of course, as a police officer, I'm certain that during your career you must have encountered mothers who quite literally would give up their last breath for their child while there are those who for different reasons, inflict physical harm upon their children or ignore their basic needs and in doing so, cause the child harm. In fact some women, who admittedly are in the minority, completely contradict the notion of maternal instinct."

"Case in point, my mother?" she sarcastically responded.

He smiled at her remark, then he continued, "Similarly, there's also the belief that we should love our parents and siblings because we are of the same blood, but believe me when I tell you," his face clouded, "I've seen men murder parents, brothers, sisters and other family members because of some political, racial or religiously motivated ideologies. So, as a health professional," he slowly smiled, "believe me when I tell you, you need *not* feel guilty about *not* loving or even liking your mother. My experience is that love and respect are not just to be given, but to be earned."

In that heartbeat, staring back at him, Mary could not explain the feeling she felt, but decided that at some point in the past, Bill Howie had himself been emotionally hurt and badly so.

Now, she wondered, where did that thought come from?

He broke into her thoughts when he said, "Is it usual for a Detective Chief Inspector to work on Sunday's?"

"Oh, you know I'm a DCI, then. I suppose my dad was boasting," she felt her face flush.

"Just a little," grinning, he held up a hand with a short space between the forefinger and his thumb.

"Well, in answer to your question, the privilege of rank permits me most weekends off; however, I'm currently running a murder investigation, so at the minute it's all hands to the pumps, as it were."

"Right, then, I'd better be off and let you get to your bed," he rose to his feet and once more, she marvelled how tall he was and to her consternation, realised she was unconsciously comparing him to Harry, her ex.

Blushing at her thoughts, she got to her feet and followed him to the door, where again she said, "Thanks for all your help, Bill. And the fish suppers," she coyly smiled.

"No problem," he stepped out into the chilly night and waving a hand behind, turned on the pavement to enter his own pathway.

Closing the door, she thought, he's a nice man, then grinned when she thought again, a *very* nice man.

It was only when getting ready for bed that she realised; unlike most people she knew or had encountered, Bill had not asked her anything about the murder investigation.

CHAPTER THIRTEEN

Once more, DS Colin Baxter was first into the incident room that Sunday morning, closely followed by DS Elaine Fitzsimmons, who greeted him with, "Any word if the boss is coming in today?"
"No word that she's *not*, so I reckon she'll be here."
"Am I hearing my name mentioned?" they turned to see Mary Wells striding into the room.
It was Baxter who asked, "Everything okay at home, Boss?"
"Fine now, thanks, Colin."
"Now, what's happening here," she settled herself down into a chair.
"First," it was Fitzsimmons who tensely began, "I told the team to come in at nine-thirty. As it's Sunday, I gave them the extra hour, if that's okay."
Mary slowly nodded then to Fitzsimmons relief, replied, "You're the deputy SIO, Elaine, so you were in charge and I'll stand by whatever decision you make. Now, Colin, how are we doing with the actions?"
From behind his desk, he began by relating DC's Tommy Maxwell and John McGhee's visit to Max Pettigrew, telling her, "All in all, a worthwhile visit, boss. I've put the word out to the team interviewing the staff to try and identify anyone they think might be easily coerced into thieving from their client's home. If we can identify one member of the gang, if indeed it *is* a gang, that'll be our starter for ten."
"Good," she nodded. "Anything else?"
The door opened to admit some of the team who began to drift into the room.
"The fingerprint on the candlestick the partial in blood. Still nothing back from the Fingerprints Department," Baxter shook his head.
"Nothing on that at all?" she repeated, though inwardly wasn't too surprised.
"Nothing, Boss," he shook his head, then continued, "I also think

we've lucked out on the door to door. There's nothing came of that, either and you might wish to consider taking the four guys left on it and adding them to the teams checking the client list."

"Do that," she agreed with a nod, forcing a smile rather than showing her disappointment.

She remained in the room till the last of the team arrived and suggested that as it was Fitzsimmons who closed yesterday, she begin with this morning's briefing.

When the last member of the team was within the room, Mary, her stomach tense and a little apprehensive, rose to her feet.

Astute enough to know that her team would be aware she left the office in response to a call to return home, she knew that sooner or later, word would leak from the Partick Police Office to Govan about what had occurred at her house and so on the way to work, decided to pre-empt the gossip by being upfront.

"Yesterday when I got home," she felt her mouth curiously dry, "I found that my parents had a set-to that carried on to my home. The police were summoned and in short, my mother is being reported by the local cops for walloping my father with her handbag. No big deal. Any questions?" she stared around the room, almost daring someone to open their mouth.

She wasn't prepared for the response to her admission.

The sudden revelation from their DCI about what had occurred in her home had more than a few of the team glancing at each other in surprise, but the silence was broken when from the back, DS Donnie Corbett, in his rich bass voice, loudly called out, "When I was fifteen, my Da came home steaming drunk when he should have been taking my mother to a family party. Ended up she scudded him right across face with a frying pan, breaking his nose and knocking out a couple of teeth. He got fifteen stitches and a right sore face and she got a night in the pokey."

The laughter that erupted stalled when waving a hand for silence, Mary, with a subdued smile on her face, said, "Thanks for that vote of solidarity, DS Corbett, and it's a bit of a relief to know I'm not the only one with a dysfunctional family. Now, people, you have your actions, so let's get out there and find our killer."

****

Elaine Fitzsimmons and her neighbour, DC Alan Hamilton, decided their first port of call would be a member of the cleaning staff, Maria

Clinton, whose address was recorded as Thornley Avenue in the Knightswood area of the city.

"According to the staff list," her head bowed as Fitzsimmons read from the sheet, "Clinton's thirty-four and been employed by the company for about three years. If her shift pattern is correct, then she's off work today. Unfortunately, no home phone number" she sighed and mentally crossed her fingers that being early in the morning, the woman was at home.

Turning off Lincoln Avenue, into Thornley Avenue, Hamilton slowed the car to a crawl and peered at the council built, four in a block flats, looking for the house number, then stopping the car, said, "Here we are. Looks like a ground floor flat."

Glancing round at the building, Fitzsimmons saw that while most of the neighbouring houses had neat and tidy gardens, the front garden for Clinton's house was overgrown with weeds and the five feet high hedgerow so neglected it was spilling out over the pavement.

Getting out of the car, they made their way to the front door that was located at the side of the house.

It was evident from the scratches on the bottom of the wooden front door, that there was a dog in the house, confirmed when they knocked by a deep, throaty barking from inside.

Seconds later, the door was pulled open by a shaven-headed man in his late thirties, wearing a stained, once-white tee shirt that showed of his numerous ink tattoos on both arms and hands, with his belly hanging over the waistband of a grubby pair of grey coloured tracksuit bottoms. The man was struggling to hold onto the collar of a large, hairy Alsatian dog who slavering at the mouth, was showing its teeth and snarling at the officers.

It would be a *bloody* Alsatian, Hamilton thought.

Fitzsimmon's, seemingly unperturbed by the dog, flashed her warrant card at the man and calmly told him, "CID here to speak with Mrs Clinton. You want to put that dog away in a room somewhere before I call out animal control?"

"Eh, what?" the man's face creased with suspicion, showing a mouth of yellowing teeth with a number of gaps.

"Hang on," he said at last and dragging the yelping dog off, closed the door.

A minute later, the door re-opened and the man, now minus the dog which could be heard barking crazily and scratching at a closed door, peered at them both, then hostilely said, "Who are you again?"

"We're the CID here to see Mrs Clinton," she patiently repeated then behind the man saw a thinly built woman fearfully staring out from a door at them.

"Ah, there she is," Fitzsimmons widely smiled then pushing past the man, entered the hallway.

Following her, Hamilton immediately gasped at the strong smell of dog faeces that was almost as strong as the body odour given off by the man who completely taken aback, stared wide-eyed at Fitzsimmons, his protest dying on his tongue.

"Mrs Clinton?" Fitzsimmons smiled at the nervous woman, "somewhere we can sit and have a chat?"

"Eh, how about in here?" she didn't wait for a response, but pushed open the door that proved to be the front room where on a couch, a young girl no more than nine or ten years of age and wearing a shabby, pink coloured, short sleeved nightdress that barely covered her thin body and under which could clearly be seen a dark pair of girls briefs, sat with her arms folded across her chest, her head down and her feet bare.

"Hello, there," Fitzsimmons cheerily greeted the girl, but her mother then anxiously hissed, "Ellie, away to your room, hen, and try and keep that dog under control, eh?"

Her head still bowed, the girl wordlessly left the room, sneaking past her father, but not quick enough for Fitzsimmons to fail to notice the fingers marks on her arms.

Entering the room, her father asked in an aggressive booming voice, "What's this all about?"

It was Fitzsimmons who steely replied, "We've come to interview Mrs Clinton about her job. I assume you're Mr Clinton?"

Glancing around him at the stained furniture and wondering where the dog had been shitting, Hamilton hoped to God that they weren't invited to sit down.

"Aye," he almost sneered, "Peter Clinton. It's my house," he haughtily added.

Staring at Maria Clinton, who like her daughter wore a knee length dressing gown with short sleeves that was both worn and the once bright colours faded, Fitzsimmons could not but help notice the bruising on the thin woman's arms nor the dull, yellow bruise under her left eye.

As if recognising what Fitzsimmons had seen, Clinton snapped, "You, away and put something on and cover yourself up."

Just like her daughter, the cowed woman bowed her head and literally fled from the room as Clinton stretched to his full five feet seven and again said, "What's this all about?"

Hamilton had worked with Fitzsimmons for a couple of months now, long enough to know that his neighbour was not a woman to be trifled with and just then, he wondered what the beefy man was going to say that would set Elaine off on one, for he had seen her when she was angry and it was not a pretty sight.

Her teeth gritted, Fitzsimmons quietly replied, "We have some questions for your wife about her employment with 'Sweeps n' Dust,' questions that won't take long."

Trying to regain some sort of authority in his own home, his lip curled to show his yellowing teeth when he said, "Well, see it doesn't because we're busy, okay?"

Fitzsimmons snapped her head around and staring at him, Hamilton's heart sank, for he'd seen that look before and prepared himself for a confrontation.

In a monotone voice, she stared hard at Clinton before she replied, "It will take as long as I say it will take and by the way," she hissed, "Where did your wife and daughter get they bruises on their arms?"

"Eh, what?" his eyes narrowed at the change of tact, then his face paling, he muttered, "I don't know what you're on about."

Turning, she saw Maria Clinton, wearing a faded cotton dressing gown that covered her arms that were now protectively wrapped about her, re-enter the room, then said to Hamilton, "Wait here with him. Mrs Clinton, you come with me," then reaching for the woman's arm, began to propel her from the room.

"Hey, you can't…" Clinton began and took a step forward, but stopped when Hamilton, four inches taller and a whole lot fitter, placed a hand on his chest and smiled, "Easy there, pal."

In the hallway, Fitzsimmons asked, "What one's your daughter's room?"

Shaking and confused, the slightly built woman pointed to a door that Fitzsimmons curiously noticed, had a door-bolt screwed on the outside.

Now why, she wondered, would they want their daughter locked in her room?
Then remembering, Fitzsimmons asked, "Where's the dog?"
"The dog? Eh, he's in the kitchen."
"Right, okay," Fitzsimmons replied with some relief that she wouldn't be facing a snarling Alsatian, then pushed open the daughter's door and entering the brightly lit room, gagged and almost immediately felt a lump in her throat.
The young girl sat huddled on a single bed, her chin resting on her bony knees and her arms wrapped about her thin legs that were tucked under her.
Eyes wide, she stared fearfully at the Detective.
One leg of the frail looking cheaply made bed was missing and propped up by a number of books. The washed-out Mickey Mouse quilt cover lay in disarray on the floor by the bed and what had once been a white, chipboard DIY wardrobe lay at an angle against the wall with a number of clothes, including a school blazer, hanging inside. Wallpaper was peeling at the corners and some prints, quite obviously cut from a young girl's magazine, were thumbtacked to the walls.
On the floor were scattered some toys that included an undressed, cheaply made doll.
The cheap, black fabric curtain over the window was torn at the bottom and instead of a curtain rail she saw the curtain was thumbtacked round the edges to the wall, completely shutting out any light.
Taking a breath, Fitzsimmons, the mother of ten-year-old twin daughters, fought the emotion that threatened to overwhelm her when she softly said, "Ellie, isn't it?"
The girl continued to stare as Fitzsimmons, tears biting at her eyes, moved closer to the bed.
It was then the Detective gave a horrified gasp and felt a cold chill sweep through her body as she stared in disgust at the stained pink sheet that lay rumpled on the bed; stains that as an experienced Detective officer, she recognised for what they were.
Barely able to speak, Fitzsimmons turned to the mother and her teeth gritted, quietly said, "Please remain here and while I'm away, find some clothes for you and your daughter and get dressed."

Without waiting for a response, she left the room and made her way outside to the CID car.

In the front room, Hamilton heard the dog frantically barking, then the front door closing and stepping towards the window, pulled aside the curtain to see his neighbour at the car, using the car radio.

"What's going on?" Clinton asked behind him, but turning, Hamilton waved him back from the window and replied, "You'll find out in a minute."

It didn't escape the younger man's notice that Clinton was now visibly perspiring.

Less than a minute later, his neighbour opened the door to the front room and addressing Hamilton, told him, "I've called for some uniform back-up and I've the mother and the daughter getting dressed. We're taking them both to Sandyford Place. We'll be met there by the local Division's FACU officer and the police Casualty Surgeon. Him," she turned and curled her lip, "for the minute he's going to Clydebank Police Office with the uniform cops when they get here."

Of course, Hamilton recognised the address in Sandyford Place as the clinic used by the police and other agencies for the examination of women beaten, sexually assaulted or for other sexually related issues and, knowing better than to ask in front of Clinton what was going on, simply nodded.

However, when Clinton angrily interjected, with, "Who the fuck are you to take my wife and kid out of here?" Fitzsimmons merely stared at him for several seconds before she replied, "You are being detained under Section Two of the Criminal Procedure (Scotland) Act of nineteen-eighty as a suspect for incestuous rape."

"For what?" his eyes widened.

Ignoring him, she felt her face pale when she snarled at Hamilton, "If he opens his mouth one more time, if he as much as breathes loudly or farts," she hissed through gritted teeth, "you have my complete authority to beat the living shit out of him," then left the room.

****

After seeing Clinton handcuffed then placed into the rear of the marked Transit van and an explanation given to the attending officers, Hamilton drove Fitzsimmons and Mrs Clinton and her daughter to the mid-terraced, Georgian building in the Finnieston area of the city.

On arrival there, they were they were met by a B Division FACU officer, who informed them the Casualty Surgeon had also arrived and was waiting to examine the daughter.

Leading the extremely nervous Maria Clinton and her daughter to an interview room and with the FACU officer present, Fitzsimmons informed the mother of her suspicions and was tearfully given permission for Ellie to be medically examined.

During this time, Hamilton found a phone and calling the incident room at Govan, informed Colin Baxter of their involvement in what seemed to be a sexual crime.

"Any idea how long you might be tied up, Alan?"

"No idea," Hamilton shook his head, "but Elaine's got the bit between her teeth, Colin, and she's not letting it go. She's already been onto the Duty DI at Clydebank and had an argument with him."

"How so?"

"Well," Hamilton rubbed wearily at his forehead, "he started off with the Pontius Pilate thing, telling her he's not got enough resources on today to deal with this, so he's wanting Elaine to go ahead with the inquiry."

"Washing his hands of it, even though it's his Division?" Baxter sighed with a shake of his head.

"Exactly."

"Okay, Alan, I'll let the boss know what's happening, so give me the number we can contact you on and I'll get back to you."

****

The examination of a weeping and distraught Ellie Clinton took just over fifteen minutes after which the young Casualty Surgeon beckoned that Fitzsimmons join him in the corridor outside.

Leaning with his back against the wall, the young doctor shook his head and stuttered, "Jesus, I hope I don't get too many of these examinations, but it's as you suspected, DS Fitzsimmons. The lassie is showing all signs of being the victim of rape, with bruising and genital injury. I would suspect too that we're talking about multiple penetration over a period of time," he sighed with a shake of his head. "That's all apart from the fact there's evidence of finger-marks on her arms and bruising, recent and historical, where she's probably been held down."

She watched him exhale when his eyes moist he again shook his head and his voice, almost breaking, said "God alone knows how that wee girl is going get over this, if indeed she ever does."
He stared keenly at her when he softly asked, "You suspect the father?"
She nodded, feeling a lump in her chest and her throat tightening when she replied, "Before you go, doctor, and with her permission, can you also examine the mother?"
****

Over and hour and a half later, both the mother and daughter, their examinations concluded and now showered and carrying clean, donated clothes, were removed to a quiet room with comfortable couches, soft furnishings, and a variety of book, magazines and children's toys.

It was then that Fitzsimmons and Hamilton learned from a member of staff that a Detective Inspector and a Detective Sergeant were looking for them.

Meeting their colleagues in the foyer, the DI rudely explained that he and the DS were now taking over the investigation, that the house at Thornley Avenue was being subjected to a Scenes of Crime examination and as a result of the evidence and verbal admissions made by Maria Clinton and her daughter Ellie, that Martin Clinton's status as a detained person was now revoked, that instead he had been formally arrested for the repeated rape of his ten-year-old daughter as well as the spousal rape of his wife, Maria.

Guessing from his attitude that the DI was extremely pissed that his Sunday evening had been interrupted by Fitzsimmons and Hamilton, neither of the G Division Detectives gave the DI any cause for further complaint, but thanked him for taking the case off their hands.

However, Fitzsimmons then politely asked, "While Alan here provides you with our statements, Boss, can I have a word with Mrs Clinton before we go?"

"And for what reason?" he stared suspiciously at her.

"To be honest, we never got the opportunity to speak with her about why we arrived at her house. I promise, I'll be no more than ten minutes, fifteen at the most."

"I suppose so," he grumpily replied, then stomped off to find a coffee machine, fortunately without seeing his DS's grin.

"He was supposed to be at a golf club dance tonight," the DS intimated, "but when your DCI called *our* DCI at home and inquired why two of her team had to deal with a B Division rape, that lazy bugger," he nodded towards the departed DI, "wasn't best pleased having to explain himself on the phone."

"Sod him," Fitzsimmon's sourly said, "That's why he's getting more money than we are. Right," she turned to Hamilton, "you give the statements and I'll see you in the foyer when we're done."

****

Even though they had been assured they were now safe from her violent husband, when Elaine Fitzsimmons entered the quiet room, she saw both Maria and Ellie Clinton startle and the little girl huddle close to her mother, their hair still damp from the shower and both now wearing the donated clothing.

Maria, sitting side by side with Ellie and tightly holding her hand, wore a rust coloured sweater that was at least a size too big for her thin frame and a red flared skirt while her daughter wore a pink coloured jersey with a rabbit motif on the front and a pair of blue jeans, turned up at the hem.

Raising a calming hand, she smiled and siting opposite Maria, said, "He can't hurt you here, Maria, and I've just learned that your husband has been formally arrested, so I'm confident he will be detained after his court appearance and will not be able to contact you."

No matter the assurance, she could see in the terrified woman's eyes that the fear still existed and it was expressed when Maria hesitatingly asked, "But when you let him go, he'll come after us, won't he?"

"No, Maria, he will not," she firmly replied.

"Now," she continued, "a Detective from the local Division will come into the room with the Female and Child Unit officer, what we call the FACU, and that'll be the policewoman who was with you when you were examined," she explained, then smiled when she added, "She seems a nice enough lassie, doesn't she?"

Maria, eager to please, hesitantly returned the smile and nodded.

"They will take your statements. You can sit with Ellie when she gives hers, okay?" Fitzsimmons continued to comfortingly smile.

"When that's all completed, the FACU officer will remain with you and there will be people from the clinic here who will help you and answer any questions you might have. Do you understand?"

"Will we need to go back there, to the house, I mean," her lips trembled.

Fitzsimmons wasn't one hundred per cent certain, but quietly replied, "Look, if you don't want to return to your own house, I'm sure that something can be arranged by the clinic here. You know, Maria, you and Ellie are not the first women to come through this place. We, I mean the police, we're starting to understand what wives go through when their husbands or their partners are bad to them," and long overdue it is, she savagely thought as she stared at the frightened woman.

Inwardly taking a breath, she continued, "There's now procedures in place to help women and children who have been, well," she shrugged, unwillingly to even use the word rape, "victimised like you and Ellie."

Maria slowly nodded, then her voice almost a whisper, she said, "He told us he'd kill us and kill himself if we ever told anyone."

A fleeting rage coursed through Fitzsimmons body when she heard those words uttered, knowing that Martin Clinton, no doubt a pathetic and cowardly man, had used the threat but never in a million years would have had the courage to hurt himself.

"Be sure to tell the Detective that," she nodded at Maria.

Other officers and predominantly men, she angrily thought, might have argued that Maria Clinton should have stood up against her husband when he violated their daughter and her; should have screamed for help, told someone, anyone rather than let the horror continue.

But staring at the mother, Fitzsimmons saw a weak and wretched woman with no self-worth, beaten down by life and domestic violence and realised she had chosen survival, no matter the cost.

"Then," she forced a smile and for Maria's sake, blatantly lied, "there was nothing you could have done to stop him, was there?"

Seconds of silence followed, broken when Maria hesitatingly asked, "It'll not be you that puts him to the court, then?"

"No," she smiled, "I come from a different area. Now, the reason that DC Hamilton and I originally came to visit you is that we're part

of the team investigating the murder of Elizabeth Bradley. Did you know Lizzie from your work?"
It was the short intake of breath, her head and her eyes dipping to the left that gave her away and Fitzsimmons realised then that Maria Clinton knew something.
Something about Lizzie Bradley.

CHAPTER FOURTEEN

DI Sammy Salmon's arrival at Pollok CID had not gone well. With one DS and two DC's on their monthly weekend off and a second DS and DC attached to the Govan murder investigation, the most opinionated of the three, DS Hugh Donnelly, greeted him that morning in the small general office with, "So what have you done wrong to get posted here then, *sir*?"
The emphasis on the *sir* rather than the CID's generally accepted and respectful term, *Boss,* immediately declared Donnelly's dislike for Salmon.
With twenty-five years' service completed, Hugh Donnelly was not a likeable man and it was even rumoured his wife couldn't stand him, though both the origin and veracity of that rumour were unclear.
Unaware, both Donnelly's DC's had in confidence individually applied to be transferred from Pollok, not as he thought because of their former DI, Martin Reilly, but because neither of the DC's could cope with Donnelly's idleness and constant sarcasm. That and he was widely suspected to be the source of false rumours or information that not only permeated throughout the Pollok CID, but curiously often found their way into the local media and in particular, the 'Glasgow News.'
Now, here he was, greeting the temporary DI with such disdain that Salmon could almost feel the displeasure emanating from the balding, overweight DS with the constant sullen expression.
With patience and without disclosing too many details and suspecting that word had already reached the Pollok CID office, Salmon courteously explained about Reilly's unexpected retiral,

concluding that the DCI had appointed him as a temporary measure till a new DI could be in place.

He didn't miss Donnelly's eyes betraying his sudden interest when the sour faced man realised there might be an opportunity for him to step up to the vacant post.

Aye, Salmon thought, dream on you fat bastard, for the DI, with a sickening feeling in the pit of his stomach, recalled that during his tenure as acting DCI, when Mary Wells was on postnatal leave, the then DI Martin Reilly and Donnelly were two of his worst critics; Reilly believing it was he who should be appointed to the acting rank and Donnelly, who took every opportunity to be just plain rude when speaking with Salmon, who he openly referred to as some sort of Johnny-come-lately, though never to Salmon's face or in the DI's hearing.

"Right," Salmon suddenly forced a smiled, "What's happening today then?"

Passing the DI the black plastic crime folder, Salmon flicked through the green copy crime reports, then asked, "Why have the CR's not been allocated yet?"

"That's usually the DI's job," Donnelly shrugged. "Reilly had his favourites and they'd get the easy CR's that might produce an arrest while the rest of us were dished out the shite that was left. That way he manipulated the statistics to indicate who seemed to have the more detections, while the rest of us looked like we were doing nothing."

Salmon's eyes narrowed, for he was unaware of such a procedure and suspected Donnelly, who was also suspected to be one of Reilly's so-called 'favourites,' was lying to cover up his own poor detection rate.

It occurred to Salmon then that the DI could only distribute the CR's when he was on duty, that otherwise it was the DS's job and being unaware Salmon was arriving today, Donnelly should have dealt with the matter. However, rather than forcing the issue, he kept his counsel.

"Well," he forced another smile, "that stops today. CR's will be distributed on a next in line basis by whoever is in the office first thing in the morning, whether that be me a DS or a senior DC. However, for now give me ten minutes and then they'll be ready for issuing."

In the DI's office, his first act was to open the window to rid the room of the strong smell of Martin Reilly's tobacco, then seating himself behind the desk, flicked through the CR folder before phoning the direct internal number for Mary Wells.
"Morning, boss," he greeted her, "that's me in situ at Pollok."
She wasn't certain, but thought she detected a lack of enthusiasm in his voice.
"Good. Anything worthy of note that I should know about?"
"No, apparently it's been a quiet Friday night so nothing other than a couple of housebreakings, one serious assault that the late shift dealt with and two car thefts, one of which is recovered. A smattering of other minor issues, but most of which can be returned to the uniformed cops to make their own inquiries."
"If my shift rota is up to date, it'll be Hugh Donnelly on duty?"
"Aye, that's correct," then much to Wells' amusement, he sarcastically added, "Welcomed me with open arms."
It was never her style to micro-manage her supervisors, but then thoughtfully shared with him, "You're long enough in the tooth now, Sammy, to ignore that bugger's insolence. Donnelly thinks because he's got a few years under his belt he's untouchable, but I'm not blind to the fact he's hardly done a full day's work while he was working under Reilly. Usually offloads his inquiries onto his team, though why Reilly let him away with it, God alone knows."
"On that point about Martin Reilly, Boss. Nothing specific, but I've a feeling that Donnelly might believe himself to be in the running to replace Reilly."
Several seconds of silence were broken when she snapped, "Come hell or high water, I'd appoint a uniformed probationer before I'd consider him."
Then taking a breath, added in a more conciliatory voice, "Don't be worrying about that, Sammy, I've got it under control."
Then, as if to reassure Salmon, she said, "One thing you should be aware of, Sammy. I know that you have intimated your desire to return to uniform, that you believe the CID isn't the route you want to take, but believe me, I have more confidence in your ability than you have in yourself. You are a far better manager than you give yourself credit for and you should also know that clowns like Donnelly aside, you are more respected than you think you are."

Her short statement took him by surprise and catching his breath, heard himself reply, "Thanks, boss, that was…unexpected."
"Well, Sammy, you should know me by now. If it needs said, it's said. Now, between us, if things work out as I've planned, your secondment up there in Pollok won't be for long, so stick with it and remember," she teased him, "you're too ugly to let someone like Donnelly get under your skin."
"Ugly?" he grinned. "I don't think you realise I'm the best-looking guy in the Department."
"Stay in touch," she ended the call with a smile, satisfied that her short pep talk had been successful.
****

Seated at her desk, she finished reading through the previous day's synopsis of actions completed by her team, frustrated that though the team themselves were out on the ground making their inquiries, nothing of evidential value was coming back in.
The one positive thing that had occurred that morning had not even been part of the investigation; Elaine Fitzsimmon's and Alan Hamilton's discovery of the house in Knightswood where the father had been raping both his wife and their daughter.
"Evil bastard!" she involuntarily snarled.
What made it worse was the DI at Clydebank Police Office trying to tie up her two officers with a C Division crime. Just as well his DCI was an old friend of hers from Tulliallan Police College, so that sorted the issue. Well, that and the statistics for sexual crimes was at an all-time low throughout the Force, so the DCI was more than grateful to have two criminal detections for the rapes, statistically separate crimes, albeit the culprit was the same man.
****

Sitting back in her chair, Wells thoughts turned to the arrival that morning of her father and Eileen, both a little nervous and apprehensive now that the dust from the previous afternoon was settled.
Her father, still dressed in the same clothes she saw, had sought her assurance that she really was okay with him having a relationship with Eileen, while the older woman had nervously looked on.
"Dad," she had first ushered the children from the kitchen to play in the lounge, then told him, "I love you and you know that. I am also aware of the life you have being living all *my* life with a woman

who, frankly, hasn't been as faithful to you as you have been to her."

"Oh," his shoulders had slumped, "you know about that?"

"Me *know* about it?" she had pretended to express a shocked face. "Dad, Alan *and* William know too. Where the heck do you think we were living at the time? With you, you dunderhead. How the hell could we have missed what was going on?"

"I'm so sorry you had to go through that," his shoulders slumped and his eyes moist, he had been visibly upset, but Mary had moved towards him and hugged him.

"No matter what you two decide," she had included Eileen in her gaze, "whatever you choose you have my unequivocal support and I feel certain I'm speaking for Alan and William too."

It was Eileen who then spoke and anxiously told her, "I'm so sorry, Mary, I still feel I've betrayed your trust. If it hadn't been for me," she had stared tearfully at Michael, "maybe the best thing is I just leave."

Pokerfaced, Mary had responded with, "Try and leave, Eileen McAulay, and I'll hunt you down and drag you back by the hair. How do you think my kids and I can possibly get by without you."

It had been exactly the words Eileen had been hoping to hear and when the older woman stretched out her arms and moved forward, Mary found herself being hugged by both her father and Eileen.

The moment was broken when a small voice said from the doorway, "I'm hungry," and the three turned to see Morven staring curiously at them.

When she'd left the house, she had daintily picked at her father's shirt then taken his house keys from him, telling him, "I'll stop by and collect some clothes for you. I imagine the last thing you want is to visit when mum's there."

"I feel such a coward, letting you do that," he had replied, but Mary shooed away his objections telling him, "The last thing you need is a confrontation. I'm guessing that mum will already be thinking about negotiating a divorce and I've no doubt either you'll be the bad guy, so she'll be thinking now what she can get out of a settlement. You turn up and she'll likely allege that you are harassing her, threatening her even."

"Do you really think she'd do that?" he'd falteringly asked, to which Mary replied, "Oh, God, Dad, even after all these years, you have no idea what she's capable of, have you?"

However, confident though she had sounded at the time, driving to work Mary considered that it might be worth having someone with her when she visited at the house in Meadowhill and smiled, because she knew exactly who'd she'd call.

****

Parking in the rear yard at Govan Police Office, Alan Hamilton switched off the engine, then asked his neighbour, "I'll grab us a coffee while you speak with the DCI?"

"Okay, while you're grabbing the coffee, I'll get a hold of Colin Baxter and bring him into the room too, then we'll both speak with the boss," Fitzsimmons had replied. "This info is from us both, Alan, so if there's any kudos to be had, we share, okay?"

"Okay," he grinned at her.

Minutes later, with Colin Baxter in tow and who carried a file, Fitzsimmons knocked on Mary Wells door and asked, "You got five minutes, Boss? Might be important."

"Come in," she waved a hand then saw Alan Hamilton appear with two mugs of coffee.

"Sorry," Fitzsimmons told her, "we've not had the chance of a break today. Hang on and I'll
fetch another chair."

Once the three Detectives were seat in front of her, Mary addressed Fitzsimmons and Hamilton with, "Our investigation aside, that was a good arrest today, you guys. The DCI at C Division was well chuffed and I hope his DI wasn't too much trouble."

"Nothing we couldn't handle, boss," Fitzsimmons replied with a shrug.

"So, what's so important?"

"The woman we went to visit, now the complainer for the rape case, Mrs Maria Clinton. One of the employees of 'Sweep 'n Dust.' Turns out she's one of the team who were stealing the ornaments and jewellery from the clients."

Mary could feel the old and familiar tingle in her guts when she heard that, the first lead in the investigation that sounded promising.

"Go on."

With a brief glance at Hamilton, Fitzsimmons continued, "Following on from what Kenny Maxwell and John McGhee learned from the resetter, Max Pettigrew, his suggestion that because of the low quality of some of the items stolen, one or some of the thieves might be easily coerced, someone not too bright. Well, his profiling was spot on because Maria Clinton, poor soul that she really is," she said with some feeling, "fits the bill to a T."

She paused as if to catch her breath, but it was Wells alone who recognised the emotional turmoil that Fitzsimmon's must have experienced when she discovered the child was being molested. "Bullied by her husband who abused her both physically and mentally," Fitzsimmons continued, "she was also being persuaded at work into thieving from some of her clients. Now, not that I'm any better than anyone else," she held up a hand to stress the point, "but Maria is a poorly educated woman with no self-respect whatsoever who when at home, lived in constant fear of her husband. Then when she was at work, she was," she paused, searching for the correct word, "I suppose what I'm trying to say she was a little overwhelmed by of one of her co-workers, a woman called Lorraine Gray, who befriended her. From what she told us, it was about three months ago that Gray," she raised her forefingers as italics, "*convinced* her and another woman, Martha Foster, to steal from their clients."

Mary saw Baxter lower his head to check his file then tell her "Gray and Foster. Got both their details here, boss, but neither has yet been interviewed. Telephone number for Foster, but none for Gray."

"Go on, Elaine."

"It seems Gray is the organiser for the thefts and had also persuaded our victim to keep the stolen property in her flat."

Her curiosity aroused, Mary's eyes narrowed when he asked, "Did this woman Clinton happen to mention or did she know why they collected the property and not just sell it off when they stole it?"

"According to Maria, Gray told her and Foster that when they had all the stuff collected, she knew of a resetter over in the north side of the city who would give them a total price for the property, then they would divvy the money up four ways which of course, included our victim, Elizabeth Bradley."

"And Clinton, she believed that?"

"Apparently," Fitzsimmons shrugged.

"To be honest and like I said, she's not very bright. I think she clung to the idea of having some money of her own to get her and the wee girl out of the hands of that *bastard* of a husband of hers," she finished with some feeling, then hesitantly added, "Sorry, Boss, but I didn't think after what she is currently going through it was appropriate to start levelling charges of theft against her. If that is to happen, I'm certain we can do that at a later date."

"We'll cross that bridge when we come to it, maybe with the PF's approval and considering what she's gone through, we might even consider using her as a Crown witness rather than an accused," Mary thoughtfully replied.

"I take it you warned Clinton off from contacting the other two?" she asked.

"I did, boss," Fitzsimmons nodded. "She's in no doubt that if she attempts to contact them to warn them of our interest in them or for any other reason, we'll be back to jail her and for what it's worth, I think she got the message."

"Colin," she turned to him, "do you have the shift pattern for both Gray and Foster?"

His head bowed as he run his fingers down the page, then replied, "According to this rota, Gray is off tomorrow and Foster is to visit a client in the morning at one-nine-o-nine, Maryhill Road."

His brow furrowed when he added, "I'm familiar with that area," and glanced up. "It's old Victorian tenements along that stretch of the road."

"Right," a pleased Wells smiled, "Early doors tomorrow morning, Elaine, I want you and Alan to collect Gray from her home address. Colin, organise a second team to be waiting at the Maryhill Road address and lift Foster from there. Bring them both to Govan under Section Two and we'll see what they have to say for themselves. Elaine, Alan," she stared at them in turn as she nodded, "good work, both in detecting the rapist and bringing back the first good lead we've had in this investigation. For now," she glanced at her wristwatch, "I'm thinking that we'll have a sharp finish. So, Colin, gather the team for a de-brief in half an hour. Thanks, guys," she nodded and smiled their dismissal.

****

It was just under an hour later when Mary Wells parked her Toyota in Meadowhill, just twenty yards from her parents' house and saw that her mother's BMW was in the driveway.

With a sense of foreboding, she was about to get out of her car when a familiar vehicle, parked behind her and glancing in the rear-view mirror, to her inner relief saw it to be the dark blue coloured Mercedes of her brother, Alan.

Greeting him on the pavement, she saw to her surprise that he was accompanied by his wife, Morag, a no-nonsense woman brought up in the tough Easterhouse council estate and often referred to by Natalie as, "…that loudmouthed fishwife."

However, the petite, blonde-haired Morag was no shrinking violet and Natalie had quickly learned that even hinting at any disaffection with or making sly comments about her eldest son, Morag was right there, defending her husband and verbally putting her mother-in-law right in her place.

"Unexpected though it is," Mary hugged Morag to her, "I *am* glad to see you here."

Following his father into accountancy, Alan had through the years built up a small but successful business that in due course, considerably improved their standard of living.

Although now relatively affluent, his wife Morag had never changed, for she still spoke with a strong, gruff Glasgow accent that completely belied her stunning good looks. Utterly devoted to her husband and their two children, she was one of Mary's favourite people and among the first to stand at her sister-in-law's side when Harry had abandoned his wife.

As Mary often jokingly related, it was only by good fortune that Harry and his new girlfriend had quickly vacated the house next door, for Morag was what Mary termed a 'black and white' woman; she could be the best friend or the meanest enemy, for there was no halfway measure with the unyielding Morag.

Making their way up the driveway to the front door, Mary saw the lounge curtain twitch and in a low voice, warned, "She's expecting us, so do not be provoked, no matter what she says."

Turning to Morag she stared meaningfully at her and smiled when raising her hands, Morag replied, "I'll not start anything, I promise, but old bitch or not, she says anything about my family, she's getting it."

By family, Mary took that statement to mean not just Alan, but her father-in-law Michael, too, who two years earlier had been there at all hours to comfort and console Morag, until her own father finally succumbed to cancer.

The door was snatched open by Natalie, who wearing a knee length white dressing robe and her hair tousled, stared at them in turn, then growled, "Why are you here?"

It was Mary who had elected to be the spokesperson and so she asked, "Come we come in?"

"No!"

Feeling her anger welling up inside her, Mary slowly nodded before she puckered her lips, then said, "Fair enough. Just to let you know that he's not coming back, mum. He's asked us to pick up his clothes and he says to tell you that in due course, you'll be contacted by a lawyer to come to an agreement about a divorce settlement."

"And he's not got the balls to come and tell me himself?"

"Might I remind you," Mary calmly replied, "that the last time you met you assaulted him?" though didn't add that she had assaulted her daughter, too.

"I didn't hit him hard enough," Natalie's eye blazed when she scowled.

Mary sensed and anticipated her brother's anger so before he spoke, she reached out her hand to grab at his arm, then quickly said, "All we want is to get his clothes. That's not too much to ask, is it?"

"Well, you're too late," she sneered through gritted teeth. "They've been barbequed."

Feeling a tightness in her chest, Mary quietly asked, "Are you telling us you've burned dad's clothes? All of them?"

"All of them," Natalie sniffed with self-righteous indignation.

It was then to their mutual surprise the door to the lounge opened behind Natalie and a man stepped into the hallway; a tanned man who Mary guessed to be at least her mother's age with silvery white hair and wearing a black polo shirt over fawn coloured chino's and who held in his hand what clearly seemed to be a whisky glass.

Visibly embarrassed, Natalie's mouth gaped open as she stared crimson faced at Mary, Alan and Morag.

"Everything all right, Natalie?" the man hesitantly called out.

"Everything's fine," she snapped back, then added, "Go back into the lounge! I'll be with you in a minute!"

The man disappeared back into the room, but before Mary could speak, Alan, his face masking his disgust, politely said, "Didn't take you long to find yourself another fancy man, eh, Mum?"

Natalie's face turned purple with rage and she hissed, "Fuck you all!" then slammed the door closed.

Stood there facing the closed door, the three of them were slightly bewildered about what had occurred, but it was Morag who broke the silence when she wryly quipped, "I'm guessing our Michael's going to be visiting Marks and Sparks tomorrow, then?"

The tension broken, a laughing Mary and Alan hurried after Morag as she jauntily strolled down the driveway.

CHAPTER FIFTEEN

Seated with them in her kitchen, Mary's father, Michael, wasn't surprised when she broke the news about their visit to his home and his wife's burning of his clothes.

"She was always telling me that the first opportunity she had to get rid of me, she'd make sure I wouldn't be coming back," he half smiled, then wryly added, "Give Natalie her due, she's a woman of her word."

It was while on her way home, Mary had thought hard about disclosing her mother's visitor and finally decided that he'd better know now rather than find out later, so told him, "There was a man there. Someone I think she was, ah, entertaining."

She saw her father quickly glance at Eileen before he asked, "About your mother's age, grey hair?"

"That sounds about right. You know him?"

"I don't know him, but I know *of* him," he shook his head. "She was recently boasting about some guy in the church who was flirting with her. You know what she's like, Mary, always thinks of herself as the bee's knees and that every man she meets is chasing her."

And that's because she makes it so easy for them, though Mary kept that thought to herself.

"Well, if nothing else, Michael," Eileen gently stroked at his back, "you've the opportunity on Monday to fit yourself out with a new wardrobe."

"In the meantime, dad," Mary interrupted, "though I've been meaning to hand them over to charity, there's still some of Harry's stuff in a box in the wardrobe up in the top bedroom if you want a browse through them."

"Might be an idea, hen," he smiled at her then said, "In fact, if you don't mind, I'll go and have a look now."

When they were alone, Mary asked, "How were the kids today?"

"Their usual mad selves," Eileen smiled, then her brow furrowing, she said "About your dad. You don't mind that he's going to be living with me?"

She stared at her for several seconds before she shook her head then replied, "Oh, Eileen, you have no idea how happy I am that he's out of that house in Meadowhill. Natalie was quite literally wearing him down. She's starved him of affection for so many years he was becoming a shell of a man, but look at him now. You and him? God, that's the best thing that could have happened to him and, dare I say it," she stared keenly at Eileen, "you too."

With unshed tears, Eileen met her gaze and nodding, said, "We're taking it slow. I mean, everything, you know," and blushed, "but I feel as if I've met my soulmate and at my time of life too," she broadly smiled. "Who would have thought it?"

They were interrupted by Morven who ran into the kitchen complaining to Mary that her brother had smacked her bottom.

"And why?" her mother quietly asked.

"He said I took his motor car."

"And did you?"

The little girl scowled with guilt then without replying, run from the kitchen.

"Justice administered," Mary grinned.

****

While she and her father cleared the table and washed the dishes, Eileen took the children upstairs for their bath, permitting Mary and Michael to discuss the events of both the previous day and that afternoon.

"I'm sorry you had to find out about Eileen and I before we were ready to tell you and your brothers," he began.

"That's not a problem Dad, and you must know that both Alan and William are as happy for you as I am and I suspect," she smiled at him, "you knew they would be. But I have to ask. Are *you* really happy now?"

He stopped drying the plate to stare thoughtfully at her before he replied, "I was a little uncertain to begin with., I mean, how you and your brothers would take me leaving your mother, but to answer your question, yes; I am really happy and in the last couple of months I feel as though I'm getting my life back. Not just that," he shook his head, "but I'm no longer walking on egg shells, worried about saying the wrong thing or wondering what kind of mood your mother might be in."

"You've really hit it off with Eileen, then?" she smiled at him.

"More than I can explain. And you," he hesitantly asked, "you're definitely okay with us being together?"

"Me? Dad, it's your life, you're a grown man and can make your own choices, but yes, I am happy for both of you."

She frowned when she continued, "I'm only concerned about the trouble mum will make for you because like it or not, she won't make it easy. She'll fight tooth and claw for what she can get out of a divorce and I'm betting too she'll go after your pension fund. That and the house, because let's face it," she grimaced, "she believes she has a certain standard of living and a social standing in *her* community, so like it or not, you'll be portrayed as the bad guy who abandoned his poor wife, albeit she's already taken up with another man."

"About that," his eyes narrowed. "Years ago I might have given in to her and just been happy to be rid of her, but today? No," he vigorously shook his head, "if Natalie thinks she can come after me and I'll just lie down to her demands, then she'd better think again."

"How do you mean?"

"I'm not giving any secrets away, but I think that now our relationship is out in the open and thankfully, you and your brothers approve, but you have to know. Eileen isn't just a widowed woman, hen, she's a lawyer, though of course she hasn't practised for some time. Not since her husband died."

Stunned, Mary stared at her father and heard herself stutter, "What kind of lawyer is she? I mean, what kind of law did she practise?"

"Corporate law for some of the largest UK firms," he said, with a touch of pride in his voice. "After her husband died," he continued, "she took a turnabout with her life and, well, I'll let her tell you the rest. However, the reason I mention it is that Eileen still has connections in the profession and is certain she can call upon them to help me in any divorce action that Natalie takes out against me."

"Oh, well that does come as a bit of a surprise," Mary wiped her hands on the dishcloth and sat back down into a chair.

The door was pushed open by Jamie, who followed by his sister and both in pyjamas, burst into the room.

Smiling widely, Eileen followed Morven into the room, then glancing at Michael and Mary in turn, her face creased when she asked, "What?"

****

It wasn't every evening the children had the opportunity for their grandfather to read them a bedtime story, but before he chased them upstairs to their bedroom squealing and laughing, it didn't escape Mary's attention that Jamie had wrapped his arms around Eileen's hips and whispered, "Good night, granny."

When they were gone, a blushing Eileen joined Mary at the kitchen table with a fresh cup of tea.

"So," Mary slowly drawled, "bigtime corporate lawyer, eh? You never thought to mention that wee titbit when we met."

"I didn't really think it was that important," Eileen shrugged. "What seemed important was that you trusted me with your children's care and well-being. Does me having been a lawyer change that?"

"No, not at all." Mary smiled, "But I am curious to know why, what did my dad call it," her eyes narrowed, "you took a right turnabout away from what I can only presume was a highly paid job."

Eileen sipped at her tea before she replied, "When Jack unexpectedly died I was in a right old mess. I couldn't sleep, I missed or was late for meetings, couldn't concentrate on my job and all in all…the truth is, Mary, I went downhill fast."

Her voice almost broke when she continued, "We had no children and I didn't have any close family and as for Jack, he was an only child and both his parents had died years before. You have no idea, Mary," she grimly smiled, "what it's like being left on your own…"

Her voice faltered and her eyes widened when she realised what she had just said, then placing her hand across her mouth, stuttered, "I'm sorry, I didn't mean…"

"It's okay," Mary leaned across the table to place a comforting hand on Eileen's arm. "Harry buggering off and your husband dying, that's two completely different situations and besides, I had my brothers and my sisters-in-law and my dad too around here all the time. You had no one to share your grief with."

Eileen nodded, then taking a deep breath, said, "Before I knew it, that downward spiral included prescription medicine washed down with alcohol, so months went by without me realising it."

"But you picked yourself up and here you are," Mary brightly said.

"It wasn't easy," she sighed, "and you of all people, left with a toddler and, after a difficult pregnancy, a new born baby and then discovering your husband had run off with someone you trusted and believed to be a close friend. I can only imagine the pain you went through."

"Yes, it was the darkest time of my life," Mary admitted. "Some of the thoughts that went through my head…" she involuntarily shivered, inwardly recalling the dark, sleepless nights alone when she believed her suicide seemed to her to be the best option for everyone.

"But then," Eileen smiled, "I met you and then the children and you have no idea what those meetings still means to me."

"Oh, and now you're a granny?" she teased.

Eileen grimaced when she replied, "That was Jamie's idea. Apparently it was easier saying to a wee pal in the playpark that I was his granny rather than explaining about me being a childminder."

"Well, for what it's worth, it suits you."

"Really?" her face expressed her pleasure.

"Oh, I think so because after all," Mary sighed, "they don't really have a granny, do they?"

"What are you two chatting about?" they turned to see Michael standing in the doorway.

It was then the front door was knocked.

****

Seconds later Michael returned to the kitchen with Mary's neighbour, Bill Howie, behind him.

Dressed in a pale blue coloured shirt open at the neck and grey suit trousers, Bill carried a small, brown leather bag and his weariness showing on his face, he explained, "Sorry to disturb you all and I didn't want to ring the doorbell in case the kids were sleeping and I saw your Beetle outside, so I guessed Michael might be here."

Setting the bag down onto the table, he gestured that Michael sit down then continued, "I won't be long, I just wanted to check your wound and redress the bandage."

It was Eileen who jumping to her feet, politely asked, "You'll stay for a cup of tea?"

Mary saw Bill glance at her before he replied, "Yeah, okay, that'll be lovely, thank you."

They watched as he gently removed Michael's dressing then after examining the wound, replaced the dressing with a fresh one.

"No headache, blurred vision, nothing like that?"

"No," Michael shook his head, "Eileen gave me two paracetamol when we got home last night and I slept fine. Had another two this morning just in case, but no ill effects so far."

"I remember you just take some milk," Eileen laid down a mug in front of Bill.

"Thanks," he slumped down into a chair and exhaled.

"Rough day?" Mary asked.

Bill stroked a hand through his thick hair then grimaced before he replied, "Busy day in the sense that the Department is underfunded, short-staffed and I'm still feeling my way around, getting to know people, that sort of thing. That and more than half the people coming in are not casualties in the real sense of the word. Most of them are just to bloody lazy to book an appointment with the GP," he irately added, then sheepishly said, "Sorry, just blowing off some steam."

She glanced at her father who taking his cue, said, "It's Sunday night, Bill, and we were thinking about getting some fish and chips in from the chippy just up the road on Anniesland Cross. Now, if you don't mind chip suppers two nights in a row and as you bought them last night, how's about you letting us treat you this time?" he smiled.

"Eh, oh, yes, well, if I'm not imposing, that would be great. In fact," he grinned, "I don't think I even had lunch today."

"Then that's settled," Michael nodded then asked, "Eileen, fancy a wee walk?"

"I'll get my coat," she stood up from her chair.

"And I'll get the table set," Mary chipped in.

Minutes after Michael and Eileen had left and remaining seated, Bill watched her set the table and said, "This is awfully decent of you, Mary. I really wasn't expecting this at all."

She couldn't explain why, but she felt a little awkward being alone with him, even though they had sat together the previous evening and shared a bottle of wine.

"Just being neighbourly," she forced a smile, "and after all, you didn't just provide us with chips last night, you patched up my dad too, so we're in your debt."

"There's no debt to repay," he shook his head. "If I'm not being too nosey, the children; do they know about your father splitting from your mother?"

"Ah, we're not telling them," she cautiously replied. "They're still a bit young yet," then went on to relate how Jamie and Morven had decided to call Eileen, granny.

She watched him smile when he replied, "Kids, they're amazing people in their own right. They see things that we don't understand or have forgotten to understand because we have matured into adults. That," he sighed, "and I've learned through the years never to underestimate just how perceptive they can be."

Her brow furrowed when she asked, "Do you have children?"

He softy smiled again when he said "I had hundreds of them, Mary, though never any of my own. The children in the camps, living through such poverty that we in the UK will never understand or hopefully, experience. Yet the camp children…" he shook his head and exhaled. "They find joy and happiness even though they might be half-starved, orphaned, sometimes limbless through conflict or a hundred other reasons being trapped where they are."

She could see the pain in his eyes and feel the emotion emanating from him and was shocked to discover that some part of wanted to reach out and tightly hold and comfort this man, this stranger who only yesterday had stepped into her life.

Instead, she took an inward breath and forcing a smile told him, "I can only imagine how difficult it must have been for you and your colleagues working in such an environment, but you're here now, Bill. Safe."

To divert him from the sombre mood he was in, she asked, "How did you come by your scar?"

"Nice distraction and by my scar, you mean the one here," he touched his forehead, "rather than the psychological ones?" he smiled at her.

She felt herself blush before she replied, "Sorry, was I that obvious?"

"A little," he continued to smile, then jokingly told her, "I fell over one night when I was pissed."

For several seconds she stared hard at him, then eyes narrowing, slowly replied, "But that's not true, is it?"

"Phew. My God, woman, you *are* a Detective, aren't you?"

She continued to stare narrow-eyed at him and after a couple of seconds, watched him defensively raise his hands when he said, "All right."

His mouth twisted as if recalling the incident, then he said, "One afternoon a couple of years ago, in a refugee camp in the Sudan outside a town that isn't even on any map, I foolishly stepped in front of a war lord, who with his rather large and armed gang had come to steal the medicines from our clinic. In my stupidity, I thought I could reason with him, explain that he would get more support from the people if he *supported* the clinic rather than robbed us. Big mistake. I found out later he didn't need the medicines for his gang. No," Bill sighed, "he wanted to sell them to use the money to buy more guns and ammunition."

"And the scar?"

"Ah, that. Well, let's just say when a forehead and the butt of an AK47…" he stared curiously before asking, "You know what that is?"

"Earlier in my career I had a spell with Special Branch, so yes, I know what a Kalashnikov semi-automatic rifle is."

"You continue to impress me, Mary Wells," his eyes widened. "Anyway, one minute I'm trying to be Mahatma Ghandi, the next I'm lying on a camp bed being stitched by…" he licked at his lips, then said, "a colleague."

She didn't miss the inflection in his voice and guessed the colleague was someone he cared about.

"I've seen a few rough scars in my time, Bill, so whoever stitched you up did so with care."

Pokerfaced, he casually replied, "Yes, well, she was very competent when she needed to be."

"Any lasting effects? From the blow to the head, I mean," and realised she was blushing and wishing she had phrased the question better.

However, Bill was way ahead of her and smiling, replied, "Not from the injury, but yes. The fallout with my colleague, *that* took some getting over."

"Is that why you've really returned to Glasgow?" she gently asked.

"Maybe that's part of the reason, yes," he stared curiously at her when he quickly added, "I'm impressed, because you are one shrewd woman, Mary. I can only imagine you must be a hell of a Detective, too."

"Perhaps, not that good because I've yet to find my murder suspect," she smiled and slumped down into the chair opposite.

They were denied any further intimate conversation when the front door was opened and they heard her father call out, "It's only us."

****

Towards the end of their meal, Mary saw Bill fighting a yawn and suggested, "Perhaps you should be getting an early night?"

"Not a bad idea at all," he smiled, then rising from his chair, asked, "Do you mind if I slip away and sorry about leaving you with the dishes."

"No, not at all," Michael responded for the three of them, then added, "Thanks again, Bill, for this," he pointed to his head.

"You're very welcome and tomorrow if you're here," he turned to stare at Mary, who responded with, "Likely, yes. Sorry dad, you and Eileen," she apologetically glanced from one to the other, "You're okay to have the kids tomorrow?"

"Of course," Michael replied and watched as her father squeezed Eileen's hand.

"Well, then," Bill smiled. "If your wound continues to heal I'll have that dressing off and let the air at it."

"I'll walk you to the door," Mary rose to her feet.

Grabbing his bag, she followed him to the front door where opening it, he hesitated before turning to nervously ask, "I know we've just met, but if Michael and Eileen are up for it and you're okay with it…"

To her complete surprise, she heard herself quietly reply, "Yes."

"Oh, right," he suddenly smiled, "Dinner some night it is, then. I mean," he shrugged, "when you're free and we're both off duty, as it were."

When the door had closed behind him, she stood with her back against it and completely stunned, thought; what the hell have I just agreed?

CHAPTER SIXTEEN

Both Michael and Eileen arrived that Monday morning wearing their raincoats over their heads and splattered with rain.

"Raincoats and welly boots day, today," Eileen grinned at the children who seated at the kitchen table were wolfing down their cereal.

"Sorry, but I can't stop, I've my guys out early today," Mary, already dressed and wearing a dark green coloured knee length waterproof raincoat, hurriedly kissed her father on the cheek then, to Eileen's surprise, grabbed and tightly hugged her too.

It was after Mary had gone that Eileen thought about the hug and realised the hug was not just a passing affection, but a complete acceptance that she was now fully a part of Mary Wells life; not her father's new girlfriend nor the paid childminder, but the children's adopted granny and, dare she even contemplate it, more than just Mary's friend.

The very thought caused her to well up and excusing herself, rushed to the bathroom where she happily wiped her eyes of some spilled some tears.

****

DC Alan Hamilton was already in the incident room and had a coffee waiting for his neighbour when Elaine Fitzsimmons arrived.

"Got us a motor," he jingled a set of CID car keys, then said, "Colin Baxter left us Lorraine Gray's address. It's a flat at number twelve, Prospecthill Crescent. Am I correct in thinking that's over in Toryglen?"

"Yep, F Division," she nodded, then slurping the last of her coffee, added, "Right, let's get cracking."

****

At Wells instruction, Colin Baxter selected DC's Tommy Maxwell and John McGhee as the team to lift Martha Foster, the woman identified as Maria Clinton's accomplice, at the time when that morning Foster was due to attend to call upon her client at Maryhill Road.

Both Detectives mutually decided that though the time noted in Colin Baxter's file for Foster to visit her client at Maryhill Road was between 9am and 10am, they would be at the close entrance for eight o'clock; early yes, but better than missing their suspect, they agreed.

Now sitting in the CID car just twenty yards from the close at number one-nine-o-nine with the rain hammering on the windscreen, both nursed a coffee and roll and sausage from the café further down the road.

"How's your missus?" McGhee opened the conversation.

"Still harping on about booking a fortnight in Majorca," Maxwell grunted, then asked, "What about you? Nobody in your life at the minute?"

The pause was enough to make Maxwell suspicious who turning towards his neighbour, grinned, then said, "Come on, who you seeing?"

"I'm not *seeing* her," McGhee muttered and dusted the crumbs of the roll of his trousers. "It's just been a couple of nights out at the pictures and the one meal. Well, two meals, if you count a lunch."

Maxwell began to grin before he pressed on, "And who is she that you're *not* seeing?"

McGhee scowled when he turned to reply, "You're not going to let this go, are you?"

"Let it go? Unless you come across with the details, I'm going to tell *everyone* back at the office you've got yourself a bird and what will that do with your Clint Eastwood image, the man alone against the world?"

With a resigned sigh, McGhee, turned to stare out of the windscreen before he asked, "You promise you'll keep it to yourself?"

"Scouts honour," Maxwell pretended to cross his heart.

"You remember when we were on the last late shift, we attended that call up in Pollokshields a fortnight ago? The break-in to the Galbraith's store?"

"Aye, when the housebreaker's got away with…wait!" his eyes widened and he smiled. "The wee hottie that came out as the keyholder, the manageress. Her with the red hair and the big glasses?"

"Jennifer. Her name's Jennifer," McGhee intimated with the hint of a satisfied grin.

"You fly bugger," Maxwell grinned widely.

"You mean you went back and nipped the manageress? Oh, and as I recall she is a *right* looker, so she is. So, you're still seeing her then?"

But McGhee didn't respond to the question.

Instead he nodded towards the close and said, "That look like a cleaning woman to you?"
Maxwell's head snapped round to see a woman with her anorak hood up exiting an old style dark green coloured Skoda saloon car and carrying a large plastic bag in one hand and a yellow coloured plastic bucket in the other.
Then he replied, "Let's go and ask."
****
When Elaine Fitzsimmons and her neighbour arrived at number twelve, Prospecthill Crescent, Alan Hamilton sighed when he said, "It's a bloody multi-storey with what," he peered up at the building, "ten or twelve flights? Here's hoping the lift's working."
Parking their vehicle in the communal car park, he turned to Fitzsimmons to ask, "How are we going to do this? Ask her about the thefts here or a straight forward Section Two?"
"Depending on her reaction, we'll play it by ear, okay?"
"Okay," he muttered.
To their frustration, they discovered that the two lifts serving the building were both tightly closed with a formal notice that said, 'Out of Order' and a handwritten note attached that declared a lift engineer was due to attend to the repairs that morning.
"What's the flat number," she asked.
"It's on the eight floor," he scowled.
She grinned at his disappointment then said, "Well, this can be your exercise for the day."
A little over ten minutes later, both puffing and panting, they arrived on the eighth floor and discovered the clean and swept communal corridor to be bedecked in assorted pieces of what seemed to be discarded furniture, laid out as though it were a family hallway, with assorted ornaments and plastic flowers in vases that decorated the furniture.
"Seems like someone like's their habitat to be cheery," muttered a breathless Fitzsimmons.
"Right, here we are," she turned to nod to the bright red painted varnished door with the nameplate, 'L Gray' on a tartan background, screwed to the door.
'The Black Bear' cheery bagpipe music ringtone was answered within thirty seconds by a small, thin woman who Fitzsimmons thought to be in her early to mid-seventies, her hair bundled neatly

on top of her head and demurely dressed in a nylon floral decorated housecoat.

Staring apprehensively at the two Detectives, she politely said, "Yes, can I help you?"

Fitzsimmons had a bad feeling in the pit of her stomach when she answered, "We're CID officers from Govan Police Office, madam, and we're trying to trace a Lorraine Gray?"

"Oh," her face registered her suspicion when she replied, "can I ask why?"

As though expecting bad news, Fitzsimmons dully asked, "You wouldn't happen to *be* Lorraine Gray, would you?"

They saw the woman's eyes narrow when she quietly replied, "That's me, yes. So, what's this about?"

****

After using their car radio to contact Force Control, Maxwell and McGhee, with their extremely nervous detainee in the rear seat, waited for almost fifteen minutes for a Traffic vehicle to be directed to their location where, after handing the Traffic cops the keys to the Skoda, they requested it be delivered to Govan Police Office.

"Now, Mrs Foster," Maxwell turned around in his seat, "like I said earlier, we're taking you to Govan where you will be formally detained then interviewed about the theft of a number of items from your client's homes. You understand?"

If he was expecting some outrage, argument or denial of the allegation, he was to be disappointed for without warning, the forty-four years old Foster bent almost double and with her face in her hands, her shoulders shaking as her body was wracked with sobs, she began to loudly wail.

Turning back in his seat, Maxwell quietly suggested, "Back to Govan quick as you can, please, John. I think our friend in the back there is about to have a stroke."

****

Mary Wells was at her desk when Colin Baxter entered and said, "Just heard from Force Control at Pitt Street, boss. That's Maxwell and McGhee on their way in with Martha Foster. I've arranged that they tape record her in the FACU room, if you're okay with that?"

"That's fine, Colin. Heard anything from Elaine Fitzsimmons yet?"

"Ah, that's the bad news. They've telephoned in from Rutherglen Police Office. It seems that our suspect Lorraine Gray isn't as she identified herself to the 'Sweeps 'n Dust' company." He glanced at the handwritten note in his hand and said, "Mrs Gray turns out to be a seventy-four years old widow who lives at the address we got from the company."

"A false name and address?" Mary's stomach churned.

"Aye, according to Elaine, the real Lorraine Gray hasn't a clue who is using her identity and has never heard of 'Sweeps 'n Dust' either. She and Alan are waiting at Rutherglen for a call back after I delivered the news to you."

"Shit!" she slapped a hand on to the desk then said, "Get someone up to the company office in Bath Street…no, wait. Tell Elaine and her neighbour to go directly there and find out what kind of background checks that tuppence-halfpenny outfit are making on their employees. I'd like to think that if they're sending their staff into vulnerable people's homes they're conducting *some* sort of vetting checks!"

Angry now, she continued, "And if they're *not* vetting their staff, tell Elaine to find out who their contact in the Social Work Department is that's *arranged* their cleaning contract!"

"Right, Boss," he slowly drawled and made a mental note to send Janey McPhee in to Wells with a strong coffee.

About to leave the room, she quickly called out, "Hang on, Colin." He turned to see her take a calming breath then she said, "You're supposed to deliver your response to the offer of promotion to the Divisional Commander, today. What time have you to see Mr Metcalfe?"

"Eh, he said to be at his room at eleven o'clock."

"And have you made your decision?"

Mary suspected he wasn't happy with his decision when he slowly nodded and quietly replied, "Yes. I'm going to accept the promotion, albeit it means a return to uniform. Me and my wife agreed with my retirement looming within the year and so many months I've left, it's the best choice."

He'd liked to have added it wasn't really his choice, but figured the DCI had enough on her plate without him whining to her.

She nodded then said, "I'll come downstairs with you when you go to see Mr Metcalfe, so knock on my door when you're ready, okay?"

"Okay, Boss. I'll head now and call Elaine back at Rutherglen. Anything else?"

"Not that I can think of at the minute, other than let me know when Tommy and John get here with their detainee."
"Will do," he nodded and closed the door.
Mary slowly shook her head.
It had seemed so simple; bring in the two suspects and in particular, the reputed brains who had organised the thefts and the storing of the property in Elizabeth Bradley's flat, but now?
Two steps forward, one step back, she angrily thought.
She stared down at her desk and wondered; how the hell are we going to find the fake Lorraine Gray?
****

In the small, CID general office within Rutherglen Police Office, Elaine replaced the telephone and nodded her thanks to the DC seated at the nearby desk.
Turning to Alan Hamilton, she told him, "Colin Baxter says the boss wants us to visit the 'Sweeps 'n Dust' office to speak to them about their vetting procedure and find out anything, if there's anything to find out," she sighed, "about the woman calling herself Lorraine Gray."
"And?" he suspected there was more.
"We've also to ask who it is in the Social Work Department that decided the company got the cleaning contract from the Council."
"How is that going to help us find this woman?"
"It's not, but Colin says the boss is really pissed and she suspects that whoever approved the contract to the company should be taken to task, because their vetting procedure appears to be shite. His words, not mine," she smiled. "Anyway, Colin thinks the boss isn't going to let it go and that she intends making waves and probably make an official complaint that the Council have approved a company to enter pensioners and vulnerable people's homes without properly vetting them."
"She's got the bit between her teeth, then," he grinned.
"Oh, aye," she soberly nodded, "and we both know what Mary Wells is like. Honesty is her middle name," she said and with a cheery wave to the seated Detective, beckoned that they leave to visit the Bath Street office of the cleaning company.
****

DC Tommy Maxwell's quip to his neighbour, John McGhee, about their detainee having a stroke wasn't completely without foundation, for upon their arrival in the rear yard at Govan Police Office and when helping her from the car, without warning, Martha Foster began to hyperventilate.

However, some quick thinking by McGhee saw him grab the empty brown paper bag from the rear seat that earlier had contained his roll and sausage, then sitting Foster down, had her breathe into the bag. Minutes later, Foster, now calmed down and breathing regularly, was escorted into the charge bar where in front of Inspector Kenny Herdman, she was formerly detained under Section Two.

Addressing Maxwell, Herdman said, "Colin Baxter says to tell you that you're expected in the FACU room where the tape recorder has been set up."

Leading the anxious woman up the spiral, wrought iron staircase that led from the uniform muster room to the CID suite, the equally anxious Detectives, fearing she was on the point of collapse, quietly debated whether or not to summon the police Casualty Surgeon to confirm if indeed she was fit for interview.

However, the decision was taken from them when a weak voiced Foster stopped in the CID corridor and with trembling lips, glanced at them in turn when she asked, "If I'm dead honest and I tell you everything, will I get out of here by tonight?"

****

"That's Tommy and John back with their detainee, Boss," Baxter informed Wells from the doorway.

"Good," then glancing at her watch, she said, "That's almost eleven o'clock, Colin. We'll let the guys get on with their interview. Are you ready to go downstairs and see Mr Metcalfe?"

"Yes, I'm ready," he exhaled through pursed lips, acutely aware that if things went as the Divisional Commander had explained, by the end of this week, if not in fact today, could possibly be his last working in the CID.

Minutes later, Baxter now wearing his suit jacket and more nervous than he expected to be, pushed open the Chief Superintendent's door to permit Mary to enter first, then following her into the room, was taken aback to see the ACC, Keith Meadows, already seated in one of the three chairs in front of Metcalfe's desk.

Meadows turned as they entered and smiled at Wells and Baxter in turn.

It was Metcalfe who opened the conversation when he formally greeted them with, "DCI Wells and DS Baxter, so glad you could join us."

"Please," he waved a hand, "sit down."

His hands folded in front of him, Metcalfe swallowed a rough cough, then staring at Baxter, said, "I understand from the DCI that you've made your decision, Colin."

"Yes, sir. If the promotion is still open, I'd like to accept the appointment to Inspector."

"Ah, well, there's a wee bit of a problem there," Metcalfe's bushy eyebrows knitted.

"Sir?"

"DS Baxter," he stared gravely at him, "at the recommendation of DCI Wells, who you should know I fully support and with the full authority of ACC Meadows, it is my pleasure to inform you that you will not be promoted to uniformed Inspector, but instead will be promoted to *Detective* Inspector here at G Division and will, in the fullness of time and at the discretion of your DCI, be appointed to take charge of the sub-Divisional CID unit at Pollok Police Office."

He watched as stunned, Baxter's mouth fell open, then quickly added, "The downside is that the appointment will occur after the ongoing murder investigation, for I understand from DCI Wells that you are an integral part of that investigation and quite simply, she cannot afford to lose you. You are then I suppose, a victim of your own success," he broke into a wide smile.

"That all said, the promotion parade that will ratify your new rank *will* occur as soon as possible at the conclusion of the current investigation. Is that suitable?"

He didn't get the opportunity to respond for he suddenly found himself on his feet and his hand being grasped by Keith Meadows who was telling him, "Congratulations, Colin. If anyone deserves this after the service you have provided to the Department, it's you." Suddenly he felt himself being turned by Mary Wells, who grinning, said, "I'm a woman, so I'm permitted to give you a wee kiss," then planted her lips against his cheek.

Leaning across his desk, Metcalfe took Baxter's hand in both of his, then vigorously shaking it, added his congratulations too.

"Right, then," Meadows took charge when he said "We'll leave you in peace, Geoff, while Mary, Colin and me head back upstairs. And thanks," he too shook Metcalfe's hand.

When the three of them cleared the room and were making their way back up the wide staircase, Meadows quietly whispered to Mary, "Is it me or is Geoff Metcalfe not very well?"

****

Seated across the desk from Wells with a fresh cup of coffee, courtesy of Janey McPhee, Keith Meadows smiled when he said, "I think that went rather well."

"Indeed it did," she grinned. "It's nice on occasion to be able to reward long and loyal service and nobody deserves it more than Colin Baxter."

"And you think he'll be able to sort out that mob at Pollok?"

The question at first took her aback, but then she realised she shouldn't really be surprised for Keith Meadows was a man with his finger on more than a few pulses, and so she replied, "I think now that Martin Reilly has vacated the position, sir, and knowing that Colin's a man who can cope with most situations, he'll be fine. That's not to say there isn't a bad atmosphere that still exists there, but right now I've got DI Sammy Salmon there until Colin takes over and if I'm honest," her brow furrowed, "Sammy's come on pretty well in the recent past and though he might be feeling a bit challenged up in Pollok, it's a good learning curve for him."

"I think you're doing a good job as DCI too, Mary, so I trust your judgement and again, that was a good call suggesting Colin for the DI position, albeit it's a little unusual he remains in the same Division."

"Now," he arched his fingertips, "How's your murder investigation progressing?"

It took Mary a little over ten minutes to fully brief Meadows and he sensed her frustration when she informed him of the subterfuge by the woman calling herself Lorraine Gray.

"And you've been unable to establish any link between the real Lorraine Gray and the suspect?"

"Not to date, no, but as I say, I've two of my guys interviewing the third member of the gang, so I haven't yet an update as to what she fully knows."

"A mystery right enough," he slowly exhaled, then reached for his coffee.

Taking a sip, he then asked, "This bee in your bonnet about the Council awarding the cleaning contract to the company. I'm guessing you suspect maybe nepotism or perhaps corruption?"

"It's a possibility," she breathed out. "I just can't get my head around the fact that the Council would approve a company who do not properly vet their staff, yet permit them to enter vulnerable people's homes. I mean, sir, what if that hits the media? There would be an outcry and I believe the Council would be open to not just criticism, but perhaps even legal action too."

"But you intend to pursue it?"

"If there's something there to pursue, then yes," she firmly nodded. Her eyes then narrowed when she tentatively asked, "You have some misgivings about it?"

"Not about pursuing an allegation of nepotism or corruption, no, but I am concerned it might cause you to deviate from your true aim, the investigation of the murder."

"Rest assured, sir," she shook her head, "that remains my number one priority."

"Okay, then I'll take that as read. Now," he grimaced, "not that I'm being nosey, but when I get home this evening and I tell Mattie about my day, she's bound to ask how you're doing and I do *not* mean professionally. What am I to tell her?"

Mary smiled, recognising the concern in his voice and his roundabout way of asking about her mental and emotional state, so without any resentment, she, replied, "I'm in a really good place now and believe me," she held up her hand, "you have absolutely no need to worry about me. In fact, if anything I owe you my thanks for, well, sticking with me through the bad patch."

"That, I assure you Mary, was a given. You are one of my brightest and best managers in the Department and I do not say that lightly. Now, before I get all mushy," he rose to his feet with an embarrassed smile, "be sure to keep me apprised of both your murder investigation and after you conclude your rant with the Council, prepare me for any fallout I might expect and *particularly* if your inquiry should reach the ears of the media."

"Understood, sir," she respectfully rose from her chair.

CHAPTER SEVENTEEN

When Meadows had gone, Mary sat back and reflected on her morning.
It had started off with high hopes that her team would detain the two named members of the gang of thieves, but ended with a sour note when Fitzsimmons and Hamilton discovered the principal character was a ghost.
However, Tommy Maxwell and John McGhee were still interviewing the third suspect, Martha Foster, who might have some information that would enable them to trace her accomplice.
In the meantime, Fitzsimmons and Hamilton were conducting their own inquiry and had yet to call in any result.
All I can do now, she thought as she sipped at her lukewarm coffee, is wait.
****
When Alan Hamilton pushed the front doorbell for the 'Sweeps 'n Dusts' premises in Bath Street, it was Agnes Flynn, the company secretary, who answered the door then without asking them to identify themselves, rudely barked in a voice full of sarcasm, "He's in. Have you come to arrest him?"
Turning on her heel, she limped in front of them then stopped at the main office door and pushing it open, stood to one side to permit them to enter.
A little confused, Elaine Fitzsimmons led the way into the large room to see the owner, Alex McLean, sat at his desk, his hair dishevelled, jacket lying untidily on the floor by the desk, his tie lying loosely, the top three buttons of his stained shirt undone and apparently the worse for wear with drink.
"Who are you?" he slurred.
Ignoring him, she turned back to Flynn to ask, "How long has he been like this?"
"Hmmm, more or less since his slut of a wife kicked him out last Wednesday," she quietly replied. "He'd been staying at the Central Hotel for a few days, but they charge like the light infantry, so instead he's been bunking down here."
"And the drinking?"

"Since last Wednesday," she sighed, "when he went home and found out from his wife, Jackie, that every Tuesday she was shagging their gardener. Wouldn't surprise me if the gardener wasn't the only one, though," she muttered almost as an afterthought.

Stifling a grin, Fitzsimmons turned to Hamilton to tell him, "I don't think Mr McLean is going to be much use until he's sobered up; however," she then turned to Flynn, "perhaps you might provide us with some information?"

****

It was Flynn's suggestion that if they were to discuss the company's business, they retire to a coffee shop a little further down the road, moodily explaining, "There's too many ears in that place and I'm not wanting someone telling the boss something that might get me fired."

She'd sighed when her face reddening, she had added, "I'm an unmarried, middle aged woman with a bad limp and not got a man in my life and I don't think at my age I will get one, Detective, so though I do hate to admit it," her brow knitted, "I just cannot afford to lose this job."

Now seated around a table in the coffee shop and their drinks ordered and while Hamilton took notes, Fitzsimmons asked, "Is your employee, Lorraine Gray, known to you?"

Flynn's eyes narrowed when she asked, "Blonde-haired woman, about forty, maybe? Oh, aye, I know her. Well," she sniffed, "when I say blonde-haired, I'm talking dyed blonde or more probably, bleached blonde hair."

"So, you do know her?"

"Only on the occasions she's visited the office, but I don't know her *personally*, if that's what you mean."

"Okay," Fitzsimmons slowly drawled, "tell me. What vetting checks do you conduct when someone applies for a job with the company?"

Flynn stared keenly at her before she slowly asked, "Do you know how much it costs to *properly* vet someone?"

"Ah, no, I can't say I do."

"Well, vetting one individual is an expensive business," she explained, "and a lot of it depends on what type of employment you are advertising. I mean, if you want to conduct a pre-employment check, you're talking about the basics that are references, then you have to be satisfied the referees themselves are suitably qualified to provide such a reference. If the job involves driving, you can also ask for DVLA check to ensure the employee has no penalty points or any disqualifications because of motoring offences, such as drunk driving, because that would affect an employer's vehicle insurance." She paused for a few seconds then continued, "If you're worried there might be a criminal record, you can, with the permission of the prospective employee, also contact the Scottish Criminal Records Office for a background check to find out if they have outstanding convictions. If your business involves handling money, you can even make inquiry with the Inland Revenue to discover if your new employee is a bankrupt or contact previous employers to inquire why they left their previous employment. There's any number of ways to check a prospective employee but," she rubbed her thumb and forefinger together, "it all costs money to make these checks and with a staff of over eighty women, can you imagine what the bill would be for conducting proper vetting checks for them all?"

"So," Fitzsimmons slowly asked, "what vetting checks were carried out for your company's staff?"

They watched Flynn smile, but not a smile that was pleasing or humorous.

No, a sarcastic smile that with a shake of her head explained her retort, when she said, "Vetting check? The vetting check, Detective, was me occasionally nipping down to the Mitchell Library with a list of names and addresses to check the voters roll to confirm that the prospective employees did reside at the addresses they put down on their application forms. *That* and the boss man sitting behind his chair at the time the women were interviewed, his fat gut telling him, 'Aye, she'll do.' *That's* what the vetting process is for the company."

"So, the upshot is there was no real vetting?"

"No real vetting," Flynn agreed with a shake of her head then added, "Though some of the women would voluntarily bring in a birth or a marriage certificate that we'd photostat and put into their file, but we never really insisted on any identification."

"Let's return to Lorraine Gray. Is there anything you can tell us about her, anything at all? Even what she was like?"

"Is she a suspect for killing Lizzie Bradley?"

If she wanted to keep Flynn onside, Fitzsimmons decided to share at least some information and so said, "We suspect that with Lizzie and another couple of women, they were stealing from client's homes.

As for suspecting her of killing Lizzie, that's what we'll be asking her when we find her."

They watched Flynn's eyes narrow in thought before she quietly repeated, "What was she like, then? Hmm, well, my first impression was she was smart. Aye," she slowly nodded, "that's the first thing I thought when I saw her. A smart, definitely intelligent woman who turned up really well dressed for her interview. So why then, I remember wondering, is she coming to work here as a cleaner to clean old folks houses and, Detective, I'm talking about old folk who half the time have soiled or pissed themselves too."

Seconds passed until Fitzsimmons asked, "You said she was dyed or bleached blonde, but did she have any distinguishing features? Something that might stand out, like a tattoo or something?"

"Don't remember any tattoos," Flynn's lip curled, "but she spoke with a plummy accent."

"A plummy accent?"

"Aye, like she was a cut above everybody else," she sniffed. "Not a woman from one of the council's housing schemes. Like she had a better upbringing, you know? Polite, that's another word I'd use to describe her. A good-looking woman, too. I'd say she was probably in her mid-forties, but definitely looked younger, as though there was money spent on fancy salons and hairdressers. As if she looked after herself. Oh, and she drove a car, too."

"Any idea of the make or model? Colour even?"

"No," Flynn drawled and shook her head, "but I once heard her offering to give her pals a lift, I remember that."

"Were the staff asked to provide their vehicle details, you know, for getting from to one client to another?"

"Not usually, no, but I can tell you from memory that when she was interviewed for the job, she said she didn't have a car, so that's why I thought it funny at the time she was offering her pals a lift."

"Her pals. Who were they, can you recall?"

"Oh, that's easy enough to remember," she grinned. "Pair of dunderheads, the two of them. That wee woman Clinton, who was as quiet as a mouse and the other one the nervous one, always taking time off with something wrong with her, but I think the something was her man giving her bleaching's because it wasn't the first time she came to work with a sore face. Martha Foster is her name."

Flynn didn't miss Fitzsimmons glance to Alan Hamilton, and cautiously asked, "Is that the other two you are talking about? Maria Clinton and Martha Foster?"

There seemed little point in denying it, so Fitzsimmons nodded and replied, "That's them."

She then stared at Fitzsimmons and Hamilton in turn before she asked, "Lorraine Gray. That isn't her real, name is it?"

"Afraid not," Fitzsimmons agreed, "and that's why it's vital we trace her."

Flynn's eyebrows knitted when she said, "I always thought there was something phony about her. "I just knew it!" she hissed as she continued, her face halfway between a grimace and a grin. "I was thinking that the three of them and Lizzie. Oh aye," she quickly nodded, "she was in on it too, whatever it was! Thick as bloody thieves the last couple of months, the four of them!"

They watched Flynn take a deep breath of satisfaction as though having been proven correct, then Fitzsimmons asked, "You mentioned to our colleagues when they came on Wednesday that your boss is a bit of a lady's man. Do you know if he tried it on with Lorraine Gray?"

Her brow furrowed when she replied, "Do you know, I would have been surprised if he didn't try it on with her."

Seconds passed as she reflected on the question then slowly nodding, she continued, "I think he did, but if I'm again if thinking correctly, she knocked him back, maybe because at that time he was shagging Lizzie."

"Would your boss have any details about her, like, maybe her motor or where she really lives?"

"So, the address is phony too?"

"Afraid so," Fitzsimmon's nodded, more than a little impressed how sharp Flynn was in picking up on things.

"No, that plonker was the owner and the boss of course, but it was me that really run the company," she shrugged with a hint of pride. "To be honest. When it came to the running of the business, aye," she nodded, "he was okay for getting the contracts, wining and dining the clients. Never invited me to any of his fancy meetings, though," she sniffed. "But when it came to the day to day running of the business, or who was supposed to be working where, he didn't have a scooby about that."

She peered myopically at Fitzsimmons when she asked, "Do you know his wife is divorcing him?"

"After the revelation that he was having an affair with Lizzie Bradley," Fitzsimmons permitted herself a smile, "I thought that was a given."

"Aye, well, he's been spouting off about counter-divorcing her, if there is such a thing. The problem is," her voice lowered as if concerned about being overheard, "though McLean is always going on about it being his company, that's not really true."

"How do you mean?"

Again in the same low voice, Flynn took a deep breath before she said, "It's his name on the paperwork, but there are three directors with shares in the company. Him, his wife and her father who is the major shareholder."

"And her father, who is he?"

Flynn slowly smiled when with a note of satisfaction in her voice, she said, "Ronnie Atkins. You might not know him, Detective, but he's better known as Ronald Atkins, the man in charge of Procurement Services for the Glasgow City Council."

****

It was Tommy Maxwell who accompanied by his neighbour, John McGhee and Colin Baxter, knocked upon Wells door, then entering, said, "That's us finished interviewing Martha Foster, Boss, if you've got minute?"

"Come away in," she beckoned them with a wave of her hand.

When the three men were seated with Baxter's notepad on his knee and readied to take notes, it was Maxwell who with a grave face, said, "We're hearing a malicious rumour, Boss, that the auld guy there," and nodded to Baxter, "is getting promoted. I mean, that can't be true, can it? Not at his age."

She smiled and shook her head, not at all surprised at the speed of the office rumour machine as Baxter, pretending to be annoyed, replied, "Cheeky bastard, DC Maxwell."

Both grinning, Maxwell and McGhee rose from their chair to shake Baxter's hand.

Then with a polite, "Can we get on, please?" from Mary, the three men resumed their seats.

"Martha Foster," Maxwell began with a brief resume of Foster.

"John agrees with me, Boss, that she's a right timid woman and easily susceptible to the slightest hint of persuasion. It also seems from her domestic situation she's married with two teenagers, that she's much put upon by her husband and her sons. She tells us she's actually holding down three cleaning job…"

"Three?" surprised, she interrupted.

"Aye, she's working for 'Sweeps 'n Dust' and also earns cash in hand for three nights cleaning after hours in a pub in Cadder, where she lives, and cash in hand three nights cleaning a shop, again in Cadder."

Wells felt her face pale when she asked, "I take it then aside from her day job, she's working *six* nights a week?"

"Aye, and to be honest, boss, regardless of what she's been up to," he risked a glance at McGhee, "I can't but help feel sorry for the poor wee woman. She's worried sick that she'll lose her job with 'Sweeps 'n Dust' and we'll inform the DHSS about her cash in hand jobs."

"I'm guessing her man's not working?"

"No," he shook his head. "She tells us that he's not worked for over ten years. His *nerves*, she says," he almost spat the word out, "but apparently that doesn't stop him hitting the bookies and the pub. That and her sons are on the dole, too."

"Right, I'm guessing that the extra cash from the ornaments and jewellery was her motivation for being part of the team thieving from the clients?"

Again, Maxwell glanced at McGhee, then nodding, said, "Her pal at the company, this woman Lorraine Gray, she persuaded Foster that if she helped her steal from the clients, she'd get a right few quid and she'd be able to give up at least one of her other jobs and have some time to herself, Gray told her."

"How did she meet Gray? Did she know her socially or before Gray commenced work at the company?"

Shaking his head, Maxwell replied, "She says it was when Gray joined the company, she suggested she take Foster for a coffee and that's when Gray put it to her, about thieving from their clients. She said Gray told her that because of their age, the clients wouldn't miss bits and pieces, that the stuff would likely get thrown out anyway, when the old yins turned their toes up, so why not benefit from it? Course like I said," he shrugged, "Foster is so easily manipulated, she didn't like to say no. One thing she did say about Gray," his brow wrinkled, "she told John and me that Gray was a hard woman to say no to."

"What, she was scared of Gray?"

"Mmmm, she didn't actually say she was *scared* of her," his face creased, "but it was like she didn't know how to tell Gray she didn't want to do it, that she didn't want to disappoint her. Stealing the stuff, I mean."

Mary glanced at Baxter then asked, "They don't know, do they?"

Baxter shook his head when Maxwell asked, "Know what, Boss?"

"Elaine Fitzsimmon's and Alan Hamilton tracked down a Lorraine Gray at the address she gave the company, but she turned out to be an elderly woman who has never heard of *our* Lorraine Gray."

"Bugger," a surprised Maxwell turned to stare at his neighbour, who leaning forward asked, "We any idea who this fake woman Gray is?"

"Not at the minute, John," she shook her head, "but Elaine and Alan are working on it, so let's keep our fingers and toes crossed they bring some good news back. Now, was Foster able to provide any information about the murder of our victim?"

"If what she told us about herself is true, Boss," Maxwell sighed, "she has no idea where Bradley lived, that it was Gray who always took the stuff from her and Clinton and just like Clinton told Elaine and Alan, Gray said she had a guy over in the north side of the city who would give them a price in total for the property, then they would divide it up four ways when they'd finished their thieving."

Her brow furrowed when she asked, "Does she know if Gray delivered the stuff to Bradley at the flat?"

Maxwell grimaced when he replied, "Sorry, Boss, never thought to ask that question, but I will do."

"Another thing, Boss, though it might not be of any evidential use," McGhee interjected, "me and Tommy don't think that Foster had a clue about any value of the items she was stealing. We're of the opinion that if it looked shiny or expensive, she'd take it without being aware of what it might be worth."

"What about an alibi for the time of the murder?"

It was Maxwell who replied, "According to her shift rota, on Tuesday morning, Foster was at the client's house in Maryhill Road, the tenement from where we lifted her, and says she went from there to another client's address in Milton. She drives an old-style Skoda motor car to get between jobs, an absolute wreck that can't possibly be MoT'd. We'll follow through with checks at both houses, but to be honest if she's our killer…" he finished with a shrug and shake of his head.

"Nevertheless, get it done," she nodded, then said, "Right now, we can't charge her with any specific thefts because frankly, we don't know what property came from which client; however, before you release her from detention, guys, I want you to explain to her that charges might later be libelled, but she will do herself some good if she cooperates. If she agrees, show her all the property and have her admit what she's stolen and from whom and in *particular*, the address. It might be that she can also identify property stolen by her accomplices. That way we can then show the complainers the property and hopefully, have it identified and if nothing else, we know where to return it. Got that?"

"Boss," they said in unison and rising from their chairs, left the room.

Mary sat back in her chair and arching her back, exhaled, then asked Colin Baxter, "Nothing in yet from Elaine and Alan?"

"Not yet, boss."

The phone on her desk rang and when she answered it, was greeted by Sammy Salmon who said, "Okay to speak, Boss?"

"Hold on," then turning to Baxter, told him, "let me know when Fitzsimmon's and Hamilton get back."

When he'd left the room, she said, "How are things in Pollok?"

"No problem, boss," he breezily replied, then asked, "I'm hearing a rumour Colin Baxter's getting the job here?"

"My God, Sammy, news travels even faster in this place than I thought. And yes, Colin's being promoted and though it usually means a transfer to another Division, Mr Meadows agreed to my request to keep him here. He's the very man who'll sort out Pollok after that bugger Reilly caused so much disaffection among the troops up there."

"Couldn't agree more," Salmon replied. "He's a good man and with his experience, he'll soon have the place sorted."

"What about you," she hesitantly asked. "Any issues this morning?"

She heard him take a breath before he said, "When I got the guys together for the briefing this morning, Donnelly tried it on, but I had to ask him to accompany me to the office here, where I regret to inform you, I told him in no uncertain terms if he was unhappy at Pollok, by the end of the day I'd have him transferred back to uniform."

"Fucking hell, Sammy!" wide-eyed, she couldn't help herself and grinned.

"How did that wee threat go down?"

"Needless to say, he thought he'd call my bluff, so you *might* be getting a phone call of complaint."

Stunned, she took a couple of seconds to compose herself, then formerly told him, "DI Salmon, you have autonomy in running Pollok sub-Divisional CID, so any decision you make for the benefit of the Department, you have my complete backing. Is that clearly understood?"

She could almost hear him grin through the line when he formerly replied, "Understood, Ma'am!"

"Now anything else doing?"

"Nothing worth troubling you at the minute. What about your end?"

The next couple of minutes were spent discussing the murder investigation, but interrupted when a fist hammered on her door that was then thrown open by a red-faced and wild-eyed DS Hugh Donnelly.

"I want a word," he growled as he strode into the room.

"I'll call you back," she calmly said into the phone, then replacing it into the cradle, stared at the angry DS before she evenly said, "Detective Sergeant Donnelly, you do not barge into my room then demand that you have a word. Is that clear."

Standing in front of his desk, she saw the venomous glare in his eyes and for one brief heartbeat, thought the sturdily built Donnelly might reach across the desk to assault her.

As subtly as she could with her eyes fixed on his stare, surprised herself that it was the silly things she noticed about the burly, hostile DS; seeing that he had badly shaved for there were tufts of bristle on his chin and one cheek, his old-fashioned tie askew and poorly knotted and his shirt collar had not been ironed.

Fearing he was about to assault her, Mary drifted her right hand the few inches across the desktop towards the round, solid glass paperweight that her son, Jamie, had bought her for fifty pence at the nursery fete, with the intention if he come any closer, he was getting the paperweight right across his face.

But then she saw his face undergo a sudden change from red to chalk white, when he hissed, "Your nancy boy up in Pollok, he threatened to return me to uniform! *Me* that's been in the CID longer than anyone here!"

Hands flat on her desktop, she realised then with some relief he was all bluster and wind and sat back before she slowly replied, "Two things, DS Donnelly. Firstly, no, you are *not* the longest serving member of my CID," she continued to calmly stare at him, "though I agree, you have been here a while. Perhaps I should consider moving you to another job to motivate you, for it seems to me that you're unhappy in your current position."

Before he could respond, pokerfaced, she stared hard at him when teeth gritted, she hissed, "Secondly, if you ever use a derogatory term for one of my officers, regardless of that officers' gender or rank, I *will* have you disciplined! Do I make myself clear!"

She saw the uncertainty in his eyes, but then as if to bolster his own defence, he sneered, "I'm taking this further."

Pretending not to understand, her face reflected her curiosity when she politely asked, "Taking *what* further?"

"I'm being picked on here, so I am," he pointed a forefinger at her, his hand shaking as he fought to control his rage. "This is bullying, so it is. You've always had it in for me."

Leaning forward onto her elbows, her hands clenched tightly to stop them from shaking, she slowly shook her head then quietly said, "DS Donnelly, in the privacy of this room, between you and me, you are a complete dick! You swan about at Pollok office, hardly do a day's work and abuse the trust of the DC's who are your team. You evade any responsibility and believe that the job owes you a living. Well, guess what, *pal*," she glared at him, "you have absolutely nothing to complain about because now that your wire, Martin Reilly, is gone, as far as I am concerned, your career as a CID officer ends here. I am recommending that as a career incentive, you be transferred to uniformed duties, effective when the personnel find a position for you. You are dismissed for the remainder of the day so I suggest you return home and await a call from the Personnel Department. Now get the *fuc*k out of my office!"

Shocked, he could only stare down at her and that's when out of the corner of her eye, she saw movement in the corridor outside, just beside her open door.

His body shaking, with one final hateful stare, Donnelly turned and stamped wordlessly from the room.

Seconds later, Colin Baxter and DS Donald Corbett strode into the room.

"You okay, Boss," Baxter stared worriedly at her.

What she wanted to reply was no, my stomach's churning and my body's trembling and my throat's parched and I really need to pee, but she forced a smile, then replied, "I'm okay, yes."

Sighing, she softly asked, "You heard all that?"

Clearly embarrassed, Baxter replied, "DI Salmon phoned down to say that…I mean, he said he'd just heard that DS Donnelly was on his way down to confront you and he was a bit worried about Donnelly's, eh…attitude, I mean. He thought Donnelly might have been, ah…"

"So, you two thought I might need handers, is that it?" she interrupted him with a smile.

It was Corbett, the shaven headed and broad-shouldered, red bearded rugby player who interjected with, "Ach, no, boss. You're Mary Wells. We were here in case it was Donnelly who needed help."

"Bugger off, the two of you," she pretended to growl, then when they were leaving the room, loudly called out, "Thanks guys."

CHAPTER EIGHTEEN

If she were honest, the confrontation with the aggressive looking Donnelly had given her a bigger fright than she was willing to admit, but smiled when she thought of Colin Baxter and Donnie Corbett outside the door, ready to come in and support their DCI.

What does that say about you, Mary, she thought with inward pride. As for her threat to return Donnelly to uniform, now that she had informed him of her decision, she had little option but to carry out the action, though instinctively knew from the grapevine that it would be a popular decision.

It wasn't in her nature to be so harsh with her subordinates and with a heavy heart realised that in one sense, though it had been Martin Reilly's failure to deal with him, it was also a failing on her part that she had been unable to motivate him.

However, some people, she involuntarily shook her head, were beyond helping and reasoned that no matter what opportunities Donnelly had been given or would be offered, he'd simply continue to shirk his responsibilities, as he so often did with his team of two DC's when he'd off-loaded his work onto them.

Reaching for the phone, she was about to dial the internal number for the Personnel Department at Pitt Street when the door was knocked, then pushed open by Colin Baxter, who entered and closely followed by Elaine Fitzsimmons.

"Wee update, Boss," Baxter said as they made for the chairs recently vacated by Maxwell and McGhee.

"Please let it be good news," she replaced the phone, then grimly smiled.

"Yes and no, Boss," Fitzsimmons began. "Let me start by saying that Alex McLean, the owner of 'Sweeps 'n Dust,' was out of his face when Alan and I got there this morning. Seems his wife has kicked him out and he's now living in the office. However, we spoke with the secretary, Agnes Flynn, who informed us that the vetting system is, quite frankly, non-existent. They check names and addresses in the voters roll in the Mitchell Library, but that's it."

"So, our mystery woman probably dug the name Lorraine Gray out of a voters roll from any library in the city and stuck it on the application form."

"Seems likely, yes," Fitzsimmons nodded.

Mary glanced up when Alan Hamilton appeared in the doorway carrying two mugs and waved him into the room.

Handing his neighbour a mug, he drew up a third chair and quietly sat down as Fitzsimmons continued.

"Flynn isn't supportive of her boss and to be honest, I think she's actually the one who's running the business. She couldn't give us much of a description of the suspect other than to tell us she's in her mid-forties, good looking with dyed or bleached blonde, well-spoken and drives a vehicle, but doesn't have a description of the vehicle."

"Nothing in the suspect's file about a vehicle?"

"No," Fitzsimmons shook her head, "we asked that, but she didn't declare owning or having access to a vehicle."

"To continue," Fitzsimmons glanced at Hamilton. "Flynn knew that the other two, Clinton and Foster, were associating with our suspect and is of the opinion that the suspect was manipulating them both."

"Thinks that Clinton and Foster are a right pair of dummies, Boss," Hamilton interrupted with a grin.

Mary stared at him before she shrugged, then quietly said, "Or perhaps they're two women who have been manipulated for most of their lives, Alan, and found themselves in a situation where a self-serving, scheming woman persuaded them that she was their friend and offered them the opportunity to improve on the humdrum and awful life they are leading?"

The tense silence was broken when Hamilton, his face pale, nodded then soberly said, "Sorry, Boss, that was completely inappropriate of me."

"It's not a rebuke, Alan," she shook her head, "but sometimes as the polis we have to look at the overall picture and from what we've gleaned so far, Clinton and Foster are not hardened criminals. They're simply two women who find themselves in a worse situation than their lives already were. I've an idea that Clinton and Foster are so used to being put down, this woman Gray, who to them probably seemed suave and smart and offering them her friendship and the opportunity to earn some cash, must have seemed like a blessing to them both. Yes," she nodded with a sigh, "they might later be charged as thieves, but the day that we as individuals forget our compassion is the day we have to wonder, are we in the right job? Now," she abruptly turned to Fitzsimmons, "you have more?"

"You asked us, to inquire about the contract that the company obtained from the Council? Well," she related that Alex McLean was a third owner in partnership with his wife and the major shareholder, Ronald Atkins, the father of Jackie McLean and the man in charge of procurement for the Glasgow City Council.

Mary slowly smiled when she said, "Right, Elaine. You and Alan take a wee turn up to the Fraud Squad at Pitt Street. Ask for…no," she shook her head, "I'll call him instead and give him a heads up you're coming. DI Fraser McManus, do you know him?"

Fitzsimmon's glanced at Hamilton and saw him shake his head before she replied, "No, can't say our paths have crossed."

"Well," Wells smiled, "tell him everything you know about this man Atkins and eh," she almost smirked when she added, "be prepared to be charmed."

When Fitsimmons and Hamilton had left, she told Baxter, "Now that besides the deceased's prints, we have Clinton and Foster's prints, have the Fingerprint Department check all the prints lifted from the seized ornaments and once they've discounted our two suspects and our victim, any common prints that are left must likely be those of our fourth woman, our suspect. I know it's a longshot, but ask the Fingerprint Department to try for a comparison with the little we know of her description."

"Will do, boss," he nodded, then asked, "Any ideas how we're going to ID our suspect?"

"I'm open to suggestions," she sighed, then eyes narrowing, added, "This reference from both Clinton and Foster about our suspect mentioning a resetter in the north side of the city. It might have been that she was trying to impress them both, but have someone contact the Maryhill and Baird Street Divisional Collators. Who knows," she shrugged, "they might just have recorded somebody in their rolodex who isn't on the PNC."

When Baxter left the office, Mary took a breath to prepare herself then lifting the phone, dialled the internal number of the Personnel Office at Pitt Street.

When her call was answered, she identified herself then said, "I'd like to speak to the Superintendent, please, regarding the transfer of one of my officers to uniformed duties."

****

DI Sammy Salmon was having a good day.

Standing in the small, general office, he was speaking with the uniformed CID clerk when a disgruntled Hugh Donnelly returned to the Pollok Office. Wordlessly, though nosily enough for the DI and the clerk to hear, Donnelly emptied the contents of his desk into a cardboard box then snarling under his breath, left the building.

"And good riddance," the clerk muttered, only to grimace at Salmon when he said, "Sorry, sir."

"No need to be sorry," Salmon grinned at him. "I agree with the sentiment."

Suspecting that Mary Wells had dealt with Donnelly, he returned to the DI's room and phoned the Govan incident room to speak with Colin Baxter, who confirmed that, "Aye, Sammy, the boss gave him his books. He arrived back there yet?"

"Just gone. Came in, collected stuff out of his desk, then went without as much as a cheerio," Salmon couldn't help but grin.

"Well, I for one am glad I don't have to deal with him when I get there," Baxter replied with some feeling. "The guy was an absolute waste of space. With Reilly away too, that should improve the atmosphere anyway."

"Anything doing in the murder investigation?"

"No, other than we're still looking for the woman who was using the name Loraine Gray."

"She a strong suspect for the murder?"

"At the minute, she's the *only* suspect for the murder."

"But if she's killed Bradley, why leave the stolen property there in the flat? Particularly that expensive ruby ring."

"That's what the boss was wondering," he heard Baxter sigh, then suggest, "Maybe she's panicked?"

"Aye, well, until she's caught, we'll need to wonder."

****

Striding through the expansive Fraud Squad's general office to the small, glass enclosed booth that was the DI's room, Elaine Fitzsimmons wasn't prepared for the man who occupied the room. Politely knocking on the door, it was pulled open by a stout, bespectacled man in his early fifties whose florid cheeks matched his loudly patterned tie and flowery red coloured braces. Loudly, but cheerfully, he greeted them with, "DS Fitzsimmons, DC Hamilton. Come in, come in."

The brightly lit, but windowless room was occupied by a large wooden desk that overflowed with beige coloured cardboard files, two grey coloured, four drawer metal cabinets and two chairs in front of the desk that DI Fraser McManus beckoned Fitzsimmons and Hamilton to occupy.

"Now, Mary Wells was on the blower," he tapped the telephone by his right hand. "I understand you might have a case for me? Something about a Council employee?"

Having mentally prepared her brief, Fitzsimmons spent the next fifteen minutes relating the circumstances of the murder investigation that brought 'Sweeps 'n Dust' cleaning company to their attention, then the interview with Agnes Flynn. Concluding her story, she informed McManus of Mary Wells concern about the complete lack of vetting for the company's staff and the allegation that the major shareholder was the Council employee, Ronald

Atkins, who was in charge of procurement for services for the different Council departments.

"The vetting isn't really my remit, but I do understand Mary's concern about any company that would permit unvetted staff to enter the homes of the elderly. If the media got a hold of *that* one," he heavily sighed as he shook his head, his mind considering the public outcry that would follow.

They watched McManus's bushy eyebrows knit when he thoughtfully continued, "If this as you say is all true and, dear lady, I have no reason to doubt the veracity of your findings," he smiled graciously at her, "then it should easily be checkable and if so, we're talking here about an abuse of power entrusted to an individual for the public good and for that individual's *private* gain; the very definition of corruption."

However, she was long enough in the tooth to recognise there might be a problem and so asked, "Something troubling you, sir?"

"You say this company employs something like eighty women or more?"

"According to the secretary, yes."

"And," he sighed, "you understand that if the individual or individuals responsible are prosecuted and convicted of corruption, there is a real likelihood that the company will fold?"

Fitzsimmon's felt her chest tighten when she asked, "You're thinking that those women will all lose their jobs?"

"Regretfully, that is more than likely," he slowly nodded, "even though they are probably all innocent of any wrongdoing."

He sighed once more then continued, "However, as police officers, we cannot ignore the fact as there is the strong likelihood that a crime has been committed and no matter the consequences, now the matter is reported to me I have no other option than to investigate the circumstances."

His eyes narrowed when he asked, "So, as I understand it, there are three shareholders. The husband, his wife and this man Atkins, the wife's father?"

"That's correct, yes."

Sitting back in his chair, he gently stroked at his bulbous nose with a stubby forefinger, then slowly said, "While I have no doubt that all three are aware and likely colluded that Atkins granted the contract to his daughter and son-in-law's company and therefore laid them open to prosecution, if the three are put before a court and charged as such, at the time of the pleading diet it is likely they will temporarily be suspended from operating the company while a trial date determines a verdict. Until that time, which might be months or whenever, is there no one who could step up to manage the company? Someone who could, say, fill the gap while the case is being considered at Crown Office?"

It was when Hamilton turned towards her, his expression already paralleling her thoughts, that she said, "There *is* a possibility, sir, that the company secretary, the woman I mentioned, Agnes Flynn, who while I'm certain she suspected the corruption, I'm just as certain she isn't a part of it. In fact, when you conduct your investigation, sir, it might be worth your while to consider speaking with her."

****

Having arrived early for her ten o'clock appointment with the lawyer, Natalie MacDonald, had taken care with her hair and make-up that morning as well as dressing in her favourite skirted suit. Accompanied by her new beau, John Green, the silver-haired church elder, she sat impatiently in the anteroom outside the lawyer's office. Aware the receptionist was watching, she loudly tut-tutted, then hissing, "That's now ten-fifteen," persistently glanced at her wristwatch.

"Go and ask that receptionist how much longer I have to wait," she waved Green towards the receptionist's desk who at her bidding wordlessly left his seat to make the inquiry.

Returning, he told her with a nervous smile, "She says it shouldn't be much longer, a few minutes at the most."

"Huh," Natalie huffed and tightened her grip on her handbag.

A little over five minutes later, they were ushered into the lawyer's office where introducing Green, Natalie spent ten minutes furthering her case for divorcing her husband and during which, she forced some tears that she gently dabbed with a lace handkerchief.

"Can I point out that you did not bring this to my attention at your previous visits, Mrs MacDonald," the lawyer politely reminded her.

"Well, I wasn't aware at the time he was fuc…I mean, messing around with another woman, that *slut* my daughter hired as a childminder," she huffily replied.

"And you now have evidence that your husband, eh, Michael, has been in a relationship with this woman for some time, Mrs MacDonald?" asked the young woman.
"Oh, months if not years," she sniffed, then arching her back, said, "And yes. I myself saw them kissing in the Kelvingrove Park."
Which doesn't actually constitute a sexual relationship, the lawyer thought, but wisely didn't comment of the alleged sighting other than to ask, "And this gentleman who has accompanied you here is…" her eyes drifting towards Green, the lawyer left the question hanging.
"Just one of my many close friends from our church," Natalie made the point with a forced smile.
"Ah, of course," the lawyer bent her head to scribble some notes, yet inwardly thought, pull the other one.
Staring at what she had written, the lawyer then calmly asked, "So, you now wish to sue your husband for adultery rather than as you previously indicated, the irretrievable breakdown of your marriage. Is that correct?"
Natalie's eyes narrowed when she asked, "My understanding is that if I sue him for adultery, I can keep the house and I'd get most of his pension, whereas if I divorce him because of the, what you said, the irritable something, I would have to share everything with him? Is that right?"
"The irretrievable breakdown," the lawyer corrected her then added, "In layman terms, that's more or less correct."
"Then I want to sue him for adultery," she hissed, her chin jutted out to show her determination.
The lawyer, a young woman in her early thirties who specialised in divorce actions, had seen and represented all sorts of individuals who had passed through her office and was not fooled by Natalie's theatrical attempt to be the wronged woman.
What she saw when she glanced at Natalie was a vengeful woman out to get what she believed she was owed, but whether that belief was genuine or not, she had no way of knowing. What for one second she did not believe, however, was that the gentleman with her, this Mr Green, was just a close friend.
Nevertheless, the angry woman *was* her client and so, leaning forward, gave what she believed to be the best advice when she began, "Adultery is a difficult thing to prove, Mrs MacDonald, and

could involve the use of a private investigator that could over a period of time, prove to be costly. If your husband decided not to defend an action against him for adultery, the divorce might be granted within six to eight weeks from the time of lodging the papers at the court and any joint savings, pension benefits or property would be awarded at the discretion of the court."

She paused to let this information sink in, then continued, "I must say that even if your husband agrees to the divorce, where there exists acrimony where money and property is concerned and if neither party agrees on a settlement, it can be a long, drawn out affair and again, I must warn you, it *will* prove to be extremely costly."

"I said I want to sue him!" Natalie surprised the lawyer by slapping her hand down onto the varnished desktop. "As far as I'm concerned, he's not getting anything and it's your job to ensure that, isn't it!"

She could see there was no reasoning with the older woman and glancing at Green, saw him staring sideways at Natalie with narrowed eyes as if seeing her for what she really was.

Forcing a smile, the lawyer drew her notepad towards her then said, "As you wish. Now, some details of where I can send papers to your husband, if you please."

****

For Mary Wells, it had been a long day and she eagerly looked forward to getting home, but not before all her team had returned to the incident room, some dispirited after a fruitless day attending to actions while others, like Fitzsimmons and Hamilton after their visit to DI McManus at the Fraud Squad, had good news to relate albeit their news did not directly impact upon the murder investigation.

So too DC's Maxwell and McGhee reported their interview of the suspect, Martha Foster, who had since been released from detention after being informed that in the fullness of time, charges of theft would be considered.

"And," Mary addressed the team as she carried on from Maxwell's short briefing, "before she was released from detention, Tommy and John had Foster identify objects that she herself had stolen and from whom and where, so that gives us the opportunity to make the rounds and interview then obtain statements from a number of complainers. I would add that it is also our intention to bring in the second identified suspect, Martha Clinton, who will also be brought to Govan and re-interviewed and likewise given the opportunity to assist us by identifying the objects she has stolen. That should again provide us with further names and addresses of complainers. I know, guys," she held up a hand and slowly shook her head, "that it's a long and laborious process, but if we can narrow down the items to our outstanding suspect, the fake Lorraine Gray, it might take us a step forward to identifying her and then interview her regarding the murder. The other positive side," she exhaled as she grimly smiled, "is that for every object that is recovered, a crime report for theft will be created and likely every Division where the theft occurred will be sending us their thanks because we're inadvertently helping with their detection statistics."

The hand raised and question asked, predictably by DS Donnie Corbett and which raised a laugh among his colleagues, was, "And does that mean a grateful bottle of the good stuff will be arriving from these Divisions, boss?"

To more laughter, she sarcastically replied, "Aye, Donnie, I can see *that* happening."

"Any questions so far?" she cast her eyes around the room.

"You weren't happy about the cleaning company staff going into old people's homes without being vetted, boss," the young female DC, Fiona McCloy, called out from the back of the room. "How are you going to deal with that?"

She glanced briefly at Fitzsimmons before she replied, "The short answer is, I don't know and to be honest, I don't think I can. DI McManus will be handling the corruption allegation against the company's directors, but whether or not he can incorporate that into his investigation, I really can't say. Yes," she nodded, "it's shameful and immoral what the company was doing, failing to vet their staff, but illegal?" she shrugged.

"Aside from the allegation of corruption, I can't think of any law requiring companies to vet their staff, that was broken, so we'll wait and see how DI McManus gets on. Anything else?"

When no one spoke up, she said, "Right, then. Before you go, you'll no doubt have heard that DS Donnelly is taking a break from CID duties and returning forthwith to uniformed duties. DS Baxter will be in charge of making a small collection to buy him a farewell gift, so I'll leave it to your discretion if you wish to contribute. Other than

that, see you all sharp tomorrow."
Ignoring the low voiced and whispered, "That bastard? That'll be right," and "No way would I even give Donnelly the time of day," among similar comments, Mary made her way from the incident room to her office, planning to shelve the rest of her paperwork till tomorrow.
In the corridor, she turned when hearing her name called.
"Ma'am, telephone call for you in the general office," Janey McPhee told her.
"Right, can you transfer it to my office, please Janey."
A minute later, she picked up her phone to hear Janey telling the caller, "Putting you through now."
"DCI Wells."
"Mary, is that you, hen?" she heard her father ask.
She knew that he'd never phone her at work unless it was urgent, so felt her chest tighten when she hurriedly replied, "Dad! Everything okay? The kids all right?"
"They're fine, Mary, it's, well," she could hear her father's intake of breath, then his voice lower when he said, "It's Harry, your Harry. He's here at the house and he's wanting to speak to you."

CHAPTER NINETEEN

Forcing herself to drive at a moderate speed, Mary's mind was awash with questions as to why her ex-husband would visit her and try as she might, couldn't come up with a viable reason.
Turning into Ancaster Drive, her mind registered Eileen's brightly yellow coloured Beetle which was parked in front of a rusting, shabby looking white coloured Ford Escort van with one black coloured rear door that clearly had replaced the original door. Mary also saw the van had sometime in the past, suffered a bump to the driver's side too and correctly guessed that's what Harry was using these days.
After switching off the engine, she sat staring out of the windscreen, preparing herself to meet the man who had deserted her and their children, the man who had tried in vain to first persuade, then took

her to court to force her to sell the house; the house in which their children had been born and were growing up in.

The man who despite Mary's lawyer's letters, refused to take or even show any interest in visiting or meeting with his children.

The man, who again despite repeated requests, refused to pay any kind of monetary contribution towards his children's upbringing.

Her teeth gritting, she fought the urge to scream out loud, to snatch open the door and march into the house and tell him to fuck off, to get out and never darken her doorstep again.

Taking a deep breath, she slowly exhaled then checking herself in the rear-view mirror, felt sufficiently composed to face him.

****

Her father must have been watching for her arriving, for he opened the door to admit Mary and nodding, told her, "He's in the front room with the weans."

Her first thought was to go straight into the room and tell the children to go upstairs, but reminding herself she would be calm, she slowly nodded before she replied, "I'll send them out, dad. You don't mind staying till he leaves?"

Michael looked at his daughter, his face pale, then said, "I'm going nowhere till that deceitful, two-timing bastard is out of your home, hen. When you send the kids out of the room, I'll be sitting in the kitchen while Eileen takes them upstairs for their bath."

"Thanks, dad," she smiled as she squeezed his arm, then handing him her coat and handbag, made her way into the front room.

The first thing she saw was Jamie, sitting on the couch, his hands in his lap and his face deadpan as he watched his father bounce a giggling Morven up and down on his knee.

Turning, Harry saw Mary and in a falsetto whisper, said, "Oh, oh, here's the boss."

She couldn't help herself when, arms folded, she said, "Hello, Harry. Introduced yourself to your daughter, have you?"

She saw his eyes widen as the snide remark hit home and gently removing Morven from his knee, he set her down to stand on the carpeted floor.

"Jamie, Morven," she addressed them with a forced smile, "away upstairs, the both of you. Granny Eileen's got your bath running."

It didn't escape her attention that while Morven looked confused and glanced at Harry; Jamie took his sister's hand then ignoring his father, led her from the room.

"See you later, kids," Harry called out with a wave, while Mary thought, over my dead body you will.

"Sorry to burst in like this without phoning first," he smiled at her. Staring at him, she could see that in the years since she'd last seen him, his hair had thinned out, his skin looked blotchy and he'd obviously lost weight. Unshaven with several days' growth, he was wearing a stained boiler suit and working boots that were both grimy and paint stained.

She decided to remain standing, that to sit down would seem like he was being invited to remain, so she replied, "And exactly why have you *burst in* like this, Harry?"

She watched his eyes narrow when staring at her, he continued to smile and said, "You're looking good, Mary, really good. The weight loss suits you and, well," he shrugged, "I don't know what it is, but you're looking younger too."

"Thank you," she coldly replied, "and I'll ask again. Why are you here?"

She saw him take a deep breath as though preparing himself to explain, then his arms wide, he replied, "I miss you, Mary. That's why."

She felt a cold chill sweep through her when stuttering, she said, "You *mis*s me? The woman who days after giving birth to our daughter who you abandoned for the woman who I thought was my close friend? You *miss* me?"

Still standing with her arms folded, she then took a few steps towards the curtained window before she continued with, "What's the real reason that you are here and please," she held up her hand and shook her head, "don't give me that old bullshit about missing me."

She saw him swallow several, times as though seeking to find an explanation for his arrival, but then his shoulders sagged when he said, "I've wanted to come by a few times, but…"

"But your new wife didn't think it was a good idea, eh?"

His startled expression confirmed what she thought.

Licking nervously at his lips, he stared up at her and for one awful moment, she thought he was about to burst into tears, but then he composed himself and said, "I fucked up, Mary, leaving you. I didn't know what I was doing. She played with my head and, well…"

His head drooped into his hands and Mary stared wordlessly at him, surprised that though she had once loved this man, she had absolutely no feelings for him now for as far as she was concerned, he was as much a stranger to her as anyone passing her by on the street.

It was then she instinctively realised why he was really here and so she softly asked, "So, you and Beth have split up?"

His head snapped up when stunned, he replied, "How did you know?"

"What happened, Harry? Why have you split up?"

She watched him gulp air before he said, "She's changed. Since the wee girl was born, she's no interest in me anymore and it's killing me."

Mary hadn't known the child was born, but guessed that like her, Beth had maybe gained birth weight or perhaps no longer was as sexually active as Harry wished and that, she further guessed, caused the rift between them.

A humourless smile played on Mary's lips when she responded with, "And now that Beth has kicked you out…oh, wait, I'm presuming she has kicked you out?"

With obvious reluctance, he nodded.

After having resolved not to be baited, not to lose her temper, she found herself sneering when she snapped at him, "So, you've been kicked out by your girlfriend and thought you'd wander back here and into my life and the lives of the children you abandoned? Is that it, Harry? Have I got that right? You've not just abandoned me and the kids, but now you're abandoning your new woman and her baby too!"

Surprised, she took a step back when without warning, he jumped to his feet, fists clenched and teeth bared, then snarled, "That's you all over, isn't it, Mary? So *fucking* righteous! Always think you're so much smarter than anyone else!"

The door flew open to admit Michael, who carrying a frying pan that he brandished above his head, cried out, "You, ya arsehole, get out of here now or you're getting it!"

Shocked, both Mary and Harry stared at him, before Harry his hands raised muttered, "I didn't come looking for trouble, okay? I'm going."

Michael, his face chalk white and physically shaking, but still threateningly holding the frying pan, stepped to one side to permit Harry to pass him by, then seconds later, the front door slammed.

No sooner had that occurred then Eileen, who had unknown to them been standing in the hallway, entered the room, an aerosol can in one hand held in front of her.

Her eyes fluttering, Mary spluttered, "What were you going to do with that?"

"Blind him," Eileen scowled.

"And you dad," she turned to him, "Really? A frying pan?"

His face creased with embarrassment when he shrugged, "I couldn't find the rolling pin."

****

Once the children were settled in bed, Mary, her father and Eileen sat around the kitchen table discussing Harry's visit.

It was Eileen, her expression thoughtful, who gave Mary cause to wonder when she said, "I don't think I knew what to expect when he arrived and said he was your husband or rather, your ex-husband, but he just didn't seem the type, if you know what I mean."

"The type?" Mary smiled.

"Well, look at you," Eileen smiled too. "You're a good-looking woman, extremely smart and dare I say it, you've come through quite a lot since he left you and not just survived, but you're back doing what you're so obviously good at and believe me, I don't say that lightly."

"Thanks…I think," Mary continued to smile, then with a sigh, added, "I was a young newly promoted DS when I met Harry. He'd just started his own plumbing business and was working every hour God sent to build it up. Police pay in those days wasn't good so every penny was a prisoner," she continued to smile. "Then, about six or seven years ago, when I'd just made DI and Harry's business had taken off, we decided to start a family and so Jamie arrived. It was a hard time for me because pregnancy just didn't suit me. So much so that we or rather Harry," she grimaced, "decided that one child was enough. Anyway, the best laid plans and all that nonsense went awry when I fell pregnant with the wee one."

Her brow knitted when she said, "I think it was about then that Harry and I started having problems though of course I didn't know about her next door, Beth, who I thought was my close friend."

"Aye, some friend," Michael muttered with a touch of derision in his voice.

"The rest you know," Mary shrugged. "I'm busy in labour giving birth to Morven, he's away canoodling with her next door and then I find the letter telling me he's leaving."

"Probably the best thing that happened to you, in a roundabout way, I mean," Eileen forced a smile, then teased her with, "Now you're a free woman, self-sufficient and a definite catch for a lucky man."

"Aye, like that's going to happen."

"Oh, I don't know, Mary," she glanced at Michael, then said, "Tell her."

"Eileen!" he glared at her.

"Go, on, tell her," she urged.

"Tell me what, dad?"

He slowly took long breath then said, "When Bill next door took me to the hospital, he was asking me about you. That's all."

"Oh," she stared suspiciously at her father, "and what was he asking or more to the point, what did you tell him?"

Michael glanced at Eileen before he replied, "I'd said you were on your own, divorced with two kids I mean, and he asked if you were seeing anyone."

Taken aback, Mary had mixed emotions about what her father told her; curiously excited that a good-looking man was asking about her, yet after her failed marriage, apprehensive too about forming any kind of relationship again.

"Well," she struggled to respond, "If he's interested I'm sure I'll find out in due course, but let's not dwell on it. Now, you two," she asked, keen to divert their thoughts from any idea about a new romance for her, "how did your day go and have you made any plans yet?"

"I spent a few bob today," her father grinned. "Eileen and the kids took me shopping for a new wardrobe that included an obligatory visit to MacDonald's, as you might have guessed."

"And handsome he looks too, in some of his outfits," Eileen reached across the table to hold his hand.

"Good for you, dad," Mary grinned.

"As for me," Eileen's eyes narrowed, "I spent half an hour on the phone to a former colleague, someone who owes me a huge favour from my days in the firm, who your dad and I are to meet on Thursday morning, where she'll discuss his pending divorce with a view to representing him."

"That's good news, dad. Thursday morning? I'll contact the local nursery and see if they'll take the kids for the day. They've been there before and enjoyed it. If you're able to drop them in about nine, the session is till four-thirty, so will that be enough time for your meeting?"

Michael smiled and then glancing at the wall clock, turned to Eileen to say, "Maybe we should be going, love. Especially if we've all got an early rise tomorrow."

"Oh," Eileen rose from her chair then addressed Mary, "I've made you a pasta that's in the fridge and there's some garlic bread too. Five minutes in the oven for them both. I'm guessing you'll not have had a full lunch."

"You're a star," Mary hugged her tightly then saw them to the front door.

Minutes later, the pasta and bread in the oven, Mary stood in the kitchen, her arms folded and her back to the worktop, reflecting on what her father had told her.

She smiled and even alone in the kitchen, could feel her face redden when she had so eagerly accepted Bill Howie's invitation to dinner. Accepted it?

My God, she blushed furiously.

He hadn't even finished suggesting it when she'd anticipated the invite and said yes.

Of course, there was no denying he was a reasonably handsome man and if his experience was anything to go by, widely travelled too. But there was something about him, Mary's eyes narrowed. Some baggage he was carrying with him that caused her to wonder; the brief mention of a former colleague.

What was it again, that he'd said?

Some *fallout* with a colleague.

Yes, that was it, she now recalled.

Could it be that colleague was the woman who had stitched his wound and that to Mary suggested a fellow doctor or maybe even, a nurse.

Was the colleague the woman who had been in his life?
Well, Mary Wells, she told herself, there's no point in guessing.
If the dinner *does* go ahead, then no doubt I'll hear in due course.
If not, what have I lost?
Turning, she bent to fetch her food from the oven.

CHAPTER TWENTY

DS Colin Baxter was in a happy frame of mind when he arrived at Govan Police Office that dull, overcast Tuesday morning.
Breaking the news the previous evening to his wife that yes, he was being promoted to Inspector, but that he was to remain in the CID had been treated first with stunned silence, then grabbing her coat she'd insisted they dine out to celebrate.
The dinner had been followed by a taxi home where the happy night had continued upstairs to the bedroom.
Pushing open the door to the incident room, he was still smiling at the memory of their drunken lovemaking, but his thoughts were rudely interrupted when behind him, Mary Wells called out, "Morning, Colin penny for them."
"Eh, morning, Boss," he replied, acutely aware his face was flushed and he reeked of peppermint toothpaste.
Staring suspiciously at him, Mary sniffed at the air and deciding to ignore his embarrassment, instead asked, "Anything from downstairs about the murder?"
"I checked the dookit, but apart from the usual morning correspondence, nothing doing."
"Right," she nodded then told him, "I'm having a coffee in my office. When Donnie Corbett gets in, ask him to pop in to see me. I've been that tied up with the murder, I'm wondering what's happening in the general office about what else has been happening in the Division."
"Will do, Boss," he nodded then sighed with relief when she closed the door behind her.
In the corridor outside, she almost bumped into her FACU Constable, Janey McPhee, who greeted her with, "Morning, Ma'am, that was DI Salmon phoning down to inquire if you were in. Asked

if you could give him a phone as soon as you arrived."
"Did he say why?"
"No, but according to the nightshift crime reports, I believe there was a serious assault up in Pollok, last night. A shooting."
"Okay, thanks, Janey," she headed into her office.
Dialling the direct number for the DI's room at Pollok, Salmon greeted her with, "Morning, Boss, have you been told about the shooting here last night?"
"Only heard a minute ago from Janey McPhee. What do we know?"
"Nothing much. It seems there's been an ongoing violent war here between two rival drug gangs…"
"Yes, I know about that, but the last information I had was from Martin Reilly who reported that the issue between the gangs had been resolved and there was no longer any concern of further violence."
"Well, he lied," Salmon bluntly replied. "The guys here tell me that Reilly, rather than confront the issue, faked the report to indicate though they were still dealing on their own patches, they'd shaken hands to defuse the situation and thereby avoid unnecessary police attention."
"The lying bastard," she angrily burst out. "That's what Reilly reported," Mary rubbed at her forehead, then asked, "What happened last night?"
"I received a call about three in the morning that a gunshot had been heard in the Househillwood Crescent area, but when the uniform cops arrived there was no trace of any culprits. However," he breathed heavily into the phone, "the reporter, a young guy on leave from the army and staying with his parents, was insistent it *was* a gunshot he'd heard. Suggested it was low calibre that in turn suggests a handgun. I'm not into firearms, but if this guy's in the army, I suppose he knows best. Anyway, the cops were a bit sceptical at first, but when they inspected the general area and remember it was dark, they discovered a massive pool of blood on the pavement, but no victim."
He paused then continued, "However, earlier that evening though we've no evidence that it is connected, there was the report of a black coloured Morris Marina stolen from outside a house in Glenlora Drive, a short distance away; the car was discovered about four hours later with the back nearside door lying open, the ignition

block torn out and indications of blood staining on the rear seat, but again, no trace of anyone at the locus. Seems very coincidental, though."

"I agree," she nodded, then asked, "Hospital checks?"

"I had the nightshift attend at both the local Casualty Departments at the Victoria and Southern General hospitals, but no trace of any wounded or dead admittances by gunshot. However, I am of the opinion," she heard him wearily sigh, "The car was used to transport whoever the victim is to some location, wherever that might be."

"How much blood was at the locus, you reckon?"

"I'd say from what I saw and remember, it's just my opinion, it seemed a substantial amount of blood and well, whoever the victim is, they must be critical, if not from the actual wound then certainly from blood loss."

She heard a door opening in his background and someone speaking, then a minute later, Salmon told her, "That's an anonymous telephone call to the uniform bar. Seems a woman called in saying the victim was taken away in a dark coloured car by two males, but no further description of the vehicle. And boss," she heard him take an intake of breath, "I didn't have you called out because frankly, there was nothing at the time to indicate we had a murder; nothing I felt I couldn't have dealt with myself."

"You've no reason to explain, Sammy. You were correct in your assessment at the time."

A thought occurred to her, then she asked, "The locus where the blood was discovered. Any trace of a shell casing?"

"No, nothing like that, though of course I'll have a wider search made now it's daylight."

She spoke her thoughts when she said, "My experience of firearms used in shootings, admittedly limited and not that extensive, is that an automatic or semi-automatic weapon ejects the spent cartridge whereas the cartridge in revolvers, once the bullet is fired, has to be physically ejected."

"So," he seized on her explanation, "you think that if the shooter used a semi-automatic, he or she must have picked up the empty cartridge or else the absence of a shell case might indicate it was a revolver that was used?"

"That's what I'm thinking, yes," she agreed.

"Right," she made a sudden decision, "I'll come up to Pollok while you gather what information you have and we'll put our heads together and see what we can decide how you can progress this." Ending the call Mary, still wearing her coat, grabbed at her handbag then hurried through to the incident room where drawing Elaine Fitzsimmons and Colin Baxter to a corner, explained what she knew of the shooting and her intention to travel to Pollok police office. "Elaine, as my acting deputy, you conduct the morning briefing and anything I should know, you know where to find me. Colin," she turned to him, "Actions as you see fit, okay?"

"Boss," they acknowledged together as she left.

****

Rather than take a CID car when she knew the vehicles were vital for her officers to continue their citywide inquiries, Mary drove her Toyota to Pollok and arrived a little under fifteen minutes later. Making her way to Sammy Salmon's office, she found him at his desk, studying a report from the nightshift CID.

"Nothing new since I spoke with you," he greeted her with a shake of his head.

It didn't escape her attention that the normally fastidiously smart DI was unshaven, his tie undone and his dress shirt now open at the collar and rumpled with his suit jacket hung over the back of the chair.

"Rough night," she smiled as she slid into the chair opposite.

"Wouldn't have been so bad, but I'd had a couple of glasses of vino with my dinner, so I wasn't expecting a two am call-out. Had to get a bloody taxi here," he scowled.

"What about local Intel regarding who might be responsible?"

He sat back in his chair and clasping his fingers together behind his desk, sighed before he said, "I spoke with the nightshift, but frankly, it seems to me that the morale in this office has been so bad the guys aren't even speaking to each other, let alone sharing their Intel. Reilly, curse him," he almost spat out, "had been so divisive in his attitude towards his staff that the atmosphere has been toxic and the DS's are more intent on one-upmanship than they are collectively working as a unit. And that," he wearily shook his head, "has definitely got to change. I had a word with them when I arrived, but the DC's in particular are so sick of what's been going on…" he suddenly stopped and stared at her, his eyes widening in disbelief

when he stuttered, "Sorry, Boss, that sounds as though I'm…"
"Blaming me?" she interrupted then nodding, continued, "And so you should be, Sammy. I'm the DCI; I'm the individual responsible for the morale and well-being of my staff, so you are absolutely correct. "I've let things badly slip and I should have known what's been going on here. If it's anyone's fault that the Pollok CID are failing, it's mine and there's no point in blaming Martin Reilly or even his sidekick, Hugh Donnelly, because I've known all along what a pair of useless and devious gits they both are."
She drew a long breath, then sighing, added, "But that stops now. When Colin Baxter's promotion is ratified, I'll be getting the DS's and DC's together and having words. However, for now, let's concentrate on your shooting."
It was then that Salmon's phone rung.

****

It was DC's Kenny Maxwell and John McGhee who were issued the action to visit the city's northside Divisions, where they were instructed to speak with the Divisional Collators for any local information those officers might have about an individual who was known or suspected to be resetting stolen property.
While both Maxwell and McGhee were a little sceptical and suspected their inquiry was a bit of a longshot, nevertheless, they both agreed it was worth pursuing.
After stopping first to grab rolls and sausage and a couple of coffees, their first port of call was the small, crowded with filing cabinets Collator's office at D Division's headquarters in Baird Street.
After identifying themselves to the large, jovial and amiable constable, "Just call me Dunky, eh?" he first insisted they had a cuppa then, when the three were seated, Maxwell explained why they'd called upon him.
"So, from the little you know," Dunky's eyes narrowed, "you suspect the resetter is working somewhere in one of the city Divisions north of the Clyde. However," he grimaced, "you're also saying that the woman you're hunting has been lying, even to her associates, so what makes you think even after her telling the other two a pack of lies, that the resetter is real?"
"The truth is, we don't know if she's been winding them up, Dunky," Maxwell shook his head, "but we need to follow up every lead, no matter what. We're pulling out all the stops to trace this

woman, because she's our number one suspect for the murder."

"Oh, I understand that, Tommy," he nodded, "but here's a thought. What if your resetter is a woman?"

Maxwell glanced at McGhee, then said, "Go on."

Dunky's eyes narrowed in thought when he said, "I'm hearing the odd titbit from the beat men who work over in Sighthill that are getting told by their informants there's been sightings of some of our regular housebreakers and shoplifters seen coming and going from one of the high rise the flats, some of whom have been carrying plastic shopping bags and bin bags, but *not* when they're leaving the flats, you know? Anyway, I've a pal from my days on the beat there who lives in the building that's been mentioned and kind of keeps his nose to the ground about the comings and goings of the tenants and their visitors. Fact is," he sighed, "he's a widower with a pair of bum legs and no family, a lonely wee guy that spends much of his day at his window and his nights just watching the television. I keep in touch and occasionally pop by with a wee half bottle for him and have a cuppa while I'm there, just to see how he's doing."

His brow furrowed when he continued, "Cutting a long story short, he more or less confirms what the beatmen are telling me, though from what he says, the neds are taking their stolen property to a woman called Alison Steele, who lives on the on the seventh floor."

It was McGhee who brow furrowed, asked, "If he's seldom out of his flat, Dunky, how does he know who the neds are visiting?"

"I asked him that. He got that from one of his neighbours, a woman that does his shopping for him. How she knows, I have no idea," he shrugged.

"Is this woman Alison Steele known to you?" asked Maxwell.

"Nothing on my rotadex for her, no, and nothing on the PNC either. But," he smiled and raised a forefinger, "I *do* have a William Steele who turned up his toes a couple of months ago. He's still on my rotadex and he's recorded on the PNC too and he lived in the neighbouring high flats with his wife and two daughters, one of whom is coincidentally called Alison. Maybe the apple doesn't fall far from the tree, do you think?" he raised his eyebrows.

"Why was this guy Steele recorded by you," said Maxwell.

"Actually, it was my predecessor who created the card and it seems that William, before he died a few months ago, was in his prime a right good and prolific housebreaker. Not local properties. Good quality houses like you'd find over in the Newton Mearns and up in Bearsden."

Again Maxwell glanced at McGhee, who muttered, "If nothing else, worth a knock at the door."

Thanking Dunky with the promise they'd let him know how they got on with their 'knock at the door,' they left his office to head towards the high flats in Sighthill.

****

Mary heard Salmon say, "Aye, Elaine, she is here," then he handed the phone to her.

"Elaine?"

"Boss, a wee bit of news re the shooting up in Pollok. It seems that the victim is Richard Bradley, the brother of our murder victim, who goes by the name of Ricky."

Mary felt herself tense when she said, "Okay, I'm putting you on speakerphone, Elaine," then turning to Salmon, said, "Your victim is Ricky Bradley, our murder victim's brother. Elaine," she addressed her, "how did you come by this news?"

There was just the slightest of pauses before Fitzsimmons replied, "You'll recall I have ten-year-old twin daughters?"

"Yes, I remember that."

"Well," she slowly drawled, "the victims daughter, Sarah, she's ten too, and to be honest, losing her mother like that I felt a bit sorry for her. My pair are spoiled rotten with clothes and so last week, I put some of the stuff they were growing out of into a carrier bag and took it up to the wee girl in Pollok."

Though it was highly inappropriate for one of her team to fraternise with the family of a murder victim, other than as investigators or liaison officers, Mary quickly realised as a mother herself, that Fitzsimmons was acting out of kindness and consideration and so glancing at Salmon, she replied, "I'm guessing that to repay your sympathy for the wee girl, someone from the family reached out regarding the shooting?"

"Yes, Boss, and I was a little surprised it was the younger brother Billy. He's known to us but I think there's a decent streak in there somewhere and there's no doubt he's very fond of his niece. He's just off the phone ten minutes ago and told me that Ricky was a member of one of the two drug gangs vying for power in the Pollok area and it was him that was shot. Billy says, though he refused to name him, a guy came to the door in the middle of the night to inform them Ricky had been shot and knowing we'd be checking the local hospitals, they took him over to the casualty at the Western Infirmary and dumped him there. Billy says he can't provide us with any statement for fear of being outed as a grass and he's worried that if anyone finds out he's spoken with me, he'll be done in and his mother's house will be torched. When I asked him, he also said he's in no doubt that his brother will know who shot him, but it's unlikely that Ricky will admit that, that like Billy, he won't want to be seen as a grass and he'll be thinking his mob will get their own revenge for the shooting."

Mary felt her stomach clench at the thought of a shooting war in the highly populated Pollok area, of the innocents who might be hurt or worse.

"Anything else I should know?"

"No, Boss, that's the lot."

"Okay, Elaine, if Billy should reach out to you again, I'll be with DI Salmon and we'll have a personal radio with us. As it happens," Bill Howie flashed through her mind, "I happen to know someone who works at the Western Infirmary, so we'll be taking a turn over there to speak with the victim."

She paused, then added, "That is, if he's still alive."

"Now, while you're on," she continued, "any feedback re the murder investigation?"

"Only a phone call from Tommy Maxwell to say they have a slight and very tenuous lead that our alleged resetter *might* be a woman who lives in Sighthill, so they're on their way to knock on her door."

"Okay, I'll get the rest when I return to Govan."

Ending the call, she turned to stare curiously at Salmon before she asked, "How you feeling, Sammy? You think you're not too tired to accompany me to the Western Infirmary or should I take one of your DS's?"

"Try and stop me," he grinned and turned to reach for his suit jacket.

****

Arriving at the door on the seventh floor with the nameplate 'Steele,' Maxwell said, "Do you think maybe we should have got a JP's warrant before we knock on the door?"

McGhee, with a half-smile, stared at him before he replied, "What, Tommy Maxwell doubting his ability to charm his way into a woman's house? I don't think so and besides, how long will that take us?"

"Aye, right enough, there's not many women can resist a good-looking guy like me," Maxwell thrust out his chin then banged on the door.

Less than a minute later, the door was opened by a frosty faced, heavy set woman in her mid-forties with cropped and quite obvious dyed black hair, who wearing a shiny and multi coloured shell suit with what seemed to be new Nike trainers, stared at them in turn, then sighed and said, "You're not getting in unless you've got a warrant."

Staring at her outfit, McGhee was surprised there wasn't tags hanging from the clothes while idly wondering what shop they'd been nicked from.

"And good morning to you too, madam," Maxwell smiled at her, then added, "We're only here for a chat, not to turn your flat over; so, what's the chance of a cuppa?"

Taken aback, she scowled, then her eyes betraying her suspicion, asked, "What's this about?"

Continuing to smile, Maxwell replied, "Trust me when I say, it's not about what you might have in the flat, hen, it's what you might know about a murder. Now, the reason we're here is to ask for your help, not to turn you over, okay?"

Still highly suspicious, it took Alison Steele several seconds before she made up her mind then taking a deep breath, stood to one side and invited them in.

Leading them through the hallway and passing the open door to the kitchen, McGhee noticed what seemed to be the top of the range kitchen units and fittings and likewise guessed a lot of money had been spent updating it from the council fitted units.

In the front room, the Detectives could not help but wonder at the money that must have been spent not only decorating the flat to such a high standard, but the cost of the luxury leather suite and unit that held the large, seemingly brand-new television and video recorder that was the focus of the room.

However, glancing around the room, McGhee thought the cheap-framed prints on the wall completely clashed with the décor and furniture and decided that Steele might have the ready cash, but simply had no decorative taste.

Indicating the Detectives sit on the couch, she glared at them when she said, "I'll stick the kettle on, but don't be touching any of my stuff, you hear?"
Raising his hands defensively, Maxwell smiled, "Of course not, Alison. Can I call you Alison and by the way, I'm Tommy and he's John and eh, just milk for me. Milk and one for him."
Still highly suspicious, she slowly nodded then left the room.
"If this stuff isn't knocked off, then whatever money she's been making from her resetting has paid for this," McGhee whispered to his neighbour with a wave of his hand.
Several minutes later, Steele returned to the room carrying an ornate gilded tray with three mugs of tea and a plate of biscuits.
Why is it always bloody digestive biscuits, McGhee inwardly groaned? Have the great Glasgow unwashed never heard of Tunnocks?
Seating herself in the armchair opposite the couch, she began, "What's this about a murder?"
His brow furrowed, Maxwell replied, "A young woman was murdered last Tuesday over in Cessnock. Do you know the area?"
"Cessnock? Is that Govan or maybe in Ibrox somewhere?"
"Aye, that's correct, over that way. Her name was Elizabeth Bradley, but she was known as Lizzie. Does the name mean anything to you?"
Watching her slowly shake her head, Maxwell had the instinctive feeling she was being truthful, then sighing, he continued, "Now, I'm not accusing you of anything here, Alison, so don't be jumping the gun and getting all defensive, okay? What I'm about to tell you is that me and John, we're more interested in finding this woman's killer than anything you might be getting up to, do you understand?"
She sniffed, then still clearly suspicious, nodded.
"We believe the victim might have been part of a gang of women who were stealing from old folks houses and while we've identified the others, we're trying to trace the leader of the gang who we want to interview regarding the murder. Now," he held up his hand, "I'm not saying *she* killed Lizzie Bradley, but if nothing else we need to interview her to eliminate her from our inquiries."
"And what's this woman got to do with me?"
He risked a glance at McGhee before he continued, "The woman we're looking for told her pals she was going to sell the stolen stuff

to someone on the north side of the city."

"Wait," Steele suddenly aware of what she might be admitting to two Detectives and regardless of how charming the big, good looking guy was, retorted, "you're trying to say I'm buying knocked off gear? I'm not…"

"Hang on, Alison," Maxwell quickly interrupted with a raised hand. "You're not listening! We're not interested in what you might or might *not* be doing, we're only wanting to find this woman, okay!"

A tense silence was broken when Maxwell, his hands splayed out in front of him, and almost a plea in his voice, continued, "Look, if I give you what little description I have, if you know who she is or where we can find her, will you help?"

He decided to play the sentiment card, then quickly carried on, "The woman that was murdered, she didn't have a husband or a boyfriend, but she did have a wee girl who's only ten. That wee lassie is on her own now," but prudently didn't mention she had a grandmother and uncles to care for her.

He let that information sink in, then seeing Steele's shoulders slump, softly added, "The wee girl, Sarah's her name, she needs justice for her mother and if helping us find this woman who might or might *not* be the killer, then you're helping that wee girl."

Several seconds of silence fell on the room, broken when she hesitantly asked, "And that's all you need, just if I know this woman, nothing else?"

"That's all, nothing else," he confirmed with a nod.

"And no matter what I say, nothing will come back to me? I don't need to give a statement or anything, that's the end of my involvement?"

"Correct."

Second passed, the slowly, licking first at her lips, then said, "Okay. What's her name?"

"We know her as Lorraine Gray?"

They saw Steele's face change to one of puzzlement then with a sigh, she shook her head and said "I don't know the name."

Thinking rapidly, Maxwell knew that the woman calling herself Gray had lied to her associates, so why not lie to a resetter and said, "We're told she's in her mid-forties, but looks a bit younger, dyed blonde hair, described as a right good looking woman and has a polite Glasgow accent and speaks as if she's not from any of the council housing areas."

It was when Maxwell mentioned the polite accent, McGhee noticed the slightest of flickers in Steele's eyes and seizing the opportunity, quickly asked, "What name did she give you?"

"She said…" Steele began, then caught herself, realising that she'd spoke in haste and with a sharp intake of breath, turned to him and grimly smiled when she added, "That was dead smooth, pal."

"So," McGhee continued, "what name *did* she give you, Alison?"

Exhaling as though caught out, Steele replied, "She said her name was Karen Silverton."

"And the description matches?" asked Maxwell.

"Oh, aye, right down to the smarmy accent. Talked like she'd a marble in her mouth, so she did."

"When did she visit you?"

Steele rubbed at her forehead, then shrugged when she replied, "Maybe two, two and a half months ago? Knocked on my door and told me she'd be coming into some property that might be worth a few bob and asked if I'd be interested. I was a bit suspicious and thought because of her swanky way of speaking she might be the CID, but then she said something that was really funny," Steeles face creased.

"Funny?"

"Aye, she told me that she'd known my Da that it was him who had said if she ever wanted to move anything, I was the woman to speak with. Course I asked her how she knew my Da…" she paused and eyes narrowing, asked, "Did you know my Da?"

"No," Maxwell answered for them both with a shake of his head.

She smiled as though at her father's memory when she continued, "He had angina for years, then a heart attack took him nearly three months ago and you know, a couple of your lot attended his funeral. I don't know if it was out of respect or whether they just wanted to confirm the old bugger had snuffed it right enough."

"And this woman, you didn't previously know her?"

"No, not at all," she shook her head.

"Have you heard from her since she visited you?"

"Not a word," she shook her head.

"Did she say where she knew your father from?"

Her mouth twisted when she replied, "That's another funny thing.

She said after he'd got the jail, he'd pop into her office and would always bring a bag of doughnuts. Well, to be honest, that kind of clinched it for me because that was my Da's style. A bit of a ladies man, so he was and he was right fond of sugary doughnuts too. I kept telling him, Da, they're bad for you, but would he listen?" she ruefully shook her head.

"Her office?" Maxwell mused, then asked, "What kind of office might that be? Did she say or do you know?"

Steele took a deep breath before she replied, "When he got the jail, which to be honest was more often than not, the only office he'd be visiting would be his lawyer."

****

Accompanied by her DI, Sammy Salmon, Mary Wells again drove her own car and arrived at the Western Infirmary hospital twenty minutes after receiving the phone call from Elaine Fitzsimmon's. Opened in 1874, the Victorian hospital had little space for visiting private vehicles and so Mary parked her car in a bay in Church Street that adjoined the side entrance to the hospital.

Making their way to the Casualty Department, Salmon casually inquired, "Who's this contact you've got in the hospital?"

"Curiously," she glanced at him, "he's a new neighbour of mine. Bill Howie is his name or rather I should say, Dr Howie. He's renting the house through the wall until he finds a place of his own. He's taken over as the head of the Casualty Department, so fingers crossed, we might be able to call upon him for some assistance, if it's needed."

Arriving at the Casualty Department, they found that unusually, it wasn't busy then identifying themselves to the young receptionist requested they speak with someone regarding an admittance earlier that morning.

"A patient who was literally dumped here and with a suspected gunshot wound," Mary smiled encouragingly.

The young woman grimaced, then asking them to wait, made a telephone call.

Less than two minutes later, wearing blue coloured surgical scrubs and with a stethoscope around his neck, they turned when Bill Howie called Mary's name.

"Well, this is an unexpected pleasure," he smiled at her, then staring inquisitively at Salmon, introduced himself with a handshake before asking, "So, what brings you guys to my world?"

"We've information about a patient who was delivered here in the early hours of this morning," Mary politely began. "Apparently he was dropped off by some associates and had suffered a gunshot wound. We've since earned his name is Richard Bradley, but goes by the name Ricky Bradley. We'd like to know if he survived his injury and if he's able to be interviewed."

Bill stared at her for several seconds then with a nod, replied, "Perhaps you might like to follow me."

He led them from the reception area into the casualty receiving corridor, then into a small office that clearly was his.

Beckoning that they sit, he occupied the chair behind the desk that Wells saw was quite literally covered with files and clipboards, then with a sigh, said, "I'm sorry, Mary, I can't help you other than to confirm Mr Bradley is a patient here in the hospital and is alive."

Surprised, she quietly replied, "Can't or won't?"

They watched Bill's face express his consternation when he said, "If you want to be pedantic," he shrugged "Then I won't help you."

She could feel her face pale when she asked, "May I ask why not?"

His hands clasped across his chest, he bit at his lower lip before he replied, "Unless the law has changed since I've been away, there is no legal requirement for me to disclose information about any patient unless it directly affects the good health of the public in general, such as a patient being a disease carrier, in which case I am duty bound to inform the authorities. In short, other than that type of diagnosis, trust is an essential part of the doctor patient relationship and so I owe a duty of confidentiality to every patient who passes through the doors of this Department. If it were to become known that I or any other physician or member of my staff was complicit in passing medical or personal information to the police without the consent of a patient, then patients may avoid seeking medical help that they require."

A tense silence was broken when Salmon, glancing at Mary, said, "You do understand that this guy Bradley is the victim of a shooting and that if we don't get the information that we need, we could be looking at a gang war with further victims, likely some fatal?"

"I'm sorry, DI Salmon," he spread his hands wide, "but I'm not in the business of predicating the future. I can only deal with my patients as they arrive, not the circumstances of how they come about their injuries nor the consequences that might result from those circumstances."

She could feel the anger well up in her when she asked, "Is there some senior medical individual to whom we could speak about this?"

"Of course, but can I just say that it's likely my boss will agree with me. I have autonomy in my Department so I really don't think you'll get any satisfaction from going over my head."

Again it was Salmon, who recognising that his DCI was becoming angry, said, "Can we formally request of you that you speak with Mr Bradley and ask if he might be willing to be interviewed?"

"He's currently recovering from surgery and is waiting on a bed becoming free in the High Dependency Unit. However, I must warn you, he has been heavily medicated, but of course, I can ask. If you wait here," he rose from his chair then wordlessly left the room.

When the door has closed, it was Salmon who said, "Well, Boss, that's a new one to me. There was me thinking the medical staff would be keen to help us and to be honest, I've never had an issue like this before. Have you?"

"No, I haven't," she muttered, then added, "But much as I hate to admit it, Sammy, he's absolutely correct. We can't force him to provide us with the information and unless Bradley makes a complaint of being assaulted, we have no legal right to interview him. Bugger it!" she suddenly hissed.

"I take it you were on speaking terms before today, then?" he suddenly grinned at her.

"Aye, though that's likely changed now," she sheepishly shook her head.

"Good looking guy, though," he teased.

Glaring at him, she then found herself smiling when she wryly replied, "Is that right? I never noticed."

Seconds later, they both turned when the door opened to admit Bill who solemnly shaking his head, softly told them, "I didn't get the opportunity to ask him. My registrar has just informed me that Richard Bradley died a little under five minutes ago."

CHAPTER TWENTY-ONE

Constable Janey McPhee told DC Tommy Maxwell, "Hold on a minute," then called Colin Baxter to the phone.

"It's Tommy, he's at Baird Street CID office," she handed the phone to Baxter.

"What's going on, big man?"

"We struck lucky, Colin," he could hear the excitement in Maxwell's voice. "The Divisional Collator here at Baird Street identified a female resetter who we're certain has met with our suspect, only now she's using the name Karen Silverton or rather, she was about two or two and a half months ago."

"Go on."

Maxwell related the conversation with Alison Steele who in exchange for an *ad hoc* immunity regarding her resetting business, provided information about the female suspect.

"And you think the suspect is somehow connected to this law firm, Burnley, Paterson and Co?"

"It's a bit of a long shot, I know, but we're thinking that we should take a turn along to their office and continue our inquiry there."

"The name doesn't mean anything to me," mused Baxter, then agreed, "Definitely go and see them. I'll create and Action for your visit, but remember, Tommy, you're visiting a solicitors, so there might be a bit of a problem when you ask about their personnel. However, I'll leave you to deal with that, but any issues, call me."

"Righto," Maxwell ended the call, then turning to McGhee, grinned when he asked, "Ready for this?"

"Oh, aye," McGhee returned his grin.

****

Albeit Richard 'Ricky' Bradley died within the confines of the Western Infirmary, the crime of being shot had occurred in the Pollok area and so it was the duty of the G Divisional CID to first seize the body on behalf of the Procurator Fiscal, then carry out the murder investigation. Thus, as the senior CID officer in charge of Pollok CID, the task of SIO fell to DI Sammy Salmon.

Formally requesting and being granted permission by Bill Howie to use his office and telephone to contact her Department, Mary Wells informed Colin Baxter that they now had what seemed to be a second murder investigation on their hands.

Turning the phone over to Salmon, he first contacted Pollok Office where he arranged for two of his officers to attend at the hospital to secure the deceased's clothing, any possessions that he might have had, but crucially important, the bullet that had been removed by Bill Howie during the emergency surgery that, unfortunately failed to save Bradley's life.

That bullet, both Mary and Salmon knew, after examination by the SOCO Ballistics officers, would be essential in both identifying the type of weapon used and, were the weapon to be later recovered, be a significant piece of evidence in any subsequent trial.

For continuity purposes, the same two attending Detective officers would then accompany the body to the city mortuary that is located in the Saltmarket area of the city.

Salmon's second phone call was to arrange for a Scenes of Crime visit to photograph and examine the body while it lay in situ within the High Dependency Unit, as well as taking immediate samples prior to the removal of the body to the mortuary; such samples being swabs of the deceased's hand for gunshot residue as well as fingerprinting and samples from under the deceased's fingernails. Though this sample taking would normally be conducted at the time of a PM, Mary suggested to Salmon that a second delivery of the body - the first being from the locus to the hospital - but now from the hospital to the mortuary, might result in the possibility of the secondary samples taken from the body, being contaminated. Her concern was that at any subsequent trial, it could be claimed by a defence team that due to the body being conveyed twice to two separate locations, any secondary samples indicating the guilt of an individual, might be deemed at the time of a trial to be inadmissible.

The phone calls made, Salmon turned to Wells, to tell her, "Can't think of anything else at the minute, Boss."

"No, me neither, but once your guys get here, Sammy, I'll return you to Pollok and you can start with your investigation."

Twenty-five minutes later, the two Detectives arrived to both seize the clothing, bullet and possessions then remain with the body till the SOCO concluded their examination.

Satisfied there was nothing more for them to do at the hospital, Wells and Salmon left Bill's office without further engaging with him, having learned he was at that time dealing with a patient.

In her car on the return journey to Pollok, she asked, "I know when I was off on the sick you acted as the SIO in two previous murders, Sammy, so are you okay taking this on?"

"Yes, more confident that I thought I might be," he nodded, though didn't add that his confidence was much to do with the knowledge that the much-experienced Mary Wells was just a phone call away. As she drove, Salmon reflected on both murders where without much difficulty, he had acquitted himself as the SIO, but was the first to acknowledge that unlike this shooting, neither had been difficult to solve.

The first, just a few months after Wells had taken sick leave, was a simple domestic where the jealous husband had discovered his alcoholic wife had been plying sexual favour with a neighbour for money to buy drink. In fact, it was the killer himself who had contacted the emergency services and sobbingly admitted to the nine-nine-nine operator he had stabbed his wife.

The second, again some months later, was a stupid neighbour dispute between the two female occupants of tenement flats where one, noisily playing ABBA music throughout the evening and night, had resulted in the other female kicking at her door to complain.

The resulting struggle, a push and shove match on the landing outside their front doors caused the ABBA fan to fall backwards down the stone, flight of stairs and fatally cracking wide her skull. Again, upon arrival of the police, the sorrowful killer immediately admitted her responsibility and later pled guilty to culpable homicide.

But now this, he inwardly breathed and confident though he had tried to sound, worried if he was really up to the job.

"You'll be needing extra resources," she broke into his thoughts. "I can't spare anyone from my investigation, but I'll phone ACC Meadows and ask if he can arrange for the local Divisions to assist with the Mutual Aid agreement," she risked a glance at him, "so that might bring in at least half a dozen more bodies. If you need more, I'll ask if the Serious Crime Squad can lend you some bodies, too."

"Thanks, Boss, that will be helpful," he cleared his throat and nodded at her.

As though sensing his mood, she smiled when she said, "I remember not long after I was promoted to DCI, I was called to a tenement flat in Golspie Street, just off the Govan Road. A woman discovered by her partner lying dead in her bed and because she was just in her early thirties, the nightshift DC's felt it was suspicious enough to call me out in the early hours of the morning."

She risked another glance at him and continued, "So there we are, the three of us, staring down at this young woman and trying to decide because she seemed so peaceful and there didn't seem any visible cause why she was dead, we're thinking, could it be a heart attack or at worse, poison or what? Three trained CID detectives, one of whom is a DCI and we're mulling over what killed her. By now, I've called out the SOCO, the Casualty Surgeon to pronounce life extinct, the duty PF; in short, the whole circus," she sighed.
"So, what killed her."
With a smile, she said, "Well, first of all the doctor pronounced life extinct and like us, for a few minutes, mulled over why she had died. It was when a young ambulanceman began to turn her over to permit the doctor to take a rectal temperature that we saw the knife sticking out of her back. God," she slowly shook her head, "talk about egg on my face."
He guessed why, but asked anyway.
"And the point of that self-depreciating story?" he turned to stare at her.
She shrugged when she replied, "I'm not saying that having achieved DCI, I was full of myself, that I was bursting with confidence, but that *faux pas* certainly reminded me that it doesn't matter what rank you are, you are always susceptible to mistakes. However, it's learning from those mistakes that make you a better individual. This is your first real whodunit, so don't think that *anyone* and that includes me," she glanced at him, "expects miracles. Just do your best, listen to advice, whether you take it or not, and don't be afraid to come asking for some."
"Thanks, Mary," he breathed out slowly, then added, "I don't undervalue the trust you have and continue to place in me."
"And that trust, Sammy, is not misplaced. You've earned the right to be the SIO, so when we get to Pollok, I'll drop you and let you get on with it."
****

Seated on the swivel stool, Bill Howie finished stitching the six-years-old girl's leg, then smiling at the anxious, teary-eyed mother, said, "It might leave a two-inch war wound that she can show off to her friends, but there's no real harm done. Give it a week then make an appointment with your surgery's practise nurse to check the wound and remove the stitches. And you," he stared meaningfully at the girl, "no more jumping from walls that are taller than you. Oh, and one final thing."

He turned to the nurse behind him and taking the large, open glass jar from her, offered it the little girl and said, "Any lollipop, but not the red ones. They're my favourite," he narrowed his eyes in warning and pretended to snarl.

He could see the devilment in her eyes and knowing she would, he watched the child take a red lollipop then again pretending anger, wagged a finger and said, "I don't want to see you in here ever again, you cheeky monkey."

Leaving the grinning nurse in the cubicle to finish bandaging the leg, he made his way to his office, but with Mary Wells foremost in his thoughts.

He had been angry with himself and now knew he had handled her request badly, refusing to permit her to see his patient; however, he stood by his decision and knew that he had been correct. Too many times men with guns, spears or machetes had demanded to search his clinics for individuals who either were of a different religion, race or creed or simply seeking men, youths and boys to swell the numbers of their gangs. He hadn't given in then, though frightening those times had been, so he wasn't about to give into his beliefs now, regardless of who might be asking or demanding.

Now sitting behind his desk, he continued to think of Mary and hoped that he hadn't ruined any opportunity of seeing more of her and curiously surprised at his own feelings for a woman he barely knew; feelings that he had not experienced for a very long time.

At least as far as he could recall, not since Sophia.

Yet, there *was* something about Mary and not just her attractiveness, he smiled and though he had no idea of her personal circumstances, other than mentioning her husband had been unfaithful, wished he knew more about her. Yes, he involuntarily nodded, there was a lot more to Mary Wells that he'd like to know, but his thoughts were interrupted when a young nurse knocked on his door and gasped, "Sorry, Dr Howie, but that's two casualties from an RTA now in an ambulance and due to arrive here within five minutes, one with apparent serious head injuries."

"No rest for the wicked," he exhaled then pushed himself to his feet.

****

Arriving back at Govan, Mary Wells thought it odd that while she and Sammy Salmon had been at the Western Infirmary, the shooting victim's family had neither attended nor, the one thing Bill Howie had admitted, there been no inquiries from anyone as to his condition.

Making her way upstairs to the CID suite, she decided that if Elaine Fitzsimmons had already been tentatively accepted as a contact with the Bradley family, then perhaps it should be she who with Salmon's permission broke the news of Richard's death.

Opening the door to the incident room, Colin Baxter glanced up then smiling, said, "Glad to see you back, Boss. I'm from hearing Pollok the shooting's now a murder."

"Correct," she nodded, then seeing Fitzsimmons, called her over and instructed she call DI Salmon and offer her services to break the sad news to the Bradley family.

While Fitzsimmons hurried off, Mary asked Baxter, "What's the latest on our investigation?"

"Tommy Maxwell and John McGhee are away to a lawyer's office where they have information our suspect Lorraine Gray, now alias Karen Silverton, might have some connection."

"Karen Silverton?"

Turning to Janey McPhee, he said, "Away and get the boss a coffee, Janey, while I bring her up to speed."

"Bring it to my office, please, Janey," Mary smiled at the younger woman then suggested Baxter accompany her.

Minutes later, back behind her desk, she listened as he recounted Maxwell and McGhee's interview with the female resetter, Alison Steele, and her information about their suspect.

His narrative had just concluded when McPhee popped in to hand over a coffee, then when she left, his brow furrowed when he asked, "What's the story about the shooting?"

Providing as much information as she knew, she described the visit to the Western Infirmary and Dr Howie's refusal to let them interview his patient.

"Is that strictly legal? I mean can he do that?"

"As far as I'm aware, yes, he has every legal right to protect his patient, but it's a superfluous issue now anyway, Colin. Even if he'd said yes, the guy had literally minutes to live so it's unlikely we would have got anything of value from him."

"And this dead guy, he's the brother of our victim? Does that mean there might be a connection with the murder of his sister?"

Her face creased and she chewed at the inside of her mouth before she replied, "We've no way of knowing at the minute, but if I were to take a leap of faith, I'd say no. It's just unfortunate for the family, for the mother," she involuntarily shook her head and imagined the woman's grief, "that she's lost a son and a daughter within a week of each other. That said," she sighed, "without hard evidence to the contrary, we cannot dismiss the possibility of a connection, but again, I'm determined to run both murders as independent investigations unless as I say, we learn otherwise."

She slowly exhaled, then asked, "Anything else I should know about?"

"No," he rose to his feet, then added, "but I'll let you know if Tommy and John hunt down our suspect."

****

ACC Keith Meadows secretary, Ellen, called him on the intercom to inform him that DCI Wells was on the phone and was he available to take her call?

"Of course," he replied and when the call was put through, he greeted her with, "Hello, Mary, I'm reading a printout that you've landed yourself another murder."

"Yes, sir, a member of a drug gang shot dead during what we've assessed to be a feud with a rival gang. As it happens, the shooting victim is the older brother of my deceased female, but I'm not convinced that his murder is connected to my current investigation. That said, I'm not closing the door on any connection, either."

"And I suppose you're about to request additional resources?"

"If that's possible yes. I have DI Salmon in situ at Pollok who will be the SIO for the shooting while I'll continue as SIO for my own murder investigation, sir."

"And how is that going?"

He heard her sigh before she replied, "Not as quickly as I'd hoped. I've two of my guys currently trying to trace a suspect who was the apparent leader of a gang of four women, that included the deceased, who we've now learned has been using at least two false names. At the minute she's a definite suspect for a number of thefts from elderly folks' homes, but we'll need to interview her before I can confirm her as a suspect for the murder."

"Okay, and the shooting?"

"Early days yet, but there's every indication that as I said, the deceased was a member of one half of a turf dispute regarding the sale of drugs. You remember DS Elaine Fitzsimmons?"

"I do, yes. A good officer," then inwardly thought, and one to watch.

"Elaine has built up a bit of a rapport with the family of the deceased, so I have her attending at the house to both break the news of his murder and to try and ascertain if the family have any knowledge of who might be responsible for the shooting."

"Okay, so you'll keep me apprised of any developments?"

"Of course, sir."

"Right, then, digressing completely. I understand you have recommended one of your DS's to be returned to uniform."

Mary didn't even try to work out how Meadows would know about her disciplinary action for Hugh Donnelly, for it was widely held that the ACC had informants in all the Division's as well as the different CID Departments and was thus able to keep a finger on the pulse of what was happening in his CID.

"That's correct, yes," she slowly replied. "Sergeant Donnelly was not only a disruptive influence at Pollok CID, but believed himself to be above taking any instruction from his senior ranks and considered himself as the obvious candidate to replace the former DI, Martin Reilly. After a rather heated discussion within my office," she felt herself licking at her lips, "I had little option but to recommend his return to uniform as a career incentive."

There was a slight pause as Mary thought Meadows to be considering her response, but was then a little taken aback when he told her, "You may not know this and I respect that you will keep it between us, but just like Martin Reilly, Hugh Donnelly has been in my sights for some time now, Mary. Had you not acted as you did, then I might have had to step in and remove him from the post."

That small statement not only confirmed Mary's decision to be correct, but caused her to believe that someone in the Pollok Office, whether a CID or uniformed officer, had been keeping Meadows informed about both Reilly and Donnelly.

Once more, the statement only reinforced her belief that the ACC had more than a few informants scattered throughout the Force.

"Now, let me get onto the surrounding Divisions to find you some support for DI Salmon and though the Serious Crime are currently

engaged assisting the Special Branch with the anti-terrorist incident from a few weeks ago, I'll try to lever some bodies from them too."
"Thank you, sir, I really am grateful."
"Keep in touch," he ended the call.
****
Parking the CID car in the roadway in Langton Crescent, Elaine Fitzpatrick and her neighbour, Alan Hamilton saw the curtain twitch as they strode towards the house, causing Hamilton to quietly comment, "Looks like we're expected."
In a low voice, Fitzsimmons responded with, "As we agreed. I'll take the mother and you speak with the brother."
Approaching the door, they saw what seemed to be several boot marks on the lower side of the white PVC door.
"That's new," Hamilton said, just as the door was pulled open by Billy Bradley who they both saw sported a fresh bruise to his left eye and a split lip.
Ushering them in, Billy told them that his niece was upstairs in her bedroom, then led the way into the front room where his mother, Angela, sat in the chair at the fireplace, her eyes red-rimmed and a handkerchief clutched in her hand.
"He's dead, isn't he?" she greeted them.
"I'm so sorry, Mrs Bradley, but yes. Ricky succumbed to his injury just over an hour ago," Elaine softly replied, then turning to Billy, added, "Stick the kettle on, son. I think your mother needs a cuppa." Taking his cue, Hamilton followed Billy into the kitchen and closed the door behind them.
Sitting down opposite Angela, she quietly continued with, "Have you any idea who might have shot your Ricky?"
She watched the older woman shake her head when she sobbed, "No, but it was because of that crowd he was hanging around with. Them that are doing the drugs."
Elaine let seconds pass before she asked, "Can you tell me their names and you have to know, Mrs Bradley, that anything you tell me won't be divulged to anyone. As far as anyone knows, we are here simply to deliver the sad news about your son being killed, nothing more."
Angela's eyes narrowed when she whispered, "I don't know their names, but they were here earlier, looking for something in Ricky's room. Something about a book, I think I heard them shouting."

"A book? What kind of book?"

"I don't know. I've never known our Ricky to ever read book in his life, Miss. He…"

She hesitated, then taking a deep breath, she slowly said, "He was his father all over, so he was. God forgive me for saying this, but he was right selfish boy and nasty, really nasty to our Lizzie and his brother, Billy. Nothing but trouble since he was a wee wean."

She stared at Fitzsimmons with tear stained eyes and her voice a whisper, hesitantly asked, "Am I a bad mother, Miss, because…well, because my Ricky, I just didn't like the man he had become."

Fitzsimmons had no answer to such a personal question and simply stared back, but then taking a deep breath, Angela continued, "My Billy, I know he's not any innocent, but he's never really given me any bother, that boy. If anything, he takes after me, thank God. He's not like Ricky at all."

Her face creased when she added, "I know it was Billy who spoke to you when you were here, Miss, but thank you for bringing those clothes for Sarah. If nothing else it took her mind off her mammy for a wee while, but then this thing happened during the night," she sobbed.

"You mean. Someone coming to your house, Mrs Bradley?"

She saw the fear in the older woman's eyes when she fearfully stuttered, "You know about that?"

"We saw the boot marks on the front door and Billy's face so yes, we know you had visitors. I assume it was someone telling you Ricky had been shot and maybe warning you to keep your mouth shut, not to speak to the police about anything?"

It was then that Fitzsimmon's realised how Billy had come by his swollen eye and so she asked, "Billy tried to stop them coming into your house?"

"Aye, but they battered him, so they did the three of them. Shouting and screaming at him and me and the wean, too."

"And this was the team that your boy, Ricky, was hanging around with?"

"I think so, aye," she nodded.

"Did wee Sarah…did she witness this? I mean did she see this happening, Mrs Bradley?"

She turned a tearstained face towards Fitzsimmons then slowly nodding, softly replied, "Aye, she did, the poor wee soul."

"Will we get into trouble, Miss, for what Ricky was involved in?"

"No, Mrs Bradley," she smiled and shook her head. "Ricky's troubles have died with him. You won't get into trouble."

****

In the kitchen, watching him fill the kettle, Hamilton asked, "Who gave you the dull one to the eye, Billy? Was it whoever tried to kick in your front door?"

"You saw that?"

"Couldn't really miss it. I'm guessing you tried to prevent whoever assaulted you from getting through the door?"

He watched Billy switch on the electric kettle then resting both hands flat on the worktop, sighed when he nodded and said, "There was three of them. I didn't stand a chance. They were after…"

He paused and shook his head.

"After what, Billy?"

He saw the younger man's shoulders slump before he replied in a low voice, "The book. Ricky kept the book for them. He's shot and away to the hospital and his so-called fucking pals," he bitterly snapped, "all they can think about is their book!"

Intuitively, Hamilton asked, "Are you talking about a tick book? The book that recorded their drug dealings?"

He turned to stare at Hamilton, then his forehead creasing, he asked, "Aye, you know about that?"

"I know what a tick book is, yes, and these three Billy. They were part of Ricky's gang?"

"It wasn't *Ricky's* gang," he sneered at the suggestion, "he wasn't that bright, pal. He was just a patsy for them, holding the book and sometimes their gear. I tried to stop him," he shook his head, "but he wouldn't listen. You know something, Detective? I didn't even *like* him and he was my brother. How fucked up is that?"

"It's the old story, Billy," Hamilton shrugged. "You can choose your friends, but you're stuck with your family."

"Aye," he humourlessly laughed. "If I had my way, I'd have had him kicked out of here years ago, but Ma?" he exhaled through pursed lips.

"He was still her son," he shook his head, then added, "And she was Ricky's mother, their so-called pal, but that didn't stop them threatening to hurt her if she opened her mouth to the polis."

"So, let me get this right. These three that broke in looking for the book. You tried to stop them, but they set about you, yeah?"

"Aye," again he shook his head. "I didn't stand a chance, not against three of them."

"Hard men the three of them, taking on one guy," Hamilton couldn't help himself and sympathised with Billy.

Then he asked, "What about your niece? Did she see this happening?"

The kettle whistled, but they ignored it, then he saw Billy's eyes fill with angry tears when biting at his lower lip, he muttered, "Sarah, she was screaming, then one of the bastards, he shoved her into my room and slammed the door shut on her. I was on the floor and they were stomping me, so I couldn't do anything about it."

Using his sleeve, he wiped at his eyes, then turning to Hamilton, he said, "They didn't find the book."

"So, the book is missing and you're worried they might come back?"

He stared at Billy and saw his expression change to one of apparent curiosity when he replied, "They'll not come back if they're in the jail, will they?"

Hamilton felt himself tense when he asked, "Wait, are you telling me you'll disclose who these guys are?"

"*Disclose* who they are? If you mean will I grass them in, you're damn right, pal! They come into my Ma's house, threaten her, push my wee ten-year-old niece about and batter the shite out of me and I'm supposed to keep my gob shut?"

"Aye," he glared at Hamilton, "that'll be fucking right! And another thing. You brew the tea for my Ma and I'll go and fetch you their tick book. That'll not just tell you who they are, but it lists every deal they've done, where they keep their gear and besides," he shrugged and to Hamilton's surprise, grinned widely when he added, "it can't hurt Ricky, can it? You can't jail a dead man."

Stunned, Hamilton stared wide-eyed when he asked, "You know where it is, where Ricky kept the book?"

Billy softly laughed when he replied, "Ricky, he thought he was being right smart, but he wasn't *that* smart. He'd been hiding it in my Ma's room, beneath her mattress."

CHAPTER TWENTY-TWO

DC John McGhee stopped the CID car on Tollcross Road, then switching off the engine, joined his neighbour in staring at the law firm's office premises located at the bottom of the tenement building adjacent to them, between a dry-cleaning shop and a common close entrance.

"Don't know what I was expecting," muttered Tommy Maxwell, "but with a name like Burnley, Paterson and Co., maybe something a wee bit more upmarket?"

He turned to McGhee to again say, "I've never heard of them, have you?"

"Nope and I can't recall ever being cross-examined by a defence lawyer called Burnley. Though," he heavily sighed, "I do I recognise the name Paterson and if it's who I *think* it is, it'll be Charlie Paterson, but she's a woman. Likely short for Charlotte."

"Oh, you think, Sherlock?" Maxwell grinned at him.

Scowling at his neighbour, McGhee added, "If it *is* her, she usually gives me a right hard time when I'm in the witness box, so she does."

"Well, time to earn a shilling," Maxwell cheerfully replied and got out of the car.

Pushing open the front door to a brightly lit and modestly decorated reception area, they were cheerfully greeted by a young woman, who learning they were the CID, politely told them, "If you take a seat I'll see if one of the partners can speak with you."

Minutes passed until the woman returned to tell them, "Along the corridor and second door on your left."

Following her instruction, Maxwell knocked on a closed door and when a female voice called out, "Come in," he and McGhee entered a brightly lit windowless office where they were greeted by an attractive woman of around forty to forty-five years of age, Maxwell thought, whose raven coloured hair was plaited and who wore a white blouse and rimless eyeglasses. A navy-blue suit jacket hung on a hanger from the top handle of a grey coloured three drawer metal filing cabinet positioned in a far corner.

"Why, Detective Constable McGhee," the woman stared at him with a wide smile. "How nice of you to pop by and visit."

"Miss Paterson," he replied in a sombre voice then in a voice dripping with sarcasm, added, "What are the odds, eh?"

"Oh, you know each other?" Maxwell glanced knowingly at McGhee and choked back a laugh when he saw the younger man blush.

"Only in an adversarial way," she replied with a grin, then with a wave of her hand, indicated they sit down in the two chairs in front of her desk.

"Now, how can I help you?" she continued to smile, though Maxwell couldn't help but notice her eyes kept darting towards his neighbour.

Explaining they were attempting to track down a suspect who went by the names Lorraine Gray and Karen Silverton, it was clear to them both that neither name meant anything to Paterson. However, when Maxwell disclosed that Alison Steele, the daughter of a former client, William Steele, had suggested the suspect might have been employed within the law firm, Paterson shook her head and told them, "Of course, I know of William as he had been a regular client, but not the woman you mention or rather, certainly not in my time and I've been here seven years."

"What about her description, then," Maxwell suggested and when he began to describe the suspect, they saw Paterson's eyes widen when she scowled.

"Her name's not Gray or Silverton. It's Joanne Wood or it was when she worked here about three or four months ago or thereabouts. Hang on a minute," she rose from her chair and left the office.

When alone, Maxwell grinned at McGhee and shaking his head, he asked, "What is it about you that the women love? My God, John, she's got the hots for you, so she has and she's a looker too."

"No, you're wrong," his face reddened. "She's just teasing me because we've had some right set-to's in the court."

Maxwell didn't have the opportunity to respond, because the door opened to admit Paterson with a file in her hand, then resuming her seat, opened the file.

Nodding, she said, "I was right enough. Just over three months ago we dispensed with her services and as I said, her name then was Joanne Wood."

"And you have an address for her?" Maxwell asked.

"Yes, but I'm uncertain about divulging personal details," her eyes narrowed.

"Okay," Maxwell drawled, then asked, "How long did she work for you and why was she dismissed?"

Glancing at the file, she replied, "Eh, she commenced working here on Monday, the sixth of April this year and worked here for just four weeks. As for her dismissal…" she hesitated, then asked, "Before we go any further and I provide information that might come back to haunt me, perhaps you might share with me what you suspect her of?"

Maxwell glanced at McGhee before he replied, "This woman you know as Wood was part of a gang of four women who were robbing old folks' homes, then last week, one of them was murdered. We need to find her to interview her regarding the murder, either as a suspect or to eliminate her from our investigation."

"The murder of the woman over in Cessnock?"

"You know about that?"

"It was on the news and crime *is* my business, Mr Maxwell," she graced him with another smile.

"Well, then," she continued with a glance at McGhee, "her, eh, dismissal. Let me say without prejudice that my company do *not* owe any loyalty or legal protection to our former employee, simply because she was caught stealing from us."

She glanced again at the file then said, "On Wednesday, the twenty-eighth of the same month, she was left to lock up the office. When my partner arrived the next morning, he discovered the safe lying ajar and a sum of money, petty cash of around two hundred pounds or so," she shrugged, "was removed from the safe. Our attempts to contact *Miss Wood* at the telephone number she provided discovered that the line was dead, if indeed it had ever been active," she shook her head. "Needless to say, she failed to arrive at work that day or thereafter and has neither been seen nor heard from since. Oh, and letters to her address have resulted in some woman claiming to be Joanne Wood phoning the office here to tell us to bugger off or she'll have the police onto us for harassment. Bloody cheek of her!"

"Was it Wood phoning you, you think?"

"No," her perfectly plucked eyebrows furrowed, "the woman sounded older, a lot older and I'm of the opinion it was probably the *real* Joanne Wood, and that seems to corroborate your information the woman who worked here uses aliases."

"Did anyone from here visit the address?" McGhee asked.

She grimaced when she replied, "To be honest, no, and let me explain, John."

Maxwell didn't miss the use of his neighbour's forename, but said nothing.

"We were worked over, pure and simple," she continued. "If word got out and particularly around here, we'd be the laughing stock of the area and it could have repercussions on our business."

"But you did report the theft to the police?"

"Ah, no," she hesitated then it was her turn to blush when she explained, "I'm afraid my partner and I decided to take the hit, as it were, rather than suffer the indignity of having the Shettleston CID laugh themselves to death that our small but *extremely* successful company, who have literally been a thorn in their side for some years, had come crawling to them to report the theft."

It was McGhee who pokerfaced then asked, "But now that you are aware our suspect might now be wanted for not just theft, but possibly a murder, you're happy to provide us with her home address?"

For several seconds, she stared at him then said, "One-o-one, Balintore Street. It's local. In Shettleston."

"One question, McGhee said. "Have you any knowledge of her arriving at work in a vehicle?"

"Eh," her brow furrowed in thought, "not personally, no, but you can ask my receptionist. She started working here a week before Wood scarpered with our cash, so she might have spoken to her and know something I don't."

"Thank you, Miss Paterson, we'll have a word with your receptionist before we leave," he replied as both men rose from their chairs.

It was as they were leaving with Maxwell just stepping into the corridor, she called out, "DC McGhee."

Turning back into the room, he saw her rise from her chair then handing a business card towards him, told him, "Just in case you need to contact me about anything, anything at all," she waved her hand at him.

"I've scribbled my home number on there too," and stared meaningfully at him.

Taken aback, McGhee involuntarily took the card from her then with an embarrassed smile, followed his neighbour out into the reception area.

****

Following her delivery of the good news to DI Sammy Salmon that the ACC would make arrangements for support officers to assist in the shooting investigation, Mary Wells, a coffee in hand, strode into the incident room to inquire of Colin Baxter about any updates.

"No word back yet from Maxwell and McGhee, boss."

"However," he continued, "We're starting to get a number of actions completed regarding the stolen property. After the suspects Maria Clinton and Martha Foster provided the addresses they had stolen items from, the teams have obtained a number of statements and one includes the granddaughter of an elderly woman with dementia, identifying the ruby ring as her grandmothers. Seems no one in the family realised it was gone."

"Really?" surprised, she sipped at her coffee.

"Aye, as you know the arrangement the boss woman had with the other three was that they passed the stuff directly to our victim. Turns out it was Foster who stole the ring and I'm guessing it's probably likely that because she passed it straight to Bradley for safe keeping, the missing suspect didn't know about the ruby ring so wouldn't know how valuable it is. Foster certainly didn't realise its value and nearly fainted when we told her," he dryly added.

"How much of the property have Clinton and Foster identified as stolen by them?"

"Roughly just over a half and to be honest, some of the stuff that pair stole is really crap that you'd find in cheap shops. That means we can probably assume that the rest was knocked off by our victim and the suspect."

"And how much of the property stolen by Clinton and Foster has been formally identified?"

"All but four items, boss. At two of the addresses there has been no response and from what neighbours tell us, we suspect the residents are in care somewhere while at the other two, the residents, both very elderly women, are unable to say if the property is theirs. I thought about having them both fingerprinted to compare with any prints that might be on the items, but at their age, maybe that's a bit extreme?"

"Aye," she sighed, "that would need to be a last resort. Try for a close relative of both the women to see if they recognise the items. As for the two no responses, contact the woman at the cleaning company, eh…"

"Agnes Flynn," he reminded her.

"Miss Flynn," she nodded. "She's been very helpful. Ask if the residents at the two no-reply addresses are still on the company's books and if so, where are they now. If Miss Flynn can't help," her brow knitted as she gave it thought, "try for a forwarding address. I'm certain they must have that information in case any of their staff need to contact a client's next of kin. Oh, and while you're on to Flynn, her eyes narrowed, "I've had a thought. Ask her how they pay their staff wages. I'd be interested to know if they pay through a bank account because if so, they must have bank details for the woman called Lorraine Gray. Might be a starter for ten if they do and she's using the same account."

"Will do, Boss," he scribbled a note onto his pad, then asked, "Anything else?"

"What was the last from Maxwell or McGhee again?"

"The last was the phone call from Baird Street and they were on their way to the law firm's office."

"Okay," she glanced at her wristwatch. "It's getting to that time. Don't be sending anyone else out this afternoon, Colin. We'll be looking for a reasonable finish this evening. No sense in knackering the team when we've still a long way to go," she smiled.

As she left the room, his eyes followed her to the door as he thought, and that's what makes you a good boss. Looking after your team.

****

In the DI's room at Pollok, Sammy Salmon listened intently to Elaine Fitzsimmons and Alan Hamilton as they recounted their visit to Angela Bradley's home.

"Billy Bradley, the brother," Fitzsimmons explained, "will attend at the mortuary tomorrow morning prior to the PM, to formally identify your victim, Boss."

"And you're telling me," he held up the tick book and stared at her, "that this guy Billy also gave up the names of the victims three drug dealing pals as well as this?"

"Yes, boss," Hamilton eagerly confirmed. "All he asks is that we keep the three of them in custody till he makes arrangements to move his mother and niece out of Pollok because he's worried that the families of the three might try to exact some sort of revenge on the Bradley's. He told me he's got family on his mother's side up in Cupar, in Fife, that will put them up until they get a place of their own."

"Well, I don't see a problem about that," he flicked through the tick book. "What about the team that shot Ricky? Does he know who is responsible for the murder?"

"Says he doesn't and I tend to believe him," Hamilton shook his head.

"Elaine?" Salmon turned to her.

"I agree with Alan, boss. Billy Bradley, for all he's known to us for minor things, seems to me to be entirely credible and don't forget, he's taken a right bleaching at the hands of those three thugs and what's worse, they shoved his wee niece around and he was raging about that. So, he owes them nothing and is looking for payback. My suggestion, for what it's worth…"

"And always welcome, Elaine," Salmon interrupted with a grin.

"Well, I think you might want to consider contacting the Drug Squad and bringing them into this too. Make plans to hit the three of them when you decide, then separate them and interview them not just as drug dealing suspects but also as possible witnesses to the murder of Ricky Bradley. They won't know you have the tick book so they'll not be expecting that Billy will have identified them or a knock on the door anytime soon, which might give you a day or so to organise your raids. Then there's the houses that are listed in the book where there's drugs stashed. You might need to call upon some extra bodies to supplement what you've got."

"On that point," he took a breath, "Mary Wells has agreed with ACC Meadows to call in the Divisional Mutual Aid, so we should be getting some extra officers as well as some from the Serious Crime Squad too. If the worse comes to the worse," his brow furrowed as he thought out loud, "I'll try to borrow some from the uniform shift as well. All in all," he tapped the cover of the tick book, "I think we're looking at simultaneously hitting about six houses, if my calculations are correct. Bit late to organise it for tomorrow morning," he shrugged, "so probably early doors for Thursday morning, I think."

"Then, Boss," Fitzsimmons grinned, "we'd better get back to Govan before you end up drafting us two into your operation."

Salmon exhaled through pursed lips before he said, "Okay, Elaine, and sincere thanks to you both. What you've dug up is really valuable and might go some way to solving the murder. When you get to Govan, please let DCI Wells know what you've learned and I'm guessing she'll want to speak with me about hitting the houses, as well as the PM tomorrow morning. Tell her when she's looking for me," he paused then ruefully smiled, "I won't be hard to find because with what's been going on, it looks like I'll be temporarily *living* here."

****

DS Colin Baxter knocked on Mary Wells door just as Elaine Fitzsimons finished her report and concluded with DI Salmon's request Mary telephone him regarding his plan of action.

"Colin," Mary acknowledged Baxter.

"That's the team all arrived for your briefing, Boss, and ready when you are."

"Fine, I'll be a couple of minutes," she nodded.

When he left, she echoed Salmon when she told them, "That was a fine piece of work, both of you," she nodded at them in turn, then said, "Alan, can you give us a minute, please?"

When he'd left the room, she said, "Did Billy Bradley say when he intends leaving Pollok?"

"No, he didn't and that does worry me," Fitzsimmons frowned.

"What's the likelihood, you think, of anyone having a go at the family before they head up to Cupar?"

"Hard to say," her brow wrinkled, "but if I were him, I'd want away as soon as possible. The three names he provided us with are well known for violence, as evidenced by them giving him a right good kicking. If they suspect he might have turned over the tick book or even grassed them in, who knows what lengths they will go to, to get their revenge."

"Yes, I agree. I'm not happy leaving the family and particularly the wee girl in that house without any protection, so I'm considering asking the Serious Crime Squad to detail a couple of authorised firearms officers to babysit them till they leave."

Reaching for the phone, she dialled the direct internal number for Keith Meadows then waving Fitzsimmons back down into her seat and pressing the loudspeaker button on her phone, related the circumstances of Fitzsimmons and Hamilton's visit to the Bradley family then quickly explained her concerns and fear of a violent reprisal.

"So, DCI Wells," he formerly addressed her, "you believe your risk assessment is worthy of a firearms operation, that there *is* a genuine risk to life?"

"Given that there is an ongoing feud between two gangs that so far has resulted in a murder by use of a firearm would infer a likelihood that there might be more firearms in play, then yes sir, I do believe there is a further risk to life."

"Then if you cause an operational report to be typed up with your concerns, I will verbally authorise two officers from the Serious to immediately draw weapons and," he paused, "where and how do you wish to brief them?"

"I'll send DS Fitzsimmons to Pollok Office," she glanced at her. "If they meet with her there, she can both brief then introduce them to the family. Oh, and sir, sorry to spring this upon you."

"It's why my wife tells me I get paid the big bucks, or so she says," he smiled into the phone.

"Now, I'll be off to get it organised. Tell Elaine Fitzsimmon's and her neighbour that was a good piece of work."

"I'll be sure to pass on your comment, yes sir."

When the call had ended, Mary said, "You heard that, so once you've been back to the house, return here and let me know how you get on. And Elaine," Fitzsimmons, standing up from her chair, paused, "don't be surprised if the family and by that I mean Billy Bradley, might *not* want armed officers in his home. If that is the case then suggest that uncomfortable though it undoubtedly will be, the two guys from the Serious take post in the vehicle outside the house. If that *should* occur," she shrugged, "we can have the Pollok CID late shift and night shift take turns past the house as back-up and request they drop them some food and hot drinks. Oh, and tell Sammy Salmon I haven't forgotten him. I'll phone him once I've been to the briefing."

"Got it, boss," Fitzsimmons smiled and left the office.

Glancing at her wristwatch, Mary muttered, "What a day," then rising from her chair, made her way to the incident room.

****

She was pleased to see that Tommy Maxwell and John McGhee had returned to the office, then standing with her arms folded and back against Colin Baxter's desk nodded that he begin.

"First things, first," he rose to his feet, "the boss asked me to contact Agnes Flynn at the cleaning company regarding how the staff were paid. The idea being," he explained, "that if they were paid via a bank account, it might be a way to trace our suspect. Unfortunately," he turned to grimace at the DCI, "it was cash in the old and traditional wee brown pay packets, every Friday."

That's when Mary noticed Maxwell lean towards McGhee and whisper to him, who nodding, turned away and quietly left the office.

"Now, about the stolen property that we continue to identify," Baxter continued and provided an update to the team. When he had concluded the update, he said, "As you all know there was a shooting in the early hours of this morning up in Pollok and the victim, one Richard Bradley, has since succumbed to his injury. The boss will tell you more about that. Boss?" he turned to her.

Wells nodded, then taking step forward, cast a glance around the room before she began with, "The murder investigation that is now ongoing at Pollok will be run by DI Salmon, whose team hopefully will be supplemented by Detectives from the Mutual Aid and the Serious Crime Squad. Now, while I'm certain word has got out that the Pollok victim is the older brother of our victim, Elizabeth Bradley, I don't not believe the murders to be linked and have decided to run them as separate investigations. That said, it's not the first time I've been wrong," she smiled, "so if you've started taking wagers, I suggest you don't bet on me."

She was pleased that her joking admittance drew more than a few smiles and laughs and again inwardly grateful that her team still retained their sense of humour, a clear indication that morale remained high.

"DI Salmon has his PM tomorrow morning at which time we will know more, but for now, can I ask that unless you receive evidence or information to the contrary, you ignore what's going on at Pollok and concentrate on what's going on here in our own investigation."

She turned to see that Maxwell still remained alone and idly wondered where McGhee had gone before she said, "Tommy and John were tracking down a lead for our missing suspect and I've not yet had time to debrief them, so Tommy," she addressed him, "tell us what you've learned."

Clearing his throat, Maxwell began by summarising their visit to the Baird Street Collator, who in turn suggested a visit to Alison Steele. "And that led us to the law firm in Tollcross where we spoke first with a partner, Miss Paterson. She didn't recognise the names Lorraine Gray or Karen Silverton, but when we described the suspect, was confident she knew her as Joanne Wood."

A ripple of whispers went around the room, but before anyone could ask, he raised a hand and proceeded to relate the theft of the petty cash.

It was Mary who asked, "Did the firm have an address for her?"

Maxwell sighed, then nodded, "Balintore Street in Shettleston, Boss. Needless to say, even though Miss Paterson said her firm had sent letters to the address, we checked it anyway and when we knocked on the door…"

"It wasn't her," a downcast Mary finished for him.

"Correct. A woman in her mid-forties," he shrugged uncertainly, "who hadn't a clue who we were looking for, didn't recognise the description, then told us to bugger off too, or she'd have the polis onto us and that was *after* we'd told her who *we* were."

"So, we're no further forward?"

"Lost a shilling, found a tanner?" Maxwell wryly smiled at her.

"You have something else?"

"Before we left the law firm, Miss Paterson suggested we speak with the firm's receptionist who spent a week working with the suspect before she scarpered. It's not much," he shrugged, "but the lassie told us that the suspect drove a bottle green coloured Volkswagen Golf; she was quite specific about the colour because it's her favourite colour, he smiled, That and though she couldn't tell us much about the motor, she thinks it was a few years old and there's something else. She's *pretty* certain the dealers name was on the back window, you know they transfer stickers they use?"

Mary nodded, her interest heightened.

"The lassie thinks it said Arrochar something and the reason she remembers it is because when she was a wee girl, she'd an auntie who lived in Summerston and she used to get the train to the railway station at Summerston and get off the train onto Arrochar *Street*," he finished with a huge grin.

She took a deep breath then said, "Well done, Tommy, to you *and* your neighbour. That might just be the break we're needing."

She glanced at her wristwatch then added, "It's a bit late now so I assume any car dealerships on Arrochar Street or thereabouts will be closed, but first thing tomorrow morning, you and John grab an action and get yourselves over there. You know what you're looking for," she nodded with a smile.

"Boss," he returned her smile just as McGhee entered the room, then raising his hand to attract her attention, said, "Following on about your idea of an employee bank account, I phoned Miss Paterson at the law firm and she confirmed Joanne Wood was paid her salary into a Clydesdale Bank account."

"And she gave you the account details?"

"Yes, boss, and of course because they're closed at three today, it'll be tomorrow before I can check with the bank."

"Good work, John, and if the bank give you any problems about identifying their client, come and see me."

"Boss," he acknowledged with a nod.

"Now," buoyed by the news from Maxwell and McGhee, she cheerfully clapped both hands and asked, "Anything else from anyone? No? Right then, home time folks and again, thanks for everything you did today."

On their way out of the room, Maxwell quietly asked his neighbour, "How did you get on with Miss Paterson?"

"You're not going to let it go, are you?" McGhee gave him a sideways glance.

"Nope," he grinned.

Seconds passed before McGhee leaned towards him to whisper, "She's invited me to meet her later on tonight in the city centre, for drinks."

His eyes widened and shaking his head in disbelief, he replied, "What *is* it that women see in you?"

CHAPTER TWENTY-THREE

After handing over the children to her father and Eileen, that bright Wednesday morning, Mary closed the front door behind her and though she hardly dare admit it to herself, glanced to where Bill had taken to parking his Ford Capri, only to see the vehicle gone. Convincing herself that it mattered not a jot to her that if anything, not seeing him that morning avoided a frosty greeting, for Mary still hadn't forgiven him, believing his downright refusal to permit her to interview Richard Bradley was just sheer bloody obstinance.

Starting the engine, she pulled smoothly away and commenced her journey to Govan.

While driving, a dozen thoughts passed through her mind; everything from her two DC's tracking down the suspects bank account details and possible origin of her vehicle, to Sammy Salmon's PM that hopefully will provide ballistic information regarding the weapon that killed Ricky Bradley.

Her brow creased when she thought of the two murder victims remaining family and all that they had been through. Idly, she wondered if she might be able to solicit some Glasgow Council assistance in getting them removed from their Pollok home and rather than have to move in with relatives, perhaps acquire their own Council home in Cupar.

But who did she know within the Council to who she could turn for such help?

Something she'd give some thought through the day, she smiled; aye, as if she were going to have the time with everything else that was going on.

As happened so many times before, she arrived at Govan Police Office with hardly any thought of the passing journey and mentally chastised herself for not paying attention, as she should have been. Getting out of the car in the rear yard, she was surprised to see ACC Keith Meadows standing in the yard, conversing with the outdoor Inspector, Kenny Herdman, who wearing his raincoat seemed to Mary about to go out on patrol.

Both men turned at her approach and greeted her.

"Morning sir, Kenny," she nodded to them in turn. "Surprised to see you here this early," she politely addressed Meadows.

"Thought I'd pop by, see how you're getting on," he smiled at her, then turning to Herdman, added, "I haven't seen Kenny for heavens knows how many years, so we were doing a bit of catching up together."

"What, dragging up sandbags and swinging the light to create the right atmosphere," she teased them.

"Young people these days," Herdman shook his head as he theatrically sighed, then warmly shaking Meadows hand, smiled, "Good to see you again, Keith, and if you're passing by, I'm always available for a cuppa."

Accompanying her through the back door and up the wide staircase, he explained, "I was Kenny's tutor cop in the old City of Glasgow Force. He'd just come down from Inverness, from the farm where he'd grown up, but he'd an older brother who was inheriting the farm, so had to find his own way in the world and decided on the polis. As I recall, when he arrived in Glasgow, as so many of the men from the Highlands did in those days," he smiled at the memory, "he still had bits of hay sticking out from everywhere."

"Now," he turned at her office door to close it, then politely indicating she sit at her desk, said, "I don't want you to think that I'm intruding on your investigations, but I heard late last night from the Media Department that the 'Glasgow News' have the shooting story and though I don't yet know how, they've connected the murder of Elizabeth Bradley and that of Richard Bradley, to the same family."

Though not certain, she sensed there was anger in his voice.

"It seems," he continued as he sat down facing her, "that they intend running a story about both murders being connected to drugs and gang violence and guns in the southside of Glasgow, presumably concentrating in the Pollok and surrounding area. My guess is they have a source and I'm told that the story will run this evening as an introduction to tomorrow mornings front page headline," he grimaced.

Mary frowned when she replied, "I can only guess that whoever their source is, it must be someone who knows the family or at least something of the circumstances of the shooting, sir. I can quite happily vouch for my staff."

"I'm sure you can," he peered at her, then quietly asked, "But what about former members of your staff?"

She slumped down into her seat as his inference struck her then she muttered, "Shit! You're thinking either Martin Reilly or Hugh Donnelly? Okay, they weren't around at the time of the shooting, but it wouldn't be difficult for either one to put two and two together."

She scowled when she added, "And they're not sticking it just to the police, but to me personally."

"I am thinking it's one or the other, yes," he agreed with a nod. Seconds passed before he said, "I have no need to explain our beloved Chief Constable and his," he paused, "how should I describe them; his *ways*, Mary. He takes any criticism of the Force as an attack upon himself and God forbid he be mentioned in the disparaging article."

Slowly shaking her head, she stared down at her desk then quietly asked, "What advice do you have for me?"

"Other than hunting those two rats down and stabbing them to death?" he grimly smiled.

Seconds passed before he said, "When the article is released tomorrow, I have no doubt that the Media Department will be plagued with phone calls seeking a statement from the Chief about a shooting war in Pollok and knowing him," his face creased, "he'll be looking for someone to hang out to dry. Regretfully, as the head of the G Division CID, that my dear Mary, is you."

"Now, as for my advice, for what it's worth, the only thing I can suggest is ignoring the media attention, don't be quoted by any journalists who phone…" he hesitated, then shaking his head, continued, "in fact, don't even answer their calls, then solve the shooting as quickly as possible."

She took a few, deep breaths to collect her thoughts then said, "Digressing, sir, did you manage to rustle up the extra bodies for DI Salmon?"

"Eight from the Mutual Aid and half a dozen from the Serious Crime Squad who I believe will be reporting to Pollok this morning. Now, the two men who you requested to protect the family. Any issues there?"

"Not that I'm aware of, no sir, but I will be contacting Pollok for an update."

It was then a thought occurred to her and so eyes narrowing as she stared at him, she asked, "You don't happen to know anyone in the Council, preferably the Social Work or the Housing, who might be willing to do you a small favour?"

****

Sammy Salmon's girlfriend, Julie, had arrived earlier that morning at Pollok police office carrying a small holdall that contained his washbag, a clean shirt, tie and underwear and to his delight, freshly cut sandwiches and a flask of his favourite coffee.

Handing the holdall over in the public reception area and slyly watched by the duty sergeant and his bar officer, the blonde and very glamourous young woman stroked tenderly at Salmon's brow and whispered, "I must dash, but please, *please*, try and get some sleep. You look awful."

"Seeing you has just revived me," he gallantly responded, then waved as she hurried out to her car.

Turning, he saw the sergeant and bar officer suddenly take an interest in paperwork they were holding, then made his way back to his office in time to answer the phone that was ringing.

"Sammy, it's me," Mary Wells greeted him, then asked, "Did you get any sleep last night?"

"I stayed here, boss, and got some kip in my office. It didn't seem worth while heading home for just a couple of hours."

"Are you fit to attend the PM today? I can handle it if…"

"No, you're fine," he interrupted her. "Besides, I've a lot happening right now and I'd rather keep the continuity going."

Not fully convinced, she slowly drawled, "Okay," then relating her conversation with Keith Meadows, she informed him to expect the arrival of the extra Detectives.

"As for this media thing, there hasn't been any phone call that I'm aware of, Boss, but I'll give the duty sergeant a heads-up not to put anything from the press through to the CID suite, but just to refer them to the Media Department at headquarters."

"Good. Now, once you have your resources up to speed, I presume that you have an operational plan for hitting the three suspects and the stash houses tomorrow morning?"

"Yes, it's all in hand," but didn't add that planning the operation was what kept him up through the night.

"Can I suggest that at this time, you don't disclose your plan or intentions to anyone? I say that because frankly, we have no idea if Martin Reilly or Hugh Donnelly, assuming one or the other are responsible for tipping off the 'Glasgow News,' might still have eyes and ears in the office."

"Good call, boss, and yes, I'll keep it tight until my briefing."

"Now, the two Serious Crime guys that were at the Bradley house last night. Can I assume they have been relieved this morning?"

"As far as I'm aware, yes, and on that point, Mrs Bradley and her son didn't object to the protection and the guys were permitted to spend the night in the house. Two of their team took over first thing. How long do you suggest I ask them to maintain the watch?"

"I'd say till you have your three suspects in custody or the Bradley's get out of town, as big John Wayne would say. Right," she exhaled, "as soon as you are finished at the Saltmarket, give me a phone and let me know the pathologist's conclusion."

"Roger, and I'm hearing you might have a trace on your suspect, the master criminal with all the aliases," he grinned.

"See, I told you how fast word gets around this Division," she sighed, then added, "Yes, with a bit of luck we might trace her today. Tommy Maxwell and John McGhee did some good work yesterday, so fingers crossed."

"Well, good luck, Boss, and I'll phone you from the Saltmarket."

"Oh, one further thing," he could almost hear her smile when she said, "If you've been sitting in that office all night, you'll probably be a bit smelly. I know the cops have a good rapport with the Fire Brigade's station across the road, so if you need to nip over for a quick hose down?"

"Now there's an idea," he replied then grinning, ended the call.

****

DC John McGhee's first task that morning was to telephone the local Divisional Collator at Maryhill to inquire if there was anything known about a car dealership on or around Arrochar Street, but the call proved fruitless, for the Collator had no knowledge of such a premises.

However, a quick search of the BT Yellow Pages disclosed an address and phone number for 'Arrochar Motors' in Drumlaken Avenue, again in Summerston.

This then, he and Maxwell decided, would be their second port of call that morning.

Rather than phone the Clydesdale Bank's head office in Glasgow city centre, Tommy Maxwell and John McGhee decided to pay a personal visit prior to making their inquiry at the Summerston address.

Parking their vehicle in St Vincent Place, the Detectives entered the large, Georgian premises and headed for the customer service desk. After Maxwell identified themselves and requested they speak with a manager, they were invited into a side office by a middle-aged woman who, a bewildered Maxwell inwardly shook his head, seemed more interested in patting at her hair and blushing at McGhee than listening to what he was asking of her.

What the hell am I missing about him, he wondered, then repeated, "As I was saying, we're trying to trace a suspect who is using this sort code and account," then handed the woman a piece of paper with the details.

"Oh," she stared down at the paper, then muttered, "I'm not sure that I'm at liberty to divulge this information."

"Not even if it pertains to a woman suspected of a number of thefts and is also a murder suspect?" he calmly smiled at her.

Stunned, her hand reached for her chest when she replied, "Oh, my. Murder? Well," she nervously glanced at the closed door, "in that case, as long as you can assure me that you will not divulge where you obtained the information. Excuse me," she rose from her chair and with a hesitant smile at McGhee, left the room.

"Didn't think it would be that easy," McGhee smiled at him.

"It isn't," Maxwell sighed. "She's just wanting to impress you."

"Aye, right," he grinned, but then his grin faded when he asked, "You're joking, right?"

"No, lover boy, I'm not," Maxwell wheezed.

They sat in silence for almost ten minutes before the woman returned clutching a file, then resuming her seat behind the desk, said, "Sorry it took so long, but we're still working with paper files at the minute. The computerisation or whatever they call it," she shook her head, "is ongoing. But there's nothing like pen and paper, I keep telling them," she smiled at McGhee who hadn't a clue who 'them' happened to be.

"Now, let me see," she fumbled with spectacles that were attached around her neck by a bright yellow strap and peered at the only page within the file.

"The account was opened on, eh…that's strange," her brow furrowed.

"Problem?" Maxwell politely asked.

"Yes," the woman's brow creased as she raised her head to stare at him. "The account was opened on the thirtieth of March this year and closed just four weeks later on the twenty-fourth of April. There was just one payment into the account on the day the account closed, from a company called Burnley and Paterson. A salary payment, it seems. How odd," she slowly shook her head.

Maxwell glanced at McGhee, recognising that after drawing the salary, the account had already been closed before the suspect emptied the safe.

Then he asked, "And the account holder. Do you have contact details, please?"

"Ah, yes," she helpfully smiled, "the account belongs to a Miss Elizabeth Bradley of 42 Clifford Street, here in Glasgow."

****

Rather than permit Billy Bradley to travel alone to the mortuary to formally identify his brother and thus be without protection, the two Serious Crime Squad Detectives took the precaution of conveying the three members of the family in the CID vehicle to the Saltmarket, confiding to Billy that while he was at the mortuary, they would take his mother and niece to a café on the High Street around the corner and wait for him there.

"That way," the senior DC explained, "we have control of the three of you and if we're stuck here with your mother and niece at the house, we don't have to worry about you being targeted elsewhere."

Initially unwilling at being what he termed, 'to be babysat,' Billy finally, though with some reluctance, agreed.

Radioing their intention to Pollok Police Office, Billy was dropped at the door of the mortuary where after being introduced to DI Salmon, he made the formal identification, then thereafter, was escorted around the corner to reunite with his mother and niece and the two Detectives.

Minutes after Billy left the building, the post mortem examination commenced.

****

Around that time, Mary was at her desk when the phone rang.

"DCI Wells, it's Mickey at the Scenes of Crime. How you doing, hen?"

Mary smiled at the familiar voice, a man she had known since her days working as a brand-new DC in Shettleston Police Office and of all the people in the world Mary happily permitted to call her 'hen,' Mickey, the senior SOCO supervisor and a High Court recognised Ballistics expert, was one of the very few. Long in the tooth and one of the cheeriest men she knew, he was close to retirement and she had already decided his was one 'leaving doo' she would not miss. "Not heard from you for a while, Mickey. How you keeping?"

"Ach, like everybody my age, hen, my back is giving me gyp, but have you a minute?"

"For you, always," she smiled. "What's up?"

"Your man at Pollok, young Sammy Salmon. I tried contacting his office, but he's away to the PM and I'm not wanting to disturb him in the middle of the examination."

"But you have something urgent to disclose?"

The slightest of pauses ended when he continued, "It was myself that attended the Western yesterday morning to photograph and take samples from your victim."

Mary felt her stomach tighten, a familiar sign to expect news, good or bad, and so asked, "Something come up?"

"Aye, it did. I'll not go into the long-winded explanation of how we detect gunshot residue, what we call GSR, on an individual's hands, but suffice to say we're fortunate that given the time lapse between the victims admittance to the hospital and my taking the GSR samples, fortunately there *did* remain some residue."

Letting that information sink in, he then added, "I also checked his clothing and discovered GSR on his jeans at the waistband and the bottom front of his sweatshirt that suggests to me the shot was fired from not just close range, but we're talking about less than six inches, perhaps even closer."

That all said, he took a short breath, then told her, "In my experienced opinion, hen, your victim either fired or was holding the firearm when it was discharged and shot him. The curious thing is, it's as if the bullet was fired *downwards*, but I have no explanation for that."

Surprised, she muttered "Bloody hell, Mickey," then added, "That I did *not* expect to hear."

"I'll send you my formal statement when it's typed up," Mickey said then hesitantly added, "I'm away in five weeks, Mary. You'll be coming to my retiral party?"

"Only if you promise me a dance," she grinned into the handset.

A delighted Mickey ended the call with a cheery goodbye, leaving Mary to contemplate, why exactly was Ricky Bradley holding the weapon? Was it possible he was trying to wrestle it from his assailant or…?

Her eyes narrowed in thought when the phone rang.

"Boss, it's me, Sammy," he greeted her.

Already suspecting what he was about to divulge, she began by asking, "Is that the PM concluded?"

She could hear the excitement in his voice when he replied, "Yes, and you'll never guess what?"

She refrained from smiling when she said, "He shot himself."

Salmon's silence caused her to smile when he finally gasped, "How the *hell* did you know that?"

"I've just received word from Mickey at the SOCO who was trying to contact you," she admitted. "So, what's the pathologist's verdict?"

Salmon wheezed, then apparently reading from his notebook, replied, "From the angle of the wound he reckons from where the bullet entered Bradley's body, its trajectory seems to have been travelling downwards, but it struck the pelvic bone then seemingly ricocheted the bullet upwards."

He took a breath and continued, "Thereafter, the bullet first pierced the intestines on the right, travelled through the stomach, then the spleen and caused a visible channel before settling in the top half of the left lung. The pathologist, he reckons that the unusual angle of the wound seems to indicate Bradley must have been holding the gun and slightly bent over when it was fired. Says too if the bullet had not ricocheted off the pelvic bone there is a likelihood and if Bradley sought treatment immediately, he might have survived the wound."

"No chance he might have been trying to wrestle the gun from an assailant?"

"I did suggest that," he lowered his voice when he added, "and he was a wee bit peeved that I actually asked it, but he thinks not. In fact, he did offer a plausible explanation. He thinks that Bradley has been hunched up when he was trying to stuff the weapon into the waistband of his trousers and it's went off. Then I asked, wouldn't the barrel have been pointing down, but he suggested the damage to the pelvic bone is consistent with his opinion that the bullet rebounded. Says it's not the first time he's had to deal with death by gunshot. Cheeky bugger asked if I wanted a *second* opinion," he fumed.

"So," her brow furrowed, "we already have the bullet of course after it was removed by Dr Howie at the Western Infirmary."

"We do," Salmon confirmed, then added, "I don't know much about bullets, but the SOCO woman here taking the photos, she told me it's a point-three-eight round, but of course, the Ballistics will confirm that."

"Again in my limited experience," she thoughtfully said, "that sounds like a revolver was used and if that's correct, that's why there was no shell case at the locus where you discovered the blood on the ground."

"Oh, and one more thing. Dr Howie, him that stymied us at the hospital? The pathologist reckons that in his experience and apparently from the emergency surgery that was performed, Howie did a remarkable job trying to save Bradley, but he doesn't believe the deceased could have survived such a devasting wound."

"Oh, right," she was suddenly distracted by thoughts of Bill Howie. "Okay, DI Salmon," she formally addressed him, "what's your intention now as the SIO?"

"Well," he slowly drawled, "I no longer have a murder to investigate, but I do have a number of houses to turn over tomorrow morning, Boss, so before I release the Mutual Aid and the Serious Crime guys back to their offices, I'm going to have them assist me take down some bad boy drug dealers."

She found herself grinning at his description of the drug gang when she replied, "And with a bit of luck, one of them should be able to tell you why they were at the locus as well as confirm it was Bradley who shot himself."

"I'll keep you posted," he cheerfully replied and ended the call.
****

Breaking their trip to visit the Arrochar car dealership located in Drumlaken Avenue, Tommy Maxwell and John McGhee stopped at Maryhill Police Office where using a phone in the CID suite, they updated Colin Baxter with the information gleaned from their visit to the Clydesdale Bank.

"And she's used our victims' details to open the account?"

"And she did that prior to being employed by the cleaning company," Maxwell reminded him, "which seems to suggest she already knew Elizabeth Bradley. We're also of the opinion that she only got herself employed at the law firm for the purpose of stealing from them."

"Which," Baxter thoughtfully replied, "makes me wonder if she's used that MO before?"

"It might be worth putting out a Force wide telex with her description, asking if any Division has information about thefts from law firms or similar companies."

"Good idea, Tommy," Baxter agreed. "Once you're back, I want you to compose a telex, then run it by the boss and get it sent. Now, you're on your way to Summerston?"

"Correct, so fingers crossed we get a result there. Cheers."

"What did Colin have to say?" McGhee asked.

"He says once we're back, you're to compose a Telex like we discussed," he casually lied.

****

Returning to Pollok police office, DI Sammy Salmon couldn't quite put his finger on how he felt. On the one hand, there was a certain amount of relief that he no longer had a murder investigation to run, yet also experienced a sense of disappointment that he wasn't able to demonstrate his ability to be a SIO in what was a noteworthy shooting incident.

Nevertheless, his thoughts turned to the task that lay ahead; conducting a drugs operation against a formidable gang who if their reputation was anything to go by, had been operating in the Pollok and surrounding area with apparent impunity during the years that the former DI, Martin Reilly, had been in charge.

Well, he grimly thought, that stops first thing tomorrow morning when six houses find their doors being knocked by size ten boots. Then, his eyes narrowed, that leaves me, or more likely the new DI, Colin Baxter, with just the one notable drugs gang to sort out.

CHAPTER TWENTY-FOUR

DS Elaine Fitzsimmons and her neighbour, DC Alan Hamilton, were called into Mary Wells office where she disclosed the findings of both the SOCO Ballistics and the pathologist.

"So, he shot himself?" Fitzsimmons could hardly believe it.

"We will need to confirm why, but my guess," Mary shrugged, "is that the pathologist is correct; that he was stuffing the weapon into his jeans and it's went off."

"Now *that*," Hamilton quipped, "is what I would call a rather dramatic premature discharge."

The disproving glance from both women caused him to blush.

"Moving on," Mary dryly continued, "as you have a personal liaison with the family, Elaine, I want you to visit them and break the news that he wasn't after all murdered, but the official verdict is that he died as a result of an accident with an illegally held firearm.

Needless to say, anything that you can learn about this firearm might be of use to Sammy Salmon when he conducts his raids tomorrow morning."

"Right boss," they were about to rise from their seats when Mary added, "One more thing," she glanced at her notes.

"It seems the bloodwork for the deceased was completed and there were traces of cocaine in his system. In short, apparently he was high at the time of his death, but the family have been through enough, so I don't believe there is any need to tell them about him being drugged."

"Boss," Fitzsimmons nodded.

"Oh, and ask if they know why Bradley might have been in Househillwood Crescent in the early hours of the morning."

"Househillwood Crescent, Boss? Is that where he was shot?" Hamilton asked.

"It is, why?"

They saw his eyes narrow then slowly nodding, he said, "Because that's awfully close to Hartstone Road, which is literally just around the corner and if I'm correct, I think Hartstone Road is where the top man in the rival gang lives with his mother."

He shrugged when he added, "I only know that because my mate's a uniformed cop on the shift up in Pollok and he was telling me that whenever they have a call to Hartstone Road, they have to go treble crewed with one man remaining in the motor, because if they leave the car unattended, there's a real chance they'll find the windows panned in when they get back to it."

Mary took an angry, inward breath then slowly exhaled.

"So," her eyes darted back and forth when she quietly said, "it's more than likely that Bradley and whoever was with him parked their stolen motor, the Marina, in Househillwood Road to walk around the corner and were on their way to shoot their rival when, to his *misfortune*," her voice rose, "he's bloody shot *himself*!"

Teeth bared, she stared from one to the other when she snarled, "I don't for one minute blame DI Salmon for not putting two and two together because he's not familiar with the characters or the topography of the area involved in this feud, nor where the gang members live, but *somebody* at Pollok CID should have fucking *known* and informed him!"

Fitzsimmons and Hamilton, shocked at her sudden rage, stood perfectly still, uncertain whether to leave or remain.

They could not know in the seconds it took her to comprehend what Hamilton had said, she suspected the DS's and the DC's at Pollok CID must have realised the geographical connection between Bradley's shooting injury and the proximity of the rival drug gang member's home. Yet whether through sheer negligence or, as she suspected, they were sticking it to the temporary DI, they failed to make that connection known to Salmon.

Then again, her blood continued to boil, that *bastard* Martin Reilly continuously asserted that there was no real drug problem in the Pollok sub-Division, that whatever was going on, he had it under control. Fuming with herself, she inwardly hissed, why the hell did I stupidly believe him?

Exhaling, she waved a hand of apology then calming herself as quickly as she had grown to anger, quietly said, "Sorry, guys, I regret my outburst. Stupidity I can deal with, but I will *not* tolerate sheer, bloody incompetence or as I suspect, deceitfulness. Someone, perhaps more than one individual in Pollok CID, has badly let down their DI and they've let me down, but rest assured, it *will* be dealt with. Now, I will ask you to keep my outburst to yourselves and for the time being, carry on and inform Mrs Bradley and her family of the pathologist's findings."

"Boss," they both responded and left the room.

Still inwardly seething, Mary took several minutes to fully compose herself, then phoned the CID clerk at Pollok and left word that Sammy Salmon immediately contact her upon his return.

Rising from her desk, she made her way to the incident room where Colin Baxter informed her of Tommy Maxwell and John McGhee's discovery at the Clydesdale Bank, that the suspect might have known Elizabeth Bradley *prior* to the suspect joining the cleaning company.

Seated in the chair in front of Baxter's desk, she quietly responded with, "Now that is interesting."

Turning, she called out to McPhee, "Janey, can you get onto the radio and before they arrive at Mrs Bradley's house, ask DS Fitzsimmons to first call in at Pollok police office then contact me here in the incident room?"

"Ma'am," McPhee acknowledged with a nod and reached for the desk phone.

Baxter, his brow furrowed, asked her, "What you thinking, boss?"

"Well, when we first interviewed Mrs Bradley, in her statement she informed us she did *not* know a woman called Lorraine Gray and also had no idea if her daughter knew a woman of that name. At that time *we* didn't know that Lorraine Gray was an alias, so when Mrs Bradley didn't recognise the name, we wouldn't have thought to give our suspect's description because after all, why would we?" she shrugged.

"However, in light of our subsequent knowledge that our suspect uses several aliases, now I'm wondering if maybe her daughter did know our suspect, but even if Mrs Bradley doesn't recognise the aliases, she might recognise the suspect's description and perhaps know her under another name, maybe yet another alias."

Baxter smiled when he slowly nodded and said, "Good one, Boss. Here's keeping our fingers crossed."

****

Turning slowly from Arrochar Street into Drumlaken Street, Maxwell asked McGhee, "Are you certain this is the address that was in the Yellow Pages, John?"

"I'm definite. Drumlaken Avenue should be up here," McGhee replied as he slowly guided the CID car through the nineteen-sixties built, Council two storey, mid-terraced flats.

The wide road between the off-white, roughcast buildings was bordered by a large number of lengthy lay-bys, though there were a few vehicles parked in the bays.

Or so they saw until they arrived in Drumlaken Avenue, where they came upon a row of a dozen cars and vans parked together in a lengthy bay; all different makes and models, but all washed and brightly polished and, they then saw, all bearing the rear window stickers 'Arrochar Motors.'

Turning to McGhee, Maxwell dryly said, "Looks like we've found Arrochar Motors, then."

Pushing open the door of the close, Maxwell led McGhee to the front door of the first floor flat where a neatly printed sign in a wooden frame announced the occupant to be, 'Arrochar Motors.'

At Maxwell's knock, the door was opened by a clean shaven, portly man in his early fifties whose thinning brown hair was gelled back and who wore a red tie with a pale blue shirt, plaid jacket, grey trousers and whose bright smile died when he saw the two Detectives.

"Oh, you'll be the polis, then?" he asked, then before either could respond, he held up a hand to say, "Look, the motors are all taxed or rather, the forms are at the DVLA and honest, officers, I'm only trying to earn a living here."

"I'm DC Maxwell and this," he cocked a thumb behind him, "is DC McGhee. You are?"

"Eh? You're the CID?" his face fell. "This isn't about that old bitch upstairs complaining about the motors being parked outside?"

"No, pal, this is about a murder."

Two minutes later, in a back bedroom clearly being used as a cramped office with a desk, a three-drawer filing cabinet, a narrow table set under the window with a kettle, mugs, coffee and tea caddies, a small fridge in one corner and two comfortable chairs squeezed into the room, McGhee handed the shaken man a glass of water.

"By God, you guys gave me some fright there," he muttered. "Murder? What murder?"

"First of all, what's your name, sir."

"Eh, me? I'm Joe McDaid," then attempting to inject a little dignity into his voice, lifted his chin when he added, "I'm the proprietor of Arrochar Motors."

"Right, Mr McDaid, we're here about a green coloured Volkswagen Golf motor that apparently you sold to a woman, though to be honest, we don't have her details. How many Golf's have passed through your hands?"

"First, though," McDaid's eyes narrowed, "Am I in any trouble or could I be? I mean, I can't just pass out a customer's details."

His chest puffed out when he brusquely added, "There is client confidentiality, you know."

Bewildered at the portly man's cheeky comment, Maxwell turned to stare at McGhee, who in a monotone voice, quietly replied, "Mr McDaid, client confidentiality can be invoked by a lawyer who is lawfully entitled to refrain from answering our questions. Then of course, a doctor can invoke patient confidentiality and again, refrain from answering our questions."

He shrugged when he continued, "A priest or a minister can assert that privilege on behalf of a penitent about information learned during a confession and so, can also refrain from answering our questions. However, you," he leaned forward as he stared menacingly at McDaid, "you're a wee fat guy operating a second-hand car business out of your flat and likely, without the Inland Revenue being aware. And," his eyes narrowing as he stared menacingly at McDaid, he leaned even further when he added, "I'm almost certain that *none* of those vehicles outside are taxed *nor* insured to be on a public road, where they now sit. So, when my pal here asks you about a Golf motor we're interested in, you have to ask yourself. Will I do my civic duty and assist the police by truthfully answering all their questions," his eyes narrowed even further, "or will I make life difficult for myself?"

They saw McDaid gulp, then turning to Maxwell, he croaked, "Did you say it was a bottle green coloured Golf?"

Maxwell, recalling what the law firm's secretary had told him, smiled, "No, what I *said* was a *green* coloured Golf but curiously, it was described to me as a *bottle* green coloured Golf."

He continued to smile when he added, "Just like you described it yourself."

****

In his office, Bill Howie took ten minutes to himself to chomp down a bland cafeteria sandwich, sip at a now tepid coffee and thought again about Mary Wells.

My God, he thought, it's just been a couple of days, but there was definitely something about that woman that got right under his skin. But now, because of the stance that he'd taken, it was unlikely that she'd even acknowledge him when passing by.

Loathe though he was and trying to fight the thought, he could not help but compare her to Sophia and inwardly sighed.

Sophia had been small, golden skinned with tight black curly hair, a willowy figure and quick to scowl when displeased, even a little petty, he suddenly thought and wondered why he'd never really considered that before.

In contrast, Mary was slightly above average height, with a fulsome figure, brown hair and a ready smile. His forehead creased when he recalled her brown eyes that flashed a warning when he'd denied her access to his patient and realised those same, lovely eyes would also issue a warning that she could be quick to anger about anything that displeased her.

Two completely different women, he sighed; one who broke his heart and another who he hadn't even had the opportunity to get to really know.

It was then he realised he really did want to get to know Mary; Mary and her children, he corrected himself.

What am I like, he thought and ruefully shook his head.

Staring distastefully at the half-eaten sandwich, he threw it in the waste bin and gulped down the rest of the coffee, then pushing himself to his feet, turned when the door opened to admit a Staff Nurse, who apologetically grimacing, said, "Sorry, Dr Howie, but you're needed."

****

Returned to Pollok, Sammy Salmon was seated at his desk, listening to Mary Wells as she recounted Alan Hamilton's information about the rival gang member living around the corner from the locus of Ricky Bradley's shooting.

"So, it's likely then that was Bradley and his pal's motive, taking a wee walk around the corner and shooting their rival?"

"That's my conclusion, yes," Mary replied. "Either shooting their rival or at the very least, discharging their firearms to scare the shit out of him."

"And no one here thought to mention to me that the rival lived just around the corner from where Bradley shot himself," he dryly added.

"Apparently not," she tightly replied.

Several seconds of silence passed before Salmon said, "Right then boss, can you give me half an hour, please. I'll be wanting a word with my team up here."

"Would you rather that I come up and roast them?"

"Oh, no," he quickly replied in the same, dull voice. "For the minute, my team, my problem."

"We'll speak later then," she ended the call.

Staring down at the phone, Mary quietly exhaled then rising from the desk, made her way back to the incident room where Colin Baxter told her, "You were on the phone, Boss, when Elaine Fitzsimmons called in. I've passed on your message to describe our suspect to Mrs Bradley."

"Good and thanks, Colin. Anything else doing?"

"Maybe ask them two," he waved a hand behind her.

Turning, Mary saw Tommy Maxwell and John McGhee enter the room, both with a smile on their face.

"Tell me it's good news," she asked them.

Glancing at McGhee, Maxwell slowly nodded when he said, "We think we might have identified our suspect."

****

Seated in the armchair opposite Angela Bradley, Fitzsimmons watched the older woman's face crease in thought when she replied, "Aye, it sounds like her pal, Monica."

"Monica? Do you have a second name for her?"

"No, Miss, all I know is she's called Monica. A nice lassie, right good looking too and posh. Wait a minute," she rose from the armchair and made her way to the door, then pulling it open, leaned out and shouted, "Billy!"

They heard the sound of Billy coming downstairs then entering the room, he stared from his mother to the Detectives and asked, "What?"

Still on her feet, Angela asked her son, "That lassie, Monica, the good looking pal of our Lizzie. Do you know her second name?"

"No," he slowly shook his head, then his face brightened when he added, "But she's a right good-looking bird, so she is."

"Billy!" his mother snapped at him with an embarrassed glance at Fitzsimmons.

"Sorry," he muttered.

"Billy," Fitzsimmons addressed him, "Can you tell us anything about Monica, anything at all?"

His brow creased when he shrugged and replied, "Not much I can tell you, Miss. I only saw her the once, when she came to give Lizzie and the wee one a run down the road."

"Wait, a run down the road? You mean she took Lizzie and Sarah in a car?"

"Aye a green motor, a Golf I think it was. Why, is it important?"

"When was this, can you remember?"

"Eh, I'm not sure, maybe a couple of months ago? Might even be three months because like I said, I'm not that sure."

Fitzsimmons glanced at Hamilton who fought his grin.

Maybe now, she thought, we've finally got a firm lead on our suspect.

****

"According to the car dealer, boss," Maxwell began, "her name's Monica Davies. She produced a driving licence with those details on it," he handed Mary a handwritten note.

"You haven't been to the address and knocked on her door?"

"No, boss," he shook his head. "We thought it better to make you aware first of what we discovered rather than go blundering in. However," he smiled again, "we did take a wee turn past her address and saw the Golf parked in the driveway, so if nothing else, that sort of confirms she's living there. Oh, and one other thing. We also PNC'd the Golf, but though she purchased the motor about a year ago, she's never registered her ownership with the DVLA," he shook his head. "In fact, the previous owner informed DVLA he no longer owns the car."

"Well done," Mary nodded. "Not knocking on her door, that was the correct decision, guys. When we go for this woman and given the time that has passed since the murder and the thefts, I want us to proceed on warrant. So, Colin," she turned to Baxter, trying with difficulty to supress the excitement in her voice, "have the typists draft a Sheriff's arrest and search warrant for Davies at her address and you two," she turned back to Maxwell and McGhee, "will serve the warrant tomorrow morning early doors and make sure you have back-up. Once she's in cuffs, bring in the SOCO to turn her place over."

Her eyes narrowed as she considered who to send, then added, "I want a female officer to accompany you, so take Elaine Fitzsimmons with you and request the presence of a couple of the local uniformed shift to protect the locus and just in case there's a kick-out."

Janey McPhee raised a hand to attract Mary's attention then said, "DI Salmon at Pollok, Ma'am. Can you give him a phone?"

"Tell him I will do in a few minutes and thanks, Janey. Now," she

glanced at her wristwatch, "time's marching on, so we'll have an early night, Colin. Once the team are all back, give me a shout and we'll have a quick debrief, then home."
She addressed Maxwell and McGhee when she asked, "Any questions guys?"
"Who'll conduct the interview with Davies, boss?"
She grinned when she replied, "You guys will have the pleasure of the arrest, but rank has its privilege, so I'll save *that* wee chestnut for Colin and myself."
****

It was a sober sounding Sammy Salmon who spoke with Mary when he told her, "For the first time in my career, I really lost it, boss. Aside from the guys on days off, I pulled the rest of the Pollok CID into the general office and gutted them. Needless to say there was the predictable 'I never thought' and 'I didn't realise,' but to be frank, they're a shower of lying gits because of course they knew."
She knew he had more to add, so stayed silent.
"In their defence," she heard him take a breath, "the atmosphere in this office since Martin Reilly was in charge; well, him and that evil bastard, Hugh Donnelly, has been so poisonous that the guys up here don't even trust themselves, let alone someone like me who's just arrived, particularly as they have their fixed opinions about Advanced Promotion candidates like me."
The brief silence was broken when she asked, "Do you want to send some of them down here, Sammy, in exchange for some of the Govan staff?"
"No, not at all," he quickly replied. "That would seem like an admission that I have no authority over them, that I can't control them. In fact," she heard him take an intake of breath, "I have a request to make of you."
"And that is?"
"I know that at the conclusion of your murder investigation, when Colin Baxter is promoted to DI, it is your intention to send him here to Pollok. Might I ask that you delay his transfer to enable me to have a go at sorting this lot out? I know it's a lot to ask of you and it's not the ideal situation having a DS promoted to DI, then serving in the same office, but I really feel that I'd be copping out if I left and I'd feel it was unfair unloading onto Colin what effectively is currently *my* problem."

Her brow furrowed before she carefully replied, "Let me give it some thought and I'll let you know tomorrow."

"That's all I ask, Boss, thank you."

The call had just ended when her door was knocked by Elaine Fitzsimmons, who standing in the door, wryly grinned then said, "Alan Hamilton and I thought we were coming back with great news, but I'm hearing that Monica Davies has been identified?"

"What did you learn?"

"Well, between two and three months ago, a woman fitting our suspect's description and called Monica gave Lizzie Bradley and her daughter a lift in a green coloured Golf. If the time frame is correct, then it sounds like she was either employed or just left the law firm after thieving from them."

"Which also suggests she knew Lizzie Bradley at that time," Mary finished for her.

"Busy girl, our Monica," Fitzsimmons lopsidedly smiled.

"Indeed," she soberly nodded, then rising to her feet, said, "Let's get the briefing done."

****

Mary arrived home a little after six-thirty that evening, to see Bill Howie arriving seconds behind her.

Realising it would be juvenile to pretend not to notice him she locked her car then stood pokerfaced with arms folded, waiting on him crossing the road.

He caught her off guard when he gave her a crooked smile and asked, "Is this about the elephant in the room?"

"Pardon?"

He stopped and audibly sighed when he softly continued, "Yesterday at the hospital. You were angry with me. Is that still the case, that you're angry with me?"

It was then she realised that no, she wasn't angry anymore, so shaking her head, she shrugged when she said, "I was doing my job, you were doing yours. I suppose that's all there is to it."

"So, still friends?"

His disarming smile caused her to grin when she nodded and replied, "Still friends."

Her front door opened and her father, his jacket over one arm, popped his head out to tell her, "Sorry, love, but Eileen and I want to head off sharpish tonight. If you recall, I've the meeting tomorrow with the lawyer and we want time to discuss how I'm going to represent my case."

"Oh, yes, of course, dad," her face flushed for the truth was, she'd forgotten all about Michael's meeting.

"Listen," she turned to see Bill grimace when he said, "I've had a rotten day and nothing to eat, but I do have a pizza and garlic bread in the freezer. How would you feel if I knocked on your door with it, I mean," he smiled, "I'll cook it first, of course."

Taken aback and without thinking, she felt her face redden when she muttered, "Yes, eh, that would be great. Give me an hour or so to put the kids down, if you can wait that long?"

"No problem," he smiled and watched as she stepped through her door.

Closing the door behind her, Michael teased, "Is that you and Bill having a date, then?"

Standing putting her coat on, Eileen interrupted with, "Don't be listening to him, Mary. He's just teasing you. I heard what Bill said, so you enjoy a bit of company and by the way, the scallywags are up in their room and they've already been bathed and had their hair washed."

"We'd no choice about that," her father grinned. "The wee devils were covered in sand from the pit at the park. It was everywhere and you should have *seen* the state of your bath," he shook his head.

She watched Eileen playfully push Michael towards the door then making eyes at Mary at her father's behaviour, smiled then said "See you in the morning, love."

But then she turned to say, "Oh, and I've taken the liberty of confirming the arrangement for the children to spend the day at the nursery and we'll be here first thing to take the kids there before Michael and I attend at the lawyer's office."

"Thanks, Eileen," Mary thankfully sighed, for with everything going on at the office, she'd forgotten all about arranging the nursery day for the children.

When they'd gone, she hurried upstairs to find Jamie and Morven, both clearly exhausted from the play that day, lying side by side on Jamie's bed while the five-year-old held a colourful book and pretended to read a story to his wide-eyed little sister.

Standing unnoticed at the bedroom door, a wave of emotion washed over her as she listened to Jamie's make-believe story of a princess and a dragon that was completely conjured from his imagination. While her urge was to rush into the room and hug them both, her heart told her that her children were sharing a special moment and so tip-toeing back from the door, she went to her own bedroom to change out of her work suit.

****

The Horseshoe Bar in Glasgow's Drury Street is one of the city's iconic and most welcoming pub restaurants and boasts to be the longest bar in Europe. Never quiet, the clientele come from all over the city and beyond and is listed as a Category A building of historic importance.

It was to this bar that DC John McGhee rushed that evening for his meeting with the lawyer, Charlotte 'Charlie' Paterson and arrived just as she was settling herself into a small and intimate booth at the rear of the pub.

"Sorry I'm a little late," he gasped, but whether his breathlessness was due to his rushing or at the sight of her, he wasn't certain, for Paterson, her raven coloured hair lying loosely on her shoulders, wore a tight, red blouse that showed off her inviting cleavage and a short, black leather skirt that when sitting, rose up to her bare thighs. It didn't escape his attention either that more than a few admiring glances came their way from the men standing at the bar.

"Wow," he muttered and sliding into the bench seat beside her, saw her coyly smile when she replied, "I take it I've impressed you?"

"Oh, aye," but before he could respond further, she quickly added when nodding at the pint glass on the table, "I took the liberty of ordering you a Tennents. Is that okay?"

"Fine by me," he toasted her wine glass with his lager, then quietly said, "I'm at a loss why you wanted to meet with me."

Her brow crinkled when he stared at him before she slowly shook her head, then sliding close to him until their thighs touched, huskily replied, "To be perfectly honest, John, even I don't know why I asked you to come for a drink. All I can tell you is, somehow or other, you get under my skin and I find I'm attracted to you."

His face reddened when he blustered, "Well, I didn't expect that, but I can't say I'm disappointed."

"And you don't object to being seen with a slightly older woman?"

"I don't object to be seen with a woman that looks as gorgeous as you," he gallantly replied.

"Well," she leaned forward to softly whisper in his ear, "that response, Detective Constable, will earn you a night of passion that you've never before experienced."

Gulping, he thought, there really is no answer to that promise.

The next half hour was spent in quiet conversation with both making an effort not to talk about their respective jobs while McGhee was desperately keen for her to finish her drink so they could return to her place.

He had just finished his pint when his brow furrowed as he stared at two men standing at the other end of the bar who head to head, were engaged in earnest conversation.

Paterson saw him staring and glancing towards the two men, leaned towards McGhee to tell him, "He's a right sleaze ball that man. Can't stand the bugger."

He turned to face her and asked, "You know him?"

"Well," she grimaced, "I wouldn't say I *know* him, but some of my clients have had dealings with him in the past and he's not beyond sticking the knife into them when it suits him. A sort of use and abuse individual, if you know what I mean," her disgust was evident.

"I've never liked him either," McGhee quietly admitted. "I spent some time working at Pollok police office and he was my supervisor. Done me dirty on an annual appraisal."

She stared curiously at him before she asked, "Are we looking at the same man, John? I'm talking about him in the blue anorak; the 'Glasgow News' chief crime reporter, Ally McGregor."

Realisation dawned on McGhee's face and with a wide grin, lifted Paterson's hand and brushed his lips against it before he parodied Humphrey Bogart and said, "Sweetheart, you and I are destined for great things."

****

Bill Howie involuntarily cursed as he brought the tray out of the oven and accidently touched the burning hot metal side with his thumb.

Lifting the tray over to the worktop, he slid the pizza onto a sheet of tinfoil then carefully wrapped it closed.

Lifting the pizza, he placed it into the wicker basket alongside the tinfoil wrapped garlic bread and the bottle of chilled wine then switching off the oven, headed towards the front door.

Dressed in a clean, light blue coloured polo shirt and khaki chinos, he made his way to Mary's front door and was about to ring the bell, but then thought the children might be asleep and instead, lightly knocked.

Within seconds, Mary, who had been listening for him calling, opened the door and beckoning him in with a smile, placed her forefinger to her lips and whispered, "They've only shut their eyes about ten minutes ago."

He stared briefly at her, catching his breath, for her hair lying loose on her bare shoulders, she wore a light coloured, knee-length floral Cami-dress that flattered her figure, her legs bare and shoeless, showed off her red coloured toe-nails.

Quietly closing the door behind him, she pointed to the kitchen, then when the door was pushed over and only slightly ajar, she asked, "Is it okay if we eat in here? That way if they waken, I can hear them."

Nodding, Bill saw the table had been set for two and included wine glasses.

"The plates are heating in the oven," Mary told him then asked, "Wine?"

"Actually, I've brought a bottle," he produced it from the basket then collecting the plates, indicated Mary sit down and began to set out their meal.

Though they were not complete strangers, Mary sensed that both he and indeed she herself were a little nervous and so to ease his tension, opened the conversation with, "Tell me about your day."

Bill exhaled as he sliced the pizza and the bread, then made her laugh when he jokingly described treating his patients and included the little girl and her wounded leg and the mother who tearfully fussed and worried that her daughter might never again walk properly.

Then added with a wide grin, "Truth be told, it was the mother who was really the patient. The wee girl took it all in her stride whereas the mother was a nervous wreck and I almost considered sedating *her*."

At last, the meal was ready and sitting opposite each other, he in turn asked about Mary's day.

She glanced at him, then decided that he could be trusted and so at length, related the hunt for a female suspect who for a week, using various aliases, had eluded all attempts to trace her.

"But today, thanks to some diligent work by my team, we found her," she smiled, then added, "and tomorrow she's getting a loud knock on her door."

Their conversation drifted to more domestic matters, Mary explaining the difficulty of being a single parent and not only raising two young children, but holding down a full-time job too.

"Well," he smiled and toasted her with his glass "from the little I've seen of Jamie and Morven, they seem to be well adjusted children so you must be doing a good job."

"I couldn't have managed at all without Eileen's help and my dad too, of course," she shrugged and slightly reddened at the unaccustomed compliment.

She couldn't explain why, but it pleased her that he had used their names rather than calling them 'the kids' or 'the children.'

"And what about you," she stared curiously at him then cheekily smiled. "No marital entanglements?"

"Ah, me," his expression changed as his face clouded over.

"I'm sorry," she feared she had overstepped the mark and raised her hand. "I didn't mean to pry."

"No, you're okay, Mary. No," he sighed, "I've not been married, but there was someone, not too long ago actually. In fact, that's half the reason I returned to Glasgow."

She said nothing, knowing that if he wished to disclose any more, he would do it in his own time and quietly sipped at her wine.

When his brow knitted, his face expressed his thoughts when at last he said, "You'll likely know from the news bulletins that back in nineteen-eighty-three, the second Sudanese War commenced. A bloody affair it is too," he bitterly added.

"I'm sorry," she grimaced as she shrugged. "I know from the news programmes there's been a war going on, but to be honest, I don't really know much about it."

"Why should you," his face registering his sadness, he slowly shook his head.

"The Western powers have no real interest in a civil war fought in a third world country, nor the atrocities that were and are currently being carried out in the name of Islam and Christianity, too. It's the usual story," then using his forefingers as italics, he sarcastically said, "More people dying in the name of *their* God than any other reason. Course it's like most wars, it's the poorest of the poor who suffer and by God, are they suffering," he added with some feeling. He paused to collect his thoughts, then staring at her, continued, "But to answer your question. I was running a clinic in a refugee camp not far from the Eritrean border, a camp that me and everyone else in the Médecins Sans Frontières community thought was relatively safe from the fighting. However, the sad truth is that there was nowhere safe from the fighting."

He paused again then sipping at his wine, continued, "At the time I was in a relationship with a fellow medic, a French doctor called Sophia Moreau. Well," he half-smiled, "I'd known Sophia for almost two years. Two *years*, Mary," he emphasised with gritted teeth, "and there was me thinking, this is it, I've found my soulmate. Unfortunately," he sighed, "just before the refugee camp was overrun by some Islamic militia, at which time I got this," he pointed to the scar on the left side of his forehead, "the love of my life decided that she was returning to France to be with her husband."

"Her husband?" Mary's eyes widened.

"More fool me," he slowly nodded. "I didn't know, of course and when she admitted she'd been married for something like five years *and* had a son, who was living with her husband; well, I just kind of lost it. Words were exchanged and quite frankly, my world came crashing down."

She saw he was clearly embarrassed at such an admittance, then watching him gulp back the last of his wine, he pushed back his chair and standing, was about to leave when Mary calmly told him, "My husband, Harry. While I was in the maternity giving birth to Morven, he was next door shagging my neighbour, a woman I called my close friend."

He stared for several seconds at her, then slowly sitting back down, raised a hand before he sighed, "Okay, you win. I cannot beat *that* story."

CHAPTER TWENTY-FIVE

The sun was shining brightly that Thursday morning when within minutes of each other Tommy Maxwell, John McGhee and Elaine Fitzsimmons all arrived at the murder incident room.

To their surprise, Colin Baxter was already seated behind his desk and greeting them with a wide grin, said, "I've been onto Shettleston Police Office half an hour ago and informed the duty officer that you're going to Mount Vernon to execute the warrant and turn a house in Dornford Avenue. He's arranged that two beat cops will meet you guys at the main gate of Mount Vernon Primary School and told me it's literally just around the corner from Dornford Avenue, so the cops should be waiting for you there."

"Thanks, Colin," Fitzsimmon's smiled, then asked, "We have time for a coffee before we go?"

Glancing at his wristwatch, Baxter, replied, "It's just turning six-thirty, so aye, grab a coffee. I can't imagine she'll be out this early, but if the Golf isn't parked in the driveway…"

"Then we abandon the knock on the door until it is," Fitzsimmons finished for him.

"Good," he smiled then turned as Mary Wells entered the room.

"All set?" she smiled at them in turn.

"I've just told them to grab a quick coffee before they set off, Boss," Baxter informed her.

"Okay," Mary frowned, then added, "but make it quick, guys. We don't want to miss this woman and have to wait all day for her to return to the house."

****

Driving to the hospital that morning, Bill Howie reflected on his evening with Mary Wells and realised that though it had just been a few hours sharing a meal, he hadn't enjoyed himself since God alone knew.

Mary, he smiled at the memory of her, was not only an extremely attractive woman, but a smart, funny and intelligent individual who as the evening progressed, through her police stories made him alternatively smile then saddened him, particularly when she recounted her struggle with her post-natal depression. That she had come through such a traumatic and lifechanging time after her adulterous husband had fled with his girlfriend, leaving her with a toddler son and new born baby, was testament to her strong character and he wondered at how she had survived.

Yes, she'd admitted her new friendship with Eileen McAulay had been of great help and the support from her father, brothers and sisters-in-law, as well as some of her colleagues, had helped her cope too, she had told him.

Sitting across the kitchen table from her, he had gently reminded her, "But it was you, Mary. You, who faced those demons that women have to suffer when they are struck down with post-natal depression. You who abandoned by your husband, had to face bringing up your children alone. You who fought your way back to your career. You who should take pride in what you achieved and I'm guessing, will continue to achieve."

He had known he was embarrassing her, yet could not help himself and ached to hold her, but also knew that to do so would cause her to think that he was taking advantage of her, that baring her soul as she did, she had left herself open to his kind words.

And so, citing the late hour, he had politely excused himself, but as she saw him to the door he reminded her she had previously agreed that they would one evening, go to dinner.

"But *not* for pizza," he had made her smile.

The short stride to his own home had taken just seconds and yet he had hated every step, for Bill Howie now realised that given even a half chance, he had wanted to spend the night with Mary Wells, then waken beside her.

****

The three Detectives passed by the target house, relieved to see the Golf parked in the driveway, then turned the corner to find the marked police Transit Van with the two uniformed officers waiting for them outside the closed school gates in Criffell Road, a mere one hundred yards from the junction with Dornford Avenue.

Thanking them for their assistance, Elaine Fitzsimmons explained to the police woman and her young male probationary cop their intention to execute the warrant at a semi-detached bungalow around the corner where they would arrest the occupant, Monica Davies, then conduct a search of the property. If need be and if required, Fitzsimmons added, they would call upon SOCO to assist with the search.

The senior cop, a woman in her mid-thirties, then asked, "Do you have any idea who else might be in the property, Sarge?"

It was Tommy Maxwell who replied, "According to the voters roll,

Davies is the only adult listed, but we've no idea if there are other adults or children within the property."

They saw the cop's eyes narrow and it was Fitzsimmon's who politely asked, "Problem?"

The woman shrugged before she replied, "I'm thinking if there are kids in the house, we might have an issue, Sarge, particularly if you're arresting the mother."

Fitzsimmons glanced at Maxwell and McGhee in turn, inwardly thinking, shit! Why didn't we take that into account?

However, she calmly said, "Let's deal with any problems as we encounter them rather than worry about them now."

It was apparent, though, her reply didn't satisfy the cop's concerns. "Right," she said, "let's serve the warrant before the public waken up to wonder why we're standing here, eh?"

Parking outside the semi-detached bungalow with the neatly trimmed hedge to the front and mown lawn, Fitzsimmons sent both cops to the rear of the house to prevent anyone leaving via the back door.

Knocking on the front door, almost two minutes of further knocking passed before they heard a woman's voice loudly call out, "Okay, okay, I'm coming."

When the door was pulled open, Fitzsimmons and her two colleagues involuntarily felt relief, for the attractive woman matched the description of the suspect they knew initially as Lorraine Gray; in her early to mid-forties, dyed blonde hair, though in slight disarray and wearing a bright yellow, knee length cotton dressing gown.

Staring tiredly at the officers, she leaned against the open door, then to their surprise, she smiled when she politely greeted them with, "So, you finally found me, then?"

****

Sammy Salmon had spent some time the previous evening preparing his briefing for that morning. After much deliberation and as much as he wanted to participate in the raids, he finally decided that after distributing the Sheriff Drugs and Firearms search warrants and issuing the various tasks to the teams that now comprised of a mixture of his own Pollok detectives and some uniform personnel, as well as members of both the Serious Crime Squad and the hastily summoned Drug Squad, that as the SIO in charge, he would be better placed remaining at Pollok Police Office to coordinate the operation. It had been decided on a six-am report for all concerned and following the briefing, the door to all six houses would be knocked or in some properties, kicked in, no later than seven-am.

Now, pacing the floor of the general office with the radio sitting on the clerk's desk and tuned to the common channel being used by the six raiding teams, he listened without comment as one by one, five of the teams declared, 'Entry gained. No resistance and search commencing.'

It was several minutes after these declarations that the sixth team radioed in, "Entry gained." However, in the background, Salmon could hear the sound of shouting, a woman screaming, a dog barking and what also sounded like an ongoing struggle as though the radio was being wrestled from the user.

Tempted though he was to ask what the hell was going on, he maintained his silence until at last, after several nerve-wracking minutes, the caller said, "Resistance overcome. One male and two females arrested, but we're going to have to take one of the women straight to the Casualty at the Victoria Hospital, Boss. She's bleeding heavily from a blow to the head."

"How seriously…" he began to ask, then changed it to, "Any risk to life?"

"No, Boss. She came at us with a kitchen knife, so got dunted over the head with a baton. Big bird, so she is," he heard the caller take a deep breath, then grunted, "Took a right good couple of blows to deck her, so it did."

Salmon closed his eyes tightly and exhaled, already imagining the complaint that was likely to be made, yet inwardly relieved that none of the team had been injured.

Then he replied, "Thanks. Salmon to all teams. Well done and when you have all concluded your searches, I'll see you when you return to Pollok. As arranged, the dedicated rooms are ready for the interrogations," but didn't add that in an office where space was at a premium, the arrangements themselves took some doing with the sub-Divisional Superintendent, the shift Inspectors and the Sergeants all whining about being evicted from their rooms. Just as well, he dryly thought, he had Mary Wells and the Divisional Commander backing him.

It was then that he was distracted when a female voice from team three, one of the female Drug Squad, he thought, radioed back to tensely ask, "Boss, can you arrange for SOCO to attend my location, please. I have a multiple code thirty-four. I say again, a *multiple* code thirty-four."

His brow knitted, aware that team three had hit the one of the houses used by the gang to store their drugs, but for those brief seconds he was uncertain what a code thirty-four was.

He turned to the clerk who pre-empted the DI when he said, "It's firearms, sir. They must have come across some firearms."

"Right," his head bounced like a Noddy on speed, he instructed the clerk. "Get on the blower and have SOCO attend and request, *urgent* attendance," then used the radio to confirm to team three their request was being dealt with.

It was then he decided to delay updating DCI Wells until he had more information about the discovery of the firearms.

****

After dropping Jamie and Morven off at the nursery for their play day, Michael MacDonald and Eileen McAulay made their way to Eileen's former company office in the city centre for Michael's appointment with her lawyer friend.

Parking Eileen's Beetle in the Anderston car park, they walked the short distance to where the prestigious, marble fronted building was located on the corner of Waterloo Street and Wellington Lane.

To Eileen's surprise and inward delight, the elderly, uniformed commissionaire recognised her then stepping out from behind his desk, greeting her warmly and informed her that Mrs Wilson had requested upon their arrival, they make their way to her office.

Exiting the lift on the fourth floor, it was evident that the commissionaire had phoned ahead, for Lesley Wilson, a medium height and slim built, dark haired woman in her mid-fifties, elegantly dressed in what Michael thought was a made-to measure, navy blue coloured, trouser suit, awaited them at the elevator.

Hugging Eileen to her, she greeted Michael with a wide smile and firm handshake, then said, "Rather than my office, I've convened our meeting for the conference room and ordered some coffee and sandwiches because quite frankly," she lowered her voice and with almost a growl, said, "I haven't had breakfast and right now, I could eat a monkey dipped in fat."

It was that comment that decided Michael he liked this woman. Once settled in the conference room and each with a plate of food and coffee before them, Lesley finished her sandwich, then to his amusement, licked at her fingers before she said, "Right, Michael, I've set the morning aside for this meeting, so from the start, tell me about your wife and your relationship and I might add," she stared meaningfully at him, "if I am to ably represent you, I do not want you to be a gentleman. Nothing worse than an opposing counsel disclosing something *you* should have told me. So, warts and all no matter how embarrassing it might be for you personally. Is that *clearly* understood?"

And so, while Lesley prepared to take notes, from the very beginning when he first met with Natalie, an initially hesitant Michael began to recount his unhappy life.

****

Colin Baxter ended the call then rising from his desk, made his way through to Mary Wells office where he told her, "That was the Divisional Controller from E Division relaying a message, Boss. The suspect was at home and has been arrested. The guys are currently searching the house and reckon they will be here with Davies within the hour."

A relieved Wells laid down her pen and exhaled then replied, "Good. When they arrive, Colin, I want you to bring her here to my office where we'll conduct the interview. When she goes through the uniform bar downstairs, if she doesn't have her own lawyer, ask the duty officer to find out who's next on the legal aid list and to be prepared to call him or her out. Now, when we're interviewing her, do you want to take notes or shall we bring one of the typing pool in to do shorthand?"

"No," he shook his head "I'll take the notes. Oh, one other thing the E Div controller told me. She says that the message included the warning that the suspect seems to be a very confident woman and apparently expected the knock on her door."

"Confident?" her eyes narrowed. "Wonder what they meant by that?"

"Actually, I asked that and what the controller said was that DS Fitzsimmons first described her as cocky, then changed it to confident."

"Oh, well that's interesting," Wells frowned and for some unexplained reason, had a bad feeling about the suspect, Monica Davies.

****

Keen though she was to hear from Sammy Salmon about his morning operation, Mary's first priority remained the hunt for the killer of Elizabeth Bradley and so refrained from pestering her DI for information.

Though she expected that after Colin Baxter informed her of Monica Davies arrest, Fitzsimmons and her DC's would be back within the hour, it was closer to two hours before Elaine Fitzsimmon's knocked on her door to tell her, "That's the guys processing her downstairs, Boss."

About to ask her why they were delayed, she held her tongue for she could see from Fitzsimmon's expression her DS wasn't at all happy and instead asked, "What?"

Without waiting for an invitation, Fitzsimmons slumped down into the chair in front of the desk then wearily rubbing at her forehead, snarled, "Davies, she's one cocky bitch, so she is. When we hit her house, she opened the door as though she was definitely expecting us, then invited us in for coffee."

"Was she alone in the house or what?"

"No," Fitzsimmons shook her head. "Two kids, a lad of fifteen and a girl of thirteen that were getting ready for school when we arrived. Of course, because they're under eighteen, they weren't on the voters roll, so we'd no way of knowing they'd be in the house too. That's what delayed us. We had to wait for a responsible adult, in this case the ex-husband, to arrive and collect the weans before we could leave."

"What was his attitude?"

"Phew," Fitzsimmons exhaled as she shook her head, "to say he was pissed off doesn't cut it. They're divorced for almost a year, apparently, and he was absolutely *raging* that he'd been pulled away from his firm and by the way, he's a bloody lawyer. A right smarmy git, I thought," she stared at Wells when she frowned.

"That said," she continued, "he told me he's in commercial law, so if he's to be believed, he utterly hates his ex-missus with a passion and from his attitude I do not envision him coming to the rescue. And," she shrugged before Wells could get a word in, "on that point, Boss,

Davies said she won't need representation."

Mary frowned then shaking her head, replied, "All the same, Elaine, I don't want to interview a murder suspect without some form of legal representation and have the defence rip me to shreds in the court, alleging we libelled verbal admissions against her, so I've had the duty officer prepared to call out the next legal aid lawyer in line. If Davies does not want a lawyer, then let *her* tell them that and if it comes to it, we can defend ourselves that we did try to have her represented."

Fitzsimmons acknowledged with a nod, then rising from her seat, asked, "I take it then you're not yet ready for Davies?"

"No, we'll wait for the legal aid person to arrive, so ask the duty officer to place her in a detention room, meantime."

"Boss," Fitzsimmons nodded them left the room, only to be replaced by Colin Baxter who told her, "Brief phone call from Sammy Salmon. Thought you'd likely be busy with the murder suspect, so he called me. Says the teams have achieved all their aims and a substantial amount of drugs and evidence recovered; however…"

Why does there have to be a 'however,' she slumped in her chair then interrupted with, "Don't tell me there's been a hiccup."

"Aye, but a good one," he happily grinned.

"Sammy says to tell you he'll give you a full result when everything is settled, but at one of the houses they've recovered four firearms, one of which is a Smith and Wesson revolver that takes a point-three-eight bullet. The SOCO team are on their way there now and maybe I'm being presumptuous, but we could be looking at the weapon that Ricky Bradley shot himself with."

"Good news indeed, Colin," she smiled and blew out through pursed lips, suddenly relieved that at least her Divisional CID had one really good result today and, if things went according to plan with Monica Davies. But then her experienced pessimism took over and she stopped daring to hope.

When Baxter left the room, she sat back and slowly exhaled, in her mind planning her interview with Davies, but then just a few minutes passed before the door was knocked by DC John McGhee, who stepping into the room, asked, "Got a minute, boss?"

"Of course, John," she forced a smile then asked herself, why do I keep telling my people I run an open door policy when the truth is, I never have a bloody minute to myself?

"What can I do for you?"

To her surprise, McGhee turned and closed to door behind him, then stepping forward to her desk, licked nervously at his lips before he said, "The 'Glasgow News' run a wee bit in their evening edition last night about our murder investigation, boss, and again a front page spread this morning about connecting it to the shooting in Pollok. Have you seen the paper?"

"Yes," she slowly nodded. "Colin Baxter showed me a copy when I got in this morning. Why do you ask?"

"Last night, I met a friend in the Horseshoe Bar in Drury Street. Do you know it?"

"Who doesn't know it?" she smiled, yet wondered where this was going as her feminine intuition kicked in and she idly wondered; wasn't that the same shirt and tie McGhee wore yesterday?

"Well, my *friend*, she saw me looking at two guys at the bar talking together; right head to head, if you know what I mean. Anyway, it might not mean much," he grimaced and she sensed his hesitation.

"Go on anyway," she encouraged him suddenly realising he was wearing the same shirt and tie likely because he hadn't made it home the previous evening.

"Anyway, my friend, she thought I was looking at the same person she knew, but it was the *other* guy I had recognised."

"And?"

"The guy *she* knew, a nasty bugger she told me, is called Ally McGregor and she says he's the 'Glasgow News' chief crime reporter. It's his name that's on the newspaper's article last night and again this morning."

Wells felt a sense of foreboding when she asked, "How sure is your friend that's who the guy is?"

"Absolutely certain," he confidently replied.

She took a short breath, then asked, "And who was the guy that *you* were watching?"

He stared down at her before he tightly replied, "It was that bastard Donnelly, boss. Hugh Donnelly from Pollok CID."

CHAPTER TWENTY-SIX

More than happy after his meeting with Eileen's friend, Lesley Wilson, Michael MacDonald was chirpier than he expected to be and with Jamie and Morven safely at the nursery, decided to treat Eileen to lunch at the city centre pub, Lauder's in Sauchiehall Street.

Now seated enjoying their food, Michael asked, "What do you make of Lesley's intention to use a private investigator to make inquiry into Natalie's current lifestyle?"

Her brow creased and she gave the question some thought before she replied, "For one, now that we've engaged Lesley, I think it only fair and proper that we follow her advice and if she think it warrants a private investigator, then so be it. Two," she reached across the table to place her hand upon his, "I don't think there is any doubt whatsoever that Natalie will lie and cheat to ensure that she wins the divorce action and like she threatened, take you for every penny that you worked so hard for. Now," she raised a defensive hand, "I'm not saying you have to be as callous and nasty as she is, but I do believe that you, or rather Lesley, needs to use every lawful means at her disposal to protect your interests."

She sat back in her chair and she smiled gently at him when she continued, "Frankly, Michael, it matters not a jot to me if you walk away with just the clothes on your back, for nothing will change between us; however, it irks me no end that spiteful woman should have treated you so unkindly through the years, then think she should benefit from it."

Her eyes sought his when she added, "Listening to the life you had with her," she shook her head, a sob caught in her throat, "I just can't imagine how you survived. Your sons and daughter are so lucky to have you as their father and it's no surprise that you have their complete support. And particularly," she didn't wish to hurt him, but it had to be said, "as you now accept that Alan is not your biological son, though you've never raised him as anyone but your own."

"They are good kids aren't they," he couldn't help but smile, "and thankfully, they've turned out to be fine people too."

He paused then with an uncommon trace of bitterness in his voice, he added, "Despite having a mother like Natalie."

"And mostly thanks to you bringing them up, literally on your own. So," she shrugged, "having done nothing other than bearing the children, what has she contributed to their upbringing or your marriage? Coldness? Bitterness? Unfaithfulness and worst of all, treated her children like pawns in some game against you."

"Yes," he sighed, "I know you're right, but there's still a part of me that thinks we should simply split everything half and half."

Eileen stared curiously at him before she replied, "But isn't that the whole point? Natalie does not *want* to split anything with you. She wants everything! My God, Michael MacDonald, you are *such* a good man, but sometimes I think you need a right good shake because…"

She shook her head and took a deep breath then smiled at him when she said, "Listen to me. Part of the reason I care so much for you is because you are so good and kind so *do not* change. Just trust me when I tell you, I am so glad we are together, that I found you."

"As I am about you," he returned her smile, then his face creasing, he slowly said, "Digressing slightly, I had a thought this morning and wondered if you might hear me out."

"Go on."

"This Saturday evening. How would you feel about us taking Jamie and Morven for a sleepover?"

"That's not a problem," her lips pursed. "You know I love those children like they were my own grandkids, but," her eyes narrowed in suspicion, "I'm guessing you have an ulterior motive?"

His face contorted when he replied, "I really like that young guy, Bill Howie, Mary's neighbour, and I'm wondering if…"

But he didn't get to finish for Eileen giggled when she interrupted with, "Michael MacDonald! You old matchmaker, you! You want to set your daughter up with the handsome doctor!"

"Is it that obvious?" he grimaced, but Eileen nodded when she said, "I think it's a great idea, but maybe *not* mention our plan to Mary?"

"Our plan?"

She leaned towards him and gently stroked at his cheek when she softly replied, "Our plan. We're a couple now, dear, so we rise or fall together."

****

Mary's call from the duty officer downstairs informed her that the legal aid lawyer had arrived and when shown into Monica Davies cell to introduce himself, had almost immediately, been dismissed by her.

"In fact, Ma'am," the Inspector continued, "she more or less told me that if I insisted on pursuing the aim to have her legally represented, she'd make a formal complaint. Never heard the likes of it during my career," he muttered into her ear.

Mary smiled when she replied, "Thank you, Inspector. I'll send Colin Baxter down to bring her up for interview, but while he's doing that, please have the lawyer, eh…"

"It's a Miss Lavery, Ma'am. Susan Lavery. Just a young lassie," his voice lowered as though she might be standing nearby.

"Okay. Please have Miss Lavery escorted to my room so that I can have a word, then when ten minutes has passed, ask Colin to bring Davies to my office."

Some minutes later, the door was knocked by the bar officer, a long in the tooth constable who cheekily winked at Wells before he said, "Miss Lavery for you, Ma'am."

The young, tall and slim fair-haired woman who seemed to be no more than twenty-six or twenty-seven years of age, stepped into the room, her dark brown hair tied back in a tight ponytail, wearing gold rimmed spectacles and a black, trouser suit and who carried her shiny new briefcase in front of her chest like a coat of armour against anything the bad police officers might say.

Clearly nervous, she glanced at the constable then at Mary Wells, who rising from her desk as the constable closed the door behind him, extended her hand and said, "So good of you to come, Miss Lavery. I'm DCI Mary Wells. Won't you have a seat?"

The three chairs had been prepared for the interview and after taking Mary's hand then sitting down, Lavery said in a high-pitched voice, "I spoke to…no," she shook her head, then corrected herself, "I *tried* to speak with Mrs Davies, but she quite vehemently told me in no uncertain terms she did not require my services. So, why then, DCI Wells, do you need to speak with me?"

"Frankly, I wish to conduct my interview with Mrs Davies as fairly as possible and though she has refused legal representation, Miss Lavery, I would be most grateful if you might therefore remain as an independent witness to the proceedings."

Lavery's eyes flickered when she hesitantly replied, "I don't think that is quite appropriate."

"Let's put it this way," Wells smiled encouragingly at her.

"You will receive the remuneration for your time as if you *were* here representing Mrs Davies. However, you will also be totally neutral to the proceedings and need not in any way consider yourself to be biased. And," she continued to smile, "if as I suspect you are relatively new to this type of proceedings, you may on a personal note garner some experience and goodwill from me, if you should ever at any time in the future require my counsel."

Lavery's eyes narrowed in doubt when she hesitantly said, "That sounds suspiciously like… like some sort of bribe, is the only word I can use to describe it, DCI Wells."

"No," Mary slowly shook her head, "not a bribe, just sound advice. All I am asking is that you ensure the interview with Mrs Davies is conducted fair and square. Let me also add that I assure you that you being a member of the Law Society of Scotland, you will be at liberty, if during my interview and you so choose, to interrupt if you believe she is being unjustly treated."

Almost thirty seconds passed before Lavery slowly nodded, then slowly asked, "And let's be clear. I am here just to witness the fairness of your interview, but not to participate?"

"That's correct," Mary nodded, then asked, "Now, before we begin. Coffee? Oh," she grinned, then said, "and that's *not* a bribe."

****

Sammy Salmon was just short of ecstatic and try as he might could not keep the grin from his face.

Not only had all the house raids yielded drugs in varying quantities, but also the three main players and their underlings were all arrested. However, the icing on the cake was most definitely the seizure of the firearms, initially thought to be four that included two saw-off double barrelled shotguns and a quantity of ammunition, but a more thorough and determined search by the SOCO team, on this occasion using crowbars, produced a further two weapons. Not only were the firearms recovered, but so too was an assortment of knives and at least two machetes, each with dried bloodstaining on the blades.

As Mickey, the SOCO supervisor later reported, he was more than confident the Smith and Wesson revolver was the weapon that had shot Ricky Bradley, though a Ballistics examination would later confirm that.

Now, seated at his desk, Salmon listened with growing delight as one of the Pollok DS's excitedly recounted his interview with one of the three leading gang members, who keen to demonstrate his willingness to cooperate in exchange for a sympathetic word to the Procurator Fiscal, confirmed that on the night Ricky Bradley was shot, it was the gangs intention was to fire warning bullets through the rivals downstairs windows.

"However," the DS continued, "Bradley had been high on cocaine at the time and apparently was giggling like a schoolgirl and playing with the firearm he carried. When he shot himself, they all panicked, then bundled him into the stolen Morris Marina and drove him to the Western Infirmary."

"Why didn't they just drop him at a local hospital?"

"He says they were worried someone might know or recognise them at the local casualties."

"Okay," Salmon slowly nodded, then eyes narrowing, he stared at the DS when he asked, "and do you believe him when he says they were intent on just shooting at the windows?"

"Not for a second, Boss. I'm convinced they were all probably armed and out to murder their rival, but we'll never prove that intent. I mean," he grinned, "he knows fine well if he admits a conspiracy to murder, it's just a longer sentence, isn't it? As it is the whole bunch are going away for a very long time."

"What about the woman in the hospital? Her with the busted head?"

"Big Jeannie? Oh, she's a real bad bitch," he scowled. "She's a sister of one of the gang leaders and after trying to stab one of the Serious Crime's DC's, we're charging her with attempted murder and with her previous convictions, I'm in no doubt she *is* going away for a long time. At the minute though, she's handcuffed to a bed at the Victoria Hospital, then tomorrow, she's going from there to the court tomorrow where I'd be surprised if she wasn't remanded to Cornton Vale."

When the DS had left his office, Salmon sat back and with some satisfaction, laced his fingers behind his head and happily yawned for not only had he been the SIO in a highly successful operation, but for the first time since he'd arrived at Pollok CID, he saw his team gelling together, smiling and backslapping each other and looking at him with a new found respect.

****

When Colin Baxter escorted Monica Davies into the DCI's office, Mary saw that the description of Davies had been fairly accurate.

Professionally dyed blonde hair that was styled to frame an extremely attractive face, even without make-up there was no denying she was a good-looking woman.

Dressed in a simple white blouse and a grey coloured, knee-length pencil skirt with black patent high heel shoes, she stood as tall as Mary.

"Good afternoon, DCI Wells," she confidently greeted Mary then frowned when she saw the lawyer and added, "I don't think there is any requirement to have this young woman present."

"Miss Lavery is here at my request," Mary smiled politely at her, then added, "Though you have refused her counsel, I have asked her to bear witness that this interview is conducted with complete fairness to you. After all," she continued to smile, "I wouldn't like a defence lawyer at any subsequent court hearing to allege we put words into your mouth, Mrs Davies."

Gesturing that Davies sit, Mary resumed her own seat.

"Now," she cocked her head slightly to one side as she stared at Davies, "when you were brought to the charge bar downstairs, you were formally cautioned, but I wish to remind you that anything you say will be written down and might later be used in evidence. Do you clearly understand, Mrs Davies?"

"Of course I do," she sighed with a smile. "I am *not* a simpleton." Then she quickly added, "I have no intention of lying, DCI Wells, for as I planned, I expected at some time the police would come for me. Now, what exactly is it that you wish to ask me?"

Though her facial expression did not change, Wells inwardly startled for it was blatantly clear that by asking *her* question, Davies was intent on controlling the interview.

To pre-empt her, Wells deliberately stared for several seconds down at her notes, then raising her head, stared directly into Davies eyes before she asked, "While you were employed as a receptionist at the law firm of Burnley, Paterson and Co. and using the alias Joanne Wood, you stole a sum of money from the safe. What is your response to that allegation?"

Though her demeanour did not change, it was the tiniest inflection in her eyes that Mary saw that gave Davies away.

However, what shocked Mary was Davies response when she calmly said, "You will be aware that I am a divorced woman?"

"I was informed of that, yes."

"To be fair to my ex-husband, though it pains me to admit it about that selfish man," she shrugged, "he does pay maintenance for our children on time, but visit them? Take them on holiday or even spend time with them? No," she sneered, "he's far too busy with his new girlfriend for that," the sarcasm oozed from her.

"And you're telling me this, why?"

"The partner of the firm, Charlie Paterson? She was one of his many *flirtations*, shall we call them, when we were still married and it was his dalliance with her that finally decided him to leave me and our children. So," her face creased in disgust, "I thought a little bit of payback might be in order. It was my intention to, let's just say, somehow make her pay for her affair with my husband, but then I come to realise she was just another string to his bow. I won't disclose exactly how I intended making her pay in case you think the worse of me, but suffice to say before I left, I simply helped myself to some cash from the company safe."

"Are you telling me that you gained employment with the firm just to get back at your husband, then decided to steal the money as some sort of revenge?"

"Oh, to be frank I didn't really need the money, DCI Wells," she widely smiled. "But yes, I knew of most of my husband's extramarital affairs, but not much about that one. I confess, my curiosity got the better of me and I wanted to see what Paterson looked like, to confront her about the affair with my husband, but…" she smiled humourlessly, then paused.

"For you see," her smile faded as she continued, "after a number of affairs, and as I said, Charlie Paterson was the tart he finally left us for. As for the money, that was just a little bonus. Spent it on a holiday for me and my children," she airily replied.

"And was it about this time that you come to know Elizabeth Bradley?"

"Lizzie? Yes, it was," her eyebrows knit when she nodded. "Curiously, we met when we were both at the same employment agency in the city centre and got talking while we waited for our interviews. Then, when we learned we had been given the jobs with the cleaning company, we celebrated by having a coffee together. A nice young woman and I was very saddened to hear of her untimely death."

Her brow furrowed in thought when she said, "I think if we had met under different circumstances, even though we came from very dissimilar backgrounds, we could have been real friends."

She took a slow breath and seemed to reflect on her statement, then she again continued, "About that time while I was working at the law firm, when I decided to steal the money from the safe it was a…what do you call it?" her brow creased. "Oh, yes a kind of knee-jerk reaction to leaving. However, while still at the law firm forking for that *tart*," she scowled, "I had already decided to take up the employment agency's offer to join the cleaning company and had formulated the plan to recruit some of my co-workers to help me steal from the company's clients."

She smiled softly as though recalling her intentions, then said, "I realised that I would need to somehow turn the ornaments and jewellery into cash. So, before I left the law firm, I had an idea and I read through their files. That's when I discovered that one of their regular clients, a nice older man called Billy Steele who when he was trying to chat me up one day, confided he had a daughter and that his daughter Alison was a resetter of stolen property."

She paused then smilingly continued, "Of course it was relatively easy to obtain her address from his file for she was listed as his family contact and so I visited her and introduced myself as Karen Silverton, a name from the local voters roll. Once I satisfied her that I was acquainted with her father, we agreed the arrangement that when I had sufficient property collected, I would deliver it all for a price that, believe me or not," she shook her head, "I fully intended sharing between my co-workers for as I've explained, I have no real need for the money myself."

Baxter stared at her and unkindly thought, aye, so you're a female Robin Hood, now.

"And these aliases, you obtained them all from the voters rolls in the public libraries?"

"A rather nice touch, I thought," Davies nodded.

"And how did this plan of yours work out?"

"Rather well in fact, at least from the beginning," she frowned, "but when I read in the 'Glasgow News' that Lizzie had been killed; well, it was a real shock and I decided that there was little point in returning to the cleaning company for I knew that though I fully intended getting caught at some point, I still had work to do."

"We'll get back to you still having work to do," Mary interrupted, but then quickly asked, "Did you kill Elizabeth Bradley?"

If she thought her quick-fire question would take Davies unaware, she was to be disappointed, for the first time since she entered Mary's office, her composure slipped when her face paled and she stuttered, "What? You think I killed Lizzie! My God, are you serious!"

The tense silence was broken when in a soft voice, Mary continued by formally asking, "Mrs Davies, you have admitted under caution while using the alias Joanne Wood, the theft of a sum of money from your former employer, Burnley, Paterson and Co."

Continuing she said, "We have evidence that using the alias Lorraine Gray, you sought employment with the cleaning company, 'Sweep 'n Dust' for the sole purpose of organising and conspiring with a team of women; namely yourself, Elizabeth Bradley, Maria Clinton and Martha Foster, to steal from the company's elderly clients, a number of valuables. You have also admitted under caution that using yet another alias as Karen Silverton, you intended resetting these valuables to a woman called Alison Steele. What is your response to these allegations?"

Watching Davies's face pale, Colin Baxter sneaked a glance at the young lawyer, Susan Lavery, and saw both her eyes and mouth open in stunned surprise and inwardly guessed she was likely relieved *not* to have represented the suspect.

"I told you when I come into your office I would not lie, so yes," she nodded, "I admit to committing those crimes. However, I quite adamantly refute *any* allegation that I would hurt Lizzie," Davies voice rose an octave.

Watching her taking a deep breath, Mary thought Davies was about to hyperventilate and quickly instructed Baxter, "Colin, can you fetch a glass of water, please?"

He almost laughed out loud when rising from his chair, Lavery squeaked, "Can I have one too, please?"

Returning a minute later with two china mugs of water, he handed them to the two women.

As she gulped down the water, they watched Davies slump down into her chair, her head bowed, her face chalk-white and all pretence at a devil-may-care attitude gone, when she muttered, "You may wonder why I'm admitting those thefts, DCI Wells."

She turned to face to Mary, her eyes wet and her cheeks red, then said, "I needed to be caught, for my plan was to be brought before an open court. You see it was all done to hurt *him*. To publicly shame him and force him to acknowledge what he had done, how he had treated me and our children."

Stunned, she realised that Davies was referring to her husband and gently asked, "Are you telling me that this double life you were living, the aliases and the thieving, it was all to get back at your husband?"

In a short second, Davies expression changed, for her teeth gritted and her eyes full of unshed tears, she snarled, "You have no idea what it's like living with an adulterous bastard like him! The lies, the cheating and all the while, his colleagues at that fancy company of his thinking him to be a *great* guy! Well, when news gets out that I'm arrested and going to court for what I did, we'll see then how many of them stick by him, particularly when I get into the witness box and publicly humiliate him! Him and those *whores* he bedded!"

It took all of Mary's reserve not to empathise with Davies about her cheating husband, but she controlled her own emotions and thought - hell hath no fury.

What did cross her mind was the thought that sadly, it was likely Davies ex-husband would be treated more sympathetically than the poor woman believed. When the news broke that being married to a woman wanted by the police for theft and possibly murder, his antics as the career philanderer he reputedly is, the media would likely describe her as a criminal mastermind or perhaps more cruelly, a vengeful harridan.

However, Mary's primary concern was finding the killer of Elizabeth Bradley and so she pressed on, "Tell me, Mrs Davies, can you account for your whereabouts between the hours of nine am and three pm on Tuesday the seventh of July? Tuesday last week, in fact."

She watched as Davies gave thought to the question, then almost with a relieved sigh, she shrugged and repeated, "Tuesday the seventh, you said?"

They watched her smile when she calmly said, "Yes, I know exactly where I was. Well, at least for most of the day."

Mary saw the hurt on her face and her eyes crease in pain when her voice, almost a whisper, she began, "One of the reasons my husband left me is that; well, he wouldn't face or rather, he wasn't interested in facing what *I* am going through. Let's just say he had other things on his mind," she frowned.

Mary's stomach lurched when her instinct kicked in and suspecting the worse for Davies, she quietly asked, "And what are you going through?"

She watched Davies glance at Baxter as though embarrassed that a man should hear what she was about to disclose, then said, "On that morning I had an appointment at the Beatson Clinic. I was there a little early, say just after nine o'clock for my nine-thirty appointment and I underwent," she choked back the memory of the experiences, "several tests, several *unpleasant* tests. I didn't leave the Beatson till well after two o'clock that afternoon and because I had been informed that I was not to drive after the tests, I caught public transport home. I didn't get back till after my children had returned from school. Believe me," she duly added, "after what I went through that day, all I wanted to do was go home and go to my bed." She took a deep breath, then softly finished with, "And that's exactly what I did."

The Beatson Clinic, Mary took an inward breath.

The specialised cancer centre for the West of Scotland that was located next to Gartnavel Hospital on the north side of the city and at least a twenty to twenty-five-minute journey by car through the morning rush-hour traffic from Clifford Street, the locus of Elizabeth Bradley's murder.

Seconds passed before she asked Davies, "You say you would never hurt Elizabeth. If I were to inform you that we have a partial fingerprint on the murder weapon, Mrs Davies, what is your reaction to that?"

To her inner disappointment, she watched Davies expression change from melancholy to a gentle smile, then holding up both hands, she thrust her hands forward, palms upwards and eagerly replied, "Please, take my fingerprints. I want you to. I *urge* you to take them and you'll see that whoever's fingerprint you have, it is definitely not mine!"

Mary glanced towards Baxter who solemnly nodded, then turning back to Davies, she said, "That'll be all for now, Mrs Davies. You'll be taken by DS Baxter to the charge bar downstairs where you will be fingerprinted and those prints will be sent to our Fingerprint

Department at police headquarters and compared against the print seized from the murder weapon. You understand too, that we will need to confirm with the Beatson that you did attend there during the hours you say?"

"Of course," she thrust out her chin as though daring Mary to challenge her story.

Staring at Davies, she sighed then said, "We have already interviewed your associates, Mrs Clinton and Mrs Foster, both of whom agreed to identify the stolen property and assist us to return it to its rightful owners. Will you also assist us with this?"

"If I can, yes," Davies calmly nodded. "The items means nothing to me."

"Then once you have done so, you will for now be released from detention; however, charges of theft will later be libelled against you and your associates and a case submitted to the Procurator Fiscal. Do you fully understand?"

"I do, yes," she nodded again.

"DS Baxter?" she nodded at him.

Rising from his chair, he politely waited till Davies stood upright then with a backward glance at Mary she was wordlessly escorted from the room.

When the door was closed, it was Lavery who timidly asked, "Do you think she murdered that woman you spoke about?"

"To be perfectly honest, Miss Lavery," she tiredly sighed. "No, I don't think she did."

It was only after the bar officer came to collect Lavery that she collected her thoughts then wondered, if Davies didn't kill Elizabeth Bradley, who the hell did?

CHAPTER TWENTY-SEVEN

DI Sammy Salmon was still on a high.

The success of his operation that resulted in the arrest of a major drugs team, a large quantity of drugs, cash and the intelligence details of the suppliers as well as the recovery of the firearms had attracted the attention of ACC Keith Meadows.

To Salmon's surprise, Meadows took time to attend at Pollok police office where gathering the weary Detectives and the involved uniformed officers together in the crowded general office, he heartily congratulated them as a team and, as the SIO who had organised the operation, the DI personally for a job well done.

Picking out some of the individuals that were previously known to him, Meadows caused laughter when he cracked jokes and with a wide smile, regretted the meeting was not being held in a pub, for he informed them he believed the team all deserved a congratulatory drink.

At the conclusion of his speech, he indicated that he and Salmon retire to the DI's room.

Carrying their coffees with them, they settled themselves at Salmon's desk where Meadows asked the younger man, "How does it feel to be in charge of such a successful operation, Mr Salmon?"

"Nothing quite like it, sir," Salmon couldn't help but grin.

Meadows slowly nodded, then in a soft voice, said, "A while back there, DCI Wells shared with me that you didn't believe your path in the police included continuing in the CID and frankly, she was a little worried about you. Permit me to say that she didn't agree with you, though she would have accepted your decision. In fact, Mary Wells thinks you are ideally suited to the Department. How would you respond to that?"

Salmon, weary though he was and his adrenalin starting to diminish, found himself smiling when he replied, "Just a week ago sir, I might have disagreed, but you're a little out of date, now. In fact, though I am aware that as a Graduate Entry Scheme fast track officer, if I choose to continue my career within the CID it likely *will* adversely affect my promotion opportunities."

He pursed his lips then with an off-handed shrug, added, "Then so be it. This last week has been something of a revelation to me and I find that I am more capable than I actually gave myself credit for."

His brow knitted as he slowly then unconsciously nodded when he said, "Prior to coming to Pollok, I lacked confidence in myself and though I'm embarrassed to admit it, sir," he frowned, "I sometimes let my lack of experience hinder me when I should have confidently been making decisions. However," he took a sharp breath, "can I say that this last week and with the support of DCI Wells, I can't explain it, but I found an assurance in myself, in my own ability that I didn't know I had. I'm sorry," he forced a smile, "maybe I'm not actual explaining that properly…"

"No," Meadows raised a hand as he interrupted, "I think you have explained yourself completely, Mr Salmon, and for what it's worth, the Department is pleased to have you. Now," he glanced at his wristwatch as he rose from the chair, "I think I'll pop by Govan and see how your boss is getting on with her murder."

****

Aware that her team would be anxiously waiting for news about her interview with the female suspect that they had been hunting for over a week, Mary Wells gathered them together in the incident room to brief them.

Her eyes darting among the crowd, she began, "I regret that subject to her alibi confirmation, it seems the woman we now know to be Monica Davies is no longer a suspect for the murder of Elizabeth Bradley.

A collective groan went up from the team, but silenced when Mary, desperately keen to keep the teams morale positive, continued, "That said, we still have work to do and while I do realise this is a major disappointment, we still have other lines of inquiry that must be investigated."

Glancing at Colin Baxter, she saw him give an almost imperceptible nod and so she explained, "Monica Davies was a woman wronged by her husband who, to put it bluntly, was shagging around and deserted his wife and their children."

To her surprise, she saw a few heads lower or embarrassedly turn away and realised that some of the team were making their own comparisons.

With a wry smile, she decided to face it head-on and continued, "Yeah, I know, that information hit a bit too close to home. However, I didn't go out thieving, because that's what Davies did, but curiously all with the intention of getting caught and hoping the resulting media attention would bring shame and embarrassment to her husband."

It was John McGhee, who raising a hand, said, "Colin had me put out a telex message, Boss, asking Divisional CID's if they had any information about a woman matching Davies description under whatever name she had been using at the material time, was responsible for thefts from any other law firms or similar firms or companies. Do you want me to issue her true details as an addendum to that telex?"

McGhee's admission he had sent out the telex caused Baxter to glance angrily at Tommy Maxwell, who took a sudden interest in the overhead lights.

"Have you had any responses yet?" Mary asked.

"No, nothing yet," he shook his head.

Her eyes narrowed in thought before she replied, "Then hang fire until you do. If any other Division has a *partial* description that might match, I don't want them dismissing any suspicious female if we send out her true details. However, if there is nothing by the end of the week, then issue a second telex informing the Divisions with Davies's details and that she's been arrested."

"What about the theft from the law firm over in Shettleston?" McGhee continued. "Do you want us to return there and inform them of her arrest, then obtain a statement from Miss Paterson?"

Unaware of McGhee's new association with the lawyer, Mary shook her head when she replied, "No, just give her a phone call to let her know we have Davies in custody and you might want her to know too that Davies apparently targeted her firm because of her belief that Paterson was having an affair with Davies's husband."

It was when she saw McGhee turn pale, his eyes widen and his mouth drop open that the penny dropped and she hastily added, "In fact, John, come and see me when the briefing is finished."

"Boss," he muttered and turned to stare at a stunned Maxwell.

She glanced to one side when the door to the room opened to admit Keith Meadows, who waving a hand to indicate she ignore him, quietly slipped into the back of the room.

"Right then," she decided to conclude her short briefing, "I'm informed that DS Baxter still had a number of outstanding actions to be issued, so see him and let's get on with our investigation. Thanks, guys."

Making her way to Meadows, she politely asked, "With respect, can I ask that you grab a cup of coffee, sir. I need to speak urgently with one of my DC's."

"Of course," his eyes narrowed, then lowering his voice, asked, "Not a problem, is there?"

"I bloody hope not," she sighed.

****

McGhee followed Wells to her room then when she sat behind her desk, sheepishly turned to close the door behind him.

"Tell me," she stared at him.

There seemed little point in denying it, so he replied, "It was just the one night, Boss. Last night in fact. When I phoned her yesterday, she suggested a drink in the Horseshoe Bar and…"

"And she was the one who told you about the reporter," Mary interrupted. "This guy, Ally McGregor?"

"Yes, Boss," he exhaled, then asked, "How did you know?"

"I'm a woman, John, so I notice things. You happen to be one of my rather more smartly turned out DC's, so when you arrive at the office wearing the same shirt and tie two days running, then I know you've not been home."

She took a deep breath, then continued, "I take it you will give serious consideration to abandoning any further *romantic* contact with this woman?"

"Definitely, Boss," he vigorously nodded.

"Then we will consider the matter to be closed?"

"Absolutely," his sigh was one of relief.

"On your way back to the incident room, please inform Mr Meadows that at his convenience, I'm at my desk."

"Will do, Boss," he forced a smile.

As he was about to leave, she couldn't help herself and with a wry smile, she called out, "John. Last night, was it worth it?"

"Oh, aye," he blushingly grinned. "I had a really good night."

"Well, if nothing else, you *did* learn some valuable information about our former colleague," she almost spat the name out, "Hugh Donnelly. However, if there should be any reason for Miss Paterson to be contacted again, I'm certain you'll ensure that Colin Baxter issues the action to someone else, preferably one of our female colleagues."

"Boss," he nodded with a wry smile."

****

When Keith Meadows had settled himself in the opposite chair, he asked, "What's your next move?"

"Honestly, sir? Right now I'm at a loss, so I'll need to give it some thought. On the plus side, we have a partial fingerprint from the murder weapon. All I need is a name. That and as a spin-off of the murder investigation and as you already know, we have wound up a small gang of women who have conspired to steal from pensioners throughout the city, though I suspect *that* investigation will drag on for a while as we have several recovered items that are still to be identified."

"However," she slowly shook her head at the thought, "our accused are hardly master criminals, so I suspect that once the dust is settled, we'll be looking at the Sheriff Court rather than a higher court."

Her brow knitted in disgust when she said, "A further spin-off, though the investigation will be dealt with by C Division CID, has identified a father who was both physically and sexually abusing his wife and unfortunately," she grimaced, "his ten year old daughter."

"Yes," he nodded, his face registering his disgust "I'm aware of that case. As I understand it, it was Elaine Fitzsimmons who picked up on the abuse when she and her neighbour called at the house on another matter."

"That's correct, yes."

He suddenly smiled when he reminded Wells, "As I said before, DS Fitzsimmons is one to watch."

She paused then sighing, continued, "On the negative side, the woman who was our main suspect is likely alibied, so it looks like I'm going to have to recommence the murder investigation from scratch and review all the actions to try and determine if we've missed anything."

"Well," he sipped at his coffee, "it's not your first whodunnit, Mary, so I have every confidence that if the killer is to be found, then you will find him or her. Now, I've just returned from Pollok and I spoke with young Salmon and his team. A good and successfully run operation that has yielded excellent results."

She watched as his expression darkened, prompting her to ask, "What?"

He took a slow breath before he said, "I haven't told DI Salmon because, frankly, I didn't want to…what's the expression? Rain on his parade, but later this afternoon, the Chief Constable intends holding a press briefing where if true to form," the bitterness of his words oozed from him, "I suspect he will take personal credit for young Salmon and his team's success."

Slowly shaking her head, Mary smiled humourlessly when she scornfully sneered, "I know I'm being disrespectful, but doesn't that smug *bastard* have any self-dignity at all?"

"Yes, DCI Wells," he pretended to be shocked, "you *are* being disrespectful, but you're also correct. The bastard has no dignity whatsoever."

Unable to vent her anger, several seconds passed before she hissed, "I can assume then that DI Salmon *won't* be invited to stand beside the Chief when he's crowing about *his* success?"

"What do you think?" Meadows humourlessly grinned.

They sat in silence for several more seconds before Mary, now composed, then said, "Speaking of media issues, sir, this morning, one of my DC's brought something to my attention."

"Yes?"

"It seems that my former Detective Sergeant, Hugh Donnelly, was seen yesterday evening in the Horseshoe Bar in Drury Street in the company of the 'Glasgow News' chief crime reporter, Ally McGregor."

She watched as Meadows eyes narrowed and his lips tightened before he replied, "Ally McGregor, that sleazy, treacherous bugger and the author of those articles linking your victim's death to the supposed murder of her brother, with the inference it was all drug gang related."

"The very one," she nodded, then asked, "I take it you know him?"

"Oh, aye, I *know* McGregor of old," he slowly nodded, "A most disreputable man if ever there was one with no journalistic pride and shunned in his own profession by most respectable reporters. More than half if not *all* of McGregor's stories originated from the Press Bar where he seldom got off his backside and telephoned them into the newsroom with the pretence he was actually at a locus. A so-called reporter who never let the truth get in the way of a dishonest story," he stared at her, then added, "However, what you have learned provides us with a tremendous opportunity regarding the Chief's press briefing this afternoon."

"How so?"

"Well," he slowly drawled as his mind worked overtime, "let's just say that if the more legitimate and factual media outlets were to learn that your murder investigation is completely unrelated to the shooting of your victims brother, that in fact what is not yet in the public domain is that the brother, a member of a drug gang, *accidently* shot himself."

She could see his eyes narrowing as he gave the idea some thought. "I would presume that your victim's family must be rightly outraged that the 'Glasgow News' has falsely associated Elizabeth Bradley's murder with her brother's death, too. I can imagine then that the owners of the 'Glasgow News' will be extremely keen to both disassociate themselves from any further reporting about the so-called drug war in Pollok, as well as extricate themselves from a possible legal action by the family for false allegation about Miss Bradley's murder *being* drug related. Therefore, we can effectively close down any suggestion of a drug related murder and perhaps even bring that bugger McGregor to heel."

"My God, sir," she stared admiringly at him. "What a devious mind you have."

He rose from his chair then with a cunning smile, said, "I think I'll make my way back to Pitt Street where I'll make a few phone calls, then have a word with the Superintendent in the Media Department who composes the Chief's speech. I'm certain that if the Chief's speech should include an official denial about your victim's involvement in any drugs, it will go a long way to scaring the pants off the owners of the 'Glasgow News' and of course ease the pain of the Bradley family, who I have little doubt, suffered when they read that article about Miss Bradley."

"On that point, sir, about the Bradley family, did you happen to have a word with anyone at the Council's Housing Department?"

"It's in the pipeline, Mary," he nodded and she had to be satisfied with that.

"One last thing, sir."

But he pre-empted her when he said, "Hugh Donnelly."

His forehead creased when standing at her closed door, he quietly thought for almost a full minute, for he knew that even the more principled reporters would consider selling their soul if it got them a scoop or an advantage over their rivals.

Then he said, "Many distinguished and reputable journalists have stood by their integrity and actually opted for a short prison sentence rather than disclose their sources. McGregor, however, is a completely different kettle of fish. Now, I assume you will treat this in confidence, because if I'm correct, then I think after a word in the right ear," his eyes narrowed in thought, "I believe I might be able to *persuade* McGregor admit that our Mr Donnelly has been providing him with confidential information about an ongoing police investigation. And, if that *should* occur, I will invoke our colleagues in the Complaints and Discipline Branch to pursue the issue. Until then, though," he smilingly placed a forefinger against his nose then left the room.

When he had gone, Mary sat back in her chair then exhaling, used her phone to summon Colin Baxter and Elaine Fitzsimmons to her room.

CHAPTER TWENTY-EIGHT

When both were seated, Mary, her hands in front of her and clasped on the desk, stared from one to the other, then said, "Between us we have several decades of police and CID experience. Right now, I am at a loss how to progress our murder investigation, so as you, Colin, a long-time serving Detective on the cusp of being a DI and you, Elaine, as my deputy SIO and with your own experience, I'm asking; what do we do now?"

Baxter breathed in then exhaled through pursed lips before he replied, "We start at the beginning. We review all the Actions and by we," he turned to her, "I mean Elaine and I swap jobs. She's a fresh pair of eyes and should sit at my desk reading the copy actions and hopefully seeing what I might have missed. As for me, with the rest of the team, I take a turn out on the ground, making the same inquiries starting from action number one, the door to door."

"Elaine?" Mary turned to her.

"I can't fault nor add anything to Colin's suggestion, boss, though" she smiled at Baxter, "I don't want to sound patronising, but I can't believe either that Colin has missed anything."

"Nevertheless, we're none of us completely infallible, so come on guys," she sat back in her chair, "there must be something else we're missing."

"There is *one* thing, boss," Baxter hesitantly began.

"Go on."

"What was your first inclination when you entered the victim's flat?

Your very *first* thoughts about her killer?"

"I'm sorry, Colin," her brow knitted, "I don't know what you're getting at."

"Well," he leaned forward, "remember, we were met at the locus by Joe Docherty and his neighbour, yes? Then when you were satisfied that it *was* a murder, we called in the SOCO."

"I remember, yes," yet still she was puzzled, uncertain where Baxter was going with this.

"Then, when SOCO invited us into the flat, what did he lead us to?"

"You're talking about the spare bedroom, the wardrobe that was filled with the stolen ornaments and the jewellery?"

"Exactly," he sat back in his chair, knowing that having sown the seed, Mary Wells would find her way to what he was suggesting. Both he and Fitzsimmons watched her closely, her eyes darting back and forth as her mind swept back to what she had seen, her thoughts at the time and…

And?

Holy shit!

Slowly, she leaned forward and placed her head into her hands then heavily sighing, she removed her hands and stared at them in turn before she hissed, "Blinkered! I was so *fucking* blinkered!"

"Boss?" confused, Fitzsimmons stared at her, then turned to Baxter who was smiling.

"Colin," she shook her head, "why didn't you mention this before!"

"Mention what, exactly?" a now clearly irate Fitzsimmon's glanced from one to the other.

Mary slowly smiled, but not a happy smile; no, a smile of understanding how stupid she felt she had been.

It was then Baxter replied to her question, "To be honest, Boss, like you, I was…to use your own terminology, blinkered too. It was less than half an hour ago I was sipping at my coffee when young Janey McPhee said something that got me thinking."

"What did she say?"

"Then maybe one of you can let me in what you're talking about," remarked Fitzsimmons, her voice sounding a little cross.

"Sorry, Elaine," Mary shook her head, then added, "Let's first hear what Janey said to provoke Colin's thoughts."

Sitting back in his chair, Baxter shrugged, "Janey, she was talking about a play she watched last night on the television, about one of the characters who at the end said, 'It was right under our noses' or something like that. Anyway, whatever the story was about," Baxter shrugged, "it seems that the main character was a conman, but nobody guessed the ending because he was so good at diverting attention away from himself."

"And that means what?" Fitzsimmons was now really confused.

"What Colin's suggesting," Mary turned to her, "is that we or I should say *me*," she angrily sighed, "because I'm supposed to be the bloody SIO, I was too preoccupied by the fact that we had discovered the items in the wardrobe and wrongly assumed the murder was all about the ornaments and the jewellery. Now, that in turn led us along the path of searching for the thief or thieves and ultimately, our main suspect, Monica Davies. A path that because it was criminal, I convinced myself the murder must be connected." She sat back, hands flat on the table and slowly shook her head, inwardly angry with herself.

"However," she continued as she stared at Baxter, "what Colin is so correctly pointing out is that since we now know the ornaments and the jewellery have nothing whatsoever to do with the murder, then perhaps the murder was *not* planned, as we already believed, but simply opportunistic. Our killer had been in the house and seized her opportunity."

Fitzsimmons eyes widened when her voice almost a whisper, she said, "Her opportunity? Oh, my God. The wee woman next door that disliked...no," her brow fiercely knitted, "she actually admitted she *hated* our victim. Surely not!"

Mary glanced at Baxter before she said, "It's somewhere to start."

Baxter's eyes narrowed when he said, "We have the fingerprint on the murder weapon, but how would we obtain the neighbours..."

"Church," Mary interrupted. "As I recall, Yvonne Church, is her name."

"Yeah, Boss, you're right. But, how would we obtain Mrs Church's fingerprints?"

She smiled then said, "Funny enough, I have an idea about that."

****

The de-briefing that early evening was short and concise.

Mary loudly clapped her hands together, then her expression solemn, began with "Now, a wee admission to make. Following a discussion with DS's Baxter and Fitzsimmons, I have to tell you that as SIO I have led you to believe, as I did, that the discovery of the stolen items in the victim's flat was an overriding factor in her murder." She paused to stare around the room, then said, "I now believe that I was wrong. If anything, and to quote myself again, I was too blinkered and did not consider there might be an alternative motive for her murder. And for that, as the SIO I bear the responsibility of misleading this investigation. However, thanks to Colin Baxter, I have now re-focused our investigation on local individuals and that begins with the neighbour across the landing, mainly due to her disparaging comments about the victim, and who now is to be subjected to some scrutiny."

She hesitated when a hand was raised at the back of the room and saw it to be her DS, Donald Corbett, who loudly said, "I wouldn't be too hard on yourself, boss. I don't think there's anyone here that thought anything different. Am I right?"

He cast a glance around the room to see heads nodding, and heard voices replying, "Aye, right enough, big man," or from DC Mary Patrick, who called out, "At the time, it seemed the logical way of thinking, boss."

Touched and her chest swelling with pride, Mary waved away the rest of the supportive comments, then said, "I appreciate your backing, guys, but the fact remains, I *am* still the SIO and if there's a fault, it lies with me; so again, I promise I'll try to be more open-minded. If any of you have any ideas, you know I have an open door policy, okay?"

She could not nor ever would know, but as Colin Baxter watched her address her team, he thought of all the bosses he had served, yet did not know of one who would so openly admit to be wrong or who had the overwhelming support or willingness of her staff to work for Mary Wells, a DCI who he recognised to be a true leader.

"And on that point," she continued with a grin as she studied her team, "tomorrow morning, DS Fitzsimmon's and her neighbour, young Alan there, are out *really* early and on a mission. More about that at tomorrow's briefing."

"However, for now," she continued to grin, "I want you all to head home and get a good night's sleep because like I said, tomorrow guys, we're back hitting the Actions."

****

When the room was clearing, Tommy Maxwell laid a sympathetic hand on John McGhee's shoulder and following him into the corridor, quietly said, "Sorry that you had to find out your new bird was doing the old fandangle with our suspects husband, pal."

"The fandangle? What century do you come from?" McGhee stared curiously at him.

"Eh, you're not upset that you're not going to be seeing that good looking bird again? Her, I mean," he glanced around him and again lowered his voice even more, "Charlie Paterson."

McGhee stopped and nodding that Maxwell join him in the gent's toilet, ensured that there was no one within before he replied, "Look, I'll tell you this and no more, okay? Yeah," he exhaled, "I had a great time with Charlie last night and things were sweet when we got back to her pad. However," he grimaced, "as fabulous as the night with her was, it was a little…discomforting, when she kicked me out at six this morning and told me I'd better skedaddle, because her husband was due back home on the overnight train from London."

"Her husband? Shit! You're kidding!" Maxwell's eyes were almost as wide as his grin.

"So, to answer your question, I won't be seeing her again unless it's from a witness box," McGhee shook his head, then humorously smiled.

****

Standing drunkenly after fetching more ice from the freezer for her gin, Natalie MacDonald's rage had not abated. Her eyes glazed and still wearing her dressing gown over her nightdress, she leaned against her worktop in the kitchen, quietly cursing.

The cause of her anger, John Green, the church elder and her latest beau, was gone.

She'd awakened that morning, confused why he hadn't attended at her bedroom with her usual coffee and toast. Eventually forced from her bed to her en-suite by her toilet needs, she then stepped next door to the room she'd persuaded him to use after she bedded him, only to find that not only was he gone, but so were the few items of clothing he kept there.

Initially confused, she had glanced outside to see his car was also gone then telephoned his house, but her call was not answered.

It was then the penny had dropped.

"Bastard!" she had screamed, her fists clenched and her anger knowing no bounds.

It occurred to her then to drive to Green's home and beat upon his door, but that would have had people talking; someone would have seen her and she refused to have those torn-faced *bitches* at the church gossiping about her being an abandoned woman *again* and that, she most certainly was not!
"Nobody dumps me!" she had hissed to the empty house.
Her body shaking with unbridled rage, she had decided to go downstairs and have herself a calming gin.
"Fuck them all!" she had sneered at the empty kitchen and in seconds, downed the gin.
"I don't need any of them, none of them!" she had roared while pouring herself a second gin.
Then, as the day passed and a second bottle of consumed gin lay on the carpet like a fallen soldier, Natalie awoke with a start in the lounge, apparently having rolled off the couch onto the floor, her head aching, her mouth dry, her back throbbing from the awkward position she found herself in and the front of her dressing gown stained with spilt gin and her own, reeking vomit.
It was several seconds before she realised she had peed herself, too, and even more seconds for her to recall why at that time of the early evening, she was not dressed.
When she remembered, her face contorted and she decided that she'd have it out with John Green, make the bastard explain why he'd run out on her.
Her body shaking, she managed to get to her feet, only to stumble and fall backwards onto the couch.
A mouthful of expletives exploded from her and it was then she felt the nausea sweep through her body.
Choking back her bile, she staggered with arms outstretched, using the furniture to steady herself as she made her way to the hallway, then upstairs to the en-suite.
Natalie hated cold showers, yet forced herself to stand shrieking for almost a full minute before carefully stepping onto the bathmat, her body shivering uncontrollably.
Ten minutes later, her stomach still in turmoil, she combed back her damp hair, idly noting that it was time for yet another expensive visit to the salon to deal with the rapidly emerging grey.

Now dressed in a gaudy, designer sequinned pink tracksuit and white training shoes that would never see the inside of a gymnasium, she took a deep breath then exhaled onto her cupped hand and sniffed. She scowled, for there was no denying her breath reeked, but it wasn't the first time she'd driven after a bevy session. After all, she turned back and forth while coyly glancing at her reflection in the en-suite mirror, what police officer would imagine that a good-looking woman like her and who drove a smart, BMW sedan, would be anything *but* sober.

And so what if I am stopped, she drunkenly sniggered, then reached for a deep red coloured lipstick.

Vanity had never been a problem with the conceited Natalie who satisfied that she was still the most attractive woman she knew and more than capable of charming any man.

Aware that her balance was a little awry, she hesitantly returned to the bedroom where to her surprise, a sudden dizziness overtook her, causing her to grab at the wardrobe door to stay upright, then arms once more outstretched, cautiously stepped across the floor to sit on the edge of the bed.

Minutes passed, then feeling better, she exhaled and gingerly stood upright.

In the hallway, her legs shaking, she used both hands on the rail to support her downward steps, then in the foyer, reached for the car keys from the drawer in the small unit.

It was then she remembered and made her way into the lunge where with one hand on the top of the fireplace, she stooped to pick up what she needed.

A minute later, unlocking the front door, she took a huge gulp of air before stepping out of the door then pulled it closed behind her and slowly teetered towards her car.

****

Bill Howie was parking his car when Mary Wells arrived home. He stood on the pavement till she alighted from her Toyota, then greeted her with, "How was your day?"

"Oh, the usual harum-scarum problems of running a murder investigation that just seems to keep growing arms and legs," she sighed, then asked, "And your day?"

"The usual bumps and scrapes," he smiled back at her.

They stood for a few awkward seconds, as if both reluctant to break off the chance meeting, then Mary said, "Well, better go in and relieve my dad and Eileen before my pair wear them down any further."

"Mary," he raised a hand.

"Yes?"

"Ah, about that dinner. You still up for it?"

"Yes, of course," she nodded.

"Well," he slowly drawled, "I'm taking my first full weekend off this Saturday, so if you're not otherwise engaged…?"

He saw her brow furrow before she replied, "Depending on what you mean by engaged and what happens in my ongoing investigation," she frowned. "I should be home on Saturday at the very latest by sevenish, if you're okay with that? Fingers crossed, that is," she hastily added.

"Yes, that sounds fine and rather than have you rush to get dressed for going out, how would you feel if I cooked and we ate at my place?"

She smiled lopsidedly before she replied, "I think that would be wonderful, Bill."

"Then it's a date," he grinned, but his face fell when he almost immediately corrected himself with, "What I mean is…"

"It's okay, Bill," she softly laughed, "I think I know what you mean."

Turning, she graced him with a wide smile then pushed open her front door, only to be met by Jamie and Morven who screaming with delight, came rushing down the hallway to greet her.

Clutching both children to her and kissing at their heads, she thought there was no finer way to be welcomed home.

Once the children had been dispatched back to their cartoon show, Mary sat with a much-needed cuppa at the kitchen table, learning of Michael and Eileen's visit to her friend, Lesley Wilson, at the law firm.

"So, this private investigator she's talking about. I can only presume they must be licensed?"

"I don't imagine for one-minute Lesley would use any disreputable investigator," Eileen shook her head.

Even with Eileen's assurance and no matter what her feelings were about Natalie, Mary was still a little disconcerted at the thought of her mother being under covert surveillance, yet inwardly argued that she had brought this upon herself by her behaviour throughout the years she had bullied and abused her husband and, yes, her children too.

"So," she asked, "when does Lesley intend commencing the divorce proceedings?"

She saw Eileen glance at her father before Michael replied, "As of tomorrow, the investigator will begin to gather evidence of Natalie's…" he hesitated, "her behaviour and statements from people who she has been seeing."

"You mean the men she's been seeing, dad?"

"Yes," he slowly exhaled. "The men."

"I'm sorry to ask this, but what about you and Eileen?"

His brow creased and he made a face when he asked, "What do you mean?"

"Well, again I'm sorry to be so blunt, but it's no secret now that you are in a relationship with another woman while you're still legally married, so how will Lesley deal with that?"

He turned to glance at Eileen, then reaching across the table to take hold of her hand, replied, "Frankly, I don't care, but if I am ever asked, I will truthfully say that after almost forty-five years of being married to a woman who treated me so badly, I have met a woman who not only cares for me, but shown me what true love really is."

Mary couldn't help but smile, though inwardly wondered what a divorce court would make of that statement.

"Well," she smiled and stared at them in turn, "If nothing else, dad, you have the complete backing of your children and that's something that mum never had nor ever will have."

With his free hand, he reached for Mary's then said, "I know that, sweetheart, and don't think I take it for granted, not for one minute. Now," he released both women's hands, "I think it's time we were off."

When he rose to his feet, it was Eileen who asked, "What about your murder, Mary? Are you any further forward with it?"

"I thought today I might be, but that fell through; however," she grinned, "like Scarlet O'Hara says, tomorrow is another day."

"Well, we'll be here bright and early at the usual time, won't we," Eileen turned to Michael, who grinned, "With bells on."

When they had gone, Mary began to organise the children's supper and as she did so, her thoughts turned to Bill Howie's dinner invitation, then she smiled at his *faux pas* about it being a date. But it *is* a date, she told herself, isn't it?

Then, to her own surprise, she rather hoped it was and distracted by that thought, idly wondered what she would wear.

****

Returning that evening to her home in Old Kilpatrick, Elaine Fitzsimmons was caught between being a little disappointed that she had such an early start the following morning, yet pleased that she and her neighbour had been entrusted by Mary Wells to carry out the task that might just break the murder investigation.

Turning into the driveway of her house, she saw her husband, Eric's, car already parked and knew that he'd have begun to prepare the dinner and likely with the help of their daughters, she smiled. Switching off the engine, she didn't immediately leave the car, but sat thinking through the day.

It had been a disappointment for the whole team when their primary suspect, Monica Davies, proved to be a washout, but more so for Mary Wells, Fitzsimmons thought.

For a woman who had come through such a traumatic personal incident, being dumped by her unfaithful husband, just as she delivered her second child, Fitzsimmon's inwardly wondered; just how had Mary coped?

Then, a little under a year later, to return to work knowing that her domestic issues were the talk of the steamie and facing up to the challenge of being the DCI running the CID Department in a Division with a seriously high crime rate. Not to mention the problems that slimy bastard, Martin Reilly, left her, with a demoralised Pollok team.

She took a deep breath and unconsciously shaking her head, promised herself that tomorrow she and Alan would get a result. It just had to come, after all the hard work the team had completed. Staring at her house, she involuntarily smiled that unlike Mary, she had a husband who wouldn't let her down.

But then again, she found herself frowning, though Eric had never given her any cause to be suspicious, just how well *do* we know and trust our other halves?

****

With her children now bedded down and sleeping, the subject of

Fitzsimmons thoughts, Mary Wells, had just completed three miles on her exercise bike.

Now, towelling herself down after a hot shower, she frowned when she heard the phone ringing in the hallway.

Wrapping the bath towel around her, she rushed to answer the call, inwardly praying it wasn't a call-out, that she didn't have yet another serious incident to attend to.

"Hello?"

To her relief, it was her brother, Alan, who brusquely asked, "Hi, wee sis, do you happen to have Eileen's home phone number handy? I need to speak to dad."

"Eh, yes, I know it if you've a pen handy," then almost immediately asked, "Why, what's up?"

There was a slight pause before he sighed heavily, then replied, "I've just had a phone call from the police in Giffnock. It's mum. She's been arrested."

CHAPTER TWENTY-NINE

After a restless night, Elaine Fitzsimmons, who had taken the precaution of laying out her clothes downstairs so not to disturb her husband who was on his uniform shift's days off,

slowly turned her head to confirm with the digital alarm clock it was now four-thirty, then slid from the bed.

Tiptoeing to the door, she was about to pull it open when Eric grunted, "Hope you get a result, darling."

Grinning, she returned to his side of the bed then bending, delivered a kiss to the top of his head and quietly replied, "With some luck, I'll be home this afternoon. I don't see the boss keeping me and Alan all day, if we're out this early."

A little over ten minutes later, showered and dressed, she poured her coffee into a flask then made her way outside to her car.

The journey time normally made through commuter traffic from her home in Pleasant Drive, within the picturesque village of Old Kilpatrick, to Govan Police Office in Orkney Street, was around twenty to twenty-five-minutes, but early that Friday morning and with one wary eye on her rear-view mirror watching for the

'Beasties,' otherwise known as the Traffic Department, Fitzsimmons arrived a little over sixteen minutes later.

Getting out of her car she was pleased to see Alan Hamilton's Mini already parked there and with her flask in her hand, hurried upstairs. Entering the incident room, Hamilton stood smiling at her and waving a set of car keys, then asked, "Ready to go?"

"Got a production bag?"

"In my pocket," he patted at his anorak.

"Then let's go," she smiled.

A little over five minutes later, she stopped the CID car in Clifford Street, some twenty yards short of the close the locus of the murder. Switching off the engine, she said, "We're early, so hopefully they haven't been on their delivery yet."

"I'll be just a minute," he replied, then getting out of the car, strode purposefully towards the close at number twelve, pulling the brown coloured paper production bag from his pocket as he walked.

A little over a minute later, he returned and holding up the production bag, then nodded, "Got it."

"Right, then, let's head to Pitt Street."

She could feel her heart beat that little bit faster when glancing at her wristwatch, she added, "Mickey at the SOCO should be waiting for us."

****

Mary Wells too had a sleepless, restless night.

Rising from bed at a little over six that morning, her thoughts as to why her mother had been arrested danced around her head.

Tempted though she had been to phone Giffnock Police Office, she knew it would be extremely inappropriate for her to make a call to ask wat had occurred, that it would rightly be seen as Mary using her rank to solicit personal information.

However, there had been no further calls from Alan or her father and she rightly assumed Michael wouldn't want her worrying, but by not contacting he, he inadvertently had caused her to worry more.

Now showered and dressed, she restlessly paced the kitchen, listening both for her children to awaken and her father and Eileen's arrival.

As it turned out, it was a pale faced Eileen who arrived alone, a little earlier than usual and it was clearly obvious to Mary that she too had not had a good night.

While the children sat in their pyjamas at the kitchen table having their cereal, Mary boiled the kettle for coffee then sat with Eileen in the front room.

"Here's what I know," Eileen began with a tired sigh.

"Your brother Alan phoned to say he had been contacted by the police from Giffnock Police Office to say your mother had been arrested for drunk driving and assault."

"Dear God," her eyes widening, Mary instinctively reached a hand to her mouth.

"Michael decided that he would go with Alan to Giffnock to find out what the story is, but he didn't want to contact you and worry you because he knows that Giffnock is part of your Division. Is that right?"

"Yes, it is," Mary sighed, already envisioning what the gossip might be, yet annoyed her father hadn't thought that a heads up might have been more appropriate. However, her DI at Giffnock CID, Gerry Turney, was not only a very capable and loyal officer, but trustworthy too and likely be keen to contact her when she arrived at work to bring her up to date on her mother's arrest.

"Do you know if she's being held in custody?" Mary asked.

"I don't," Eileen shook her head, then continued, "but before Michael left to meet with Alan, he said he'd likely stay over with Alan and Morag, but he told me that he'd phone me here this morning with any news he has. I expect because I'm early, he won't phone for another twenty minutes or so. Do you want to wait till he calls, or what?"

"No, I'll just head into work and get the bad news there," she frowned.

Leaving Eileen to finish her coffee, she returned to the kitchen then forcing a bright smile, kissed both her children before calling out, "Cheerio," to the three of them.

****

After handing the production bag over to Mickey, the SOCO supervisor, Fitzsimmons told Hamilton, "It's unlikely anywhere is open at this time of the morning."

Turning to Mickey, she said, "We'll head up to the canteen and have a coffee," and held up her flask. "If you need us, just phone us there."

"Righto, Elaine," he peered into the brown, paper bag, then added, "I shouldn't be too long processing this and when I'm finished, I'll take it myself up to the Fingerprints Department."

Her eyes narrowed in curiosity when she asked, "Are they open for business at this time of the morning?"

He smiled when he said, "I'm owed more favours than I can count by that mob, so trust me; when I ask for one of them to come out and do a comparison, the bugger better be there. Besides," he shrugged, "it's not often that Mary Wells asks for a favour, so good guy that she is, believe me when I tell you, *nothing* is too much bother."

Fitzsimmons and Hamilton both grinned at the big man's sincerity and left him to do his work.

****

DI Gerry Turney, a former Lanarkshire Constabulary police officer who had been rejected by the City of Glasgow Police because he was half an inch below the required height, had turned forty-two just a week earlier. Turney was prematurely bald with a ready smile and easy-going attitude that hid a razor-sharp mind and had served him well during his twenty-three years of police service.

Happily married for nineteen years to a midwife and with three teenage children, the DI was an admirer of his DCI, not least because Mary Wells had returned to work following a disastrous domestic situation and, if he were honest, she seemed not only to have turned her life around, but her whole being too. A faithful and devoted husband, Turnery was still a man, so even he admitted to his wife that his DCI, who just months previously had been a woman on the brink of obesity and had completely let herself go, was now looking like a mature model from a woman's magazine.

"As long as you admire from afar," his wife had jokingly chided him.

"Hey, hang on," he had retorted with a grin, "you're always window shopping, but you don't always buy, so can't that apply to me, too?"

Now, sitting in his office at Giffnock Police Office in Braidholm Road, he read a summary of the report against Mary Wells mother and sighed.

Reaching for the desk phone, he dialled the internal number and when Mary replied, said, "Boss, it's Gerry Turney. You'll have heard the news?"

"I have, Gerry, but not the circumstances. I take it you have the custody report in front of you?"

"I'm afraid it doesn't make for good reading," he replied, then when his door was knocked, Mary heard him loudly call out, "I'm busy. Come back in ten minutes."

"Sorry about that. Never a minute's peace here," he groaned, then began, "The accused is Natalie MacDonald, aged sixty-eight…sorry, what am I thinking? You'll know that. Anyway, the summary reads that the late shift uniform cops were called to the report of a disturbance at a property in Merryvale Avenue, here in Giffnock. Do you know it?"

"I'm not familiar with the area, no."

"Literally just down the road from the office here. It's a nice bit, nineteen-fifties built semi-detached bungalows and relatively affluent," he explained, then continued, "It seems it was neighbour who made the nine-nine-nine call and when the cops arrived, they found a sixty-nine-year-old man, John Green, sitting on his doorstep with a broken nose being tended to by the said neighbour. He seemed out of it and so the cops called an ambulance. Green identified your mother as his assailant and said that up to the previous day, they had briefly been in a relationship, but he had ended it due to…" he paused.

"Look," he suddenly said, "I'm sorry to be telling you this, are you sure you want me to continue?"

"Yes, Gerry," she sighed. "I'd rather hear it from you than the gossipmongers."

"Okay, then," he unconsciously nodded.

Taking a short breath, he continued, "Green told the cops that your mother was a controlling woman and he feared she was violent too and he couldn't take it anymore, so he had left her house the previous day. It doesn't say in the report because the cop that wrote it is a useless git, but the inference is that they must have been living together. Anyway, the neighbour apparently witnessed your mother making off in a silver coloured BMW and gave the reggie number to the cops. They put out a lookout for the motor and knowing the registered address from the PNC, the local cars headed for that area. Cutting a long story short," he paused and took a breath, "they stopped the motor and discovered your mother was, well, she was definitely over the limit. That said she refused to be breathalysed at the locus. When they brought her back here to the office, she again refused the breathalyser a second time. According to this report, she had blood staining on her tracksuit that she was wearing, though she had no visible injury. Green's blood, I suspect, and her tracksuit top was seized for analysis. Anyway, the Casualty Surgeon was called out to examine her, but she refused to be examined by him, screaming they should call out her own doctor, which of course, the Duty Sergeant refused to do."

"How badly hurt was the victim, this man John Green?"

"Initial report from the casualty at the Victoria Hospital is a broken nose and a laceration where the poker hit him. I had a look at it in the production store and it's one of them…Sorry, Boss, you likely know the one I'm meaning?"

"I think I do, yes. It's a reproduction thing, one of a companion set from her house that sat by the gas fire. Purely ornamental."

"Sounds like it, yes," he nodded at the phone. "Anyway, it has a bit of a rough edge on it and when your mother clobbered Green, it's the rough edge that seems to have caught his cheek, because he suffered a three-inch laceration that needed stitching. I don't have to tell you, boss, that going equipped with an offensive weapon to assault Green doesn't help any defence she might put forward."

"Dear God, it gets worse," he heard her angrily exhale.

"Boss," he quietly said, "the rest doesn't make good reading."

"Go on," she softly asked then quickly added, "Wait a minute."

He heard her ask, "Who is it?"

A slight pause followed that ended when Turney heard her say, "Tell him I'll call him back."

Seconds later, she said, "Sorry, Gerry, that was one of my team telling me my father was on the phone looking for me. Probably to give me the bad news as well. But please, continue."

"Right, where was I? Oh, aye, anyway, the cops stopped your mother on the Ayr Road and according to the report, she was bawling and shouting and using your name, threatening them that they'd lose their jobs because you are a DCI and you'd see them getting the sack."

"What? They actually put *that* in the bloody report?" she was outraged and started to curse.

"Mary! Listen to me!" he snapped at her then when she'd quietened, he drew a breath and quietly said, "Sorry, but you need to *listen* to me, okay? You know as well as I do that there are arses in the job, both uniform and CID. Well, this guy that done the report. I know him. A right lazy bastard if ever there was one; that and he's a whining bugger as well. He likely thinks by adding that little gem that he's sticking it to the management and the management, unfortunately, is you."

A short silence ended when he continued, "Oh, and there's a further bad news, I'm sorry to say."

"How much worse can it be," she sighed.

"Well, when they tried to put her in the back of the Transit van, she *allegedly* kicked out, so she's also been charged with resisting arrest. However," she heard him irritably sigh, "given that she is a sixty-eight-year-old woman and she was apparently pissed, I can't imagine how much damage she could have inflicted with a pair of training shoes on the four burly polis that apparently were witnesses to the resisting. Sounds to me like they were just too eager to add further charges to their report."

He heard her exhale before she asked, "And the report, I assume it's already winging its way to the Fiscal's Office over in Paisley?"

"Sorry, aye, it's already gone. However," he breathed into the phone, "when we're finished this call, I'll be phoning the Fiscal myself and believe me, as for your mother using your name, I *will* get that sorted. We both know she was a drunk woman and there was absolutely no need for that to be reported. Anyway, to summarise," he said, "in the late hours of this morning and once she provided a negative breathalyser, she was released for report, though I think the Duty Sergeant did so out of respect for yourself and who, I believe I'm correct, is ex-CID. As you know, the assault and the resist arrest would usually have warranted an overnighter, then an appearance this morning at the court."

"Thanks, Gerry," she sighed, though inwardly thought it might not have done her mother any harm getting a night in the cells. "I owe you one and the sergeant too, if you could pass my thanks."

"Of course I will," he grimly smiled into the phone, then added, "Is there anything I can do to help?"

"Do you know any hitmen that work on the cheap?" she irately asked, then more calmly added, "No, but thank you for the offer and anyway, you've already done enough for me."

"Now," he heard her take a breath, "while you're on. Anything else doing up in Giffnock?"

"Nothing that we can't handle, Boss. You just concentrate on yourself and for what it's worth, I'm sorry you're going through this. With your mother, I mean."

"Gerry, I appreciate that, but we both know there's more than a few people had a lot more to contend with than a relative who thinks because their daughter is a senior police officer, it entitles them to be an arse," she said with some feeling.

"Oh, one more thing, Boss. Your mother's car's still here in the back yard. Do you want to make an arrangement to have it picked up?"

"Frankly, Gerry, it can rust away until such time the sub-Divisional Officer decides to get rid of it. I am taking nothing to do with her or her motor."

"Fair enough, Boss," he grinned.

"Right, I'd better be off and contact my dad. No doubt he's as angry as I am. So, again, thank you and stay in touch," she said with some feeling.

When the call had ended, Turney stared at his desk, more angry than he had admitted to Wells that a cop in his office should make an already difficult situation for her that much worse by officially reporting the ranting of a drunken woman, for he knew that such reporting was completely unnecessary and nothing more than simple malice.

Well then, the reporting officers face jumped into his thoughts, once I've phoned the Fiscal to explain the vindictiveness behind those comments in the report, I'll be keeping a very close eye on its author. And though not by nature a vindictive man, he thought, I'll be waiting for the first, slightest mistake the lazy and useless bastard was bound to make.

****

For the second time in a week, Mary Wells found herself standing in front of her team who by now having heard through the Divisional grapevine, were all aware that the DCI's mother had been arrested the previous evening for serious assault, resisting arrest and drunk driving.

It was no wonder that Mary, staring around in the silent room at some embarrassed and some curious faces, considered that maybe she should lock herself in her room and let Colin Baxter take the briefing.

However, the fortitude and resilience that had brought her through a disastrous marriage and severe post-natal depression once more came to the fore and so, staring at her team, she sombrely said, "First, let me get this off my chest. It's no secret that my mother has once again attracted the attention of the police, on this occasion with our colleagues at Giffnock Police Office. I regret that…"

"Boss?"

Taken aback at the sudden interruption, Mary saw that once more her DS, Donald Corbett, was standing at the back of the room and holding up his hand.

"Yes, Donnie, what is it?" she stared inquiringly at him.

"Boss, I was thinking," the large, broad-shouldered man began to thoughtfully stroke at his thick, red beard, then exhaling through pursed lips, said, "Now, maybe I'm out of line here, but I don't really give a flying fuck what happened up in Giffnock, pardon my French. I'd rather hear what is happening about our murder investigation, here in Govan."

Seconds of tense silence passed as a murmur went round the room and before she could respond, the cry went up, "Aye, me too," and "That's right, well said, big man," then the room as a whole were agreeing that whatever her wayward mother had done, it had no relevance to their investigation.

Tears biting at her eyes and unable to respond for fear of embarrassing herself, Mary took a deep breath and turned to stare at Colin Baxter, who taking his cue, quickly rose to his feet, then raising a hand to quell the good-natured outpouring of support, said, "I'm sitting here waiting on a phone call from Elaine Fitzsimmons and Alan Hamilton."

The team turned their attention to Baxter, who continued, "As the boss told you yesterday, she had an idea that maybe we as a team could not see the forest for the trees. In short, were we looking for a motive for Elizabeth Bradley's murder because of the items we discovered, rather than seeing what is under our noses."

He turned to softly smile at her, then realising she had composed herself, said, "It's your idea, Boss, if you want to share it with the guys."

"Thank you, Colin," she smiled gratefully at him, the smile meaning more than just the opportunity to disclose her plan.

"As you are all aware, we obtained a partial fingerprint from the murder weapon that does not compare with our three suspects involved in the thefts from the elderly clients of the cleaning company. And, like I said yesterday, it was my decision that on hindsight was not my *best* decision, to put all our eggs into the one basket. But that has changed."

Her eyes searched the room when she said, "Now, I decided yesterday that we should first look at our victim's neighbour, the woman across the landing who quite openly and freely admitted she disliked Bradley, even suggested she hated her, for no other reason than Elizabeth Bradley was a single and unmarried parent who though she was employed by a cleaning company, was not herself a particularly tidy individual. A woman who, and again according to Mrs Church, lived in a pigsty, who was slovenly and sloppy about putting her rubbish out in the bins at the rear of the building."

She paused to let her words sink in.

"But what we…" she hesitated, then said, "or rather, what I didn't pick up on was, how did Mrs Church know our victim lived in a pigsty other than if she had been in the house, which she previously denied. In fact, she *told* me that she would not step into a pigsty like the victims flat, so how could she possibly know what the interior of the flat was like?"

Once more, she paused before she asked, "Is that reason enough to murder someone? I really don't think so, but then again I don't see myself as an uptight, righteous snob who also looked down on our victim simply because being on a low income, she rented rather than bought her flat."

She let her statement again sink in before she continued, "On my attendance at the locus last Tuesday, I happened to notice that Mrs Church still had her milk delivered in a glass bottle, unlike most of us who probably buy our milk in cartons. However, what was interesting was that after the bottle was empty, it was washed out and left on the doorstep, presumably to be replaced by a full bottle and that got me thinking."

She paused again then staring round the room, said, "Early doors this morning, Elaine Fitzsimmons and Alan Hamilton conducted a wee bit of subterfuge."

Now seeing she had their undivided attention, she inwardly smiled when she continued, "At my instruction, Elaine and Alan stole," she smiled again, then corrected herself, "I mean, *borrowed*, the empty milk bottle from Mrs Church's doorstep. The milk bottle was then taken to Pitt Street where Mickey, the SOCO supervisor,

fingerprinted it and as far as we are currently aware, it's at the Fingerprint Department right now being compared to the print seized from the murder weapon. So, guys, fingers crossed."
****
Sitting in the empty canteen and sipping at the remains of their cooling coffee, both Fitzsimmons and Hamilton startled then turned together to stare at the far wall when the phone rang.
It was far too early for the canteen staff to have arrived, so both immediately realised only one individual could be calling.
It was Hamilton who waving her back down into her chair, sprung to his feet and raced towards the phone.
"Yes, Mickey," she heard him answer.
Turning towards her, her stomach lurched when she saw him suddenly grin and give her a thumbs-up.
Taking a deep breath, she slowly exhaled and uncharacteristically found her two fists punching the air.

CHAPTER THIRTY

After identifying himself to the bar officer, Michael MacDonald sat nervously in the foyer of Govan Police Office for a couple of minutes before a smiling young woman appeared before him, who then said, "Mr MacDonald? I'm Janey, if you'd like to follow me, sir?" then escorted him upstairs to his daughter's office.
When Janey pushed open the office door then indicated he enter the office, he saw Mary seated behind her desk who rising, thanked Janey, then watched her pull the door closed behind her.
Taking the chair Mary indicated, she saw her father seemed to have aged several years since the previous day, then wearily sitting down, he hesitantly said, "I'm so sorry to come here to your office, sweetheart, when I know you're so busy, but I wanted to apologise in person rather than over the phone. I assume by now you will know all the details?"
Resuming her seat, Mary stared curiously at him before she asked, "I do, but why are you apologising, dad? What is it you think you've done wrong?"
Slumped in his chair, Michael replied, "Your mother, Mary. If I'd

been a stronger man, a better father who'd stood up to her…"

"Now," she raised her hand and harshly interrupted, "stop right there. You have absolutely nothing for which to apologise, dad, other than perhaps for marrying that woman in the first place and let me tell you right now, you are not the only one who is divorcing her. As far as I am concerned and I likely speak for my brothers too, we are *all* divorcing Natalie."

Catching her breath, she continued, "I admit I was apprehensive about how difficult it would be for you obtaining a divorce, how messy it might be, but after learning of her behaviour today as well as coming to my home and assaulting you; well, she doesn't deserve to have you, me Alan or William and *definitely* not *my* children or my brother's children in her life!"

She took a few seconds to compose herself then in a quieter voice, she continued, "I also have to inform you, dad, that I have no compunction about contacting Sergeant Cowan, the officer who took the report of your assault. He warned *Natalie*," she stressed the name, now inwardly refusing to call her mum, "that if she should continue her behaviour, he would with hindsight inform the PF that rather than a warning letter, he will recommend the PF pursue a charge of assault against her, albeit it was relatively minor compared to her actions yesterday evening. Nonetheless, it will be a further charge that even if it is a minor assault in the scheme of things and the PF does not take it up because it will be retrospectively submitted, it demonstrates a pattern of her violent behaviour and if nothing else, can be useful for indicating to a divorce court the life you suffered with her."

Michael sat straight back in his chair and stared at his daughter, for this was not turning out as he had anticipated. He'd thought Mary would be angry with him, at his failure as a husband and a father, but her anger was solely directed towards her mother.

And suddenly, tears biting at his eyes, he felt an overwhelming pride in her, for she had so correctly convinced him that he was better off without Natalie, that he no longer felt any guilt about divorcing her nor any doubt he was also correct in pursuing the action against her for what was rightly his property.

"Now, dad," she forced a smile, "As much as I appreciate you coming to visit me here, I have an ongoing…

"Yes, yes, of course," he almost leapt to his feet. "I'll be off and Mary," he stared down at her with a smile.

"Thank you, sweetheart."

She rose from behind her desk, then stepped forward to warmly hug him, just as Colin Baxter knocked on her door to soberly inform her, "Sorry to interrupt, Boss. She's here."

****

Regardless of Chief Constable Charles Pettigrew's previous evenings media briefing at Force Headquarters, when Pettigrew suggested that it was he who had been responsible for planning the Pollok operation that netted a drugs gang, the true architect for the arrests, DI Sammy Salmon, was still on a high and had no genuine interest in being awarded plaudits for his successful operation.

It was enough for Salmon that he had a team who were now bonding and for the first time in a very long while, their morale as well as his own, was at an all-time high.

However, to those members of Strathclyde Police who were well acquainted with Pettigrew, the headquarters media briefing had merely reinforced their opinion that the publicity seeking Charles Pettigrew was a narcissistic waste of space.

A conceited individual whose sole desire, that bizarrely he openly admitted, was to be offered the position of Commissioner of the Metropolitan Police, Pettigrew had, as already predicted by ACC Keith Meadows to Mary Wells, alluded to the attending journalists and both the STV and BBC television crews, that it was indeed he who had organised the successful operation leading to the arrest of a number of individuals engaged in operating an illegal drug ring in the Pollok area.

"Not only was there a large quantity of drugs seized," Pettigrew turned towards the cameras and proudly smiled, "but a number of illegal weapons were also recovered."

However, it all started going wrong when a reporter for a rival newspaper of the 'Glasgow News' then asked, "And what about Richard Bradley, the man who was shot dead, Chief Constable? Is there any truth in the previous reporting by the 'Glasgow News' that his sister Elizabeth, a murder victim too I understand, was also involved in the drugs ring?"

Standing a little behind Pettigrew, the Superintendent in charge of the Force's Media Department tensed and for those few seconds, mentally crossed his fingers and literally stopped breathing, for he had clearly underlined in the Chief's briefing paper that the sister's murder was not in fact connected to her brother's shooting, that Richard Bradley's wound was not murder, but an accident; a self-inflicted wound.

However, the Superintendent also knew that the Chief was notorious for *not* properly reading his briefing paper and had a tendency to 'wing it' when asked awkward questions…or on occasion, simply lied, leaving the Superintendent struggling to pull Pettigrew's arse out of the fire.

Of course, not having fully read his brief and unaware of the true circumstances of Elizabeth and Richard Bradley's deaths, to hide his ignorance of Elizabeth's demise, Pettigrew *was* aware they were brother and sister and so confidently replied, "Oh, yes, of course she was. A family business, eh?" he jocularly laughed.

It was at the point the Superintendent turned pale, then seriously thought he might interrupt the Chief and explain to the attending media that the stupid bastard was a lying git, that there was absolutely no truth *whatsoever* in Ally McGregor's article and that Elizabeth Bradley's murder was an ongoing and *completely* separate investigation.

However, the Superintendent then inwardly startled as a deep calm overtook him, for it was just then that he involuntarily smiled.

In that instant the Superintendent had realised it was highly likely an official complaint from Elizabeth Bradley's family would be lodged against Pettigrew; particularly now as there was both video and corroborative reporting evidence that without confirmation to the contrary, the Force's Chief Constable had publicly slandered an innocent woman by stating that her death was attributed to her involvement in a drugs gang.

And, he breathed a sigh of relief, the Superintendent knew that to protect himself against any allegation by the Chief Constable, he had printed numerous copies of his briefing paper that were sent to senior officers of the Force and which categorically stated Elizabeth Bradley was *not* involved in her brother's gang.

Struggling to keep his face straight, the Superintendent thought, let's see Pettigrew squirm out of this and any hopes he has for the Commissioner's job must surely be finished.

The downside, his brow knitted and he inwardly groaned, is that Pettigrew might survive the complaint and remain as the Chief Constable of Strathclyde Police.

****

When ACC Keith Meadows arrived that morning at his office, his secretary, Ellen, who herself having watched the Chief Constable's disastrous briefing on television, had already guessed her boss's sombre mood and had coffee waiting for him upon his arrival.

"Did you see him on the telly?" Meadows ranted as he slumped down into his chair and rubbed at his weary brow. "Did you hear him take the credit for the operation, an operation that a young DI put together? Did you hear him declare that young woman, the lassie that was murdered over in Govan, was part of a drugs gang?"

"My God," he almost spat in anger, "That poor, murdered lassie was a complete innocent," then ruefully shook his head when he muttered, "What were the Committee thinking when they appointed him to the Chief's job?"

"Yes, sir, I understand," she sighed, then laid the mug down onto his desk, "but there's little point in you having a stroke because of him. I mean you already know what he's like. The man's a buffoon."

He stared up at her, then broke into a wide smile and softly laughed when he repeated, "A buffoon? My God, Ellen, when was the last time I heard anyone called a buffoon."

"Well, Mr Meadows," she sniffed, "for your information, I went to a good school, now drink your coffee while it's hot and I'll bring your mail through."

It was as she turned to leave, he called out, "Ellen. I haven't told you enough, but thank you. I appreciate what you do for me and we both know that I sometimes need to sound off and well," he shrugged, "I know that you're here to listen to my moans and groans and that, believe me, helps a lot."

She permitted him a soft smile, then she thoughtfully asked, "Will he survive this, accusing the poor young woman of being in a drugs gang when clearly, from what you have just shared, she was not?"

Slowly shaking his head, he replied, "Frankly, I don't know. What is likely certain is that some enterprising law firm will persuade Elizabeth Bradley's family to formally complain and, on their behalf, perhaps even sue either Strathclyde Police as an organisation, or Pettigrew personally."

He stared at her, then sat back in his chair, comfortable in the knowledge that whatever he shared with Ellen would go no further, then said, "We both know that previously on a couple of occasions, he's been publicly caught out lying, but so far he's survived."

He shrugged when he continued, "Will he survive this time, I really don't know. My feeling is that the Police and Fire Committee do not want to admit their mistake in appointing him, so while I'm certain there will be a meeting to discuss his future, I regret that he'll either be asked to step down and offered a bloody gratuity the size of a small countries annual budget or the family will be paid off with a generous sum and *he'll* remain in situ. Either way, our police budget will take a hammering," and again, he ruefully shook his head.

It was then Ellen heard her desk phone ringing and excusing herself, left his office.

Seconds later, she returned, her face grim and irately told him, "That was the Chief's secretary, sir. He *requires* your presence."

****

With Colin Baxter seated opposite, Mary Wells discussed the forthcoming interview with Yvonne Church, who at that time was seated in a detention room downstairs, awaiting the arrival of a legal aid lawyer to represent her during the interview.

"Right, Colin," she rubbed at her forehead as she stared down at her notes, "we're dealing here with a seventy-two-year old woman who may or may not have health issues, perhaps if her attitude can be described as peculiar, even mental health issue. What do you think? Should we have her medically examined before we conduct the interview? I don't want any future defence lawyer to claim we did not acknowledge any health issues she might have or even the worst scenario, her taking a bad turn during the interview."

"I'd not thought of that, Boss, but given her age and the fact a lot of pensioners are on some sort of medication, that's not a bad idea. What it does unfortunately, is put back our interview until the Casualty Surgeon gets here."

"Right," she reached for her desk phone, "decision made and while I'm making the arrangements, you see that she has something to eat and drink and made as comfortable as being in a detention room possibly can be. In fact on hindsight," her brow knitted, "take her out of the detention rom and have her sit in with the female turnkey. If nothing else, it's a bit more comfortable for her.

Baxter nodded, then listened while she called down to the Duty Inspector to request the attendance of the Casualty Surgeon, then heard her acknowledge that the duty lawyer might be delayed for half an hour.

"You heard that?"

He nodded.

"If nothing else, the lawyer being late works in our favour for it avoids her legal representative from complaining about having to hang around here. Now on another issue. I've decided that Sammy Salmon will remain as the Pollok DI, while you will remain here at Govan and be my deputy. I hope that doesn't disappoint you?"

She thought that breaking the news, he might be a little disappointed, but her surprise, he smiled then nodding, said, "No, Boss, that suits me down to the ground. To be honest, I think Sammy deserves the Pollok job after his operation and the word is from the team here is that the guys at Pollok are boasting about what they did. That sounds to me like they're a happier bunch up there."

"Indeed," she nodded, then said, "Thanks for accepting the job here. To be frank, I wasn't sure how you'd take it."

He nodded then asked, "If I'm not overstepping the mark, can I ask how are you feeling? I mean, since you learned about your mother?"

"Bruised and more than a little embarrassed, I think is the words I'd use. She's always been a loose cannon, my mother. A complex woman, as my dad describes her. That said," she flushed, "I was really pleased about how the team took the news. I kind of half expected them to joke about it or…"

"Then you really don't know your team, Mary," he shook his head, his voice a little annoyed with her.

Her eyes flickered at the use of her forename, but then exhaling, he continued, "Do you recall when Fiona McCloy's young brother died in that RTA? You sent her on compassionate leave for six weeks to look after her mother, but didn't put her time off through the books and you visited her, what, three or four times to see how she was getting on?"

"Yes, but…"

"But nothing" he snappily held up his hand, then said, "And what about when Donnie Corbett's wee boy went through that serious operation at the sick kids hospital over in Yorkhill? Who was it that phoned Ibrox and put the squeeze on the manager there and got him to arrange for some of the Rangers players to visit the wee guy in the hospital? Then recently, what about that carry-on with Janey McPhee and her belief that guy from Pollok, I forget his name, didn't kill his wife? What other boss would have listened to a young, uniformed lassie who had doubts about the guy's guilt?"

"Okay, okay," she smiled, "I get the picture, Colin."

"I sincerely hope you do, because on a personal note, Mary, you have to know how highly your staff rate you. Yes," he nodded, "you've had your personal difficulties, but the very fact you come back to work and you treat your people fairly and sympathetically; there's not a lot of bosses have your consideration for their staff, so don't be surprised when they're pleased to get the opportunity to support you."

"Okay, okay, enough" she grinned widely. "Any more of that, Colin, and you'll have me applying for sainthood."

He smiled then said, "Right. The interview. How do you want to introduce the fingerprint evidence?"

"Well, we can't use our ploy in how we obtained her fingerprint, so as she is a person lawfully detained, I want her fingerprinted while she's in detention and have it rushed to the Fingerprint Department for confirmation it matches the print from the murder weapon. In fact, while you're making arrangements for her comfort, see to that now, please."

"On my way, Boss," he rose from his chair.

****

While Eileen stayed at Mary's house with the children, Michael MacDonald visited his lawyer, Lesley Wilson, and informed her of the circumstances of Natalie's arrest.

As she listened, Lesley took notes then with a smile, informed him, "I'll get right on to our investigator. I suspect that while John Green is feeling sore and vulnerable from the assault, he'll be more than willing to provide a statement and maybe even permit our investigator to photograph his injuries. Perhaps even share details of any other men that he knows Natalie might have been involved with."

"And will this help my case?"

"Michael," she smiled, "this information might even win you your case."

****

While Colin Baxter was downstairs arranging the fingerprinting of their suspect, Mary Wells, true to her word to her father, contacted Partick Police Office and left a message for the off-duty Sergeant Cowan who had attended Michael's assault at her home, that he contact her as she had some relevant information.
When the call had ended, she sat staring into space, trying to focus her thoughts on the upcoming interview with Yvonne Church.
From the brief time she had spent with the woman, Mary suspected that Church, surprising herself by comparing Church to Natalie MacDonald, was an opinionated individual who likely would refuse to believe that she was ever wrong.
The PNC check had proved negative, that Church was not known to the police, yet she wondered what opinion her neighbours might have of the older woman and with that thought in mind and mentally berating herself for not previously considering it earlier, rose from her desk to hurry through to the incident room.
As luck would have it, Tommy Maxwell and John McGhee were just arriving from an Action inquiry and so beckoning them to her, said, "Here's what I need, guys, and as a matter of urgency. Don't hang around waiting for an Action to be written up, but get yourselves up the locus and bang on the doors in the close. If you can, maybe even the closes on either side of number twelve, too. I know it's a working day and there might not be many people at home, but ask those who are at home if they know the suspect and what their impressions are of her and any issues they might have had or currently have with her. Don't bother rushing back here, but use the radio to pass the information or, if you can get the use of a phone, call Janey and she'll pass the word to Colin and I. Got that?"
"Boss," they nodded together then hurriedly left the room.
After briefing McPhee to expect the radio messages or a phone call, Mary stepped back into the corridor where she met Elaine Fitzsimmons and Alan Hamilton.
Grinning, she said, "You pair look like you need your beds."
"It's been a long day, boss," Fitzsimmons smiled.
"Well your day is over. Get yourselves home and I'll see that you both get a phone call to let you know how the interview went. And thanks, both of you, you did well," she smiled.
Watching them walk off, she sighed then wondered; have I forgotten anything?

Well, if I have, it's too late now and I'll just need to go with what I know.

****

Entering the outer office to the Chief Constable's inner sanctum in the Command Suite, ACC Keith Meadows saw that the Media Department Superintendent, a young man he liked and valued as good at his job, was already present.

Greeted by the Chief's secretary, a long serving and in recent times long suffering, lady of mature years, expressively raised her eyebrows when she greeted Meadows to inform him, "Good morning, sir. Mr Pettigrew will see you, shortly."

He was tempted to lighten the tense atmosphere by using the tired old joke, not to call him 'shortly,' but instead smiled, then acknowledging with a nod, sat down next to the Superintendent.

"Any idea why we're here?" he politely asked the Superintendent.

"Not officially, sir, but I can make a good guess," the younger man dryly replied, then leaning close to Meadows, his voice low, he continued, "With respect, Mr Meadows, you know what the Chief's like. He didn't read his briefing note and, well, all morning I've been receiving and fielding requests for comments about his, eh, rather misguided statement."

He lowered his voice to a whisper, when he added, "I fear that we as a Force are in for a good kicking because of what he said about the murdered woman, Elizabeth Bradley."

Before Meadows could comment or ask more, they both began to rise to their feet when the buzzer on the secretary's desk sounded and when she nodded, made their way through the door into the chief's office.

Even though the room was uncommonly warm, Pettigrew, wearing his tunic with a row of medal ribbons that Meadows believed were service awards rather than earned, sat with his hands below the surface of his desk and glowered at his visitors.

It was immediately clear to Meadows too that the absence of any chairs indicated they would not be invited to sit.

"Sir," they both spoke at the same time, but neither was acknowledged for several seconds until Pettigrew finally growled, "Which of you is responsible for setting me up to look a fool in front of the media?"

If Pettigrew thought that his rank and his privileged position would intimidate his ACC, he was to be sadly mistaken, for Meadows, recalling his secretary's description of Pettigrew as a buffoon, inwardly smiled, then politely responded with, "Exactly what are you referring to, Chief Constable?"

His face reddening, Pettigrew first raised then slapped his hands hard onto the desk and snapped, "I was duped by your CID or *him*," he angrily pointed at the younger man, "into giving out false information to the bloody media! *That's* what I am referring to!"

Assuming a face of pure innocence, Meadows slowly took a deep breath, then pursed his lips before he calmly replied, "Like you, sir, as is standard procedure to all senior staff, I received a copy of your briefing note from the Superintendent here. It seems to me that when you presented the information to the attending journalists and TV crews, you either misread or misinterpreted the brief it contained. So, again sir, what exactly are you referring to when you accuse the Superintendent and I of being responsible for duping you?"

It was at this point that Meadows thought Pettigrew's face was about to explode and so turning to the Superintendent, he coolly suggested, "Can you wait in the outer office, please while the Chief Constable and I have a private word?"

His face betraying his nervousness, the younger man nodded, then wordlessly left the office, quickly closing the door behind him.

In those few seconds, Keith Meadows, now approaching his fifty-third birthday and with thirty-two years police service under his belt, much of it spent as a Detective officer, decided he had enough of this bumptious, excuse for a police officer and staring down at Pettigrew, recognised that his lengthy and distinguished career was no excuse for standing here taking *shit* from a man who had no inkling of how to be a leader, let alone a Chief Constable.

Accepting that his career was about to be over, his face expressed his sarcasm when he said, "Duped into making you look a fool? No," he suddenly snarled and stepped forward to place his hands flat on Pettigrew's desk as he bent over to stare down at him, "there was no need for either of us to do that simply because you *are* a fool! That young man out there provided you with all the information you needed to convey to the media, but you? You *fucking* idiot," he saw Pettigrew's face pale as he flinched at the harsh words, "you couldn't be bothered to read the brief! You winged it, didn't you and now that you've been caught out and as usual, you are looking for a scapegoat! Well, *Chief Constable*," he hissed at him, "Neither the Superintendent nor I will *be* that scapegoat for I'm going from here straight to whatever news outlet will give me air time when I will use my position as an Assistant Chief Constable of Strathclyde Police to out you for the bullying fool you are! I will also inform the media that unlike you publicly claimed, you had neither knowledge nor any part of that successful operation, that the whole thing was managed by a young Detective Inspector, whose name you never even bothered to find out!"

"How dare you," Pettigrew blustered, at last finding his voice, only to be shouted down by Meadows, who banging a fist on the desk, continued, "I *dare*, sir, because unlike you, I *am* a real police officer, not a pen pushing clerk who likely has *never* in his administrative career seen or had to deal with an angry man!"

As Pettigrew's mouth fell open, Meadows stood upright and with one final sneering glance, turned on his heel to march from the room. Pulling open the door to the outer office, he saw both the secretary and the Superintendent gaping at him, then their heads turned to the door from where they could hear Pettigrew screaming that Meadows return.

Ignoring the screams, it was however when he started towards the outer door the presence of the two middle-aged men in business suits that attracted Meadows attention; two men he immediately recognised from previous meetings.

Striding past the men, he curtly nodded at the Chairman and the Deputy Chair of the Police and Fire Committee.

****

It was Colin Baxter who informed Mary Wells that both the lawyer and the Casualty Surgeon had arrived, that the doctor had examined Yvonne Church and found her fit to be interviewed.

"Good, then bring her and her lawyer here to my room, please Colin."

In the few minutes before they arrived, she prepared herself and once more, checked her notes.

When the door was knocked and they were all seated, Mary saw that Church, her grey, wispy hair bundled up on top of her head, seemed to be wearing the same all-encompassing, ankle length black dress, then addressed Church by remind her that she had been formally cautioned and…

"Yes, yes, I know all that," the older woman rudely interrupted with a wave of her hand, then asked, "But just because I disliked that woman, you can't honestly believe I am a murderer?"

"On the contrary, Mrs Church, we not only believe that you simply disliked Mrs Bradley, but have evidence that you killed her."

The lawyer, a harassed looking man in his late forties or early fifties, interrupted with, "May I inquire as to what evidence you do have, DCI Wells?"

"I'll come to that shortly," she replied with a soft smile, then turning back to Church, said, "When I spoke with you, Mrs Church, just after your neighbour's body had been discovered by her ten-years-old daughter, I recall you told me that you had never been within Mrs Bradley's flat. Is that correct?"

Church's eyes narrowed as though trying to remember the conversation, then she slowly nodded and sneered, "*Mrs* Bradley, you say? Huh, I don't *think* so. Anyway, that's correct. I have never been in that woman's house."

It didn't escape Mary's attention that the lawyer shot Church a sharp glance at her sneering mockery of Elizabeth Bradley's marital status as he made a notation on his pad.

"So," she slowly drawled, "You have never been in Mrs Bradley's flat. Correct?"

"I just said so, didn't I?" Church sniffed.

"Hmm, yet I distinctly recall you telling me Mrs Bradley's flat was a complete pigsty. Those were the words you used, or am I mistaken?"

"Yes, the place was filthy. Absolutely filthy," her derision was clear.

Again, Mary sneaked a glance at the lawyer and saw him pass a hand across his face at his client's obvious error.

"So, Mrs Church, if you have never been inside Mrs Bradley's flat, how would you know it was a complete pigsty?"

As if realising her blunder, Church stuttered, "It was the way that woman looked. You're just trying to trick me," she tried to rise from her chair, pointing an accusing finger at Mary while behind Church, Colin Baxter also rose from his chair to restrain her, but sat down again when she subtly waved at him.

"Please, Mrs Church," she politely asked, "Sit down."

The door was knocked then pushed open by Janey McPhee, who was waved in by Mary.

"Ma'am," Janey handed Mary a sheet of paper, then left the room.

"Excuse me," she smiled at the lawyer then glanced at the handwritten notes.

"What's that? What do you have there?" Church, back in her chair, demanded of her.

"This, Mrs Church," she waved the A4 sheet of paper at her, "is information that seems to indicate Mrs Bradley was not the only neighbour you disliked."

"It says here," she read from the paper, "that two of your upstairs neighbours argued with you because you cut their washing lines that at the time, were full of clean washing. Is that correct?"

"They shouldn't have had their washing out after six o'clock at night," she sniffed again, then added, "That used to be against the byelaws when people did as they were told."

"Did as they were told," Mary softly repeated, then continued, "And one of those women, again your upstairs neighbour, alleges you pointed a knife at her when she caught you and protested at you cutting down her washing line. Is *that* correct?"

"Like I told you. If they didn't leave their washing lines out after six o'clock, they wouldn't be breaking the law."

"You mean, *your* law, Mrs Church?"

Church didn't respond, simply glanced away as Wells continued, "Another neighbour, this time in the adjacent close, alleges that you dumped filthy rubbish on her doorstep. Is *that* correct?"

"The bins round her back were full, so she thought she could use the bins for my close. If she'd asked," Church shrugged, "I might have said yes."

"And speaking of bins, Mrs Church, you had a grievance about Mrs Bradley and the bins, didn't you?"

"If I may, DCI Wells," the lawyer intervened and leaned forward, "may I ask where this questioning is leading?"

"I'm trying to demonstrate that your client has a history of forcing her neighbours to comply with her demands. If you bear with me?"

"Yes, of course," he sighed, happy for the moment that he had asked a question and so done his job.

"And lastly, Mrs Church, what about the neighbour in the next close? The elderly woman you threatened. What was that about?"

"That was just a joke," she slumped back in her chair.

"Oh, nothing to do with the excrement you smeared on her door, then told her if she reported you that you would burn her out of her flat?"

"That woman," she bared her teeth, "permitted her dog to wander the street and into the other closes including *mine*! Doing its business everywhere and I *mean* shitting and peeing! Someone had to deal with it!"

"And that someone, you believed, was you?"

Behind Church, Colin Baxter hastily took notes and wondered, when is Mary going to mention the fingerprint?

She stared at Church for several seconds before she said, "The day you killed Mrs Bradley…"

"I did *not* kill that harlot!"

"The day you entered Mrs Bradley's flat, the day you lifted the candlestick…"

She saw Church's eyes flutter.

"The day you argued with her and were sickened by the state of her flat…"

"I'm telling you…"

"What angered you so much that you decided to teach her a lesson?"

Church's eyes widened and she clutched at her chest with her bony hand, then softly whispered, "Forty-three years I have lived in my home. For forty-three years I've watched the area decline. People not tending the gardens like they used to, rubbish being scattered about without going into the bins. *Coloured* people," she almost spat, "moving in with their smelly food and their children running riot, screaming and shouting in their foreign tongues and worshiping their false Gods. Forty-three years and I can't even walk my own street without some stranger watching me and I'm wondering, are they waiting to break into my home?"

Her voice began to rise as she continued, "Then the flats being bought by absent landlords who don't give a fig about who they rent to. People such as unmarried mothers like her! *Bradley*!"

"And is that why you decide to teach her a lesson, because she wasn't up to your standard, Mrs Church?"

She stared curiously at Mary, then drawing herself up, her eyes narrowed when she hissed, "Oh, aye, I taught her a right good lesson. Told me to get out of her flat, that she'd report me to the polis!"

"Mrs Church," her lawyer raised his hand and tried to interrupt her, but she ignored him when she hissed, bobs of spittle dripping from her mouth, "Report me, to the polis? Me? A God-fearing woman? As if the police would do anything to me! I'm a law-abiding citizen so I am. I have nothing to fear because my God is on my side!"

"I'm wondering, though," Mary injected some curiosity into her voice, "if you disliked, even hated Mrs Bradley so much, how is it that you come to be in her house?"

Church stared at her and though she would never describe herself as any kind of medical expert, Mary inwardly shivered because she suspected that behind those watery, almost oblique eyes was a touch of madness and mentally reminded herself that she should suggest in her report to the Fiscal that Church be psychiatrically examined.

"She said, she wanted us to be friends," Church huffed, her hands now bunched into fists in her pal, then added, "As if a good Christian woman like *me*," she stabbed at her chest with a bony forefinger, "would ever be friends with a woman like that! Said when saw her at her door after she'd seen her daughter off to school that we should have a word, that she wanted us to be good neighbours and invited me into that pigsty of a home."

She stopped speaking, then drawing a deep breath, carried on with, "Good neighbours? *I am* a good neighbour. She was just a slutty, dirty *cow*! When I told her she should start with cleaning her filthy house, she told me to get out!"

"So, you hit her with the candlestick?"

"DCI Wells, that is simply speculation," the lawyer hastily interrupted.

"Not so," she shook her head, then addressing Church, said, "When your fingerprints were taken earlier, Mrs Church, we sent them to police headquarters to be compared with a fingerprint lifted in blood from the murder weapon. Your fingerprint, Mrs Church, that matched sixteen points of similarity with the fingerprint we obtained from the murder weapon."

"Oh, dear," the lawyer almost whispered.

To her surprise, Church then angrily sneered, "I'm not sorry. You'll see. Nobody who believes in the true God will ever convict me. That woman, that *harlot*, she deserved everything she got and I'm not sorry I killed her, so there!" she sat back in her chair and with childish petulance, folded her arms.

Seconds passed, then turning to the lawyer, Mary softly breathed out and politely told him, "I assume that you will wish to accompany DS Baxter and I downstairs to the charge bar, where I will libel a charge of murder against your client."

CHAPTER THIRTY-ONE

Returning to his office, ACC Keith Meadows was fully aware that the Chief Constable, Charles Pettigrew, would now be in the process of suspending him, then arranging his dismissal.
Clearing out his desk of his few personal belongings, he stuffed them into his suitcase then calling his secretary, Ellen, through to his office, asked her to bring with her from the cabinet, a resignation form.
He first apologised that he had not given her any forewarning and quickly explaining his utter act of madness, assured her that whoever was to be appointed as his successor, he would contact them to ensure that she was kept on in her position.
"For what it's worth, sir," she grimly smiled, "it was about time someone took that incompetent bugger to task. Just a pity that you're losing your job for it."
"Aye, well, I can't really complain, Ellen, I've had a good run. Anyway," he forced a smile, "give me a minute to complete this form and make a phone call before I say cheerio."
When she'd left to return to her desk, he called his home number, then greeted his wife, "Hello, Mattie, wee bit of bad news I'm afraid."
"Don't tell me, you've run away to join the circus. I always knew there was something strange about you, Keith Meadows."
He smiled then said, "I'm afraid I kind of lost my temper, dear, so I'll be coming home a wee bit early today. Eh, now, in fact."
The tense pause was broken when she asked, "What have you done?"
"I called the Chief Constable a fucking idiot," he calmly replied or rather, more calmly than he felt.
Another tense few seconds was broken when she said, "About time someone did. Has he sacked you?"

"I'm going to complete a resignation form and have Ellen run it to the Personnel Department before he can sack me, so hopefully I'll leave with some dignity."

"Bugger your dignity," the ever-practical Mattie responded. "What about your pension and your lump sum?"

"Well," he drawled, "if I can get my resignation in *before* he sacks me it should be okay, so I'll hurry that up and see you when I get in."

"If you don't get the form in on time, don't bother coming home." He knew she was joking and smiled then ending the call thought, I *hope* she's joking.

Folding the form, he grabbed his overcoat and briefcase then pulling open the door to the outer office was surprised to see the Chairman of the Police and Fire Committee standing with his deputy and speaking to Ellen.

Turning, the Chairman frowned when he said, "Ah, Mr Meadows, can we have a word?"

****

The team stood chatting in the incident room, but turned and went silent when a pokerfaced Donnie Corbett entered the room.

Stepping forward to stand in front of Colin Baxter's desk, he turned then glancing around the room, broke into a wide smile then said, "The boss and Colin are downstairs right now with the suspect. We have a confession and Yvonne Church is being charged with Elizabeth Bradley's murder."

The cheers and hand clapping that followed faded when Corbett waved his hands for order, then added, "We've to hang fire here until the boss comes up to have a word."

Just over ten minutes later, when Wells and Baxter entered the room, there was a second loud cheer and much hand clapping.

Calling for silence, she loudly called out, "Right, as far as I'm concerned, it's an early night now for you guys, though Colin has a few things to clear up and I've a case to report, I want you all to know how grateful I am that you stuck with this and it's down to you that we have a result."

She paused and glancing around the room, continued, "With Pollok CID's successful operation and our murder solved, I rather think we have done ourselves proud. Thank you again, guys, and as of tomorrow, we're back to our normal shifts. For those of you off the weekend anyway, enjoy yourselves while those of you on shift tomorrow, I'll see you all no earlier than ten o'clock."

That simple reward of just an hour and a half was greeted good-naturedly by cheers too and when the room emptied, she told Baxter, "If you phone Alan Hamilton and tell him the news, I'll give Elaine Fitzsimmon's a call then meet you in my office for coffee."

"Boss," he nodded and reached for his phone.

Returning to her office, as promised she phoned Fitzsimmons at home, but learning she was asleep, informed her husband, Eric, of Yvonne Church's confession and arrest.

When the call was finished, she contacted the Procurator Fiscal's Office and though Church should have been held in custody at Govan till her appearance on the forthcoming Monday, Mary explained the accused was a seventy-two-years-old woman.

The Fiscal Depute she spoke with understood the implications of keeping a woman that age in a police cell for three nights and agreed an arrangement to have her brought before a special sitting of the Sheriff Court the next morning, at which time she would thereafter be remanded to the more suitable accommodation of the women's prison at Cornton Vale, in Stirling.

She just ended the call to the PF as her door was opened by Baxter who carried in two mugs of coffee.

Settling himself into a chair, he handed her a mug, then said, "I took five minutes to send out a telex to the Divisions in your name, Boss, thanking them for their assistance and letting them know that we've arrested a suspect for the murder. I've also copied it to the Media Department and the ACC's office."

"Good, I hadn't even given that a thought," she admitted.

"Look," he could see how tired she was, "if you want to get away home, I can draft the report to the Fiscal for tomorrow morning."

"Thank you, *DI* Baxter, but I'll hang fire and do that myself."

He smiled a little uncertainly when he asked, "DI Baxter?"

"Wasn't that the arrangement, Colin? You continue to act as the DS incident manager for the duration of the murder? Well," she slowly drawled and toasting him with her mug, said, "we've concluded our murder investigation, so as far as I'm concerned, you are now a DI. All that remains is for it to be ratified by that git who is currently the Chief. Until that date arrives, I supposed you're really an *acting* DI, but either way, your promotion is guaranteed."

"DI Baxter," he slowly shook his head as he mused. "To be honest, I never really thought it would happen."
"It's well deserved, Colin, so hopefully it will keep your missus happy."
"The extra *money* will keep her happy," he grinned.
"Right then, DI Baxter, your first order from me is to get your coat on and away home. I don't need you tonight, so like the rest of the guys, I do not expect to see you tomorrow till ten o'clock, okay?"
"Not often I get a lie-in, Boss, so I might just take you up on that," he wearily pushed himself up from his chair, then waving goodbye, left the room.
Left alone, Mary grabbed at her pen and pad and began to compose her report to the PF.
****

A full hour had passed and her report to the Fiscal completed and passed through to the typing pool, Mary grabbed at her coat, but turned when to her surprise, Keith Meadows stepped through her office door.
"Sir? What you doing here on a Friday evening?"
"Thought on my way home to the Mearns, I'd pop by and congratulate you on finding your murderer. A seventy-two-years-old woman? Who'd have thought it," he shook his head.
"Can I get you a coffee or something?"
"No," he raised his hand towards her, "Mattie will likely have the dinner on and she does *not* like me being late."
Mary sensed there was a reason he had visited her, so hesitantly asked, "Is there something I can do for you, sir?"
Seeing her holding her coat, he replied, "If I'm not keeping you back, can we sit for a minute?"
"Of course," she rehung her coat and stepped back to sit at her desk. When they were seated, he stared grim faced at her, then asked, "Likely I can I assume that you watched the television report yesterday, the Chief Constable's briefing about the successful Pollok operation?"
"I did, yes," she dryly replied, then added, "As likely did most if not all of the Force."
Her expression changed to one of anger when she continued, "I know I'm out of line criticising a senior officer and particularly the Chief, but how *dare* he presume to suggest my victim was engaged

in illegal drug activities! That and claiming credit for his organising the operation! It beggar's belief that he would be so bloody crass as well as completely ignoring the effort and risks taken by junior officers in bringing those thugs before the courts! I mean sir," she angrily tossed her head, "even though they knew a firearm had already been used, my guys were going through doors with no idea what might have been behind the doors; it could even have been someone pointing the gun at them that Ricky Bradley shot himself with, you know?"

She could feel her face flush as Meadows stared impassively at her. Seconds passed before he said, "How dare he indeed, Mary, and I do agree with you; your anger is completely justified."

He paused, then continued, "However, as of tomorrow morning you'll find you have a new boss."

"Sir?"

"Let me explain," he frowned then proceeded to relate his summons by the Chief Constable to his office and the one-sided confrontation that ensued.

Mary's eyes widened in horror when she gasped, "Oh, no, sir, don't tell me that you've been sacked!"

Meadows blank expression slowly changed to a wry smile when he shook his head, then holding up his hand, the forefinger and thumb a mere inch apart, he explained, "Actually I was this close to submitting my resignation when the Chairman of the Police and Fire Committee and his deputy visited me in my office. Cutting a long story short, he told me that subsequent to the Chief Constable's disastrous media briefing that already followed on from numerous complaints," he held up a defensive hand, "and believe it or not, which curiously even with *my* sources I was unaware of. It seems that several of those complaints had reached the ears of both the Minister of State for Scotland and, curiously, the Lord Advocate."

He took a short pause, his brow knitting as he reflected on what had occurred, then continued, "It also seems that after my rather unprofessional outburst, for which I admit to being totally embarrassed and even though it needed to be said, Mr Pettigrew was visited by the two aforesaid gentlemen who offered him the option of what I believe these days is termed as gardening leave, that in turn, was to be followed by a discreet retirement; an offer that he rather unwisely point-blank refused."

He shrugged, then shaking his head, he said, "According to the Chairman, apparently Pettigrew, arrogant man that he is, thought them to be bluffing and so having refused that offer, he was instead required to immediately resign and without reference. I understand his resignation without reference will certainty scupper his opportunity to be being appointed to the Commissioner's job in the Met."

"Bloody good riddance too!" she vehemently snapped back, then sheepishly added, "Sorry, sir, but you know what I mean."

"I do indeed, Mary," he smiled at her.

"But what do *you* mean," her eyes creased with suspicion, "when you say I'll have a new boss tomorrow?"

"As likely you know, the Deputy Chief has been on a six-month secondment lecturing at the Police Staff College at Bramshill, down in Hampshire. Well, he's been summoned back to take on the acting Chief job till a replacement can be appointed. Between you and me I'm predicting it will be himself. As for me," he sighed, "it seems for the time being I'm now to assume the role of acting Deputy Chief Constable."

Her delight was reflected in her broad smile when she asked, "And who is my new boss?"

"For the time being and strictly between us until it's published on Monday?"

"Of course, sir."

"Detective Chief Superintendent Les Scullion will assume the role of acting ACC (Crime)."

He watched Mary frown and knew it was because it was widely held among the Divisional CID that Scullion, currently serving as the Head of the CID for the City's southside Divisions, was an acolyte of Charles Pettigrew who had been brought north from Pettigrew's former English Force and with very little CID experience. That and it was also widely rumoured Scullion seldom left his Pitt Street office to visit the Divisional CID units he was nominally in charge of.

However, to her surprise, Meadows said, "Between you and I, Mary, when he arrived up here, I was not initially impressed by Mr Scullion and more than a little prejudiced when he joined the Force to be promoted by Pettigrew, his golf pal. However," he took a soft breath, "in the recent months he has come a long way and in fairness to the man, accepts he lacks CID experience, but *is* open to suggestion and advice. In short, I will ask you and doing the rounds to speak with my other Divisional heads to give him a chance to settle into his new role for in my humble opinion, he is keen to make an impression among the officers he now commands."

Though Mary would never previously question Keith Meadows opinion, she already had distinct reservations about Scullion and having met him on just a few occasions, had not been immediately impressed by him.

But then again, she inwardly admitted, I had formed a similar opinion about Sammy Salmon and look how he turned out.

"Okay, sir," she nodded, "if Mr Scullion wishes to pop in to Govan at any time at his convenience, he'll get nothing but cooperation from me and my team."

"As I already believed and expected of you, Mary," he smiled at her, then getting to his feet, added, "Again, congratulations to you and your team for a job well done."

"Sir," she acknowledged with a nod as he left the room.

****

Driving home that evening, Mary yawned widely and realised she was more tired than she had originally thought.

Knackered, more like, she shook her head before turning into Ancaster Drive and decided that after her father and Eileen left, she'd spend some time with the kids and later, have a long soak in the bath, then an early night.

Or so she'd planned.

Parking her car in her usual spot, she glanced across the road to see Eileen's Beetle parked directly behind Bill Howie's black coloured Capri.

Opening her front door, she was surprised to see that both Michael and Eileen already had their coats on prior to their departure, but even more surprised to see that the kids too were dressed in coats and carrying their small, colourful children's backpacks.

"Eh, what's going on?" she stared suspiciously at her father, who raising both hands, palms towards her, replied, "Not my idea. It seems that your childminder wanted to take these scallywags for an overnighter tomorrow, but has since decided that you need more than a single one-night break, so they coming with us for two nights. How I'll cope, I have no idea," he theatrically sighed, to the children's giggles.

Before she could respond, Eileen stepped forward and placing her hands-on Mary's arms, softly stared into her eyes before she said, "Look, darling, you're completely exhausted with the hours you've been keeping as well, as the stress you've been under and you need a good night's sleep too. Yes," Eileen nodded, "I know you're up early tomorrow for work, but let your dad and I take the weans tonight to let you have some time to yourself. Now, I've made a lasagne that's in the oven and it's ready to eat with the garlic bread that'll just take five minutes to heat up. That and there's a bottle of white wine cooling in the fridge," she smiled. "So, am I right or what?"

Mary returned Eileen's smile, then her face squinted, pretended to think when she said, "This is July, so why not bring them back, say around September?"

"As if you'd let them stay away for more than a couple of days," Eileen pretended to scold her, then added, "You know that a couple of days to yourself won't do you any harm, don't you?"

"I know," she nodded then glancing at them in turn, sighed. "Thanks, guys, I think I hear a glass of that wine shouting my name."

Bending to hug her son and daughter and securing the pinkie-promise from both that they'd be good for granddad and granny Eileen, as she was now being called, she watched her children, each held by a hand, happily skip across the road to Eileen's Beetle. When the four had driven off, she sighed and as promised, headed towards the kitchen for her glass of wine.

No more than two or three minutes passed before the doorbell and muttering, "Bugger," made her way into the hallway.

Pulling open the door, she saw Bill Howie standing there who slightly embarrassed, told her, "Half an hour ago, Eileen turned up at my door and told me when she and your dad and the kids had gone, I was to knock on your door to tell you the dish of lasagne is far too much for one person to eat. So, what is that about?"

Mary fought her grin then blowing out through pursed lips, replied, "She did, did she? Okay, give me an hour to get myself together, then pop back. It seems you and I have been set up for a date."

****

Across the city at her home in Newton Mearns, Natalie

MacDonald's anger at what she perceived to be as her unjust treatment at the hands of the police, had not abated.

Nor had her drinking.

Now wearing a once clean scarlet coloured tracksuit, she sat glassy-eyed and slumped in her favourite armchair in the front room, her hair in disarray, her legs splayed out before her and with a tall glass of neat gin clutched in her hand, she stared morosely at the unlit fire thinking vengeful thoughts on each and every one who had through her life, betrayed her.

Her thoughts ranged from the memory all those years before of the handsome, Spanish man who had impregnated her, then left her to fend for herself until she hooked that useless sod Michael, to the police sergeant who had with complete disdain forgetting who she was, refused to call her a taxi, then wordlessly thrust her out from the back door and into the cold rain of the rear yard at Giffnock Police Office.

Her lips tightly compressed, she inwardly vowed no matter how long it took and if it was the last thing she ever did, she'd get some sort of payback for the way they had treated her.

Gulping at her gin, she convinced herself that she was the victim; that she, who had clawed her way up the social ladder, was the one that everybody was jealous of, that nobody liked her because she was such a looker and smart too.

Taking a second gulp at her gin, she neither noticed nor cared about the liquid that spilled down and stained the front of her blouse.

Bastards! She drunkenly muttered at them all.

I'll get my own back, you just wait and see, she thought.

But first, with some difficulty she pulled herself to her feet and decided, I need to collect my car.

Staggering to the visitor's cloakroom toilet with her handbag, she stared bleary-eyed into the mirror and made an attempt to apply some blusher and lipstick, then drew a comb through her tousled hair.

Satisfied she was once more the glamorous woman she believed herself to be, she returned to the lounge and staggering across the room, reached for the telephone to summon a taxi.

****

Almost to the minute, the door was knocked and pulling it open, Mary saw that Bill had quite obviously changed into a light blue coloured polo shirt and fawn coloured chinos, though she refrained from laughing when she saw he was sockless, but wore well-worn, open-toed leather sandals on his feet.

As for Bill, he almost gasped when he stared at Mary and his eyes widening, the thought rushed through his head that he wanted this woman.

No, he *really* wanted her.

Her hair freshly washed, lay loosely on her shoulders and it was clear she had taken some time with her make-up. Wearing a strapless, knee length, Leopard print, summer mini-dress that complimented her hourglass figure and sandals on her bare feet, he took a deep breath then heard himself mutter, "You look amazing." Without thinking and as if it were the most natural thing to do, he stepped forward then his hands holding her lightly by her arms, bent forward to gently kiss her on the cheek and involuntarily inhaled her fragrance, a Dior Sauvage that Mary had sprayed and not used since…God, she had bizarrely thought at the time, I can't even recall when.

For her part, Mary was taken aback by his kiss, and though a woman who exuded confidence when performing her job, surprised herself even more when she didn't resist and in turn, found herself inhaling Bill's sandalwood aftershave.

As they parted, she flushed then said, "Dinner's all set to go, if you're ready to eat."

Almost as if they were newly met strangers, he followed her into the dining room where she had formally set the table and lit a matching pair of candles.

"Take a seat and pour the wine," she smiled a little bashfully at him. "I'll fetch our meal through."

When she had left the room, Bill let out a relieved sigh, for like Mary, he'd felt unusually anxious and after pouring the wine, nervously drummed the fingers of his right hand on the table.

When Mary returned holding a plate in each hand, Bill jumped to his feet to take them from her when she said, "I'll just fetch the garlic bread."

"Garlic, not the best aphrodisiac is it?" he jokingly replied, then stared in horror at Mary's stunned expression.

"Sorry," he stammered, "it just came out."

A smile played on her lips when she calmly asked, "Oh, is that another pun?"

His shoulders slumped, then realising he was being teased he joined her in laughter.

All tension now gone, she grinned, "I'll get the bread."

****

The private hire driver, realising his passenger was just short of being completely pissed, was curious to ask why she wanted to visit the police office, but said nothing.

Though a normally courteous man, particularly to the elderly, he took his fare from her shaking hand then stared through the front windscreen, deciding that since the old cow had been cheeky throughout the journey, she could get herself out of the back door. He half turned in his seat when he heard her yelp and saw that she had landed on all fours, on the pavement.

Shaking his head, he opened his door to exit the vehicle, his hand outstretched to assist her until she pushed his hand away and drunkenly slurred, "Get off me."

"Suit yourself, hen," the driver shrugged and when he was satisfied the old woman was clear of his vehicle, he turned and awkwardly reaching behind his seat, pulled the door closed before speeding off.

Sitting sprawled on the pavement, Natalie MacDonald pulled the spare set of car keys from the pocket of her slacks, unaware that they were now scuffed at the knees with dirt and with a lopsided grin at her daring, turned onto all fours and managed to scramble to her feet. Lurching towards the police office's dimly lit vehicle entrance, she recognised the narrow path that led to the rear yard from where she had been ejected in the early hours of that morning.

But it was the cars parked in the forecourt that attracted her interest. Rubbing the back of her hand across her now dry mouth, she could not know that she'd smeared her lipstick across her cheek and so fixed was she in trying not to sway like the drunk she was, she failed to see the middle-aged couple who arm in arm as they passed her by, slowed their pace, then stopped and turning, saw her enter the forecourt and make towards a white coloured BMW car.

As they stood watching, they saw the drunken woman unlock then enter the driver's door, then heard the roar of the engine. Realising that the woman intended driving the car, the shocked man hurried into the police office's foyer, but the duty constable was through in the kitchen brewing a cuppa and was only alerted to the problem by the man's finger continuously pressing the bell as he shouted for help.

When the constable irately pushed through the door into the public bar and as the man garbled out what he and his wife had seen, they both heard the loud roar of the engine and the high-pitched squeal of tyres.

Rushing through the door and out into the forecourt, the constable was in time to see the BMW with a loud screeching noise, strike the stone perimeter dwarf wall at the exit when being driven out of the yard.

His mouth agape, he watched the vehicle turn left towards the traffic lights, but fail to stop at a red light before again turning left again into Fenwick Road, then was gone from his sight.

"Bloody hell!" he involuntarily muttered before rushing indoors to inform the control room at Govan Police Office.

CHAPTER THIRTY-TWO

When Mary opened her eyes that Saturday morning, the digital clock read six forty-three.

As she slowly came to consciousness, she saw a dagger of light shining through her curtains onto the wall opposite.

Then her eyes widened when she realised that for the first time in years, she was not alone for not only was she completely naked, but a hand lay on her left breast.

Oh, my God, she wondered as she slowly turned to stare at Bill, his eyes flickering in REM sleep and her thoughts turned to the previous evening.

Their meal finished, they had retired to the lounge where Bill had selected the 'The Sound of Bread' album, then with an enticing smile, invited her to dance.

Perhaps it was the wine, the ambience of the evening or simply having a handsome and attentive man pay her attention and hold her close; whatever the reason, Mary knew then it was inevitable they would make love and so halfway through David Gates second song, her heart racing, she took him by the hand and led him upstairs.

It had been years since Mary had undressed before a man and a little shyly, turned away from him, only to find him behind her, his hands on her shoulders and softly whispering to her, "Only if you're comfortable, Mary."

For her, the first minutes of their lovemaking had been awkwardly tense, but then found herself relaxing as his lips and hands explored her body and sighing, she gave him her all.

Now, lying here beside him, she realised with a start that though she had known him just a few short days, Bill Howie was to become a part of her and her children's lives and for that she was not only glad but also so very, very happy.

The memory of their lovemaking still fresh in her mind and after those years of sexual abstinence, Mary was now a little embarrassed when she recalled her enthusiasm.

Tightly squeezing her eyes closed, she fought the giggles that threatened to erupt from her. However, try as she might and though she covered her mouth with her hand, she could not help herself and her body shook with unrestrained laughter.

The slight motion of her body wakened Bill, who sighed, "What the…who…eh?"

His eyes flickered opened and turning his head, he too suddenly grinned when he muttered, "Morning."

"And good morning to you, Dr Howie," she finally erupted into a fit of giggles.

He continued to grin when he quietly said, "Thank you."

"Oh, I think it's me who should be thanking you," then leaning towards him to kiss on the mouth, grimaced, then pulled slightly back and made a face when she said, "You were right about the garlic."

It was Bill's turn to laugh, then he said, "If I were to nip into your en-suite and run a finger of toothpaste across my teeth, will you still be lying here and naked, when I get back?"

"Why," she grinned coyly at him, "what do you have in mind?"

Lifting the quilt that covered them both, he peered under it before he slowly replied, "Well, it's early and you're not in a hurry to get up from bed, are you?"

"And I'll ask you again" her eyes narrowed with eager anticipation, "what do you have in mind?"

He adopted a thoughtful expression when he replied, "I'm thinking that to pay you back for a lovely evening, good food, nice wine and an extremely delightful if rather exhausting physical workout, I should repay you by offering you a complete body examination, perhaps starting with those lovely breasts."

Then before she could respond, he lowered his head and closing his mouth around her left breast, used his tongue to tickle at her nipple. Mary gasped, then closed her eyes and sighed contentedly.

Stroking at his hair, she felt his hand move slowly down her stomach and his fingers walking towards her groin.

Parting her legs, her eyes tightly closed, she took a soft breath when she felt him probe gently at her…

But then the phone rang.

EPILOGUE

Returning to work was a difficult time for DCI Mary Wells, who on that Monday morning, the third of August and already having had her name appear on the front pages of the media and linked to her mother's actions, had in the intervening weeks given serious consideration that she might perhaps request to either take a step back from operational police duties, maybe return to uniform or ask for a leave of absence.

It was no surprise to Mary, or anyone who knew her, that whoever was providing the "Glasgow News' with the scandalous comments about her had some knowledge of her as well as of her personal life. On that warm summer morning and three days prior to the cremation service of Natalie MacDonald, Mary was visited at her office by her new boss ACC (Crime) Les Scullion.

An imposing and handsome man turned forty-four who stood six feet tall and with a rugby player's build and a shock of greying, groomed hair, Mary quickly sensed that Scullion was a little anxious, though why, she had not a clue.

"Can I get you a coffee, sir?" she invited him to sit.

"Ah, yes please, just milk," he replied in a surprisingly soft, Sussex accent and with nervous smiled as he watched her phone through to request two mugs.

When the coffee had been delivered, she asked, "So, what can I do for you, sir, and before we begin, I'd like to thank you for your telephone call regarding my, eh…my mother's demise."

He waved a dismissive hand when he said, "You are one of my senior officers, DCI Wells, so I felt obliged to support you," yet almost immediately regretted his reply, thinking it to be a rather off-hand response.

But then his eyes widened, when grimacing, he added, "I'm sorry, that came out wrong. I don't want you to think that I phoned out of duty."

He sighed when he shook his head and leaning forward, said, "Look, to be blunt, the reason I'm here…" he paused to ask, "Can I call you Mary?"

A little bemused, she nodded then replied, "Yes, of course, sir."

He took a breath, then licking nervously at his lips, his eyes narrowing in thought, continued, "The reason I'm here is that I want you to understand that your family relationship to your mother will not in any way," he crossed his hands over and over, "affect your career. Not at all."

Mary felt her body go cold.

"Yes," he nodded, "I know the media and particularly that rag, the 'Glasgow News,' made a big thing about your family connection with your mother, but believe me," he paused again and to her surprise, smiled.

"Let's not beat about the bush, Mary. Our former boss, Charles Pettigrew, was a complete arse. So, bringing me up here and promoting me into the CID, a job I'd never done before, what did that say about me? What did *real* Detectives like you make of that?"

She realised his question was rhetorical and remaining silent, watched him shaking his head when he stared meaningfully at her, then said, "What I'm trying to say in my blustering way is that Keith Meadows didn't hold my background against me, no matter what *I* thought of myself, so do not think anything the media have written or broadcast will affect you whatsoever. I'm here to tell you, no matter what is publicly said, to go on doing what you are good at and also to inform you that Keith Meadows considers you to be one of his brightest senior Detective officers."

He stopped then continuing to smile, added, "And from what I hear of you, so do I."

A little taken aback at his forwardness, Mary was about to respond when he continued, "I can only imagine that you'll be thinking…" his brow creased in thought when he asked, "What is it you people up here keep saying? Something about being the gossip of the steam?"

She couldn't help but smile when she replied, "I think you mean, the talk of the steamie. It's Glasgow parlance, sir. It means to be the subject of scandal or gossip."

"Yes, well, one day," he drolly smiled, "I'll maybe understand what you people are talking about, but in the meantime, you're doing good work, Mary," he nodded, "so it's my wish that you remain in situ and I hope that we can continue to have these chats."

"Yes, sir," she lifted her mug and with a new found respect for his honesty, toasted him, then smiled, "I'm sure we will."

****

The following Monday, the tenth of August, a service was held at the Linn Crematorium.

Roughly four weeks previously and as was reported by most of the West of Scotland media, a drunken Natalie MacDonald drove her BMW on the wrong side of the road, then at the junction of Ayr Road and Davieland Road, side-swiped a double-decker bus before careering sideways into a lamppost and killing herself outright.

Among the small group of ten mourners who passed through the doors of the building for the private cremation, were her estranged husband, Michael MacDonald, their sons Alan and William, both men's wives and their daughter, Mary.

Michael's partner, Eileen, had chosen not to attend Natalie MacDonald's cremation service, believing that because of the circumstances of her and Michael's relationship, it would be inappropriate and so elected to remain at Mary's home with the children, Jamie and Morven.

Mary was accompanied by her neighbour and new friend, Dr Bill Howie.

Seated with acting Deputy Chief Constable Keith Meadows in the seats to the rear of the small chapel were the acting ACC (Crime) Leslie Scullion and DI Colin Baxter, who had chosen to represent DCI Wells staff.

The short service concluded after ten minutes, but there was to be no purvey, for Natalie's estranged husband and her children had decided that to arrange such an event would be insensitive, given that Michael and their children had decided to have nothing further to do with Natalie when she was alive.

However, taking their farewell of the three police officers at the crematorium, Michael and his family, who he noted with inward satisfaction now seemed to include Bill Howie, returned to the former family home in Meadowhill, for a meeting.

Arriving there, the two sisters-in-law, Morag and Kathleen, ably assisted by Bill Howie, busied themselves in the kitchen preparing tea, coffee and sandwiches while Michael and his sons and daughter retired to the lounge.

Glancing around him, he sighed when he said, "It seems that Natalie had let herself go a bit. The place isn't usually this untidy."

It was William who with raised eyebrows curtly replied, "Don't kid yourself or us, dad. That's because you weren't here. We all know it was you who cleaned the house. Natalie never got off her backside and why would she when she had you to order about?"

They watched their father sadly smile when nodding, he said with an ironic smile, "You're right, of course. Natalie hardly knew where the dusters and the hoover were kept, let alone how to use them."

Alan, turning to Mary, then asked, "You've already gave us the bones about how she managed to get her car out of the police yard, sis, but what's the meat? I mean," he shrugged, "don't your lot disable seized motors to prevent the owners taking them without authorisation?"

"Maybe in TV shows," she smiled, "but not in reality. The BMW was parked in the public bays in front of the office, but it's not as if we demand the second set of keys," then inwardly thought, though it might now be an idea to do so.

"Only twice in my career" she continued with a shake of her head, "Have I been aware of someone illegally recovering their car from a police office, Natalie being the second. From what I was told and remember," she cast a glance at the three men, then raised her hand when she continued, "and mind, because she was family I can't be involved in the investigation. Anyway, apparently she ordered a taxi from here to the police office, then with the spare keys, drove out of the yard like a bat out of hell and so quickly that she run the car alongside the small dwarf wall at the pavements edge, damaging the wall and the car. That didn't stop her though, and she continued driving at speed along Fenwick Road, straight through the McDonald roundabout and onto the Ayr Road, where as you now know," she paused, "she collided with the bus, lost control, spun twice during which she collided with another vehicle, then the car ended up wrapped around the lamppost."

She slowly exhaled as her father and brothers conjured in their minds the image of the crash, then continued, "The PM, for what it's worth," she glanced at them in turn, "concluded that not only was she four times over the limit, but death must have been instantaneous. Oh, and the only good news is that thankfully, no one else was injured."

A short silence followed, broken when Morag and Kathleen carried through trays with four mugs and plates of sandwiches, then Morag brightly said, "We're having ours in the kitchen to let you guys have a chat among yourselves and besides," she glanced mischievously at Mary, who guessing what was coming, felt her face reddening when she added, "it gives Kathleen and I a chance to get to know Bill."

"There's no need…" Michael began, but was waved down by Morag who said, "No, we believe that you need to chat among yourselves. We can hear later what you've talked about."

When she left the room, Michael raised a hand and said, "I've made a decision and before I tell you, I will not hear any argument against it."

"Dad?" William stared curiously at him.

The watched their father glance around the room before he told them, "As you know, Eileen and I are a couple now and we're very happy living in her comfortable home. With your mother's death, the divorce action is now irrelevant and so I inherit everything."

He sipped at his coffee, then licking at his lips, said, "I have decided to sell this…this mausoleum," he waved a hand round the room, "that has too many unhappy memories for me and I'm certain, you three as well. I'm pleased to tell you there is no mortgage," he smiled, "so the profit from the sale will be divided equally among the three of you."

After their initial surprise and intake of breath, they began to protest, but again holding up his hand, he firmly said, "Enough! I've made my decision, so that's it. With my savings and my pension, I have no need for the money, but I'm certain you three will put it to good use."

For Mary and her brothers, glancing at each other, they knew there was nothing more to say, other than thank you.

****

As Keith Meadows had predicted, some six weeks after the Deputy Chief Constable was summoned home from Bramshill to assume command after the departure of Charles Pettigrew, he was formally appointed to the position of Chief Constable of Strathclyde Police. What Meadows did not predict was his own position being ratified as the Deputy Chief Constable and in turn, to the surprise and perhaps also the disappointment to many of his peers, the appointment of Chief Superintendent Les Scullion to ACC (Crime). One of Meadows first act when appointed as the Deputy Chief Constable had been to instruct the Superintendent in charge of the Complaints and Discipline Branch to instigate an investigation into the allegation of collusion between Sergeant Hugh Donnelly and the 'Glasgow News' report, Ally McGregor.

Three weeks later and following both overt and covert surveillance, Meadows received official confirmation that Donnelly had and was currently providing confidential police information to McGregor. Immediately arrested and brought before Meadows, Donnelly was suspended prior to a discipline hearing, but later that day attempted to resign rather than be sacked.

However, Meadows was himself instrumental in blocking the attempt which had he been successful, seen Donnelly retire with a pension and all his benefits.

A hurried disciplinary board was assembled at which an aggrieved and confrontational Donnelly, regardless of his protests, found guilty of a number of serious contraventions relating to the Police (Scotland) Act of 1967 and was summarily dismissed from the Force.

As a result of his dismissal, Donnelly forfeited all pension and lump sum benefits due him.

In essence, he left the police without any financial benefit to show for his lengthy service with no expectation of any kind of reference and in disgrace.

****

Acting on DCI Wells recommendation and while on remand in HMP Cornton Vale, the murder accused, Yvonne Church, was examined by two psychiatrists who independently concluded that she was unfit to stand trial.

In agreement with her defence counsel, Crown Office arranged for Church to be transferred and detained without limit to the State Hospital at Carstairs, the institution that provides care and treatment for the criminally insane.

****

True to his word, Keith Meadows pulled in some favours from his contact within the Strathclyde Council that enabled Angela Bradley, her son, Billy, and Elizabeth Bradley's daughter, Sarah, to transfer from their Council property in Pollok to a Fife Council property in the town of Cupar, where they now reside among their relatives. However, before the family travelled to the north-east and unknown to her colleagues, DS Elaine Fitzsimmons took an excited ten-years-old Sarah Bradley for a lunch and shopping trip to Glasgow city centre where once more, she called upon her sister-in-law, Jill McGillivery, to extend the hospitality of the BHS store.

The day ended with the excited and happily exhausted little girl being dropped back to her grandmother clutching several bags of new clothes.

****

Some weeks later, appearing together for their pleading diet at the Sheriff Court, the accused Monica Davies, Maria Clinton and Martha Foster, were formally charged with a large number of thefts. Asked to plead, both Clinton and Foster pled guilty to all charges. Mindful and mainly due to the sympathetic police report submitted by DI Colin Baxter, that recognised both women's difficult backgrounds, their susceptibility to persuasion and their admittance to the crimes as well both the full recovery of the stolen items and their complete cooperation when arrested, the Fiscal Depute presenting the Crown case against both Clinton and Foster, requested the Sheriff give consideration that both women be admonished.

The Sheriff, like his fellow judges, already under political pressure to deal the backlog of cases as quickly was possible, agreed to the Depute's request and both women *were* admonished then summarily dismissed from the dock.

Not so, Monica Davies, who against the advice of her counsel, pled *not* guilty and so her trial date was set for two months later.

On that date and what the PF's Department were unaware of was that prior to appearing at the Sheriff Court, Davies had contacted several newspapers to inform them of her intention when in the dock to provide salacious information about her unfaithful husband, a man well known throughout the Glasgow legal and business establishment.

And so when the Fiscal Depute led evidence of her guilt, to the court's surprise, her Counsel, already clearly instructed by his client, led no defence to each and every allegation.

The purpose of this strategy soon became clear to the court and the Sheriff in particular when her Counsel at last called her to the witness box.

Her blonde hair pulled back into a tight ponytail, her make-up professionally applied and wearing a white blouse and sober, grey skirted business suit, those present saw her to be a remarkably attractive woman who hands demurely clasped in front of her, confidently stared down at the assembled journalists.

"Yes, I committed those crimes," she brazenly admitted to the court and the watching reporters, "but perhaps you might be interested in why I did it."

There followed a brief, four-minute tirade against her unfaithful husband during which time Davies intimated her husband's abandonment of both her and her children, then managed to mention at least six names of women with whom he had been unfaithful, three of whom were lawyers themselves and included Charlotte 'Charlie' Paterson of Burnley, Paterson and Co.

Among other names mentioned were three business associates, two of whom were also unfaithful husbands and one an unfaithful wife.

The court now in an uproar as Davies continued to scream out the names and the company's employing them, officers were instructed by the Sheriff to physically remove her from the witness box.

While the court officers struggled with the uncooperative Davies, the Sheriff, now on his feet and banging his ceremonial gavel on his desk, loudly called out to her, "This court is not a platform for your revenge!"

However, no one heeded the bewildered, elderly judge for the journalists were far too busy writing down the names she had called out, then rushed from the room to catch the evening edition of their respective newspapers.

As for Monica Davies, still hysterically screaming, she was dragged from the box and removed to the court cells where a further charge of contempt of court was libelled against her.

Later that afternoon, she was conveyed to HMP Cornton Vale for the night.

Appearing again the following morning before the same Sheriff, but on this occasion in a closed courtroom, a much subdued and rather more dishevelled Davies, without makeup and her business suit creased and showing signs of being slept in, changed her plea to guilty and pled guilty too, to the charge of contempt of court.

Addressing her, the Sheriff calmly explained, "While I do sympathise with your marital predicament, Mrs Davies," he briefly paused to collect his thoughts, then continued, "the extent to which you went to conceal your identity, while recruiting women who regretfully had neither your educational opportunities nor your relatively affluent lifestyle, was both cunning and manipulative. The lengths to which you went to revenge yourself on your husband had far reaching consequences; consequences that if this morning's shameful newspaper headlines are any indication, will affect more than just your own family. Such consequences that you set in motion are truly disgraceful and I, as an appointed Sheriff, cannot ignore that your actions might have caused possible harm to others."

He paused and stared solemnly at Davies before he thoughtfully continued, "However, while the law does permit me a number of penalties that I can award you, I am also aware that you have never previously come to the attention of the police and that your husband, I am told in good faith, refuses to accept his children into his new life, whereas you quite obviously care deeply for them both."

To his credit, the elderly Sheriff recognised a woman cruelly betrayed and taking cognisance of the fact Davies, who had no previous convictions, had admitted her guilt to the police and like her fellow accused, also cooperated with the return of the stolen items.

However, what he did *not* disclose in open court was he had been discreetly informed by her Counsel of her ongoing health issues. And so, he decided on a far lesser sentence than her Counsel anticipated.

"It is therefore my solemn duty to sentence you to twelve months imprisonment," but just as she gasped and felt her legs go weak,

causing her to grasp at the railing around the dock, the Sheriff raised a hand to quickly continue, "However, in sentencing you I believe I am also depriving your children of the one parent who seemingly cares for them and I have no desire to cause *them* further grief. So, on this occasion, the sentence will be suspended, pending your good behaviour during the period of the twelve months. Do you fully understand, Mrs Davies, the opportunity this court offers you?"
Openly distraught, tears freely rolling down her cheeks and unable to speak, she nodded and mouthed the word, 'Yes.'
"Then you are free to go," the Sheriff indicated to the court officer to lead her down from the dock.
****
Though her fellow accused were now free from the judicial system, Maria Clinton was not.
Just two weeks after her own appearance at the Sheriff Court, Maria and her thirteen-year-old daughter, Ellie, were called as prosecution witnesses to the High Court sitting held at the city's Saltmarket.
Maria sat anxiously within the room reserved for witnesses with her arm thrown protectively around her daughter's thin shoulders, ignoring the glances and rough humour of the witnesses who were crowded in the room.
The dimly lit room with dark green walls that quite obviously had not been painted for many years, was furnished with scratched and uncomfortable decades old wooden bench seating along three of the walls, in the centre of the large room sat an overflowing tin waste bin and a long wooden table that itself was scratched and vandalised and the air reeked with the pungent smell of cigarette smoke.
Holding tightly to her mother, Maria's daughter shook with fearful anticipation of the ordeal she was about to undergo.
One long and tense hour passed, then the door opened to admit a man wearing a legal wig and dressed in a black coloured, flowing robe who called out, "Mrs Clinton?"
Nervously rising to her feet, the man beckoned both Maria and her daughter to him, then led them to the corridor outside.
"Case against Martin Clinton?" he glanced at his clipboard and asked for confirmation, but so uptight was Maria she could not respond other than to simply nod.

"Right," the man, who did not identify himself, peered down at the clipboard, then brusquely said, "Clinton changed his plea to guilty, so you're free to go."

He was about to turn away when Maria found herself to be unusually angry that he was being so uninformative and dismissal of her and Ellie.

Furiously, she grabbed at his robe and hissed, "What do you mean, we're free to go? For Christ's sake, can't you tell us what's just happened?"

Taken aback, the man stared at her, then calmly replied, "Your husband has pled guilty, Mrs Clinton, so there's no need for you or your daughter to give evidence. Like I told you, you're free to go."

Maintaining her vice-like grip on his sleeve, she asked, "And is he getting the jail? Tell us!"

The man, an extremely busy clerk of the court though she couldn't know that, saw the panic in her eyes then glancing at the young girl, saw the same fear there too.

Aware of the charges Martin Clinton was facing, in a rare moment of compassion, he sighed when he replied, "Come with me and please, *be* quiet."

Leading them a short distance along the corridor, he stopped at a large, old-fashioned wooden door and with his forefinger to his lips to ensure their silence, slowly pushed open the door.

Silently ushering them inside, Maria, not knowing the word alcove, saw they were standing in what to her seemed like a small wooden enclosure and glancing to where the man pointed, saw her husband Martin, pale faced and visibly shaking.

Shaved and his bald head glistening with perspiration and dressed in an ill-fitting blue suit and uncommonly, a white shirt and blue tie, he was standing between two uniformed prison guards in a small, raised wooden box a mere twenty feet away.

Tightly gripping her daughter's hand, Maria shrunk against the wall behind her, fearing that Martin might turn and see her and Ellie, then heard a bewigged and robed Judge speak, who she now noticed was sitting in a large, ornate chair behind what she thought to be a big desk.

Though Maria did not understand many of the things the Judge was telling Martin, she understood the words, 'evil,' 'depraved' and most telling of all, heard the Judge describe Martin as "…the worst

kind of immoral man who has ever darkened this court."
Desperate to know what was going on, she turned to the man and was about to whisper, but once more with his forefinger at his lips, he hissed, "Shhh!"
It was then the Judge spoke again and uttered some more words she didn't really understand, but then she almost fainted when she heard him sentence Martin to eighteen years in prison.
Her body shaking, Maria almost collapsed in a dead faint and was supported from the alcove by the man to the corridor outside, where he led her and Ellie to a bench, then lowering her down onto the bench, gently said, "Wait here. I'll fetch you a glass of water."
He was gone but a minute when Maria, taking a huge breath of air, grabbed at Ellie then hissed, "Let's go, hen. Let's get out of here, eh?"
In the fresh air, she took a further gulp of air then seeing the Glasgow Green, the large park on the opposite side of the road from the High Court, grabbed at Ellie's hand and hurried her daughter through the traffic and across the road, then in through the large, black painted wrought iron gates to the park.
When they'd passed through the gates and stopped almost fifty yards into the park, Ellie hesitated, then her voice quivering and her eyes wet with unshed tears, asked, "Mammy, is he really going to the jail?"
Maria stared at her daughter, then her voice breaking gently as she gently stroked at Ellie's brow, she replied. "Aye, hen, he's away for a very long time. He'll not hurt us anymore."
****

Not related, but in a spin-off from Mary Wells murder investigation, DI Fraser McManus of the Strathclyde Police Fraud Squad, spent some weeks compiling a substantial amount of evidence against the Directors of the 'Sweeps 'n Dusts' cleaning company.
The evidence clearly indicated Alex McLean, the so-called owner, his now estranged wife Jacqueline McLean and her father, Ronald Atkins, the Senior Procurement Officer for Glasgow City Council, colluded together to obtain the contract for the company of which they as Directors, were mutually responsible.
After reporting the circumstances to Crown office, criminal indictments were issued for the three of them.

At their pleading diet and on the advice of their lawyers, all three pled guilty to the charges of corruption.

As an alternative to prison, the trio were fined by His Lordship for sums totalling three hundred and twenty-five thousand pounds, which in effect not only wiped out their ill-gotten frozen bank accounts, but also resulted in the seizure of their vehicles, goods and purchased properties that in due course, were to be sold at public auction to pay towards their fines.

Further to his financial sentence, Atkins was also barred from holding any position of trust for public office for a period of ten years.

As for the company, 'Sweeps 'n Dusts,' His Lordship recognised that closing down the company would result in not only the loss of gainful employment by a large number of staff, but might cause hardship for a large number of its elderly clients.

With this in mind, His Lordship agreed ownership of the company that had been seized by the Crown, could be purchased by Glasgow City Council for the sum of one Sterling pound to enable the continuing employment of the staff and the good work the majority of the women carried out.

At the suggestion of DI McManus and because she had a working knowledge of the company, as well as for continuity purpose, the Council were also persuaded to recruit Miss Agnes Flynn, the former company secretary, as the new, employed managing director.

****

A little over seven weeks after their date night, Bill Howie informed Mary that though they had only been together for a short time, he believed it was pointless renewing the tenancy of the house next door when they were already discussing living together, though that would mean a new start; a new home together and somewhere local that suited them both.

The doubt she initially had, whether he would accept her children as his own was quickly settled, as far as Mary was concerned.

Now standing in the doorway, her arms folded and watching Bill lying on his back on her lounge floor and attempting to fend off her giggling children who were climbing all over him, she instinctively knew that he was the one.

Yes, she felt her heart beating in her chest, he was definitely the one and she had no doubt he felt the same about her.

"Right, you lot," she clapped her hands and loudly called out, "bath time."

"Does that include me?" Bill, grinning, stared up from the floor at her.

"No," she coyly replied, "you and I get to shower later."

****

Once again, the storyline and the characters in '*DCI Wells*' are completely fictitious and do not represent any individual, alive or deceased.

As I have likely mentioned previously, writing crime fiction is my hobby and so while I recognise that it is not ideal to self-edit one's own work, I accept that any spelling, grammatical or other mistakes are mine and mine alone. That said, I hope that you might forgive such mistakes and that they do not interfere with the storyline.

As always, I will be grateful for feedback in the form of reviews and if you are able to do so, kindly submit a review.
I promise you I will be appreciative, regardless of the comments.

Kind regards,

George Donald

Printed in Great Britain
by Amazon